I0822304

GUARDIAN

OTHER FICTION BY A.J. CALVIN

THE RELICS OF WAR
The Moon's Eye
The Talisman of Delucha
War of the Nameless

The Ballad of Alchemy and Steel

Serpentus

THE CAEIN LEGACY
Exile
Guardian
Harbinger
Legend

HUNTED

WRAITH AND THE REVOLUTION

PRAISE FOR GUARDIAN

"Guardian felt like a soothing balm after the events of Exile. There is still plenty of excitement but tonally, I found it to be the perfect follow-up for book 1 in the Caein Legacy."

– *C.B. Lansdell, author of Far Removed*

"Guardian is an excellent sequel in The Caein Legacy series and one that will expand your understanding of the world and stakes."

– *Under the Radar SFF Podcast*

"AJ Calvin has written wonderfully deep and complex relationships within the family, as well as fantastic world building."

– *Kat Kinney, author of The Everwood Falls series*

"Guardian reminded me of The Witcher series at its best. Other than some surprisingly dark scenes, the tone is rather whimsical."

– *Timothy Wolff, author of The Legacy of Boulom series*

GUARDIAN

THE CAEIN LEGACY
Book Two

A.J. CALVIN

GUARDIAN

ISBN 979-8-9883193-5-1

Cover illustration and design by Jamie Noble (www.thenobleartist.com)

Map illustration by Dewi Hargreaves (www.dewihargreaves.com)

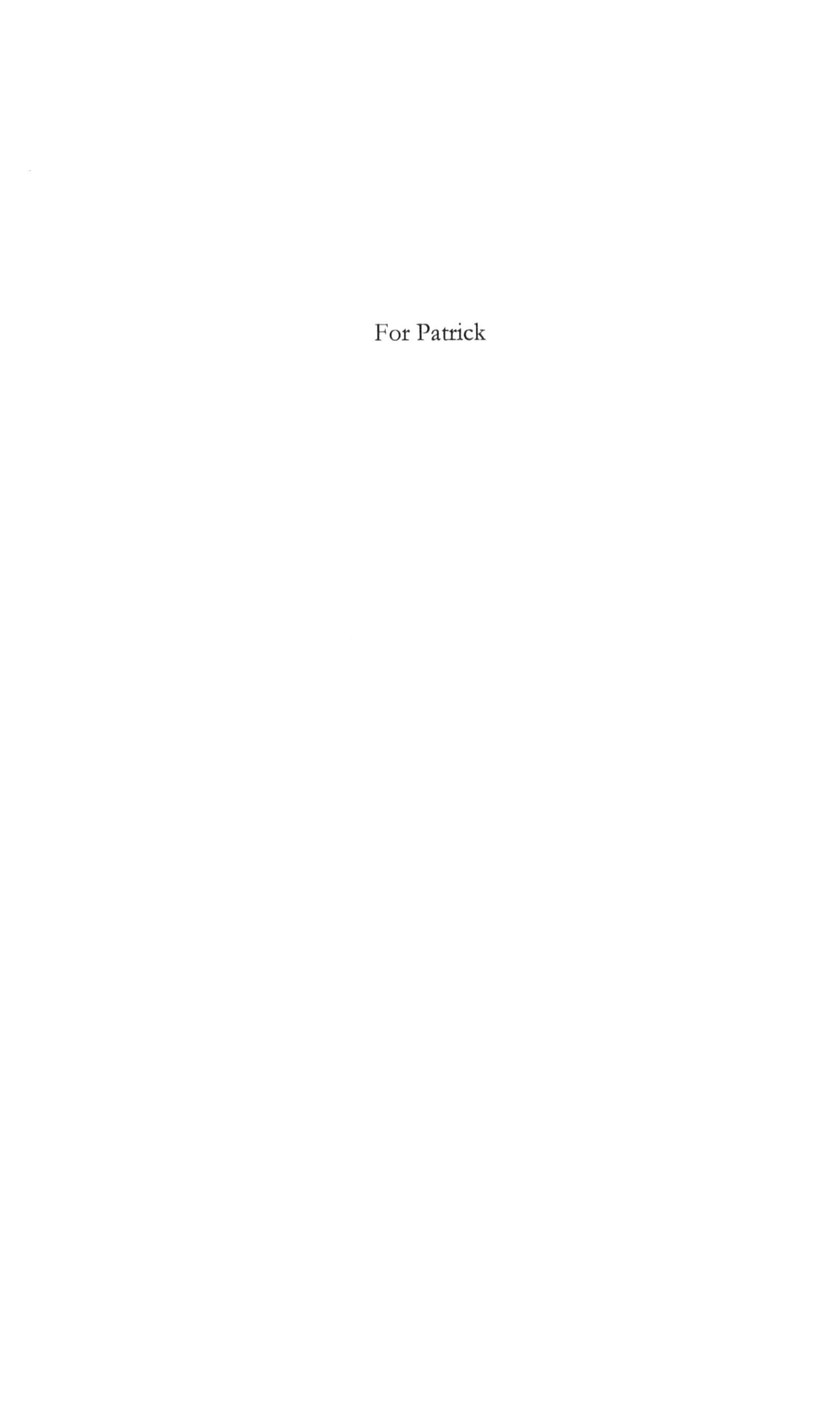

For Patrick

AUTHOR'S NOTE

Guardian is ultimately a story of siblings, of the elder looking after and protecting the younger, even into adulthood. But more than that, it's the story of the elder sibling watching their brother grow and find their own path. It mirrors much of my own experience.

Many of the interactions (and banter) between Andrew and Alexander were inspired by the relationship I share with my brother. While he may not have known it at the time, he was a major influence on that aspect of this book and the overarching series. The bond between siblings is often a strong one, and I certainly can't escape my own, even while writing.

The entirety of this story is set in the Southlands, but a return to Novania will happen in book three. For now, I hope you enjoy what is truly Alexander's journey, though it's told through Andrew's perspective.

Thank you and happy reading,
A.J. Calvin

SOME FURTHER NOTES ON THIS BOOK

The Caein Legacy hosts a wide array of characters, but I have chosen not to include a character glossary in the text of the book. The story is told solely from Andrew's perspective, and all of the other characters are seen through his eyes.

I have set up a page on my website with a list of characters (including pronunciation guides) for those interested. You can find it at the following location: www.ajcalvin.nct/books/the-caein-legacy/the-caein-legacy-character-glossary/

Additionally, Guardian contains some language, content, and situations that may not be suitable for some readers. I write for mature audiences, so please bear that in mind as you proceed.

NOVANIA AND THE SOUTHLANDS

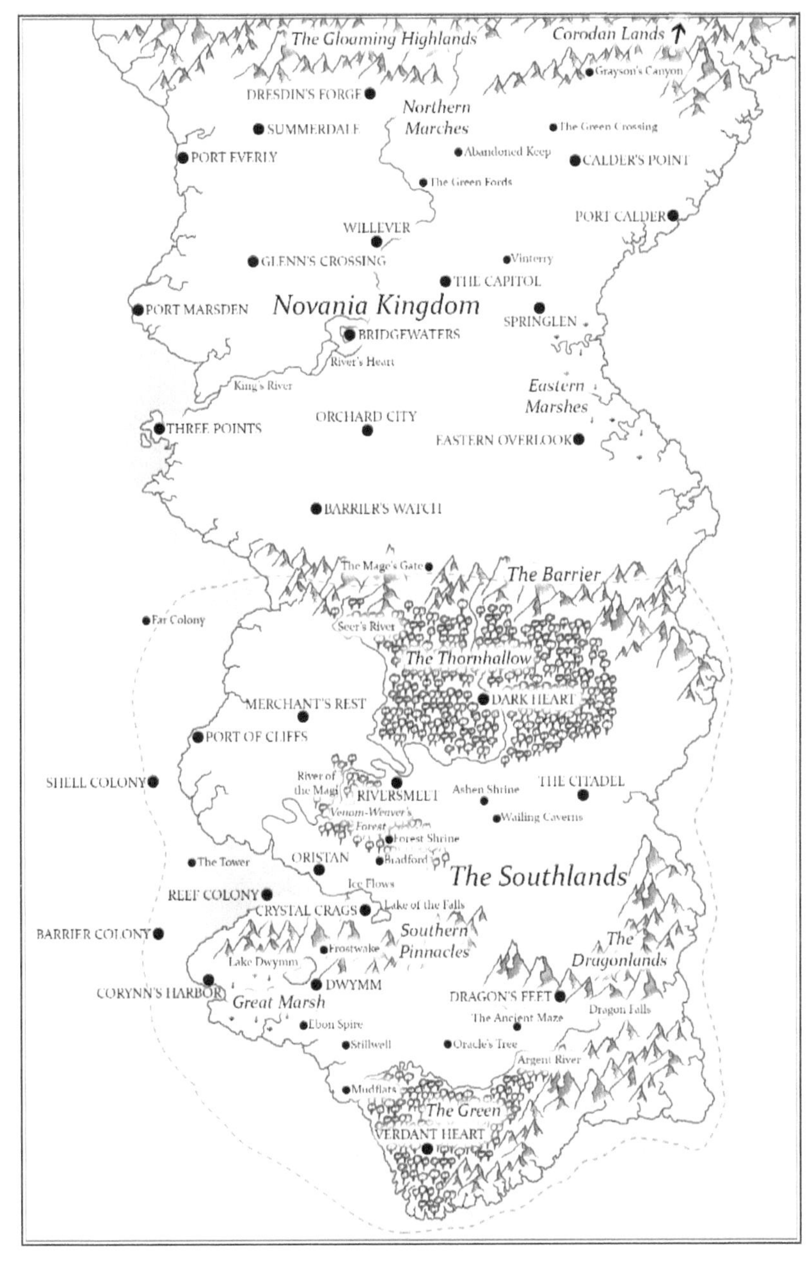

ONE

Dawn painted Alexander's face in lurid and bloody shades of crimson, a portent of events to come if the Oracle was to be believed. I turned away from my brother, troubled by the implications.

We stood on the outskirts of the Citadel. The sky was awash in color, thin bands of clouds illuminated by the first rays of an early summer's sun. In the distance, a graceful white tower rose from the city's center. It was the home of the Oracle, the woman who had sent us on our latest journey. The tower was wide at its base, tapering as it rose skyward, only to flare outwards again near the top. Below the tower, the city was beginning to awaken. I could hear the sounds of the distant marketplace as merchants began to shout their wares to passersby, while the scent of baking bread wafted on the summer breeze.

"I thought she would have been here by now," Alexander grumbled. "This is where we were to meet."

I glanced at my half-brother. We were much alike in appearance, though I was several inches taller than he; we both had blond hair and green eyes, courtesy of our mother. His eyes were ringed with dark circles, a testament to his poor sleeping habits of late, but they were also alight with anticipation. Today we'd embark on his pilgrimage. It was little wonder he was impatient to be off.

"Relax, Alex," I replied. "She'll be here. She said she'd need to acquire a horse and cart. Perhaps she was forced to wait for the merchants to awaken before she could carry out her business."

He sighed in frustration. "I know. I'm just eager to be off. With all that's going on back home, I want to help Tom as soon as I'm able."

I nodded, sharing his sentiment. The latest news we'd received from Thomas had been worrisome. War was coming to Novania, and though I wished I could aid Thomas in his plight, my first priority was to see Alexander through his pilgrimage. I'd given my word I'd do so.

The damned Oracle had seen to that.

Alexander had inadvertently accessed his magical gift on at least one occasion, placing him in danger until he learned to control his abilities. Despite my own innate gifts, I simply couldn't be present to help both of my brothers at once. I'd assist Thomas once Alexander's safety was assured.

The Oracle had provided supplies and a guide to lead us through the journey, and it was the guide we currently awaited. I had volunteered to guard my brother against the threats we might face along the way; after all, there were few others as well suited to the task as I.

"Hmm," Alexander said after a few moments, "I think I see her."

He shaded his eyes with one hand to shield them from the sun while he pointed to a cart moving in our general direction. I could not make out the features of its driver from our present distance, but I could see the unmistakable wide-brimmed hat she wore. It was Chela, our appointed guide.

"The sun hasn't fully risen yet," I replied with a smirk. "She isn't late, you know."

He shrugged, seemingly uncomfortable. "I know. I'm ready to be away from this place. There are too many unpleasant memories in the Citadel."

He referred to his tense relationship with the Oracle, and the recent sacrifice I'd made on his behalf.

I rolled my shoulders experimentally. The wound at the center of my back ached dully with the motion as the flesh pulled and stretched uncomfortably, but it didn't split open. It had healed significantly in the last ten days, but it would still take several weeks before I was fully recovered.

He frowned, his green eyes narrowed as he observed my motions. The armor that had been crafted for him would be on Chela's cart, and I hoped he would use it when necessary. I remembered little of the process of its creation beyond the excruciating pain I'd endured. If it meant Alexander would be protected, then my ordeal had been worth it.

While I understood Alexander's position, I didn't share his bitter outlook on the events that had transpired. Rather, they'd provided me with a measure of hope for our future. We'd been welcomed—and accepted—in the Southlands, a marked contrast to the common sentiment in our homeland to the north. There, we were considered dangerous anomalies, unfit to live amongst the populace, though neither of us had ever caused the people any harm.

Shading my eyes from the glare of the summer sun, I watched as Chela approached our chosen location. She was clad in a leather jerkin and pants, and her dark eyes sparkled at the prospect of adventure. Her face appeared ageless, neither old nor young—one of the hallmarks of a trained mage. The cart she'd procured was large enough to accommodate our supplies but held scant room within for passengers. She was perched at the front, driving the sturdy workhorse that dutifully pulled the wagon behind it. The beast was built for labor and didn't look as though it could be coaxed into moving much faster than its current plodding pace. It was just as well; Alexander and I had fled our homes with nothing, and we had no means of attaining horses to ride ourselves. We were relegated to making the journey on foot.

"Good morning, friends!" Chela called as she drew up the wagon nearby. "Are we ready to be off?"

When Alexander nodded, she urged the workhorse forward once more. The path we were to take made its way west from the Citadel, disappearing into the forest not far ahead. Chela gestured that we should take the lead and she would follow behind with the horse and cart.

"We'll be traveling through the wood for the better part of two days," she said. "This close to the Citadel, the roads are free of danger, but as we near our first destination, we may run into some trouble. We'll be passing through the Wailing Caverns on our way. There are always a few bandits and such hiding there, looking to waylay unsuspecting travelers."

"And how long will it be until we reach that point?" Alexander asked.

"Hmm. Five or six days," Chela replied.

"Let's hope we don't encounter any bandits," Alexander said as he cast a worried glance in my direction.

I sighed in exasperation. "I can handle a few bandits, Alex. In five or six days, the healing will be farther along. I'll be fine."

He frowned, his expression skeptical. "Belora said you needed at least another two weeks."

I crossed my arms, unyielding. We'd discussed and argued the same points the previous evening. The Oracle had named me Alexander's guardian, and I would do everything in my power to ensure he made it through his pilgrimage safely. Ideally, we would have remained in the Citadel for another week before departing, but due to something the Oracle had seen in her visions, she'd urged us to leave sooner.

There was also the looming threat from Novania—and our brother, Colin—that we would be forced to deal with eventually. I felt my blood run hot with rage each time Colin entered my thoughts. What he'd done at Vinterry was unforgivable. I'd make damned certain he faced justice, despite his present status as king—even if it proved to be my final act on this world.

"A single bandit, or perhaps two, you might handle on your own," I conceded, "provided that you are wearing your new armor. But I will not sit idly by if it comes to a fight, and you know that. You may be an excellent swordsman, but you're not invincible."

He rolled his eyes and muttered something under his breath that I didn't catch, though I distinctly heard the word "impossible."

I shrugged and chose to ignore him, then turned my attention back to our guide. "We'll travel through the forest for a couple of days, then travel another three or four to reach these Wailing Caverns. What then?"

"The caverns can be difficult to navigate," she replied. "Luckily for you, I know my way through them. The bandits usually don't stray far inside. It's too easy to become lost. I believe we can make it through the caverns in a day if we don't encounter any trouble. Once on the other side, we'll descend into a broad valley, and at its far end, we'll find the Ashen Shrine. It's our first destination."

"That's an odd name," Alexander commented.

"Not as strange as you might think," Chela replied with a grin. "There was a great wildfire that swept through the valley many years ago. The shrine is still intact, but the exterior was charred. The building was once white and had another name, but it has been lost to the endless march of time. I've only known it as the Ashen Shrine."

Our path had taken us into the forest proper. The summer air was considerably cooler beneath the canopy of branches that interlaced their leafy fingers above our heads. As the sounds of the Citadel faded, a deep and profound silence took hold, broken only by birdsong and the hum of insects, the creaking of the cart, and our own footsteps. Chela removed her hat to place it carefully in the cart behind her, revealing her tawny hair was pulled into a thick braid.

"The Oracle informed me that you know little of these lands," Chela continued after a time. "You've come from the north and will require more guidance on this journey than most."

Alexander snorted in frustration but made no reply. I sighed, knowing I'd be forced to explain our situation yet again. I understood he remained angry with the Oracle over what had occurred between them, and though he had apologized to her for his behavior, he was still bitter. It was our lack of knowledge about this land that had led to their rift.

"We've been told little," I replied while Alexander continued to brood. "Alex must undertake this journey. Along the way, he'll learn how to use his magic. What it entails has not been explained to us."

"Hmm." Chela frowned in thought. "We have at least a few days until we reach the Wailing Caverns, and there will be little to occupy our time beyond idle conversation. I'll explain what I know of the trials."

"Trials?" Alexander asked over his shoulder, his tone moderately curious.

"Yes. At each destination, you must complete a trial. Each trial is unique to the mage who enters and can only be determined by the elders upon your arrival," Chela replied. "There will be elders at most of our destinations. There may also be others undertaking the pilgrimage, but in my experience, it's rare. It seems fewer magi require this journey of late. It may be there are enough others about who can teach, or perhaps our numbers are slowly waning. I don't know." She shrugged.

I studied Alexander as we walked. An array of emotions flitted across his features as Chela spoke before they settled into an irritated frown. There was much about the Southlands we didn't know, and its denizens often seemed to forget we were newcomers. The Barrier had shielded them from Novania for generations, and likewise, the people of our homeland feared traveling too near it. There had been little crossover between the two lands for centuries; our arrival had been unusual.

We'd been taught that magi were terrible beings to be feared, and Novania's laws stated that anyone bearing the Mark must be put to death. Alexander had managed to hide what he was for most of his life, but once his Mark had been revealed, we'd been forced to flee. It was only through my intervention that he was alive at all.

Though we both understood the significance of his Mark and the necessity of his training, the details had been largely glossed over by the Oracle and her associates. Alexander resented her—not only for her lack of explanation, but also for her manipulations. We'd both been coerced by the Oracle, and while I believed she meant well, she'd left us mistrustful of her motives.

"Can you explain the elders? What purpose do they serve?" I asked.

Alexander glanced in my direction briefly, then nodded once to indicate he understood I was trying to help him. It had been difficult for me since our arrival in the Citadel; I was out of my element with the mysticism that had enveloped us, and I struggled with the concepts of magic. I was a warrior, a career soldier. I didn't know how to help my brother with what he must do, but I was trying.

"The elders are exactly as they sound," she replied. "They are the oldest and wisest of the magi and have chosen to dedicate what remains of their lives to teaching others. At each destination, save one, Alexander will speak with the elders upon our arrival. The elders may choose to examine his Mark. They'll ask him questions to learn more of his personality or past—then they'll determine some of what his trial will entail. Each location has a special significance in the history of the magi." She paused and looked at us quizzically. "Do you know the details of the Mage Wars?"

I shook my head, but Alexander stunned me with his answer.

"I read a book on its history," he replied. When he saw my surprised expression, he chuckled. "It was in Vera's library."

My heart ached at the mention of Vera. I nodded and looked away, reluctant to pursue the topic further.

"Who was Vera?" Chela asked, curious.

Her question was innocent, but it rankled. She was unaware of our history, but I didn't want to relive the pain I'd endured at Vera's loss. I'd loved her dearly, but now she was gone, killed at the behest of Colin, the tyrant-king and my ruthless half-brother.

I shook my head again, unwilling to respond. I wasn't certain I'd manage a sentence without grief cracking my tone or tears stinging my eyes.

"Ah, Vera was Andrew's wife," Alexander said quietly after a moment. "Her estate had a library with many old books—some of which should have been destroyed under the laws of the kingdom. Our brother Tom spent hours in there, reading everything he could get his hands on. Vera was a good woman. She's…dead."

Chela was silent for a moment, then said, "I'm sorry. I didn't know."

"I don't blame you," I replied thickly. "I was unable to protect her from Colin, and one day I intend to make him pay." The last came out as a growl as my temper flared.

Chela nodded but did not reply.

We walked without speaking for a time. I listened to the sounds of the forest creatures in the trees and allowed my thoughts to drift to happier times. A time before Colin's ascension, when I'd been at peace, Alexander hadn't been hunted, and Vera had been alive.

Damn Colin. And damn Novania's outdated laws.

The past few weeks had been the darkest of my life. I longed for the days that once were.

TWO

"The trials often begin simply enough, but they won't remain that way." Chela peered at Alexander from beneath the brim of her hat.

We'd been traveling for two days and had not yet exited the forest. During that time, Chela had spoken often of magic and its nature, but this was one of the few times she'd mentioned the trials outright.

Alexander shrugged. "Countless others have passed. I'm confident I'll be no different."

Chela lifted her eyebrows, nonplussed. "Some don't survive their pilgrimage. You'd do well to remember that."

I narrowed my eyes but didn't interrupt. Alexander tended toward recklessness, and during his trials, I'd be helpless, unable to intervene. It wasn't a situation I was accustomed to; I'd always been my brother's protector.

"If they're so dangerous, perhaps you ought to enlighten me." Alexander kicked at a loose stone in the road but didn't look up to meet her eye.

"As I've said, the trials are unique to each mage. You'll be tested, pushed to your limits, and perhaps challenged to harness your magic or die. I can tell you little more until you've completed a few." Chela flicked the reins, but the horse, whom she'd dubbed Sienna, didn't increase her pace.

"You're as vague as the damned Oracle." Alexander released a sigh and kicked another stone. "I'll survive this. I have to."

We fell into a tense silence and continued on. By evening, the trees had begun to thin and a carpet of knee-high grass had sprung up between them as the forest slowly gave way to the plains. Chela pointed to the dark outline of a rocky outcropping far to the west as we made camp. It was the only natural feature that arose out of the landscape as far as the eye could see.

"The Wailing Caverns are located there," she said. "It will take another few days before we reach them."

Alexander busied himself with setting up our tent and didn't reply.

I groaned, weary of his surly demeanor. "I'll gather firewood."

Chela nodded and began to explain her own experience during the mage trials, undeterred by my brother's dour attitude. I glanced at Alexander; he'd paused in his task to focus on Chela, finally keen to hear what she had to say.

I took a small axe from the cart and strode toward a thick stand of trees while they discussed magic. Alexander needed to learn all he could from Chela, and though I'd tried to reason with him, he remained stubbornly resistant after his dealings with the Oracle.

I'd collected an armful of branches and had turned back toward camp when I realized the nearby forest had fallen eerily silent. The birds had ceased their twittering songs and even the insects had stopped their buzzing drone. I paused to listen intently while I wondered what predator was responsible for the abrupt and profound disruption. After a few seconds in which I strained my ears, the sound of heavy footfalls became clear, marking the passage of a large creature speeding through the undergrowth.

I placed the branches on the ground and gripped the small axe in both hands, steeling myself for the appearance of the beast. Judging by the noise, it was headed directly toward my location. If the axe proved an insufficient defense, I could shift into my dragon form, though I wanted to avoid a rapid change if I was able. I only had one other set of clothing, and I didn't want to ruin this one.

As the creature drew nearer, its heavy and labored breathing could be heard over the sound of its passage. It was puzzling; most predators were built for sprinting, not distance running. Something must have been driving the beast. I adjusted my grip on the axe and drew a breath as I prepared to face it.

An instant later, a brown bear burst through the trees and stopped abruptly as it spied me. A petite Merael girl perched atop the bear's broad back, her dark hair loose and tangled from their rapid passage through the woods. She grinned broadly, waved to me, then hopped to the ground.

"Emmarie?" I asked, stunned. I was delighted to see her again. I relaxed my grip on the axe and dropped it to my side.

Emmarie smiled proudly and nodded once. She was smaller than an average human, and like all of her people, her skin was a shade of deep green, akin to that of the leaves overhead. Dressed in natural leathers, she blended into the forest with ease.

She turned toward the bear, then made a series of growling noises it seemed to understand. It nuzzled at her hand briefly before trundling back into the forest. She turned to face me once more, a smirk playing at the corners of her mouth.

"Andrew, it's good to see you." She flashed a grin. "I followed you here."

I shook my head, baffled, and began to collect the branches I'd abandoned on the ground. "Why?"

"I ran away," she replied with an unconcerned shrug. "My uncle sent me to the Citadel, but the Oracle assigned me to help that message-writing mage, Bryson Feige. Do you know him?"

I nodded. I'd visited Bryson twice during my stay in the Citadel. He'd sent messages to my half-brother, Thomas, and had even arranged for Thomas to send replies in return.

"Then you know what his ability is," she continued. "I was *bored.* He didn't need my help, and I didn't want to be there. When I heard you and Alex had left, I asked around the city and learned which direction you'd traveled. I hadn't gone far into the forest when I met Kavar, and he agreed to help me reach you."

"Is Kavar the bear?" I asked. I motioned that she should follow as I made my way back to our camp.

"Yes, that's what he called himself," she replied.

"Why did you want to follow us?" I asked, still confused by her decision.

She was young, an adolescent, and was often impatient, much like her human counterparts of the same age. I was uncertain if she'd followed us for a significant reason or if it had simply been on impulse.

She rolled her eyes and made a sound of exasperation. "Your brother is going on a pilgrimage," she explained as though speaking to a child. "I wanted to leave the Thornhallow to see more of the world, and accompanying a mage on a pilgrimage is the best way to do so. Regardless, you could use my help. You'd never know if one of the wild creatures has important information that could help you along the way."

As we neared the camp, Chela looked up from where she was slicing potatoes and frowned in confusion as she noted I was no longer alone. Alexander had finished setting up the tent but faced away from us, his arms crossed and expression thoughtful as he contemplated something they'd likely discussed. I set the branches down a short distance from the cart, then began to stack them in preparation for a campfire.

"And who might you be?" Chela asked Emmarie.

I heard Alexander turn and glanced up in time to see his face break into an amused smile. "Emmarie! I wasn't sure we'd see you again," he said.

"That's because you don't know me very well," she replied with a smirk. "I wasn't going to sit around the Citadel when something much more exciting was going on."

While Emmarie was introduced to Chela and explained to Alexander why she'd come, I worked to start the fire.

"While joining us in this manner is unorthodox, I won't deny that your abilities will be welcome along the way." Chela appeared confounded by the Merael girl's decision but seemed to have accepted it.

"Of course, I can help you," Emmarie replied matter-of-factly. "You know, my uncle told me that long ago, it used to be standard practice that the Oracle assigned a Wild-kin to each mage's pilgrimage. Why do you suppose that changed?"

Chela shook her head. "I'm afraid I don't know the answer."

Chela didn't comment further until Alexander had drawn Emmarie away for a time, leaving us alone to prepare supper.

"I don't know if it's wise to allow Emmarie to undertake this journey. It will be dangerous, and she's young."

"I know. But if we send her away, she'll only come back, and that could prove more dangerous than if she stays with the group." I shrugged uncertainly. "What little I have learned of Emmarie is that she'll do as she pleases, no matter what we tell her. If she's determined to join us, I don't see any way to avoid it."

I was concerned by Emmarie's decision myself, though for different reasons. She'd proven impulsive, and at times had been irreverent to those in positions of authority. I didn't know her history beyond our brief interactions prior to our arrival in the Citadel, but I sensed she'd been unhappy with her uncle's decision to send her to work for the Oracle. She clearly craved adventure, but would her desire to explore new surroundings become problematic for our journey? I didn't know.

"So long as she doesn't prove difficult, I suppose it can't hurt to have her with us," Chela conceded after a moment. "I hope she'll heed my warnings. I don't speak lightly of the danger we'll face, and you aren't healed yet."

I shrugged. "I'm better each day. I'll be back to full strength soon enough."

She shook her head. "That wasn't my point, Andrew."

She was worried what it would cost me to ensure the protection of yet another person, but I didn't share her concerns. I knew my limits and trusted my strength would see us through the dangers ahead. Chela hadn't yet experienced my dragon form, and I suspected she wasn't aware of the sheer power I wielded. Few people were.

"I can manage," I replied. "I should be fully healed before we reach the Ashen Shrine."

She frowned, her gaze level and expression stern. "While I understand you are capable of some incredible feats, *skin-changer*, I will not put your brother's life in danger due to the impulses of a mere teenager. She will mind herself, or she will be left behind."

I clenched my jaw, frustrated she'd even suggest I'd place Alexander's safety behind that of anyone else. She clearly didn't know me, nor did she understand the enormity of what we'd already endured—or the lengths I'd go to for my brother.

"Alexander is—and has always been—my first priority," I growled. "I assure you, the sacrifices I've made to get him this far were not made on a whim. You would do well not to question me when it comes to my brother's welfare. I will protect him at any cost—even if it means no one else on this expedition survives."

I glared a challenge, daring her to contradict me a second time. She met my gaze for a few seconds before averting her eyes, then nodded in resignation.

"You have no *inkling* of the hell we've been through," I added vehemently. "Don't presume to speak of what you don't know."

We didn't speak until well after we'd broken camp the next morning. My temper had cooled somewhat, but I remained irritated by our previous conversation. I kept my distance, leaving Alexander to take up the post alongside the cart. Emmarie accompanied me a short distance ahead, though she said little. I wondered if she'd overheard Chela's words and my own response, but she didn't mention it.

The landscape faded from the dwindling forest to a vast plain. The dark ridge that I'd glimpsed the previous evening remained prominently in our view but was a significant distance from our present location. The sun was high in the cloudless, late summer sky, and the air had become uncomfortably warm as the morning drew on. There were few trees and little respite from the sun's intense rays. I grew thirsty and stopped walking to allow the cart to catch up.

"What is it?" Alexander asked, curious.

"I only need some water," I replied, to which Alexander laughed and nodded.

Chela pulled Sienna and the cart to a halt, then reached behind her seat, producing a pair of water skins. She handed one to Alexander and the other to me. As I began to move away from her, she grasped my hand.

"Andrew, wait," she said hesitantly.

I handed the water skin to Emmarie and met Chela's gaze unflinchingly as I waited for her to continue.

"Alex told me your story." She looked away, sorrow in her eyes. "I knew you'd lost your wife, but I didn't know the circumstances. I know why you reacted as you did. I'm sorry."

I nodded once, jaw clenched. "Alex and Tom are all I have left. Colin has taken everything else, and I don't intend to lose any more."

"I understand," she said as she released my hand.

I recognized the empathy in her gaze, and the last vestiges of my fury rapidly dissolved. I realized she'd simply misunderstood my intent the previous evening, and a pang of guilt shot through my core. I had once again allowed my temper to take control of a situation where I should have known to rein it in. I sighed and raked one hand through my hair.

"It's alright," she said after a moment. "I won't hold your anger against you. I would have reacted in much the same way had our circumstances been reversed."

While her words were meant to console me, they only made me feel worse about the situation. I sorely needed to be more mindful of my temper. It pushed people away, even those seeking to help, and that was something I could not afford. We'd come to the Southlands with nothing, and it was only by the charity of others that we'd managed to survive so far.

I nodded and took the water skin from Alexander when he offered it, drinking deeply. "I'm sorry," I said finally, "but I meant what I said."

"As did I," she countered.

I understood she referred to Emmarie and the possibility of leaving her behind should she prove "problematic." While I hoped it wouldn't come to that, it was difficult to judge how Emmarie would handle herself when faced with certain danger.

I frowned but nodded an acknowledgment. We now understood one another, and I didn't believe we'd have any further disagreements.

I glanced at Emmarie. She'd wandered a short distance away and was gazing toward the dark ridgeline that marked our next destination. I wondered if she knew what we'd discussed and if she had, what her thoughts were. Her features were expressionless and betrayed no emotion beyond mild curiosity directed toward the landscape spread before us.

"I'll speak with her," I promised while Alexander strode ahead to accompany her.

"Perhaps you can do so later. I'd like to speak with you regarding my earlier conversation with your brother."

I lifted my eyebrows in silent question as she flicked Sienna's reins.

"I've been a guide to six other would-be magi prior to Alexander," she said after a moment's pause. "Four completed their journeys successfully, but the other two… They did not."

I frowned and glanced at Alexander. He was laughing at something Emmarie had said, seemingly carefree.

"What happened to the other two?" I asked.

She shook her head, a pained expression on her weathered features. "There's a dreadful place we'll be forced to pass through after Alexander finishes his trials at the Ashen Shrine and the Ivory Spire. We call it the Venom-weavers' Forest, after the arachnids who reside there." She paused, her gaze locked on something far away as she recalled unpleasant memories. "One of my charges never made it through. We weren't even within the confines of the forest when we made camp that night, but I awoke to screams just before dawn. Some of the spiders had come to investigate, which was unusual but not unheard of. The screams had come from the guardian as she defended our camp, but there were four Weavers to one woman. She didn't survive."

"I'm sorry."

She sighed and looked away. "I tried to persuade the mage to retreat. We weren't far from the spire, but when his guardian perished, he went berserk. I couldn't stop him. He was far more powerful than I'd believed, and his ability enabled him to conjure fire and bend it to his will. He summoned his magic but drew too much power. He lacked the training to properly handle it. He killed the spiders but sacrificed himself in doing so. It was a terrible tragedy, one I don't wish to relive."

"It must have been difficult to lose them both," I replied, though my thoughts were focused on how I'd handle a similar situation. I needed to learn more about the spiders.

"It was that incident I recalled when we spoke last night," she continued. "The Venom-weavers should not be taken lightly, although I believe we have a greater advantage over them than the typical group of travelers can claim." She glanced at me appraisingly. "The spiders fear dragons, you know."

I raised an eyebrow. "I didn't. Truthfully, there is still much I haven't learned about myself. I never had the chance."

She nodded. "It's understandable, given your upbringing. Alexander said you've both visited the Stone Grove and that you've spoken with your father."

The memory brought a faint smile to my lips, though the meeting had been bittersweet. "I spoke with him at length. He gave me his surname—something I didn't have when we came to the Southlands." I paused as I considered what she'd said regarding the spiders. "Why do the spiders fear the dragon-kind?"

"Dragon scale is one of the few materials their fangs cannot penetrate," she replied with a shrug. "Coupled with the strength dragons are rumored to possess, I believe they simply know when they're outmatched."

"Hmm."

Her explanation seemed too simple, too straightforward. The Corodan also feared the dragon-kind; I'd led many battles against them, but it had taken years before I learned they were fearful of my dragon form. Their leader had summarized the encounter with three words: *Danger. Power. Death.*

"You think it might be otherwise?" she asked, genuinely curious.

I shrugged. "I'm not certain. I fought against Corodan for much of my adult life. I killed the Hive-queen in my dragon form, which resulted in peace for the first time in my memory, but it left a lasting impression on them. They feared me, but I don't believe it was simply because I'm dragon-kind. The scene was…brutal."

She nodded thoughtfully. "I'd heard the Corodan also feared dragons, though perhaps there's more to it." Her gaze drifted to the path ahead as she considered her next words. "I suppose you'd like to know what happened to the other mage who failed to complete the pilgrimage?"

"Yes. I need to learn what we'll face. If I'm to protect Alexander, there is much I can learn from the failures of others."

"Wise words." Her eyes had drifted toward the horizon line once more, her expression distant. "The other mage's tale is one that still confounds me. I wish I could give you a better account of what occurred, but I don't know all the details." She released a weary sigh, then pressed on. "We were nearing the end of the journey—the final destination upon the pilgrimage is in the highlands, far to the south and east, in the ancestral home of the dragons. Since the dragons' departure, the trek has become arduous. I've been told there is a second passage, one which can only be opened by the dragon-kind, but it's been inaccessible to us. I plan to lead Alexander to that entrance. It will save us much time. I believe you can open it."

When I nodded, she continued. "Without a dragon or a skin-changer to aid us, we were forced to take the long road to the highest peaks. We had perhaps two more days of travel, and all seemed well. The mage wasn't acting strangely, and her guardian had done an excellent job throughout our journey. I was confident the pilgrimage would finish successfully within the week. But it was not to be."

She shook her head sadly. "Something happened while we were camped for the night, but I don't know what. When I awoke in the morning, all seemed well. The guardian awakened sometime later and mentioned it was unusual for our mage to sleep so late. He felt something was wrong, then went to her tent to wake her. She was gone. We searched our campsite for any sign of her departure, but we found nothing to indicate which direction she may have gone. We searched for several days but never found her. I don't know what became of her."

"Does that happen often?" I asked, suddenly concerned for Alexander in a way I hadn't been previously.

"No, but it isn't unheard of. Sometimes a mage falls into madness without any warning. I fear it's what happened to her, though I'll never know for certain. Magi are particularly vulnerable in the last stages of their journey."

She peered at me, her eyes boring into my own. "Andrew, if the madness strikes your brother, there is nothing that you—or anyone else—can do to save him. And I fear he will be more susceptible than most. His power is vast. He's tapped into it at least once without knowing he did, based on what he's shared of his imprisonment. The only way to prevent the madness entirely is to complete the pilgrimage."

She shook her head, her expression fearful. "But you must realize that completion does not rely solely on surviving the physical dangers of this land—he must also survive the danger he poses to himself."

I nodded and averted my gaze as the unfamiliar sensation of helplessness washed over me. What good was a guardian who could not protect their mage from *every* danger they encountered?

The spiders I could deal with. Bandits, too. But I was powerless against the forces of magic.

THREE

The afternoon was fading into evening when I finally spoke with Emmarie. We'd stopped for the night, the tents were erected, and Chela was stoking a campfire. Alexander had departed to fill our water skins; a lake glimmered in the fading light a short distance south of our campsite.

I drew Emmarie aside, dreading the pending conversation. I hoped she'd understand Chela's concerns, but I wasn't certain how she'd react. She'd remained unusually quiet throughout the day, and I wondered once more if she'd overheard what had been said the previous evening.

Before I had the opportunity to broach the subject, Emmarie blurted, "I know why you want to talk."

I raised my eyebrows. "Then you understand why Chela is worried."

She sighed heavily. "Yes, and I'm sorry. I know I can be impulsive, but it only happens when I'm bored. I've been dreaming of an adventure like this since I was a child, and I won't let the opportunity pass me by!" Her dark eyes shone with emotion while her lower lip began to tremble.

"I don't want to leave you behind," I replied evenly, hoping my words would ease her fears. "I truly believe you'll be of great help, but I gave Chela my word that I'd speak with you. She's concerned for Alex's safety, as is her duty."

She swallowed hard and nodded, her eyes brimming with tears. "I promise I won't do anything to put us in danger. I *know* what lies ahead just as well as she does. I've heard many tales from the birds I've befriended." She hung her head as the tears began to fall. "I…I only wanted to help!"

I drew a breath and put one arm around her narrow shoulders in an attempt to comfort her. "Emmarie, I understand. I *do*. And I truly believe you have nothing to fear from Chela. I'll watch over you."

She sniffed and raised her eyes to meet mine. "Do you truly mean that, Andrew?"

Her voice held equal notes of desperation and hope. She'd wagered everything in her young life to follow us on this journey, and if we sent her away, she'd return home in disgrace. I'd met her uncle briefly in Dark Heart; he'd seemed an influential man amongst the Merael, but Emmarie had alluded to his strict and unyielding nature on more than one occasion. I didn't believe her people would take her disobedience well, and even less so if we refused her offer of aid.

I didn't possess the constitution to knowingly ruin her young life. She'd stay with us, no matter how vehemently Chela might argue against it.

"Yes, I mean that," I replied. "You should speak with Chela and explain this to her exactly as you did for me. She *will* understand."

She swallowed again, then nodded, blinking away her tears. "I hope so." She drew a shaky breath and pushed herself away. "Thank you," she whispered before turning back toward our camp. She squared her shoulders and strode toward Chela, determined to explain herself and secure her position within our group.

I managed a faint smile. I had no doubts Emmarie would prove herself to Chela in the days to come.

Three days passed. We trudged through the grassland toward the dark ridge that loomed ever closer as the miles disappeared in our wake. I asked Chela a myriad of questions regarding the Venom-weavers, the caverns that lay ahead, and the bandits we might encounter there. She answered patiently, understanding my unspoken desire to glean every tidbit of knowledge she had to spare regarding Alexander's defense.

On the evening of the third day, we reached a location a short distance from the ridge where a grove of trees surrounded a small pond. Chela indicated we should make camp for the night, and as Alexander and I set up the tents, an eerie, keening wail pierced the air.

I froze, unnerved by the sound. The land immediately surrounding us had fallen still and silent as the wailing drifted to us upon the breeze. I was unable to determine the source of the noise and hoped it wasn't a sign of trouble. Alexander paused as well, his eyes wide as he surveyed our surroundings.

"Don't concern yourselves with the sound," Chela called as she waved one hand dismissively in the air. "That's merely the caverns. The rocks are porous. When the wind blows past the ridge just so, it creates that noise. It's why we call it the Wailing Caverns." She flashed a knowing grin.

"It's unsettling," Alexander grumbled before returning to the tent.

I agreed. The sound was akin to the cry of someone in the throes of anguish. If the wind continued to blow and produce that unearthly racket, I'd manage very little sleep during the night.

"We're near enough to the caverns that we ought to post a watch overnight," Chela said after a moment. "There may be bandits nearby. It would be wise to remain vigilant."

I glanced toward Alexander, who nodded once in confirmation. We had long ago determined when we needed to post watch, he'd take the first, and I'd take the second. It had been our routine for years while on campaign for the late Novanian king. Chela's eyes darted between us, uncertain as to what had transpired, and I broke into a grin.

"We've followed the same plan countless times," Alexander said for her benefit. "I'll take first watch, he'll take second. That's our arrangement."

She blinked once, then nodded. "I'm unused to a mage participating in the watch on these journeys," she replied with a laugh. "Most magi aren't trained warriors."

He shrugged. "I'm capable enough with a sword. I'm not as effective as my brother, but I'm better than most."

What Alexander had omitted was in terms of technique, he was often superior, but I possessed a decided advantage due to my unusual strength and longer reach.

Chela arched one eyebrow at Alexander. "I doubt there are any left who can rival your brother in combat."

"My uncle used to tell me stories of the Mage Wars," Emmarie broke in. "He told of the dragon-kind descending from the highlands to make the journey north, toward the Barrier. A pair of skin-changers once came through Dark Heart. They weren't welcome in the Thornhallow, but one of our people accompanied them on their journey. The story claimed they were unmatched on the battlefield."

Finished with the tent I'd been assembling, I straightened and met the Merael girl's gaze. "This isn't the first time since we met that I've been told my kind aren't welcome in your forest. Why is that?"

She sighed and looked away. "My people have always felt a union between two different species is fundamentally wrong, that it should not be. A dragon should not pursue a human romantically, but it was once commonplace. Skin-changers are a reminder of what such a union can produce, and my people have always believed it unnatural, that it defies the laws of nature." She shook her head, her dark hair falling to obscure part of her face. "I think those beliefs are old-fashioned and based on superstition. I don't share them, Andrew."

When we'd passed through the Thornhallow, I'd been instructed to remain in my dragon form for the duration of our journey. If what I truly was had been revealed, the Merael would have been furious. I had no doubt they knew the truth now, and it was unlikely I'd be welcomed a second time.

"I won't be able to return, will I?" I asked.

It was irksome I should be made an outcast due to the choices of my forbears. It wasn't the first time such a situation had arisen, and I knew it wouldn't be the last, yet it rankled all the same.

She shrugged. "I'm certain they know what you are now, but since you're the last of your kind, they may make an exception. I don't know. It will be up to the Elders to decide."

"Fortunately, none of the sites we seek will take us that far north," Chela replied cheerfully. "Negotiating passage through the Thornhallow with the Merael will be a task for a later date."

While I'd known little of the history surrounding the dragon-kind prior to our exile from Novania, I'd gleaned some information during our travels and more from speaking to my father. I understood skin-changers had always been a rarity; the circumstances between the dragon-mage and their chosen partner had to be aligned precisely, else nothing would come from the union. My father had insinuated skin-changers had always been considered outcasts by larger society and had only been welcomed by the dragons themselves.

My experience had shown some humans revered me, the Merael believed I was an abomination, the Corodan feared me…

It had only been my father, Caelmarion Zorai, and Vera who had seemed to accept me as I was without hesitation. Even Alexander had been fearful when I first revealed my dragon form to him.

Thoughts of Vera stirred the deep anguish I'd been attempting to bury over the past few weeks. I'd been so fortunate to have met her, so happy sharing my life with her. She had not only accepted what I was, but she'd encouraged me to learn more about my dragon half. Colin had ordered her death and left me reeling, even now. I was hollow, angry, heartsick, and bitter.

I missed her calming presence, her inquisitive nature, the beautiful smile that lit up her face and sparkled in her eyes. For weeks, I'd been plagued by nightmares, forced to relive the devastation Colin had visited on Vinterry and the discovery of her lifeless form amongst the charred vineyards.

The wound he'd rent in my heart flared. Tears threatened, but I refused to let them fall. Damn Colin for all he'd done.

I sighed and turned away from the others, my thoughts focused on the memory of the woman I'd lost and continued to mourn.

Sleep proved elusive during the night. The unearthly keening from the nearby ridgeline was impossible to ignore. When I did finally drift off, my dreams featured the unsettling sound, and it was a relief when Alexander awakened me to take over the watch. We spoke briefly before he turned in for a few hours rest.

"All has been quiet if you discount the wind," he said. "I'm not certain I'll sleep with that racket." He glanced toward the cart, where Chela was asleep amongst our supplies, unperturbed by the noise. "At least someone is getting rest."

"Relax, brother," I replied, trying to make light of the situation. "You'll be asleep in no time."

He snorted and rolled his eyes in response, then ducked into the tent I'd just vacated.

I sat alongside the dying embers of our campfire but didn't bother to stoke the flames. The air was cool but not cold, and I didn't require the heat to keep warm. I listened to the other sounds around our camp; the chirp of crickets, the occasional call of an owl, the buzz of some insects high in the trees. I peered at the sky and noted the moon had shrunk to a thin sliver, its pale light so faint most of the stars outshone it. Nothing stirred across the landscape. All was well, as Alexander had indicated.

I'd been at my post for perhaps an hour when I heard rustling from Emmarie's tent. I turned to note she'd emerged to study the campsite. Her eyes were rimmed in red and her face was haggard.

"May I join you?" she whispered after a moment. "I can't sleep."

"Of course."

She shuffled forward and sat down carefully near the remnants of the fire. "I'd hoped the wind would stop during the night, but there is just enough breeze that it continues." She shook her head, her jaw set in an expression of frustration. "That sound is unnatural."

"I didn't sleep much, either," I replied.

"Chela said bandits often lurk in the caverns. How can they stand the noise?"

I shrugged, knowing well what desperation could force a person to endure. "I don't know the history of these bandits, but if they're like those I've encountered from Novania, they're here to avoid someone or something. If they're determined to remain hidden, they're likely to push themselves farther than most when it comes to enduring hardships. The sound may have become nothing more to them than the crickets' chirping seems to us."

She tilted her head to one side, her brow furrowed in thought. "I didn't consider that." She looked up at the starry sky and was silent for a time.

"What is the land north of the Barrier like?" she asked after a while.

I chuckled. "The land itself isn't much different than this one. The people are different, to be sure. There are only humans, unless you travel far enough to reach the Gloaming Highlands. Those belong to the Corodan. I don't know what lies north of their lands."

"There are Corodan in the southern reaches, beyond The Green," she replied. "I've never met one. Have you?"

"Some. Often, our meetings were bloody. Novania was at war with the Corodan since before my birth. Before my tyrant half-brother took the throne, I spent most summers traveling north toward the highlands to fend them off. They'd often raid towns and villages, killing the inhabitants senselessly and burning what structures they could before fleeing to the highlands."

"I didn't know the Corodan were violent," Emmarie replied thoughtfully. "They aren't here. The Merael of The Green trade with them. Why did those in the north attack?"

I shook my head. "I don't know. A little more than a year ago, we negotiated peace with them. When we fled Novania, the Corodan had kept their word. It was still peaceful."

"How did you do that?" she asked, genuinely curious.

I smiled grimly into the darkness and shared the tale of what had transpired in the frozen north of Novania kingdom. The Corodan had sought to draw me out, as I'd been the commander of the king's army. They believed if they killed me, it would throw our forces into turmoil. The Corodan hadn't known I was anything but human, and it had been the downfall of their devious plan. I'd met with their Hive-queen, on their terms, and had walked directly into an ambush.

Unfortunately for the Corodan, I wasn't visible to my own forces and wasn't averse to shifting into my dragon form to defend myself. I'd slain the Corodan responsible for the ambush and their Hive-queen. The next day, a new emissary from the Corodan arrived, seeking peace.

Emmarie's eyes widened as I described the devastation I'd left in my wake. It wasn't a moment I was proud of, but I'd acted out of necessity. She was silent for some time, gazing into the darkness, her expression troubled. I wondered what she thought of me now that she understood the horrors I was capable of.

I listened to the sounds of the night creatures and realized belatedly that the moaning of the wind had ceased, and the first glimmer of dawn was beginning to lighten the eastern horizon.

"I understand why you reacted as you did," she said, "but I think I'm beginning to understand why the Elders of my people have always feared your kind. If what you said is true, your power must be terrifying." She looked down, a range of emotions playing across her features. "I know you're a good person and that you try to do what's right. I know you fought the Corodan in self-defense. But… It goes against everything I've been taught. The Merael believe all life is sacred, even that of our enemies. The life you have led is so different than the one I've known." Her tone became somber as she spoke.

I sighed and leaned back. "I've always been a soldier, a warrior. Alexander's father tried to negotiate with the Corodan several times, but to no avail. When they began to attack settlements, we were dispatched to end the threat. On the battlefield, there is little room for peaceful negotiation. You fight to the death against each and every opponent. If you don't, it's your blood that's spilled."

"My people avoid conflict," Emmarie replied somberly. She hugged her arms around herself and refused to meet my eyes. "I don't know if I could stomach such violence. Do you think we'll be forced to fight the bandits?" When she raised her eyes to meet mine, they were shiny with unshed tears.

"I don't know," I replied gently, "but I am prepared for that eventuality. I've sworn to protect my brother."

She nodded. "I know, but I'm afraid."

"I won't let anything happen to anyone in our party, Emmarie. I promise I'll do my best to keep you safe."

She shook her head. A single tear escaped the corner of her eye to trace its way down her thin cheek in the gray pre-dawn light. "No, that isn't what I was referring to. I'm afraid of *you*."

I looked away, ashamed and at a loss for words. I couldn't help being what I was, and I'd never taken a life without reason, but I didn't know how to allay her fears.

I felt light pressure on my arm and turned to find she'd placed one of her small green hands there.

"This isn't your fault. Please understand." She looked away for a moment, appeared to steel herself, then continued. "Your ways are so different from the Merael's. Alexander's as well. He is so much like you. I suppose I misspoke when I said I was afraid of you, because it isn't *you*, but what you represent. The thought of war coming from the north frightens me."

I nodded, a small part of me amused that our conversation had shifted from my attempts to console her to her doing the same for me.

"War is ugly, brutal, and terrifying," I replied grimly. "Even with my enhanced abilities, I was fearful each and every time I stepped onto a battlefield. Even the most well-laid plans can disintegrate into chaos in a matter of seconds. There is little one can do when that happens but do their utmost to survive." I shook my head. "I also fear what war would do to this land. The people here are innocent, trying to live their lives in peace. Colin won't allow it if he has his way. He'll never stop his pursuit of us. Not until one or the other of us falls."

"I promised Alex that I'd help as I can throughout his journey. I want to travel with you as long as you'll allow it." She looked down. "When I spoke to Chela, she seemed to understand, though I still don't think she trusts me. She said I was impulsive and flighty."

Emmarie made a face of disgust, and I chuckled.

"You are young," I said when she frowned at me. "I don't think she knows what to make of you."

"I want to *help*," she replied fiercely. "I may be young, but I know what I'm capable of. And I will help, even if it means you'll be traveling north after the pilgrimage is done. Alex told me what the Oracle said to you. No matter how terrifying the prospect of war is, I think it's also inevitable. The Oracle said it herself, and she's rarely wrong. If I let my fear stand in the way, what good am I to anyone? I must do this."

I admired her determination. I decided in that moment that if she should ever require my assistance, she'd have it. After all, we'd only been brief acquaintances prior to our arrival in the Citadel, and she'd defied her uncle's orders to follow us and offer her skills. She'd risked her future to join us on Alexander's journey.

And I believed her heart was in the right place, even if I secretly agreed with Chela's assessment of her character.

FOUR

We reached the entrance to the Wailing Caverns by midmorning. The ridge of dark stone rose abruptly from the surrounding grassland and stretched in either direction for countless miles. The stone was rough, but the rockface was sheer and nearly vertical, leaving no choice but to travel through the caverns. On closer inspection, the stone was pitted with innumerable pinpoint holes, the source of the eerie noise from the previous evening. At present, the air was calm, and the only sounds beyond our muted conversation were the calling of birds and the hum of insects.

Alexander and I donned our armor before breaking camp at Chela's behest. She remained concerned about the possibility of bandits, though there was no sign of them at the caverns' entrance.

I was pleased at how well Alexander's new armor fit him, and equally so that he hadn't argued against wearing it. He believed the dragon scale I'd sacrificed to have it crafted had been too costly, but I disagreed. I was recovering from the ordeal well enough, and he'd be better protected than any adversary he faced. Nothing else truly mattered.

We prepared torches, binding cloth strips around a few sturdy branches before dousing them with oil. As we approached the caves' entrance, Alexander lit a pair with a bit of flint, then handed one to Chela while keeping the other for himself. The entrance was twice the size of our small cart, and it seemed Sienna was unafraid of proceeding. Emmarie clambered into the bed of the cart and wedged herself between crates of rations as Alexander and I led our group into the gloom.

The air within was dank and smelled of mildew. A thin sheen of condensation coated the walls and floor, and other than the faint dripping of distant water, it was silent. Our footsteps echoed eerily.

It wasn't long before the passage opened into a vast chamber. The ceiling rose abruptly, disappearing into shadows even our torches couldn't penetrate, while the walls arced away from our path to dissolve into the gloom.

I paused to survey the area warily. Natural columns of stone rose from the floor to vanish into the darkness overhead. The path we'd taken was clearly visible, threading through columns and stalagmites that punctuated the cavern's floor. Where the path led, the stone was worn smooth by countless generations of footsteps from travelers like ourselves.

Alexander extended his torch in a vain attempt to locate the roof. As he gazed into the shadows above, a raucous chittering erupted, momentarily deafening us and startling Sienna.

From the cart bed, Emmarie laughed cheerfully. "They don't like your light, Alex," she said.

He lowered his torch in response but appeared disconcerted.

"What's up there?" I asked.

"Bats," she replied with a shrug. "I'd like to speak with them for a moment."

She peered into the shadows, and I wondered if she could see the creatures clinging to the stone high above. She made a series of chittering noises and clicks, and a moment later, the sound of leathery wings flapping in the darkness could be heard. A solitary bat flew into the circle of torchlight and lit upon Emmarie's forearm. They conversed for several seconds before the bat departed, rising back toward the shadowy recesses and its unseen brethren.

"She says there is a fork in the path ahead," Emmarie said. "If we take the left path, it leads to a camp. She called it a 'man-place.' It may be where the bandits reside."

Chela nodded, then closed her eyes briefly. A scent akin to cinnamon permeated the air as she drew upon her magic. The odor caused my nose to itch, and though I tried to avoid it, I began to sneeze.

Alexander smirked at me knowingly. The magi we'd encountered could not smell the magic they wove as I did. Some scents were pleasant, but most caused me to sneeze. Alexander found it amusing. I glowered at him in response.

After a moment, the cinnamon scent began to fade and Chela opened her eyes. "There is no way through the caverns to the other side if we take the right-hand pathway," she stated, her tone dismayed. "We must take the left path. Be prepared for anything."

I nodded and drew my sword, then moved a few paces ahead of Alexander. We made our way through the vast room, winding through the columns as the bats continued to chitter in the shadows overhead. When we reached the opposite side of the chamber, the branching of the path was clearly visible as the bat had described it to Emmarie. The trickle of water echoed from the path leading to the right. To the left, it would lead us through a narrow gap that looked only just wide enough to allow the cart passage. Beyond the gap, darkness obscured my view.

I motioned for Alexander to stay close as I passed through the gap into the space beyond. I found myself in another chamber, much smaller than the last. The path curved along one wall, and where the torchlight managed to penetrate the gloom at the center of the chamber, delicate, glittering formations of crystal in a variety of colors were visible.

Overhead, the rocks began to moan as the wind outside passed over and through them. The sound was muted within the heart of the ridge, and I abruptly understood how the bandits resided here without the noise driving them to madness. It was but a whisper compared to what we'd endured through the night.

"I've always found this chamber fascinating," Chela said softly after a time. "It's a wonder how these crystals formed. It's almost as though they were wrought by a great artist and left abandoned here for reasons unknown."

As the path led further into the crystal chamber, the sound of water began to fade behind us, only to be replaced with the muted keening of the wind above. The path ran straight for a time, then turned sharply to the left as it wound between two massive stone columns and into another chamber.

As we made the turn, the acrid scent of a campfire hit my nostrils, and I signaled to the others to wait as I moved ahead to investigate. I didn't bother to take a torch with me; I could see almost as well in the darkness as I could in the light. The path led deeper into the next chamber, and I noted the flickering light of a fire some distance within. I moved slowly and kept to the shadows as I neared what appeared to be a small camp.

A pair of tents were erected near the fire, and three men huddled around its flames, their faces bathed in the dancing, orange light. Their conversation was subdued, and they appeared weary and troubled. There were no weapons amongst them nor any sign of provisions. I decided they posed little threat to us. I slipped away from the camp and I made my way back to the others.

Alexander appeared relieved upon my return. "What was it? I haven't heard or seen anything, Andrew."

I described the camp and the men I'd observed. "I don't think they'll be any trouble."

"It has been a number of years since I last traveled this way," Chela said, "but I find their camp troubling. From your description, I don't believe they are bandits, but we should remain wary."

I led the way, retracing my steps toward the small camp. Two of the men remained at the campfire as we neared, but the third was nowhere to be seen. With the horse and cart in our midst, our presence was noted by the men as we approached their location. One of them stood as he spied our group, and he held his hands up to demonstrate he meant no harm. The other ducked inside one of the tents and began to speak in a low tone.

"We don't want trouble," the man stated as he moved away from the campfire. He walked with a noticeable limp.

"We aren't here for trouble," I replied. "We're only passing through on our way to the shrine."

He nodded, and understanding crossed his grizzled features. He shuffled closer to the path and grimaced.

"You're hurt," Chela stated. "What happened to you?"

The man smiled wryly. Behind him, the other man exited the tent, followed by the third, who carried an unmoving child in his arms. As they neared, I noted all three bore injuries in the early stages of healing.

Bruises crossed their arms and lacerations peaked from beneath their sleeves, clear indicators of recent fighting.

"There was a plague in the main settlement," the first replied. "Some of our number disagreed when we told them we planned to leave. The plague claimed the lives of every person it infected, and I was not going to sit idly by and allow that to happen to myself." He sighed with a shake of his head.

The man bearing the child spoke next. "Nor was I. We left the settlement at night, hoping we wouldn't attract notice, but the guards learned of our plan. There was a bit of an altercation." He smirked. "What you see is the result of that, but we have not taken ill as the others did." He looked down at the small girl he held in his arms, and his expression became grave. "My daughter took a knife wound during our escape. It's beyond my skill to heal."

I glanced at Chela; she appeared pensive.

"I'm afraid I have no healing abilities," she replied. "Mine lay in navigation."

"You misunderstand me," the man replied with a tired smile. "It would have been nothing short of miraculous if a trained healer-mage came through on a pilgrimage. I ask only that you carry my Rina to the shrine. Elder Mallora has the healing gift, or so I've been told."

The tale the men told seemed plausible, and I detected no deception in their eyes. I was willing to take the child to the shrine, for it was clear she required aid. The girl was pale and appeared stricken as she slept in her father's arms, but the decision could not be mine alone. Chela was our guide, and I would defer to her judgment.

Chela sighed, then nodded. "You're certain she doesn't have the plague?" When the trio nodded, she said, "We'll take her to the shrine, but no further. She needs help, and I'm not one to turn my back on a child."

The man's rugged features dissolved into tears as emotion overcame him. "Thank you, thank you," he said, genuinely grateful. "Rina is the only family I have. Those bastards hurt her—and I was only trying to save her! Thank you."

Emmarie made room in the cart for the sleeping girl and hopped down once Rina was settled within. I asked the men for further information on the settlement they had spoken of, hoping our path would not lead in the same direction. From what Chela had told us, our journey would prove dangerous enough without exposure to a deadly disease.

The first man answered my inquiry. "Your path won't lead you through the settlement. Albrecht here," he gestured to the emotional father, "returned last night to check on the state of things." He sighed with a shake of his head.

"They're all dead," Albrecht stated, his tone hollow with grief. "All of them. Whatever that plague is, you'd best stay clear of it. Stick to the main path. It'll take you back to the surface, then on to the shrine. And tell my Rina that I'll come for her once we've healed and can travel again."

"I don't believe he told us the full story," Chela stated sometime later.

The path had led us through a series of narrow chambers, then began to slope gently upward. Rina slept fitfully in the cart bed, at times moaning softly as though she were in pain. Despite her father's tale, we failed to locate any evidence of her supposed knife wound. Emmarie had examined her in the dim torchlight once we'd traveled some distance from the camp and found nothing more than a fading bruise on one of the girl's knees.

I agreed with Chela; there was something more to the tale than they'd shared.

"Have you ever heard of a plague like that?" Alexander asked. "Andrew and I survived a few summers when plague was rampant in the Capitol. Many died, but there were always survivors. I find it difficult to believe their story."

"As do I," Chela replied with a frown. "It also troubles me that this girl appears unharmed, but something obviously ails her. Her father was genuinely grateful that we agreed to take her to the shrine, but something does not add up."

"Perhaps the girl can tell us more when she wakes," I suggested.

"*If* she wakes," Chela countered. "I'm not certain she will before we're forced to part ways."

I nodded, worried for the fate of the child that had suddenly come under our care. "How much farther to the shrine?"

Chela closed her eyes briefly while the cinnamon-scent of her magic caused my nostrils to twitch. I managed to stave off a second bout of sneezing.

"We should be outside of the caverns by nightfall. It's perhaps another hour. We'll make camp outside, and we'll be at the shrine by midday tomorrow."

Alexander groaned. "I'm not looking forward to another night listening to the wind's infernal howling."

Chela chuckled. "Do as I do—plug your ears with a bit of cloth. It works wonders."

FIVE

As Chela had predicted, we arrived at the Ashen Shrine just after noon the following day. The remainder of our journey through the caverns had been uneventful, though Chela's advice for blocking the wind's howling had done little to aid me in falling asleep. I'd taken the second watch again, but the keening of the wind as it passed through the porous stone persisted even through the cloth, and I'd been unable to rest before my turn to guard the camp arrived. I was glad to be away from the caverns and on to less noisome surroundings.

Rina had not yet awoken. She continued to produce weak moans and looked to be in pain, though there was nothing we could do to assist her. When we arrived at the shrine, Chela explained our situation and that of the girl's to the two magi who greeted us outside the entrance.

The shrine was a small building nestled at the back of a broad, forested valley. It was two stories tall, but was dwarfed by the trees that surrounded it. The walls appeared charred, and I recalled Chela's tale of the wildfire that had struck the area years ago. Decades must have passed since that time, for the forest had completely recovered.

As one of the magi retreated into the shrine, the other spoke to us and asked of news from the wider world. Alexander and I had much to share, but had only just begun our tale when the other mage returned.

"Elder Mallora asks to see the girl," he stated. "I'll take her within. Elder Vincent will be downstairs presently. He wishes to speak with you, Alexander."

I glanced toward my brother, who bit his lower lip and nodded. He scratched at the nape of his neck, a clear indication of his nerves. I was confident Alexander would succeed, but this was new territory for him. I understood his anxiety.

Rina was taken into the building while we awaited Vincent. I hoped for her sake she'd recover to reunite with her father at a later date.

Chela turned to face Alexander. "He may wish to begin your trial immediately, so be prepared for that possibility. It will depend on what he gleans from speaking with you. Most likely, he'll also ask to see your Mark."

Alexander sighed and raked one hand through his blond hair. I noted it had become shaggy since our flight from Novania, but visiting a barber had been the last thing on our minds.

"I should have expected that," he replied with a frown, his tone sharp with irritation. "Everyone wants to see it."

"You know the reason for it as well as I do," I reminded him. "The Oracle claimed your Mark is unusual, and that you'll be capable of greater feats than most. They're curious, nothing more."

He crossed his arms and glowered for a moment before relenting. "I know, brother, but I'm growing tired of it. I feel as if I'm on display."

I resisted the urge to roll my eyes. "Believe me, I understand how you feel. It's not something you'll ever grow used to."

He nodded and looked away. "I'm sorry. I know we're in this together—"

At that moment, the door opened to reveal a tall, lanky man. He stepped into the late summer sunlight, one hand raised to shade his eyes. His face appeared ageless, though his hair was starkly white and his eyes glimmered with a wisdom that could have only come from the passage of decades. He nodded once to Chela before turning his piercing gaze on Alexander.

"My name is Vincent," he said, his voice a strong baritone. "I'm an elder, and have made it my latest purpose to serve this shrine. I oversee the initiation of the magi who travel here to begin their trials." His gaze swept from Alexander to study me, then back again as he scrutinized what he saw before him. "Brothers. Interesting."

"Andrew is my half-brother," Alexander replied.

Vincent narrowed his eyes and focused on me. "You appear strong enough to act as an adequate guardian," he said after a time, "though I sense there is more to you than what my eyes perceive. And you," he said, turning once more to Alexander, "come bearing one of the most powerful Marks I have ever sensed on a fellow mage. Hmm."

Alexander scratched at the back of his neck again, uncomfortable with the assessment. He did not respond.

Vincent continued to study him for several long moments, then seemed to come to a decision. He nodded his head slowly. "I think it best to begin your trial immediately. Please, follow me."

When I moved to follow them inside, Chela stayed me with a hand. "No, Andrew, we must not enter. It's forbidden. Alex must complete the trial on his own, and we should not interfere."

I took a reluctant step backward. Alexander nodded to me once before he disappeared inside with Vincent, his expression one of silent determination coupled with unspoken fear. I didn't know what would befall him during his trials, and I was unused to stepping aside. I'd always considered it my duty as the eldest to look after my half-brothers, and being forced to wait and do nothing while Alexander underwent this challenge was difficult.

Chela sensed my unspoken frustration. "Let's set up camp," she suggested. "We can't go inside, and it may take a significant amount of time before he returns."

"How long?" I asked gruffly.

She began to lead Sienna and the cart toward one side of the shrine. "For some, it's a few hours, but for others, it can take several days. It depends on what the elders see in your brother and what they believe is the best path to embark upon. They'll test his abilities. He'll be forced to prove himself time and again at each stop on our journey."

"I hope he understands it's merely part of the process," I replied as I removed the tent stakes from the cart. "He's frustrated, and we've only arrived at our first destination. Alex isn't known for his patience."

She smirked briefly. "The trait must run in your family. I know it's difficult for you both, having grown up in the north. I understand your concerns, and I thought I was finally explaining things well enough that you'd know what to expect. But I fear you're right. He's frustrated." She looked down and shook her head. "What Alexander doesn't realize is that his Mark holds such vast power, it draws other magi to him. We can't help but react to him as we do. I've never encountered anyone with a gift comparable his."

"Will it always be that way?" I asked. "Once his training is complete, will the affect he seems to have change or disappear?"

She offered me a weary smile. "With training comes greater control over the power and greater confidence in one's abilities. We can sense that as well. Alexander will always have an effect on other magi. With further training, it will only intensify."

I resolved to speak with Alexander during the next leg of our journey. He needed to know if he didn't already, and I wasn't certain Chela had shared that bit of information with him. Perhaps, I conceded, the magnetism he projected had been partially to blame for the Oracle's actions toward him as well.

I wondered what sort of leader he would become. We planned to return home to confront Colin one day, and we'd need allies to aid in the inevitable conflict. If Alexander's mere presence held such a draw for other magi, it could bolster his role as a potential commander within their ranks. He held the potential to act as a bridge between the magi of the Southlands and the people of Novania, something neither Thomas or myself could claim.

"Look!" Emmarie cried out, breaking my reverie.

I turned to find her pointing into the sky. I could just make out the form of a large bird circling above; a hawk or an eagle, perhaps. The creature was silhouetted against the midday sun, making it difficult to distinguish any notable features beyond its size.

"A gray eagle," the mage at the doorway called over to her with a smile. "It has been some time since I've last seen one here."

"Is the eagle's presence significant?" I asked Chela as I continued to work on setting up the tents.

When she did not immediately respond, I looked up to find her gazing at the circling form of the bird, a troubled expression on her face. When she dropped her gaze and met mine, it was clear she was fearful. Her reaction puzzled me.

"Chela? What is it?"

She steeled herself then began to speak, her words tumbling out in a rush. "The gray eagles have long been considered portents, omens.

It's said they're drawn to magic and often herald the coming of the most powerful magi. The eagle's presence here, so soon after Alexander was taken inside for his trial, cannot be a coincidence. It's here because *he* is here."

I shrugged. I didn't understand why the eagle's presence was a source of distress. "We both know Alexander's power is significant."

She sighed, exasperated. "Andrew, the gray eagles have not been active in *years*. It has been rare to catch a glimpse of one—" She broke off, her eyes widening as she spied something else in the sky. I turned to see three more eagles soar into view above the treetops.

"And what does it mean if there are four?" I asked slowly, both curious and fearful of her answer.

She shook her head. "I don't know. So many… After so long…"

"You were going to say something before the others arrived," I pressed.

She nodded slowly, her eyes wide with wonder. "The eagles have not been active—and not in great numbers—for hundreds of years. It is said they often followed mage-warriors into battle. If what the Oracle sensed about your brother is true, then perhaps they are drawn here because that's what he's destined to become." She shook her head again, as though clearing her thoughts. "The gray eagles have long been omens associated with war. We've been at peace for generations, and the very notion of such conflict, such strife… It fills me with terror."

It had been a common sentiment among those we'd met in the Southlands. Alexander and I were no strangers to battle. We'd been trained as soldiers from a young age, and even though he was the king's son, he'd often accompanied me on campaigns. I'd always ensured his safety—as much as one could during the chaos of battle—but he was skilled enough with a sword that he'd rarely faced an equal.

Since we'd fled Novania, I knew it would only be a matter of time before Colin ventured south behind us. He would not relent in his pursuit, and I believed that in time, we'd be forced to confront him. I also knew there would be no reasoning with him, and it was inevitable the confrontation would turn bloody. Those thoughts forced me to recall what the Oracle had shared of her visions—a battlefield strewn with bodies, Alexander in their midst, while a black dragon flew overhead.

I met Chela's gaze evenly. "If war is coming, then Alexander and I must meet it head-on. There can only be one man behind the threat, and that man is Colin Marsden. He is *our* responsibility."

She nodded hesitantly. "Alexander must finish his training first."

"I know." I paused in my work to cross my arms. "I fear Colin won't wait, and I can't protect the Southlands from him until this journey is done. Will the Barrier hold?"

Chela blinked, startled by my question. "I… I have never even questioned it. The Barrier has withstood the elements for centuries, but I've never heard of anyone attempting to break it. The notion is unthinkable."

I frowned. I required further information on the Barrier and its capability for defense, but I wouldn't learn what I needed from Chela. It wouldn't surprise me if Colin attempted to break through it, discarding its legendary impenetrability as mere myths. If what Chela said was true, however, the Barrier's strength had never truly been tested.

"Will we travel anywhere that might have information regarding the Barrier?" I asked. "While Alex is busy with his trials, perhaps I can learn more about the defenses of the Southlands."

"You truly believe your brother will attack," she breathed, eyes wide.

"So long as we remain here, I do."

Evening had fallen before there was any further movement at the entrance to the shrine. Emmarie assisted Chela with supper preparations, while I paced along the perimeter of the clearing that surrounded our campsite and the shrine. I was filled with nervous energy as I wondered how Alexander fared, but I'd been unable to learn anything from the mage who stood vigil at the shrine's entrance. The man was friendly enough, but he could tell me nothing of what occurred within. Perhaps he didn't know.

The gray eagles continued to soar above, and several more had joined the initial four. Emmarie tried several times to communicate with the birds, but they either didn't hear her calls, or were uninterested in speaking with her. As the sun began to set, she gave up on the endeavor entirely.

A tall, slender woman with a commanding demeanor strode outside as twilight enveloped the valley. She was dressed in a tunic and leggings, and her raven-dark hair was swept up into a tight bun. Her skin was the color of mahogany, and her face had the ageless countenance that marked her as one of the magi.

Her dark eyes scanned the campsite, then came to rest on me as I continued my restless patrol. She beckoned to me as she strode toward the others, indicating she preferred to speak with us as a group.

"I am Mallora," she said. "I know why you've come. I wanted to speak to you about the girl."

"She was in the caverns," Chela replied. "A man who claimed to be her father asked us to bring her here, to you. He'd heard you were a healer."

She nodded slowly. "I am, but how is it one of the bandits knew this? They do not travel this way."

I glanced at Chela, recalling our previous conversation and our mutual agreement that the men we'd encountered had not given us their full account. In turns, we told Mallora what we knew and what we'd learned from the trio of men. Emmarie chimed in to share that she'd found no marks on the girl's body and didn't believe she'd been wounded as the man claimed.

"This tale is concerning," Mallora stated once we'd finished. "She was bleeding internally. I have repaired the damage as best I can, but her recovery will take much time. You did her a service by bringing her to me. She would have died within another few days without help. She will remain here, until such time as her father arrives to retrieve her." She shook her head. "But the plague the men spoke of does not follow the traditional progression of natural disease. It gives me pause. I wonder if one of the bandits angered the wrong sort of mage? It sounds like a curse has befallen them, not a natural plague."

I raised my eyebrows. "Such things exist?"

She chuckled humorlessly. "Oh, yes. There are very few magi with the power to cause such maladies, but they do indeed exist. Most learn to channel their abilities into doing good, but on occasion, one will arise with malicious tendencies. Perhaps this is what occurred within the caverns."

A shiver traveled the length of my spine and I shook my head, both awed and appalled by the notion. Perhaps some of the tales we'd been taught as children held grains of truth after all.

"I do not mean to alarm you, but I hope you stayed clear of the settlement," Mallora continued after a moment.

"Yes, we stayed on the direct route to the surface after our encounter," Chela confirmed. "I felt there was something the men weren't telling us, and I didn't believe it safe to explore. The Oracle was very clear in her instructions: Alexander's journey is paramount, and I should not do anything to compromise his chances of success."

Mallora's gaze traveled skyward, and she nodded in agreement. "Yes, it seems he has already gathered a following. His power is immense. I have not seen the like of it before in a man." She turned her penetrating gaze upon me once more. "The two of you share a mother, if I am not mistaken. Did she bear the Mark as well?"

"I don't know," I replied. "If she did, she never mentioned it, though Alex might know the answer. She is why we both survived to adulthood."

"It would be incredible if she were *not* Marked," Mallora replied. "It was rare for a Marked woman to bear a skin-changer, and unheard of for one without the Mark to do so. Coupled with Alexander's power…" She shrugged. "She must have been."

I recalled the last time I'd spoken with our mother. She'd been gravely ill and had passed only a few days after she'd summoned me to her chamber. She insisted that I look after Alexander, and confided that he bore a Mark. He had not learned of my own secret until several years later, when I finally summoned the courage to share it with him.

"We may never know for certain. She passed away nearly seven years ago."

"I'm sorry to hear that," she replied softly. "I didn't know."

I shrugged; her inquiry had meant no harm. "Can you tell me how Alex fares?"

She smiled ruefully. "Not yet. He was still within the trial chamber when I came to speak with you."

Noting my confusion, she continued. "Within each of the pilgrimage sites, there is a sealed room we call the trial chamber. The magi who embark on the pilgrimage will speak with the elders.

Sometimes we dictate what the trial will entail, but with some mages, we are unable to determine the best path for their ability. Your brother fell into the latter category. His gift is one we have not seen in centuries, and even as an elder, the last of the mage-warriors passed long before my time. You see, we have no experience with his brand of magic. He must learn how to harness it on his own." She paused to glance skyward once more, her eyes locked on the eagles as they circled through the twilight. "Those who must follow their own path are taken into the trial chamber. What they experience within is often very personal. Few ever deign to speak of it. Many learn to control their abilities through the process, but it takes time—which is why there are so many pilgrimage sites. Your brother showed much promise, and I am confident he will go far."

"Do you believe he will complete his training successfully?" Chela asked.

Mallora tilted her head slightly in thought, then shrugged. "It's too soon to tell, but I'm certain he will make it to the Frostwake. Beyond that, I cannot see." She glanced toward the shrine's entrance, then said, "I'd best go inside and allow Vincent a break from his vigil. He has monitored Alexander for some time while I tended to the girl."

"What is the Frostwake?" I asked Chela as Mallora departed.

"It is the half-way mark of our journey," she replied. "The Frostwake is a shrine, much like this one. It sits high in the southern mountains, in a place where the snow falls even at midsummer. The pass leading to it is treacherous, even in the best of times. It's heartening to know she believes he'll make it that far." She smiled faintly.

Emmarie appeared at Chela's side. "The stew is ready," she said. "I don't know about you, but I'm famished."

I chuckled at the distraction. "Very well."

We followed Emmarie to the campfire and ate in relative silence. I was lost in my own thoughts as I considered the implications of the gray eagles and what would lay in store for us during the journey ahead. I could not help but wonder how the experience might alter my brother; there was no doubt in my mind that he *would* change, but if it would be for good or ill was yet to be determined.

SIX

I was awakened roughly sometime before dawn. I'd been sleeping soundly, much to my own surprise, and it took several moments to realize who was shaking me from slumber. I blinked blearily several times before my eyes focused on the silhouette leaning over my prone form.

"Alex?"

He rocked back on his heels, laughing, a mischievous light in his green eyes. "I've completed my trial." He grinned. "I wanted to tell you first."

I sat up and reached for the shirt I'd discarded the night before, where it lay crumpled in one corner of the tent. "And you had to wake me from a dead sleep to do so?" I asked, feigning annoyance.

He laughed again. "I thought I'd spare Emmarie and Chela the discomfort of hearing your snores. I could hear you from the shrine's entrance, you know."

I rolled my eyes in mock-exasperation, but didn't respond. He'd teased me for years about snoring, though I'd never been able to corroborate his claims.

I dressed and followed him outside into the gray predawn light. Clouds had blanketed the sky during the night and they now threatened rain. I noted the eagles were no longer present; they'd either moved on or taken shelter for the night.

"What was it like?" I asked after a moment.

He shrugged. "It's difficult to describe. It began with a series of questions from the elders, which were simple enough. They asked about our upbringing and were particularly interested in you for a time, but I suppose that's to be expected." He smiled ruefully, then his eyes focused on a point far in the distance. "When it became apparent that my abilities were outside the scope of their combined experience, they led me to the trial chamber. It reminded me somewhat of the Barrier. It's a room constructed purely of magic. I was told I must go inside alone."

He looked down, his expression thoughtful. "Vincent has an ability akin to Gwerin's. He opened a doorway in the…magical field. Once I entered, the door closed behind me, and I was left alone… And yet, there were others inside. Not people, exactly, but the *spirits* of magi. Some had chosen to be there, but others… They were the spirits of those who didn't survive the trial here."

My eyebrows rose. "Chela never mentioned that."

I glanced toward the cart where she lay sleeping, my thoughts a whirlwind of troubled emotion. Had she withheld the information on purpose, or did she simply not know? Mallora had indicated the trials were often a private affair and most magi refused to speak of them afterward, and Chela's ability seemed so *ordinary*. I didn't know for certain, but I believed she may not have gone through the more rigorous version of the trials. She was a wealth of knowledge, but even she had limits.

And she often forgot we weren't from the Southlands, that we didn't understand so much of the process.

"The spirits aren't dangerous, Andrew. I understand that now," Alexander said. "The danger comes from within. I must show a measure of control over what I do when I use my power. If I lose control even for a moment, it can end in disaster. The trials are meant to guide me through the process of learning how to control it… By the end, I will no longer be a threat to myself." He sighed, and his shoulders slumped. "I must learn incrementally, which is why there are so many destinations along the journey. It takes time and can't be rushed. Going too fast presents its own set of dangers."

I nodded, trying my best to understand a process that I had no experience with—and never would. "Then we'll move forward only when you're ready. This journey is yours, after all."

He snorted a laugh. "I'm fine. We don't have to remain here any longer. This trial is complete, and I've been given leave to move on to the Ivory Spire. Mallora said it should take no more than two days to reach it."

"Will your next trial be similar to this one?" I asked.

"I don't know. It was like an incredibly vivid dream, and at times, it didn't truly feel *real*. The Elders claim it's a common perception. The whole process was nothing short of surreal." He shook his head, bewildered. "Sometimes I wonder if we made the right decision by coming here. And then I think of Colin and remember I wasn't given any damned choice." His voice took on a hard, unyielding edge laced with bitter emotion when he mentioned our brother.

"Colin will pay for what he has done," I replied in a low growl.

"I plan to make certain of it," Alexander agreed. "He'll rue the day he set his plans in motion and killed our father."

The vehemence in his tone was unsurprising. Colin had put us through an ordeal, and we were lucky to have come away relatively unscathed. I wanted to act on the notion then and there, but the Oracle's words—and the promise she'd coerced from me—forced me to focus on the task at hand. Alexander's journey must come first. My thirst for vengeance could be sated later.

"Your training must be completed first," I said. "Only then can we bring Colin to justice. And we will, brother."

He opened his mouth to reply, but was interrupted by Chela as she called our names from across the campsite. When I turned to peer over my shoulder, she was striding toward us, smiling broadly.

"Alex! You've finished!"

He returned her smile with a sheepish one of his own. "I did. And we can be off to the next destination as soon as we've broken camp."

Chela nodded and paused to examine his face closely. "It seems everything went well. For your sake, I'm pleased."

The threatening clouds made good on their promise of a storm at midday. A steady rain began to fall and our path became slick with mud, making footing treacherous. We pressed on through the rain until it strengthened to a deluge a few hours later.

Sienna began to struggle as the path became increasingly hazardous, forcing us to stop and wait out the storm. The rain continued through the afternoon and did not let up until well after night had fallen.

We passed the evening huddled within our tents in an attempt to keep dry, though our clothing was sodden and our boots caked with mud. We took a meal of hard cheese and dried strips of venison as the clouds darkened into a murky expanse with the onset of twilight. Alexander and I talked amicably, though at times the rain striking the canvas of our tent threatened to drown our conversation with its own relentless chatter. We could hear nothing from the other tent where Emmarie and Chela had retreated, despite its proximity to our own.

"I hope Tom's well," I said after a time.

Alexander nodded. "As do I. His last message was concerning."

"I'll ask Chela if there's a messenger-mage in Riversmeet. I'd like to hear from him again." I leaned back and stared at the canvas ceiling above.

"You'll have plenty of opportunity while I'm in my next trial," he replied with a grin. "Chela mentioned we'll need to resupply while there as well. Perhaps she'll help you with the message if you lend your strength to toting provisions."

I rolled my eyes. "You know I'd help if she asked, even if I didn't require something in return."

He snickered. "Then she may as well put you to work, brother. What else would occupy your time while I'm otherwise engaged?"

"Clearly not you." I smirked and reached toward my satchel of belongings before I realized I'd never replaced my last deck of cards. They'd burned along with Vinterry. My previous good humor fled with the realization.

"Andrew?"

"I'm fine." I shook my head, shoving my grief aside. "I need a new deck. It's perfect weather to trounce you in Cabal's Thrall."

Alexander's grin faded. "I should have thought of that while you were recovering in the tower. I could have surprised you." He crossed his arms and scowled at the tent's entrance. "Damn Colin."

I nodded a silent assent. Colin needed to be dealt with.

The rain faded and finally stopped near midnight. We hadn't posted a watch since Chela assured us the road was safe, but I slept lightly nevertheless. Lifelong habits are often difficult to break.

The morning greeted us with another overcast sky, but the clouds were not as dark as the previous day's and I doubted it would rain. The condition of the road had deteriorated during the storm, making our progress slow. We did not reach Riversmeet until the following afternoon.

When the city finally came into view, the land had been sloping for some time as it descended from the now-distant ridgeline. The forest had once again given way to plains; this stretch was greener than those we'd traversed previously, and broad swaths of farmland stretched on either side of the road. A river ran parallel to the road as we neared the city, its flow gentle as it snaked its way across the landscape.

The city was a sprawling expanse of homes and businesses that even from a distance rivaled Novania's Capitol in sheer size. Most structures were built of gray stone with thatched roofs, but at the heart of the city, an enormous yellow-white tower thrust skyward in stark contrast to the buildings around it. The tower was rounded with a pointed roof of white tile. I assumed it was the Ivory Spire—Alexander's next destination.

Like the Citadel, Riversmeet wasn't enclosed by a defensive wall. As the road led us into the fringes of the city, we were met with the noise, bustle, and odors typical of a human populace. Some residents greeted us, while others simply observed our progress toward the city center with mild curiosity. As we neared the spire, the buildings gave way to a large expanse of well-tended garden plots filled with late-summer blooms and lush carpets of grass.

Chela selected an inn on the perimeter of the gardens where we would stay while Alexander completed his next trial. It sported a flower garden of its own adjacent to the entrance and an airy stable at its rear.

"I'll go to the spire in the morning," Alexander said. "I'd like to rest first, and perhaps have a good, *hot* meal."

I chuckled, and Chela said, "We're in no rush. Approaching the spire after a good night's sleep is a wise decision."

We went inside once we'd secured Sienna and our cart at the inn's stable. The establishment was clean and well-kept, and the aroma of baking bread and roasting meat permeated the common room. We were assigned rooms, then instructed to return to the common room once we'd settled in, where we would receive the evening meal.

Alexander and I would share a room, while Emmarie and Chela shared another. The innkeeper was apologetic, but given the crowded state of the common room, I wasn't surprised by the limited space we were offered.

Our room was furnished with a pair of small beds, one pushed to each side of the cramped space. I'd be in for an uncomfortable night; the beds were only just long enough to accommodate Alexander if he lay diagonally across the mattress. I was several inches taller and would be forced to sleep with my feet hanging over the edge or curl unnaturally on my side. I shook my head and suppressed a groan as I stashed my belongings against the wall.

"Just like old times, brother," Alexander said with a laugh. "This reminds me of the inn from Calder's Point. It's clean and nice enough, but they never account for the taller folk."

"There are few places prepared for someone my size. I suppose that's to be expected. There were never many of my kind, even before the dragons fled."

He nodded absently, clearly distracted. "Let's go downstairs. I'm famished."

I laughed and followed him back to the common room. It was packed with travelers and locals alike, many of whom seemed to be regular patrons stopping in as they made their way home from the day's work. As we entered, several turned to observe our passage as we made our way to an empty table near the far corner of the room. After we were seated, I paused to observe the crowd while Alexander ordered us both a pint of ale to go with the steamed fish being served.

One man seemed to have taken a greater interest in us than the rest. He sat alone at the bar, the frothy pint of ale before him nearly untouched. His clothing was of higher quality than most, and though he attempted to fit in, he appeared nervous and edgy. He continued to glance furtively in our direction, but looked away when he met my gaze. I pointed him out to Alexander, who merely nodded in acknowledgment.

A few minutes later, a serving woman returned with our supper and two tankards of chilled ale. Alexander began to tuck in immediately, the nervous stranger seemingly forgotten. I took a few bites before I noticed the man was making his way toward us. I met his gaze as he neared our table and pushed my food aside.

"Which of you is Andrew?" he growled, his hand straying toward the fringe of his cloak.

He wasn't there for a friendly visit, and the fact that he knew my name spoke volumes.

I narrowed my eyes. "I am."

He moved swiftly, drawing a knife from beneath his cloak. I reacted in time to block the blow with my left forearm, deflecting it from its intended trajectory. The blade sliced into my flesh, and blood spurted from the wound to stain his garments.

With a snarl, I rose to my full height and gripped his arm with my right hand so tightly his bones snapped beneath my fingers. With a startled cry, he dropped the knife. He gaped at me, eyes wide with fear.

I kicked the fallen blade beneath the table toward Alexander's chair, but did not release my assailant. A warm trickle of blood ran the length of my left arm, but I ignored it to focus on the stranger. The wound would close on its own, given a few minutes' time.

"Who are you?" I demanded.

Several of the regular patrons had risen from their seats to stare and whisper as the scene continued to unfold.

"My arm!" he cried. "I think it's broken!"

I tightened my grip, relentless in my rage. "Who the hell are you?"

"I'm nobody!" he wailed. "A minor merchant. The king sent me... Aaargh!"

I struck him in the abdomen. The blow caused him pain but would not result in any lasting damage.

"You're a damned fool," I spat. "You can't trust a word Colin says. I can assure you, whatever the treacherous bastard promised you is nothing but a pack of lies."

"Stand down!" Another voice interrupted.

I looked up to find a portly man striding toward us, a club gripped firmly in one hand. I met his gaze unflinchingly but made no move to release my attacker.

"I'm the lead constable of Riversmeet," the man stated. "I saw what happened, and I overheard what he said to you." He shook his head. "To think, I was about to go home to my wife, and then someone has to go and stir up trouble. I'll be lucky to get home before midnight." He turned to the man still writhing in my grasp. "You, sir, will spend the night in the city jail."

"I was only following orders!"

"Your king has no jurisdiction here. My men and I can take it from here," the constable said to me.

I released him. With a whimper, he drew his injured limb into his chest, where he cradled it gingerly. Alexander handed the constable the bloodied knife, while two other locals assisted in rounding up the would-be assassin and led him outside.

"I'll come back in the morning to take your statement," the constable said. "By then, I should have a better understanding of that man's story. My wife is an apothecary should you need her assistance."

I pushed up my torn and bloodied sleeve, inspecting my forearm. The wound had already begun to close. In another few minutes, no sign of it would remain.

"That won't be necessary," I replied.

The man's eyebrows rose. "You aren't what you appear to be, but I think that's a discussion for later. I'll ensure he doesn't try anything else while he's in my city."

"Thank you," I replied before taking my seat once more.

"How in hell did he get here? How did that man pass through the Mage's Gate?" Alexander hissed, his tone fraught with worry.

"I don't know, but I think our days of sleeping without a watch posted are over. If Colin has sent one assassin, he has sent others." I smirked as a thought occurred to me. "At least we know one thing, brother. He's angry enough about my stunt at the tourney field that he's decided to target *me.* That should keep you a bit safer."

Alexander snorted. "Colin has wanted your blood since the day he was named father's heir. What you did to save me only added fuel to his fire." He groaned and looked down, his expression abruptly downcast. "I hope you can send a message to Tom while I'm in the spire. He needs to learn about this. And I'd like to know he's well."

I nodded. "I agree. I'll speak with Chela tomorrow."

SEVEN

I accompanied Alexander through the carefully tended gardens that lay between the inn and the Ivory Spire early the next morning. The sun was newly risen, wreathed in an array of thin clouds tinged in orange and pink. The sky was otherwise clear, the remnants of the storms that had plagued us long gone.

A pair of magi greeted us as we neared the spire's entrance, garbed in identical tunics. I recognized the crescent-and-stars motif that decorated their sleeves as the same the Oracle used in her tower. I swallowed my questions and focused on Alexander.

"Good luck, brother," I said.

He flashed a grin, though his eyes belied his inner turmoil. "I'll see you once I'm finished."

I stood aside as he followed the magi inside. As I retraced my steps to the inn, I glanced skyward, noting several gray eagles had appeared. The birds soared on invisible air currents, spiraling high into the air, their forms dark against the bright expanse of the dawn sky.

I frowned and shoved my unease aside. Alexander would emerge hale and whole without me; he must. There was nothing I could do to assist him.

I was greeted by Chela and the city's head constable when I reentered the inn. They'd been awaiting my return, though for different reasons; Chela had not been present the previous evening when the would-be assassin had made his attempt on my life, and I had not yet spoken to her of the incident. Emmarie was some distance away, perched on a stool in the inn's relatively empty common room with a plate of fruit and toasted bread before her. She waved as she saw me and flashed a bright smile. I waved in return, then focused on the others.

The constable spoke first. "I'm Berric Vance. I'm afraid we weren't properly introduced." He offered his hand.

We shook, and I said, "Andrew Caein. And this is Chela." If he recognized my surname, he gave no indication he did so.

Berric glanced over his shoulder. "Let's sit down while we discuss last evening's incident."

I followed him to a table on the far side of the common room where we would not be overheard by the handful of other patrons. Emmarie remained where she was, though she followed our progress with curiosity in her dark eyes.

"The man we apprehended calls himself Dorian Silver," Berric said as he sat down with a groan. "He had an interesting tale to tell once we'd settled him in a proper cell."

"I have no doubt." I sat across from him and folded my arms. "From what little he said, I believe I know his motive."

"How is your arm?" he asked, lifting one eyebrow in question. "Has it healed?"

I pushed up my sleeve to reveal my forearm. It was unblemished, unscarred. "As I told you last night, I'm fine."

He nodded, satisfied.

Chela cut in, tired of the suspense. "What happened?"

I recounted Dorian's attempted attack and our brief conversation the previous evening.

"You should have told me," she scolded. "I know you're capable of defending yourself, but as your guide, I must be apprised of these things. There are paths we can take to avoid any would-be assassins, ones they'll be unlikely to follow."

I shrugged. "At least he was here for me rather than Alex."

She rolled her eyes, exasperated. "Regardless, I ask that you keep me informed."

"I will." I turned back to Berric. "Did you learn anything else from him?"

"Oh, he certainly had a tale to tell," Berric replied with a nod. "He's from Novania, which I found unusual—until he mentioned you and your brother are from there as well. He's a merchant with too much debt but was promised a tidy sum from the king if he returned with proof of your death. He claimed the king would pay all of his creditors, and he had written documents to prove it. If that wasn't incentive enough, the king is holding his young daughter hostage. The girl bears the Mark."

I closed my eyes briefly and suppressed a groan. "He was here in a futile attempt to save his daughter. Colin likely had her killed as soon as Dorian left the castle."

"It seems the king didn't tell Dorian who he'd be facing," Berric replied. "Judging by your speed, you have experience with combat. Given how rapidly you healed and the amount of damage you inflicted on the poor man's arm, I believe you are no mere man." He paused to size me up, his expression shrewd. "We've had news from the Citadel that a skin-changer recently came to the Southlands, and I'm familiar with the Caein name."

I chuckled. "I suppose you've found me out then."

"It caused quite the stir. It's been nearly forty years since any of the dragon-kind were last seen."

"Thirty-eight," I replied automatically, suddenly wishing the conversation would end. I was uncomfortable discussing my origins, and though I knew most of his interest was borne of mere curiosity, I didn't enjoy the attention.

"Well," Berric said as he rose to his feet, "I need to finish writing my report detailing last night's incident. I pity that poor man for the situation he's in, but he must answer for his actions. It's the law."

"What will you do?" I asked.

"In Riversmeet, we take attempted murder seriously. He'll do penance for his crime. Hard labor." He shrugged. "It's better he's kept busy. He won't have the opportunity to try again."

I thanked him, and after he'd gone, I turned to Chela. "I won't go another night without posting a watch. This won't be the last assassin Colin sends after us. He won't stop his attempts on my life—or Alexander's—until he succeeds. Damn him. I won't give him that satisfaction."

She nodded in understanding even as her face paled at my words. "We must be more careful in our travels. That much is certain."

I followed Chela through the bustling marketplace of Riversmeet a few hours later. I'd agreed to help her secure supplies in exchange for her assistance in locating someone with the means to send a message to Thomas, as Alexander had suggested. She was grateful for the assistance.

Emmarie elected to remain near the inn. She was enjoying the gardens and had renewed her efforts to speak with the gray eagles, though the birds continued to remain aloof and seemingly uninterested. I was relieved someone would be present to greet Alexander should he finish his trial before I returned. While I refused to admit it openly, I worried for my brother more than ever before.

Chela visited several provisioners, a baker, a smith, an apothecary, and a chandler. I stood by as she negotiated payment and secured the supplies we required for the next leg of our journey. Most shopkeepers understood the nuances of a mage's pilgrimage. They were amenable to delivering the goods to the inn, though I was required to tote several satchels of various items, most notably from the apothecary's shop, our final destination on Chela's shopping expedition.

"We may need those herbs if the Weavers are active and prove unfriendly when we reach the forest," she said as we exited. "Which reminds me of another matter. I'd like to look at the wound on your back before we depart. We must ensure it is fully healed, and I won't take 'no' for an answer."

The wound was closed, and there was no longer any risk of it tearing open should I need to react to a threat. The previous evening's events had been a testament to that.

I wanted to protest, to assure her all was well, but I'd also come to expect Chela's stubborn streak when it came to her duty as our guide. She'd stop at nothing to ensure Alexander was protected, and if baring my skin was the price I must pay to alleviate her concerns, I'd do it, though I didn't have to like it. I reminded myself I was here for Alexander—and I would do anything for my brother.

I ran one hand through my hair and sighed in irritation. "Fine. You can look once we're back at the inn."

"Good." She nodded in satisfaction. "We'll visit Ilia now. She should be able to send a message to your brother if the mood strikes her."

I lifted my eyebrows in question.

"She's…eccentric," Chela replied with a wave of her hand. "You'll see."

Chela led me through several winding streets lined with merchant stalls. The marketplace was a sprawling complex that ringed the city, accessible by myriad twisting paths that I'd have easily become lost in. I was grateful Chela knew our route and doubly so that she navigated without the use of her magic.

Finally, she turned down a narrow path just wide enough for us to pass through singly. It led toward the outskirts of the city, threading between buildings that stood two- and three-stories high. It eventually ended near what appeared to be a smaller version of the gardens surrounding the Ivory Spire. On the far side of the carefully manicured greenspace was a small stone cottage with what appeared to be an aviary attached. As we approached, dozens of bird calls issued from within.

"Ilia is not a mage," Chela said. "She has befriended many birds and has earned their trust. They will take messages from her and deliver them to others if she asks—even those as far away as your brother."

Her description reminded me of Emmarie. "Is she Merael?"

Chela laughed, pleased by my question. "She is a Wild-kin. There is hope for you yet, Andrew."

I frowned at her gentle mockery, though I wasn't upset by it. There had been so much to learn since we'd fled Novania. At times I felt I'd never fully understand the intricacies of the Southlands or its people.

The door to the cottage opened before we reached it to reveal an older Merael woman. She was smaller in stature than Emmarie, her skin was olive-green, and she was dressed in a billowing frock dyed a brilliant yellow. Her dark hair was streaked with white and was swept behind her head in an elaborate twist. Though her face was lined with advanced age, her dark eyes were clear and sharp, intelligent and calculating.

"Have you need of a message?" she asked. When I nodded, she offered a smile. "I'm happy to be of assistance if you have the means to pay."

"We do," Chela assured her.

"Then you are welcome here." She motioned for us to follow her into the aviary.

I rolled my eyes but followed as requested.

"Relax, Andrew. She is always like this," Chela hissed. "She dislikes visitors, and her demands seem to be the only way she can deter some of the more persistent folk. She's the best option we have to send a message to your brother, like it or not."

"Perhaps I should have asked Emmarie," I replied. "It didn't cross my mind."

Chela shook her head. "Emmarie lacks the connections Ilia has. I doubt any of her bird acquaintances would risk the journey to Novania."

Ilia led us to a small protected alcove just within the entrance. A rickety writing table and a wicker chair occupied the space. Beyond it was another door leading into the aviary proper. The cacophony of birdsong, squawks, and various twittering chirps was nearly deafening.

Ilia withdrew a slim box from beneath the table, which contained thin sheets of parchment, a quill, and a pot of black ink. She placed the implements on the table, then gestured to the chair.

"While you write, I'll speak with the birds. Tell me the recipient's name and where they are located."

"My brother, Thomas. He's in Novania." I studied her reaction carefully and noted she registered only a brief flicker of surprise.

She nodded once. "Very well. I'll return presently."

She disappeared into the aviary as I began to write. I summarized our journey from the Citadel, the appearance of the gray eagles, and Alexander's continued progress. I detailed my encounter with Dorian Silver the previous evening, then finished by stating I hoped Thomas was well and I'd write again when I was able.

I sat back to study the message once I was finished, then released a heavy sigh. I wished there was a means to receive a message in return, but I doubted it was possible. I signed my name at the bottom of the sheet with a flourish, smiling faintly as I did. It was the first time I'd used the Caein surname; it was nice to feel I belonged to a proper family again.

When Ilia returned, a falcon was perched on her forearm. "This bird is swift and agile and used to long journeys," she explained. "She has agreed to take the message to your brother. You must describe his appearance and what his surroundings may look like."

I described Thomas to the bird, stating that although he was my half-brother, we looked little alike. Thomas had brown hair and blue eyes, and when last I'd seen him, he'd sported a beard. His whereabouts were more difficult; his last message had come from the city of Bridgewaters, but I didn't know if he remained there. When I said this, Ilia interrupted me.

"It is a starting point. This bird is intelligent. She will find your brother even if he has moved on."

I found her confidence reassuring, though her overall demeanor was somewhat abrupt and off-putting. I described Bridgewaters to the bird as well as its surrounding landmarks.

"That will be sufficient." Ilia waved her free hand, cutting me off. "She will find your brother. If he wishes to send a reply, she will seek you again."

Ilia took the message and carefully folded the thin sheet before rolling it tightly. She slid it into a tiny glass tube, which was then attached to the falcon's leg. We walked outside the aviary, where the bird shrieked once before leaping into the air, then disappeared rapidly from our sight as she soared beyond the nearest buildings. Chela paid for Ilia's service, and we took our leave.

"I hope Tom can write back," I said as we wound our way through the city and toward the Ivory Spire once more. "The last message we received from him bore ill tidings. He'd fled the Capitol and was staying with his uncle, hoping to remain out of Colin's sight. He said Colin was mustering the army in pursuit of us." I sighed and raked a hand through my hair. "I wish there was something more I could do to help him, but as everyone continues to remind me, Alexander's journey must come first."

"You can't be in both places at once," Chela replied gently. "I believe Alex needs your help now more than either of you realize. The time will come when you can go to Thomas' aid." Her words were meant to console me, but her expression belied her unspoken fear.

I nodded. She was correct, though it did little to ease my mind. I lamented my inability to help Thomas, but I would never abandon Alexander. We'd always been close, despite our ten-year age difference.

Thomas was nearly three years younger than Alexander, which made our time together markedly different. By the time Thomas was old enough to walk, I was spending my summers on campaign and my winters with the castle garrison in the barracks. We had no shared childhood memories, whereas with Alexander, there had been a few years in which we'd formed a lasting bond. Alexander had chosen to follow a similar path to my own, taking lessons from some of the kingdom's finest swordsmen, and once he'd been deemed skilled enough, he'd often accompanied me on campaign.

Alexander was more than simply my younger half-brother. He'd become my greatest friend and ally.

"I'll be there for Alex until the end of his journey," I replied. "He wants to go north as badly as I do. Once he's trained, it will only be a matter of time before we make that trek."

Chela's face fell, and she bit her lower lip. Her voice was little more than a murmur when she spoke. "I dread that day, for it will mean war has truly come to us at long last."

Alexander hadn't emerged from his trial by the time we arrived at the inn. The gray eagles continued to soar overhead, and their presence had drawn a sizeable crowd to the gardens. Emmarie met us near the inn's stables with a wave. I deposited the satchels I carried in the cart, then followed the women inside.

"I haven't managed to speak with any of the eagles," she said, crestfallen, as we entered the common room.

"If they're as rare as the magi from the Ashen Shrine led me to believe, they're most likely unused to speaking with anyone," I replied in an attempt to buoy her spirits. "If you continue to try, surely one of them will take notice and come down to investigate."

When Emmarie shrugged dejectedly, Chela added, "Alexander still has far to go. The eagles will continue to mark his progress—I'm certain of it. You'll have ample opportunity in which to speak with them."

As the afternoon drew to a close, many of the goods we'd purchased began to arrive. Chela oversaw the deliveries and organized the cart, but when I offered to help, she declined.

I was restless and began to walk the perimeter of the gardens in a repeated circuit around the Ivory Spire, hoping to spy Alexander. Emmarie accompanied me for a time, but eventually she grew bored and wandered away to renew her efforts with the eagles.

As I walked, Alexander was foremost in my mind, though Thomas remained a close second. And Colin's threat loomed, his cruelty to the Novanian people a constant source of concern. I needed someone to speak with, but there was no one who would fully understand, save Alexander. Since he had other matters to occupy his time, I was left alone.

When evening fell, I retreated to the inn to join Chela and Emmarie for supper. I surveyed the other patrons of the common room surreptitiously, wary of another attempt on my life. The evening passed without incident.

Alexander didn't emerge from the Ivory Spire until after noon the following day. The eagles rapidly dispersed minutes before he stepped into the gardens, and I wasn't certain if he'd been aware of their presence. Emmarie and I awaited him not far from the spire's entrance; she'd been attempting to attract the birds' attention once more, though her efforts remained unsuccessful. When I spied Alexander walking toward us, I waved.

He returned the gesture, but as he approached it was clear he was exhausted. He stumbled when he was a few steps away but recovered with a weary laugh. Dark circles ringed his green eyes, and his face was pale.

"Alex, are you well?" I asked, immediately concerned.

He nodded. "This trial was difficult. I need to rest."

I nodded, keeping pace with him as we returned to the inn. I wondered if this was a typical reaction to some mage trials; it was markedly different than when he'd emerged from the Ashen Shrine. He didn't speak again until we were at the door to our shared room.

"I'll be fine, Andrew. I'm just tired. After a few hours of sleep, I'll be ready to move on." He forced a smile for my benefit.

"I'll be in the hallway if you need anything," I promised. "After what happened two nights ago, I'm not leaving you alone."

He snorted. "Ever the protector." He disappeared into the room and closed the door.

I leaned against the wall, prepared to remain there as long as Alexander was within. If Colin had sent any other assassins after us, they'd be forced to confront me before they reached my brother. As his guardian, it was my duty to ensure his safety; as his elder brother, I *wanted* to protect him.

As daylight faded into dusk, Alexander emerged from the room. I'd maintained my vigil throughout the afternoon, but there had been little activity in the hall aside from a few of the inn's staff going about their usual business. Alexander appeared refreshed when he stepped into the corridor, though his clothing was rumpled and his hair mussed. The dark circles that had ringed his eyes had receded. He greeted me with a mischievous smile.

"Please tell me you didn't spend your entire day sitting here," he said, though he knew the answer. When I shrugged noncommittally, he laughed. "Some things will never change."

"Let's head downstairs for supper," I suggested. "You can tell me of your latest trial, and I can regale you with the tale of wandering the marketplace with Chela to replenish our supplies."

He laughed again. "I know how much you hate going to market, Andrew. I'm surprised you accompanied her at all."

"As we discussed, it was the bargain I made in exchange for sending a message to Tom."

His eyes lit up at the mention of our younger brother. "Did Tom send a reply?"

I shook my head as we took the staircase to the lower level. "There wasn't a mage with the right talent available. A Merael woman arranged the message's delivery. If Tom replies, it'll be some time before we receive it."

His face fell, and he looked away. "I suppose I can't always expect there to be a mage around. From what I learned yesterday, the greatest concentration of magi lies within the Citadel. The farther we travel, the less likely it will be to encounter others bearing the Mark. And I—" his voice faltered, and I looked over at him sharply.

"Alex? What is it?"

He sighed, squared his shoulders, and paused to look me in the eye. "I'm not like the others, Andrew. My power is unique, according to the elders at the spire. Even if there were other mage-warriors alive,

I'd stand out." Fear and worry warred within his eyes. "They seem to know that I'll succeed through at least the first half of the journey, but they can't see anything beyond the Frostwake. And the more I pursue my magic, the greater the risk I will become to…myself. I'll never be safe until the last trial is complete. For the first time in my life, I'm truly afraid of this Mark."

"I'll make damned sure you survive to the end, Alex." My tone was grave. "No matter what happens in the north, I'll be here with you until the end. We'll get through this together."

He nodded, and some of his fear seemed to dissipate. "Thank you, brother."

We remained in Riversmeet for another day. Chela insisted Alexander take the additional time to recover before we departed for our next destination. Alexander protested at first, but when I sided with our guide, he relented. I understood the reason for his urgency, but I also believed he needed to be alert and hale enough to survive the passage through the Venom-weavers' Forest.

That evening, Chela examined what was left of the wound on my back. She followed us into our room after we'd eaten supper, where she ordered me to remove my shirt. Resigned to my fate, I complied with a groan.

She was silent for several long moments, and I began to fear something was amiss. "Chela?"

"It's completely healed," she replied softly, her tone full of wonder. "When we left the Citadel, you were bandaging it daily. Now, there isn't even a scar left to mark your sacrifice."

I turned to face her as I pulled my shirt on once more. "I said I was fine."

She lifted an eyebrow, unimpressed. "And I know the dangers we are likely to face in the coming days. I needed to make certain you'd be up to the task."

"I heal rapidly," I replied with a shrug. "Although you aren't the first who has refused to accept my word on the matter."

My words brought with them a flood of emotions as I recalled Vera's reaction to my healing on a distant winter's night. Damn, but I missed her.

"It seems you do," Chela said. "I'll leave you now. Rest. I can't guarantee you'll get any sleep once we reach the forest."

EIGHT

We followed a road through the southwestern sector of Riversmeet to a broad stone bridge that spanned one of the two rivers giving the city its name. I could make out a few farmsteads on the far bank, and beyond, a large expanse of empty grassland that ended abruptly at the edge of a dense forest.

Even from a distance, the forest seemed to possess a sinister and primeval nature. The shadowy trees stretched toward the horizon in both directions, and it was clear we'd be forced to travel *through* the forest in order to reach the lands beyond. During our trek, Chela explained what she knew of the Venom-weavers and instructed Emmarie on the use of the herbs we'd acquired. The Weavers' venom was potent and often fatal to those afflicted.

Chela halted our progress midafternoon. We'd arrived at a point a half mile from the trees, but she seemed reluctant to go any nearer. The ground was carpeted in short scrub grass, and our campsite would be open to the sky. There was no cover unless we journeyed beneath the ominous eaves of the forest, but as I recalled Chela's story regarding the failed mage, I believed it wise to rest outside of the spiders' lair. Fortunately, the sky was clear, and it was unlikely we'd see rain.

"We'll camp here tonight," Chela said as she adjusted her hat. "It would do us no good to enter the forest this late in the day, and I'd like to monitor the activity within the trees. During certain months, the spiders are more active. If this is one of them, we need to be prepared." Her usual confidence was gone, replaced by unspoken anxiety.

I caught her gaze and held it for several seconds. "Would you like me to shift?"

She averted her gaze and did not immediately respond. The area held unpleasant memories for her, but her warning regarding the spiders' activity was more concerning. I decided it didn't matter what her response was—I'd shift to provide the best protection possible for our group. I began to unbuckle my armor while Alexander removed the tents and stakes to begin setting up our campsite.

By the time I'd removed my armor and boots, Chela had moved some distance away to stare intently into the trees. Her face was drawn and pale, her eyes wary. I glanced toward Alexander, who nodded once. He was in agreement with my plan. Emmarie assisted Alexander where she could, seemingly unconcerned by our proximity to the forest. I wondered fleetingly if she was capable of communication with the Venom-weavers. I'd ask her later.

I stripped off my underclothes and stowed them inside the cart with my armor, then moved a short distance away to shift forms. I felt the familiar expansion and elongation of my body, accompanied by a sensation of raw power. I flexed and stretched my wings before folding them over my scaly back. Despite the awkwardness I experienced with the increase in my size, I'd missed this form and the heightened senses that came with it.

I lumbered toward Chela and seated myself nearby to peer into the gloom beneath the forest canopy. Most of the trees were enveloped in thick strands of spider silk; some were covered so thickly I wondered how their leaves captured any sunlight at all. Though there was ample evidence of the Venom-weavers, I detected no movement within the shrouded trees.

Chela glanced at me briefly, then refocused her attention on the forest. "I've seen no movement so far." Her voice held an edge, a tremor that betrayed the depth of her fear. "Thank you for changing. This place has always terrified me. It's comforting to know we have a dragon along for the journey. I hope your presence will deter the spiders."

"Tell me of them. The Weaversss."

I grimaced. It was the first time Chela had encountered me in this form, and speech was often difficult. I'd yet to find a method that didn't involve me hissing like a serpent, and I was forced to concentrate on the pronunciation of my words, making everyday conversation taxing at the best of times.

"The Venom-weavers are enormous. Sienna will be smaller than most," she replied. "They are vile, ruthless creatures. They've been known to lay traps—and they're not always visible. Just as ordinary spiders have a tough outer carapace, so do they. And as you know, they're highly venomous. A single bite has been known to kill a man." She yanked the hat from her head and twisted it in her hands. "They are vulnerable to fire, as I've mentioned before. When we enter the forest, you should take the lead. Alexander and I will carry torches, and I hope Emmarie will have the sense to remain inside the cart where she will be safer."

"If the danger isss ssso great, can we not *fly* beyond the foressst?"

Chela shook her head, a sad smile playing on her lips. "I'm afraid not, though I wish it were otherwise. Alexander's next destination lies in the very heart of this forest. It's protected from the spiders by a barrier much like the one that protects our lands from the northerners. Part of this trial is surviving the journey to the shrine."

I scowled, unable to hide my irritation.

My reaction caused Chela to laugh, though the sound was strained. "I find it fascinating you appear so different in this form, yet your facial expressions remain much the same. And that was definitely an expression I've come to expect from you." She laughed again, easier this time.

"You'll find he makes faces quite often," Alexander cut in as he came to stand between us. "He's the same now as he was a few minutes ago, only much larger and a bit terrifying if you aren't used to him." He chuckled. "He'll also have an enormous appetite."

I sighed in mock exasperation. "I'm right here, brother."

He'd picked up the habit of answering for me when I was in this form, for which I was grateful—most of the time. He knew my struggle with coherent speech, and though I was capable of holding a conversation now, I preferred to speak only when I had good reason to. Perhaps one day communication would become easier.

Alexander laughed. "I know, and I'm glad of that." His tone became serious. "I wish we could avoid this place. It has an ominous feel."

"I'll keep watch tonight," I replied. "We'll get through it."

"In the meantime," Chela said, "we should gather as much kindling as we can before nightfall. I understand you see quite well in the dark, Andrew, but a blazing campfire will keep the spiders at bay. I won't take any unnecessary risks." She paused and looked away. "I don't believe I can cope with a repeat of my last pilgrimage."

Alexander glanced at me, and I nodded, indicating he could speak for me. "Andrew will protect us. Have no fear."

The others spent the remaining daylight hours gathering kindling. They moved in a group toward the trees, collected armfuls of branches, and scurried away while I continued to monitor the forest for any activity. Once a sizeable stack was gathered and additional branches placed in the cart for the journey through the forest, Chela deemed us ready.

As the sunlight began to fail, Alexander built a roaring campfire. Scrabbling noises issued from within the confines of the trees not long after, accompanied by dry rasping sounds.

The noise was chilling in its own right, but was made even more so when Emmarie sat down at my side with a troubled expression. "They're speaking. I didn't know they'd talk."

She huddled at my side, clearly frightened by the Weavers' conversation. Long after the others turned in for the night, she remained awake, stoking the campfire each time it began to grow dim.

"I don't think I'll sleep until we're through," she murmured after a time. "They refer to us as 'prey.' Even you." She shuddered and hugged her arms tightly to her chest.

"Do you believe they'll attack?"

I'd intended my words to come out in a whisper, but hushed vocalizations were impossible as a dragon. I heard Alexander stir within his tent and hoped I had not awakened him.

"I don't know. They're watching us. Their voices are…terrible. They say such awful things!" Abruptly, she reached up to cover her ears with her hands as tears spilled from her dark eyes. "I wish I could not understand their speech!"

I drew my tail around her protectively in an attempt to comfort her. She peered at me and managed a tremulous smile before she dropped her gaze once more, then rested one of her small green hands near the ridge of black spines on my tail.

My dragon form not only sported a fine suit of natural armor in the form of its scales, but it came replete with weaponry as well. The spines were but one such weapon; my feet were tipped with talons and my teeth were akin to daggers, as Alexander was fond of reminding me. I'd keep her safe and was confident the Weavers could do little to harm me.

"I don't want to ride in the cart when we travel through the forest," she blurted, her voice panicked. "I'll be vulnerable. They know... *They know I'm afraid.* They'll target me!"

"Emmarie, look at me." I feared the Weavers' voices would drive her into a panic if I didn't intervene.

She swallowed hard, then slowly craned her neck to meet my gaze.

"I'll allow you to climb on my back. You'll be with me. I *will* protect you."

She swallowed again, then nodded. "Chela won't like it. It goes against her plans."

While she may have been correct, I believed Emmarie would pose a greater risk to the group if she were forced to ride in the cart, alone with her fears. The spiders' speech was clearly unpleasant, and she was on the brink of hysteria. If by staying with me she would remain calm, we'd be better for it.

"I will tell her of our arrangement," I promised.

I glanced skyward. The moon was a few days past full, yet bright enough to illuminate the open land between our position and the forest. While the chittering and rustling continued from within the trees, there was no movement across the plains.

As the moon crept nearer to its zenith, the noise within the forest began to subside. I wondered if the spiders were affected by the brighter light; we'd observed no activity before the sun had set, and now that the moonlight was at its strongest, they appeared to be quieting once more. If light was a source of discomfort for them, fire should deter them as readily as Chela had suggested. While the thought gave me comfort, I refused to relax my guard.

I felt Emmarie shift slightly. Peering down, I noted she'd fallen into a restless sleep. Her head rested on her hands as she leaned against the curl of my tail. I smiled faintly, relieved she was finally at ease. In the flickering firelight, her face appeared younger than her sixteen years, and I experienced an unexpected surge of fatherly affection toward her.

I'd continue to protect her regardless of Chela's inclinations otherwise. She was far too young to be left alone in the world, and I'd accept the task. I wouldn't send her away. I couldn't.

As the moon began to drift toward the western horizon, the activity within the forest resumed at a more frenzied pace than before. Emmarie moaned in her sleep as the noise penetrated her dreams.

A short while later, Alexander emerged from his tent and came to stand at my side. Noting Emmarie's slumbering form, he said nothing for several minutes and merely gazed away from the campfire toward the dark line of trees. Finally, he turned to stoke the fire, his features drawn into a troubled frown.

He seated himself a few steps away once he'd finished with the task. "I can take over the watch, brother. You'll need sleep too. Perhaps more so than the rest of us."

I nodded and carefully settled myself while I did my best not to disturb Emmarie. Despite the chilling sounds that drifted to us from the forest, it wasn't long before I was asleep.

I was awakened by the first rays of the morning sun as it peered over the eastern horizon through a haze of red-orange clouds. Alexander stood a few paces away, his back toward me as he surveyed the forest ahead. In the light of the new day, the trees appeared less menacing, and the forest's denizens had fled back into the shadows. It was eerily quiet; not even birdsong greeted the dawn. The silence was more unnerving than the constant chittering we'd endured through the night.

I sat up, noting Emmarie continued to sleep. Her breathing was deep, her face relaxed and peaceful.

I stretched my wings gingerly. The muscles had become stiff and knotted during the night while I'd kept them folded tightly at my sides.

Alexander turned to face me with a half-smile. "I'm glad you got some rest, brother. Those creatures didn't venture from the trees, but after the moon set, they became…agitated. I don't want to know what they did—or said."

I nodded and glanced at Emmarie as she stirred and slowly opened her eyes. "We will be in for an interesssting day."

"That isn't the term I would use to describe it," Emmarie replied in a quavering tone. "At least they've stopped speaking." She pushed away from me and moved toward the fire.

I leveled my gaze at Alexander. "I need to hunt."

He nodded in understanding. He'd experienced first-hand the quantity of food I was required to consume as a dragon, and I wasn't willing to deplete our rations to sate it. We'd spied game on the plains previously; I'd satisfy my hunger by that means.

"All is in order here, brother. Go."

I flashed a grin, grateful, then spread my wings and leapt into the air. If there was one aspect of my dragon form I truly loved, it was flight.

I circled the campsite once while I surveyed the landscape. I reveled in the sensation of the cool morning air as it rushed across my scales and buoyed my wings, and relished the warmth of the sunlight as it struck my scales. *This* is what the dragon-kind were built for.

Spying a few deer in the flat lands to the north, I turned to pursue them. I could not tarry; Chela would seek to depart as soon as I returned, and I hoped to be through the forest as swiftly as she did.

NINE

My hunger sated, I returned to camp. From a distance, I could see the tents had been dismantled, the fire had been doused, and the others were awaiting my return. Chela paced rigidly along the length of the cart, pausing every now and again to check supplies or ensure Sienna was properly hitched. She was clearly impatient and agitated, despite her misgivings regarding the upcoming trek through the forest.

Alexander stood to one side, arms crossed, his expression one of poorly concealed exasperation. Emmarie was beside him, gazing skyward. When she took notice of my return, she raised her hand in greeting and grinned.

I had only just touched down when Chela strode toward me, her jaw clenched and nostrils flaring in anger. I didn't understand the reason behind her unexpected rage, but I drew a deep breath and steeled myself for the inevitable confrontation.

"Where were you? Your duty is *here*, with Alexander. I woke up to find you gone! Given our proximity to the forest, I expected you to take your responsibility as his guardian seriously. What were you thinking?!"

"As I've said, Andrew needed to eat. We don't have enough provisions in the whole of this damned cart to sustain him for even one meal, let alone several," Alexander cut in, his voice tight with fury.

She focused her ire on Alexander and stormed toward him. She stopped inches away from him, her spine erect in order to maximize her height, her hands clenched at her sides. The top of her head only reached his collarbone, but she glared into his eyes, unyielding and undeterred.

"Leaving you alone is unacceptable," she seethed. "You should not defend him!"

"Would you rather I lead you into the foressst weakened from hunger?" I asked.

It was an effort to keep my tone neutral, but if I attempted to reason, perhaps my words would diffuse her simmering temper before it boiled over.

"I require much more to maintain my ssstrength in thisss form," I continued. "I believed it better to hunt now rather than attempt it later."

She turned to glare at me, but her expression softened. I'd made an impact.

She stepped away from Alexander with a shake of her head. "I suppose you're right. I apologize."

"I will not fault Andrew for his decision," Alexander replied with a sour expression.

He continued to fume; it would take time for his own temper to cool. It was proving a trying day already, and we weren't in any danger—yet.

Chela grunted, then strode toward the cart without another word.

"Emma, it isss time." I lowered myself to allow Emmarie to clamber onto my back.

Chela scowled but held her tongue. I peered over my shoulder once Emmarie had settled herself between my wings to ensure she was in no danger of falling. She smiled shyly as I rose to my feet, then patted my back twice, the same signal Alexander often employed to communicate he was ready to move on.

A glance toward my half-brother confirmed my suspicions. He grinned at Emmarie knowingly; clearly, they'd discussed the signal while I was away.

"Now that everyone is settled, we should be off," Chela stated, her tone clipped.

I didn't know what else had been said while I'd been hunting, but it seemed my unexpected departure was not the only topic that had sown discord between the others.

"We'll discuss it later," Alexander said in a low tone before he made his way toward Chela and the cart.

I suppressed a groan. This was not how our journey into the forest should have begun, with Chela enflamed and resentful and Alexander equally furious. We needed Chela's guidance to navigate the Venomweavers' lair, and though she feared the area, I still didn't fully understand the source of her present anger. I understood Alexander's. I hoped that with time, their tempers would cool and the remainder of the journey would pass without further argument.

It took less than a quarter-hour to reach the eaves of the forest. As we began to pass beneath the silk-enshrouded branches, a deep and foreboding silence settled over our group. I heard no movement in the trees, but the sensation of being watched was tangible. The sunlight dimmed beneath the canopy, and in some places, the path was engulfed by shadow. Gossamer threads of webbing spanned the distance between trees on either side, but the road remained clear at present. While I hoped it would remain so, I believed we'd be forced to cut our way through before long.

I slowed my pace to allow the horse to keep up, though Chela struggled with the frightened beast. Sienna visibly shuddered, her eyes rolled with terror, and she refused to move forward for some time. Emmarie spoke to her in soothing tones, and after a few minutes, Sienna calmed enough to reluctantly plod forward. Chela muttered her thanks in a trembling voice while her eyes darted almost as wildly as the horse's had moments before.

Alexander strode alongside the cart, a lit torch in one hand and his sword in the other. His face was grim, but outwardly he remained stoic. He was clad in his dragon scale armor, though he'd opted to leave his helm in the cart.

As we'd agreed the previous evening, I walked ahead of the others. With my increased size, the path was only just wide enough to accommodate my passage without disturbing the web-shrouded trees on either side. I hoped it would not narrow any further. I didn't relish the notion of disrupting the foliage.

The forest remained silent for most of the morning, the only sound that of our passage. The spiders appeared to be nocturnal, and I hoped for our sake they were soundly asleep. Chela's anxiety grew the farther we delved beneath the eerie canopy of leaves and gossamer thread. Our conversation, limited as it had been at the start of the trek, rapidly dwindled, then faded into nothingness. We strained our ears, seeking any aberrant noise that might indicate the Weavers' awakening.

The silence stretched on while our nerves continued to fray.

We reached a small clearing as noon approached. The path widened into a small deforested meadow carpeted in grass. After a cursory inspection, we determined it was safe to rest for a time near the center of the clearing. The others took a meal of dried meat and hard cheese. While they ate, I studied the perimeter of our temporary refuge, seeking signs of the forest's denizens.

I spied a small pond on one side, but the water was green with algae and gave off an unpleasant odor. It would not be safe to refill our water skins here.

I paused for a moment to study my reflection in the stagnant water. There was little resemblance to my human form, though my eyes were the same mossy green color. I wasn't certain I'd ever grow used to seeing myself as a dragon, covered in glossy black scales and sporting leathery wings. It was surreal, yet oddly titillating.

I turned away from the pond to inspect the trees that ringed the tiny meadow. A few branches had managed to escape the Weavers' snares, though most were heavily webbed. The sun was directly overhead, and I gauged we had perhaps four hours of travel before it would disappear prematurely behind the trees.

The route leading deeper into the forest was cast in shadow. Peering into the gloom, I noted we'd be forced to cut through large swathes of spider silk not far ahead. Strands of tattered web crossed the path in a haphazard fashion and effectively blocked the path.

When I relayed this information to Chela, she frowned in dismay and swore under her breath.

"Finish your lunches quickly. There is another clearing we must reach before sundown, and the snares will slow our progress significantly." Chela eyed the surrounding forest suspiciously. "It has a spring where we can refill our waterskins. The water is clear and fresh, not like the cesspool that lies over there." She gestured to the green pond dismissively. "It's the best place to stop for the night, though it isn't without danger."

"I will guard you through the night," I promised.

She nodded absently, then turned toward Alexander. "I hate to ask this of you as our untrained mage, but are you willing to forge the path ahead?"

I narrowed my eyes in suspicion. I was reluctant to place Alexander in harm's way, and I didn't understand why she would ask this of him after her lecture earlier in the day. "I can tear through them."

She shook her head. "No. We can't risk you becoming entangled. Your strength may be unparalleled, but I have watched others fall victim to the snares… Steel is best suited for cutting through them. I don't doubt your talons are powerful, but they aren't steel and I'm not certain we're equipped to free a creature of your size."

"Hmm." I eyed them skeptically.

"I'll be fine," Alexander replied with a smirk. "Chela knows this forest. I think we need to trust her judgment." He strode to my side, and in a lower tone only I could hear, he said, "I know it's hard for you to step aside, brother, but I trust you'll have my back. I won't stray from your sight."

I nodded, resigned. Perhaps my presence alone would be sufficient to keep the Venom-weavers at a distance. I hoped it would be so.

As we moved away from the clearing, Chela urged us forward at a brisk pace. The path wasn't wide enough to allow Alexander to walk at my side, and he took the lead as we marched forward into the shadows. We paused only when Alexander began to cut through the silken barriers blocking our passage. The webs obstructing our path were tattered and appeared to have been woven some time ago. They rose no higher than a handspan above Alexander's head, and his blade sliced through them with ease. They fell away to hang limply amongst the shrouded tree trunks, and we moved forward without further delay.

Chela drove Sienna as closely behind me as the horse was comfortable with, though I wished for her sake Chela would relent. Sienna was clearly frightened of me, though her fear of the forest's denizens propelled her to obey despite my proximity. I'd always had that effect on horses, even in my human form.

As the afternoon wore on and the sun drifted ever closer to the uneven line of the forest's canopy, Chela became increasingly anxious. Each time I glanced over my shoulder, she was pale, her breaths shallow and labored.

The sun was beginning to sink below the treetops when we arrived at the clearing Chela had described. She and Alexander worked in silence as they built a large fire and lit new torches. Chela brandished one in her hand, then gave another to Emmarie, who remained perched between my shoulder blades. I turned my back on the fire to preserve my night vision and peered into the dense foliage surrounding our meager sanctuary. The spiders began to stir, and as the last of the sun's rays faded, their chitinous cacophony resumed.

When they'd remained at a distance, the sound had been unsettling. Surrounded by the creatures, the din was almost unbearable. It set me on edge.

I began to circle our campfire as I peered into the darkness. Emmarie tensed and gripped the spines on my back as she was assaulted by the hideous, rasping voices of the Weavers. They didn't enter the firelight, but I glimpsed flashes of movement within the trees accompanied by the periodic shine of ink-black eyes reflecting the firelight. They did little to conceal their proximity, and I sensed it was an act of intimidation.

Would they escalate into outright aggression? Or would they remain in the shadows and allow us to pass the night without incident?

Alexander gripped his sword in one hand and brandished a torch in the other. He paced the perimeter of our fire opposite my location, his expression fierce. Chela huddled in the cart and attempted to calm our terrified packhorse with trembling hands and faltering whispers. Emmarie clung to my back, and I could feel her body tremble as the spiders' voices increased in volume.

It was only dusk. We'd be in for a long night.

Chela periodically stoked the fire, which kept the spiders at bay. As the night wore on, heavy clouds obscured the sky. Without the moon to cast its calming light over the forest, we received no respite from the constant chittering and rustling of our unseen adversaries.

I was grateful they didn't attempt an attack that night. Without a good look at one of them, I wasn't certain what I'd be facing. While Chela's descriptive warnings proved helpful enough, I'd never been one to engage an enemy without first assessing their capabilities. Until one of the spiders stepped into the light, I was effectively blind.

When the sky mercifully began to lighten, the spiders' activity diminished, though it didn't stop as it had on the previous day. The clouds that blanketed the sky provided deeper shadows which emboldened the Weavers. They scuttled and chittered just beyond our sight, their rasping voices a counterpoint to our movements. The notion of traversing the narrower paths while they remained active set me on edge. It didn't help that none of us had received any sleep since the previous night, and I was rapidly growing hungry. There was nothing I could do but ignore the pangs until we'd safely reached our destination.

"How far to the shrine?" Alexander asked of Chela as we prepared to depart the clearing.

"If we travel swiftly, we'll be there before noon." Her tone wavered, and her eyes darted anxiously.

"Then let's go," Alexander replied. "No one wants to prolong this experience."

The path bent away from the clearing and was free of webbing, allowing me to resume the lead. I set a fast pace, and occasionally glanced over my shoulder to ensure the others maintained it. I would not leave them behind.

An hour later, Emmarie tapped my back urgently. The Weavers had begun to chitter with what I could only describe as excitement. While I'd silently questioned the change, her next words made their intentions clear.

"Andrew… They're going to ambush us," she hissed. "I can hear their plans!"

I halted abruptly. Behind me, the cart lurched to a stop.

"Go on," I said.

"They said the 'open place' near 'the wall.'" She squeezed her eyes shut with a grimace. "They plan to attack you first. You are the 'greater prey.' They fear you, but… It isn't enough to stop them."

"We must hurry," Chela replied. "The place they speak of is no doubt the clearing at the shrine's entrance, and the wall is the barrier. If we reach there, we can run to safety. There is no other way."

"We should go ahead of you," Alexander said, chewing his lower lip in thought. "If they plan to attack you first, we have a better chance of making it to the shrine. They should fear you more than they do, brother. It will be the downfall of their plot."

I didn't share his confidence, but I'd do my best to ensure their safety, and I could see no better alternative. If the Weavers wanted a fight, I'd give them one they'd never forget.

I indicated to Emmarie that she should join Chela in the cart. She'd be safer there if I was forced to do battle. Reluctantly, she complied.

"I'll protect you," I said to Alexander as we resumed our trek. "If they attack, get them to sssafety. I'll join you when I'm able."

Alexander nodded and motioned to Chela. I waited for her to pass with the cart, then took up a position at the rear.

The Weavers continued to move unseen through the trees but at a more frenetic pace. The path ahead remained clear of spider-silk, and I wondered how intelligent these creatures truly were. Was it an attempt to lure us into a false sense of security before they sprung their trap?

My thoughts flashed back to the pitfall I'd walked into during the last battle I led against the Corodan. When they'd cornered me, I'd shifted and slaughtered the lot of them, saving myself and effectively ending the decades-long war.

But this time, circumstances were markedly different. I'd been fighting the Corodan for over twenty years by the time they'd attempted their ambush. I was familiar with the enemy.

It was not so here.

I'd yet to catch more than a passing glimpse of the Venom-weavers, and while I believed I held the advantage, I wasn't certain. My claws had rent through Corodan carapaces with ease, but would the Venom-weavers' prove similar?

Regardless, I would fight to protect Alexander and the others. I'd heal from any injuries I might sustain—I always did. Determination to see my brother succeed drove me forward, despite the unrest brewing in the silken maze of the trees.

Hours passed before we entered the clearing Emmarie had described, while the Venom-weavers became ever more restless in their anticipation. The path opened abruptly into a wide meadow, carpeted in scrubby grass and devoid of webbing. I paused at the edge of the trees, silently willing the others to move more swiftly. On the other side of the meadow was the shimmering, green-gray barrier, our salvation from our arachnid tormentors.

Beyond the barrier, I spied several low brick structures surrounding a central building, and a number of people went about their business safely within. The scent of ozone wafted through the air, growing stronger with each step I took toward the barrier.

The spiders fell ominously silent as we entered the meadow.

Alexander broke into a sprint once he was in the open, while Chela urged Sienna forward to keep pace with him. The terrified packhorse didn't resist and broke into a near-gallop.

I drew a breath and paused as I counted slowly to ten, allowing the others time to reach safety before I entered the clearing and sprung the trap. They were half way across when I emerged from the trees, moving swiftly.

A burst of chittering accompanied the unsettling sound of many chitinous limbs as they simultaneously unfolded and leapt into action.

I turned abruptly to face the Weavers, skidding on the grass underfoot. Dozens emerged from the trees to form a half-circle around my location. I backed toward the center of the clearing, feigning uncertainty, though I was merely moving into the open where my abilities wouldn't be hindered by the overgrown forest. Let them believe I feared them; it would provide me with the advantage of surprise.

Each Weaver was the size of a large horse. I'd encountered countless small spiders during my lifetime, but seeing them enlarged to this scale made it clear just how grotesque arachnids could be. Their bodies were smooth, glossy, and gray, but coarse hairs jutted from between the joints of their legs. Their mouthparts were likewise covered in hairs and tipped with a wicked pair of fangs nearly as long as a human's forearm. Each Weaver glared through an array of six ink-black eyes. They pressed closer, chittering amongst themselves in their raspy, unnatural tongue.

I lashed at the nearest spiders with my tail, making it clear I was as dangerous from the rear as I was from the front. They skittered away, nimbly avoiding the blow. I took another step backward and tensed, awaiting their first move.

"Andrew!" Alexander called, his voice distant.

I wanted to look back, to see for myself that he was safe, but turning my attention away from the spiders for even a second could prove deadly. I took another step backward, edging toward the barrier. Alexander shouted something more, but I was unable to make out his words.

In the same instant, the Weavers pushed forward in unison. Some leapt over others in their sudden frenzy to attack.

I roared a challenge, tearing at those foolish enough to engage a dragon. Their tough outer carapaces were no match for my strength, and I dispatched them several at a time. Yet they continued to pour into the meadow from the forest, undaunted by my ferocity or the deaths of their brethren.

It wasn't long before I'd entered the familiar rhythms of battle—slashing, tearing, and rending. The spiders became no more than faceless foes, enemies to be dispatched as I tried to protect the others.

I didn't know how many Weavers I killed. After a time, there was a break in their ranks, and I used the opportunity to peer over my shoulder. The barrier was closed, but I could see the others watching from the opposite side.

I moved toward them but stumbled, unexpectedly dizzy. Belatedly, I noted the ground was slick with yellow-green ichor, and bits of gray chitin littered the meadow in all directions. I shook my head in an attempt to ward off my lightheadedness.

More rustling erupted in the trees.

I urged myself forward, though my limbs were heavy, and I was growing inexplicably weak. I would not fall within the meadow. I would not become overwhelmed by the next wave of spiders if I failed to reach the barrier.

It opened as I neared. I didn't wait for those within to move aside. I charged through and stumbled, falling to my scaly knees.

Alexander ran toward me, his eyes wide with concern.

Something was wrong, but I was unable to piece it together. I wasn't injured, yet my strength was depleted. My vision swam, and I shook my head again. What had happened?

"Alexsss…" I managed.

My limbs trembled, and I was helpless to stop them. Darkness began to encroach on the edges of my vision.

"Are you hurt?" he asked, his expression stricken.

"I don't...know..."

I was losing the battle with consciousness. I should have continued to fight it, but could not. I was too weak, too weary, too *drained.* I was only dimly aware of collapsing at my brother's feet before I succumbed.

TEN

I slept fitfully. Others walked past, disturbing my restless slumber, but it took an enormous effort of will before I mustered the energy to open my eyes. I was exhausted.

Though I'd endured many battles in my life, most had been longer and more grueling than my skirmish with the Venom-weavers, yet it had taken a significant toll. The spiders had fallen in droves in the face of my wrath, much like the Corodan before them. Yet something had been different with this fight, something I'd failed to account for. I couldn't fathom what it was.

When I finally gathered the energy required to open my eyes, it was morning. The sun shone above the tree line, the day was warm, and Alexander sat cross-legged within my field of view. As I began to stir, he leapt to his feet with a wordless exclamation of joy.

I was pleased to see my brother, but puzzled. He should have been in his trials.

I blinked several times and grimaced. There was an unpleasant, sour taste in my mouth, and my mind was hazy. My eyes refused to focus, and Alexander's figure remained blurred and indistinct.

"What happened?" My voice came out in a low rasp.

"You've been out cold for two days, brother." He crossed his arms, his brow etched with concern. "The magi said you'd recover given time, but I've been worried."

I frowned, and my stomach rumbled loudly. If I'd been unconscious for two days, that meant it had been nearly four since I'd last eaten. I didn't relish the idea of taking another meal in my dragon form, and I didn't possess the energy required to fly, regardless. I needed to shift.

"I have your clothing," Alexander said, reading my thoughts. He gestured to the pile of garments folded on the ground next to where he'd been seated. "I'll tell the others you're awake. Emmarie will be glad to hear it."

I shifted and dressed, fighting fatigue and dizziness all the while. I scowled as I realized Alexander had not answered my question. What had gone wrong during my fight? I didn't seem to be injured, but if it had been two days since my collapse, any wounds I may have sustained would have healed.

I was pulling on my boots when Alexander returned with Emmarie. She darted ahead of him, a grin plastered across her green features.

I attempted to stand, but immediately stumbled. Alexander sprinted to my side and circled his arm beneath my shoulders. I leaned against him, unable to keep my feet without his assistance. I groaned and lifted my free hand to my forehead. I felt as though I'd been drugged.

"Let's get you to the healer," Alexander said with a troubled frown. "She's prepared a meal for us, and she said you'll feel better once you've eaten. I made certain she's cooked enough for seven," he added with a smirk.

I nodded and ignored his jibe. "Damn, I feel…strange."

"You killed too many of them," Emmarie said, her tone somber. "We didn't know what happened until the magi explained."

"Lydia—she's the healer—told us the Weavers' ichor contains toxins," Alexander continued. He led me toward the nearest brick building, where a woman awaited us in the doorway. "While it didn't penetrate your hide, there was so much spilled during your fight it produced fumes even you couldn't overcome. You breathed in too much of the toxin."

"The meadow is unsafe," Emmarie added. "They posted a sign for other travelers to be cautious when crossing. The ichor in the ground is still releasing fumes."

I grimaced. It was taking me longer to process their words than it should have, but at least now I understood why I felt so damned wretched. I'd been poisoned by my own success.

Once we reached the building's entrance, the healer stepped aside to allow us entry. She was of average height and thin, with light brown hair that flowed almost to her knees. Her eyes were pale blue, set into a pretty, oval-shaped face that bore the ageless countenance of a mage.

She offered me a smile as she led us to an oaken table in the next room. Several platters had been laid out, piled high with various items. Cooked eggs, roasted meat, pastries, fruit, charred vegetables… My stomach rumbled in response to the sight, but this time, Alexander didn't seem to hear.

"Andrew, this is Lydia," Alexander said with a gesture to the pretty, long-haired woman. "She's a healer."

Lydia smiled. "Eat as much as you like. You'll need it to replenish your strength, and afterward, you should feel better." She disappeared into another room, leaving me alone with my half-brother and Emmarie.

I took a plate and filled it with a sampling of everything. Only after I'd done so did the others begin to eat as well.

I had a score of questions for Alexander, but wanted to speak with him alone. Instead, I turned my attention to the food. After a few bites, I realized how ravenous I truly was. I cleaned the plate and took a second helping of everything.

As I ate, my head began to clear, and my weakness diminished. If I had known of the spiders' toxic innards, I would have taken more care when dispatching them. I hoped they'd learned their lesson and wouldn't attempt another attack on travelers again. Their first had proven far more costly to their numbers than ours.

Emmarie watched me intently after she finished her portion, her dark eyes wide and her expression pensive. It was clear she wanted to speak but was uncertain how to begin.

I set my fork down deliberately though I wasn't finished eating, and focused on her. "What is it, Emmarie?"

She bit her lower lip apprehensively. "I wanted to ask you something." She glanced at Alexander, who nodded his encouragement. It seemed they'd discussed her question previously.

"I…When I saw you fight the spiders, I realized why the Oracle chose you as Alex's guardian. It was like watching a dancer, only you're much more deadly." She looked down, a light flush rising in her cheeks.

"I've trained in combat since the time I could walk," I replied with a shrug. "Battle is all I've ever known."

"Hmm." She frowned but didn't look up. "Alex says you're just as good with a sword. I mean, as a human."

I arched an eyebrow at my brother, who smirked, unable to hide his amusement.

"I can only imagine the fabricated stories my brother has shared," I replied. "He's as skilled as I am with a blade."

"Skilled, perhaps, but I lack your experience," Alexander replied. "Tell him, Emmarie."

She drew a breath and seemed to brace herself before she lifted her gaze to meet mine. "I want to learn how to fight. I know it's against the teachings of my people, but I believe what the Oracle said is true. I believe there is going to be a war, and I need to know how to protect myself. I want to help you and Alex."

I studied her thoughtfully. Her words were earnest, sincere. "I suppose we can arrange lessons in the evenings. It'll give us both something to do each night after we make camp."

Her face lit up. "Truly? I…I didn't think you'd say yes."

"Why would I say no?" I countered. "I happen to agree with you, and it might force others in our party to accept you."

Emmarie's expression soured at my words. "Chela." She crossed her arms, her jaw set in anger.

"Chela wanted to press on, to leave you behind," Alexander said uneasily. "I wouldn't stand for it. I knew you'd catch up once you were recovered and rested, and I knew you'd understand, but… It wasn't right. And after what you did for us..." He shook his head, frustrated.

I frowned. Prior to entering the forest, Chela had berated me for leaving the campsite for less than an hour. To learn she'd considered leaving me behind… I stifled a growl. There was no pleasing the woman.

Rather than stoke my temper any further, I picked up my fork and resumed my meal.

"I'm certain the Oracle chose her for a reason, but it wasn't right to leave you behind," Emmarie continued. "I told her if she went ahead, I'd remain here with you. Someone needed to be here when you awakened."

"When she broached the subject with me, I said I would not leave without you," Alexander added. "She believed I was making a foolish mistake. Each day I spend waiting is one more day I remain at risk. Holy hell, I've been reminded of the danger I pose to myself every time I meet another mage!" He stabbed at his eggs with unchecked ferocity. "I won't leave you behind, consequences be damned."

"I don't believe you'll need to," I replied. "I'm stronger every second."

He managed a smile and shook his head, mildly amused. "I'm glad for that, but you gave us all a scare. It wasn't until Lydia examined you that we understood what happened. Seeing a dragon collapse at your feet is more than a bit terrifying, brother."

"He's right," Emmarie said. "It's good to see you awake. Thank you for agreeing to teach me." She rose from her seat and began to move toward the door.

"The training won't be easy," I warned.

She smirked. "Few things are. I'm ready." She flashed a final grin, waved, then skipped from the room.

"I take it you completed your trial," I said to Alexander once we were alone.

He nodded. "I meant to tell you earlier. I was so relieved you were awake it slipped my mind."

"I'm sorry, brother. I didn't mean to cause such an uproar."

He laughed. "I'm simply grateful that you're mending." He paused to glance at the door, and I noted Lydia had returned.

"You're looking better," she said matter-of-factly as she sauntered across the room. "I assumed a good meal would restore your strength. It was remarkable to observe how your body heals itself. If I'd waited to examine you any longer than I did, it's unlikely we would have learned what caused your collapse at all. Your body purged most of the toxins within a few hours. Had it been anyone else, they wouldn't be sitting here as you are." She sat gracefully in the chair Emmarie had vacated only moments before. "You must have questions regarding what occurred while you were asleep."

I nodded. "Alex told me some."

"Of course," she replied.

Her mannerisms were formal, much like the noblewomen from Novania, though I doubted she'd come from there. I didn't know if the Southlands had anything akin to royalty; so far, we had not encountered any, but her erect posture and careful gestures would have been at home in a royal court.

"He knows what we spoke of," Alexander said. "Since I was sent off to my trial, I'm sure there is more to the story than I know. I missed a day and a half."

Lydia nodded once. "Yes, there is more." She turned to face me directly. "Because of you, we have gleaned a new understanding of the Venom-weavers. We didn't know their blood contained toxins, nor did we know if concentrated, they could kill a man. Fortunately, you are half dragon. And thanks to you, the Weavers have withdrawn from this area. Your Merael friend claims they fear you. Rightly so."

I smiled. After the terror Emmarie had endured listening to the spiders' rasping voices, she'd been given a long overdue respite. I was relieved for her sake.

"Before we entered the forest, Chela said she believed the spiders would keep their distance," Alexander said. "She believed they feared dragons."

Lydia smiled sadly. "Ah, they used to. The Venom-weavers don't live as long as humans do, and they've grown bold as their memories fade. Several generations of Weavers have lived and died since the last dragon-kind passed through their domain. They've forgotten the wisdom of their forebears and instead turned their malice upon a target they should have avoided. They don't bury their dead as we do. The bodies of their fallen remain in the meadow and will until they decompose. We've decided to leave them as they are to serve as a reminder to the Weavers what the cost of their treachery was."

I looked at Alexander warily. "I don't know how many there were…"

He snickered. "I thought as much. I'll show you when we're finished eating."

"There were other events that transpired while you were both occupied," Lydia continued. "The Merael girl was loath to leave your side once it was made clear to Alexander that he must complete his trial and leave you in my care. I permitted her to remain with me. She seems to think of you as the older brother she never had. Do you know much of her history?"

I shook my head. Emmarie had traveled with us to the Citadel when we first met with the Oracle. She'd been sent to the Oracle's tower by her uncle, an elder amongst their people, but I knew little more. She had not divulged any other personal information and preferred to keep her past to herself. I respected her privacy and wouldn't press her for details.

"She'll tell you in time," Lydia replied. "It isn't my place to reveal her story." She paused to gather her thoughts, then said, "The guide who accompanies you is an opinionated and stubborn sort. I understand she knows the lands well. In fact, she has been here before, on two occasions that I recall. Her skill aside, I don't like her. I dispatched a message to the Oracle regarding her abhorrent behavior."

I raised an eyebrow. I suspected she referred to Chela's attempt to leave me behind.

"Has the Oracle sent word back?" Alexander asked. He was curious but not surprised by her admission.

"Yes, though her response was not what I'd hoped." Lydia frowned imperiously. "She stated Chela must remain as your guide. She has foreseen something that requires that deplorable woman's singular talent. Now that you're through the forest, I don't see why her particular skill should be required." Her tone dripped with contempt.

I glanced at Alexander, but he stared at the tabletop and failed to catch my eye. If Lydia's words were true, the only reason Chela's skillset would be required was if more of Colin's minions were due to appear. Had the Oracle seen more attacks in our future? Chela's guidance would prove beneficial if we needed to follow an alternate route between destinations, and without her, I was certain we'd become lost.

While I didn't always agree with Chela's reasoning, I couldn't muster the same level of animosity that Lydia seemed to possess. I believed there was something more to her feelings than what she'd chosen to reveal.

"I will join you on the next leg of your journey, and the Oracle has approved of it," Lydia continued after a moment. "While I don't trust your guide, I also need to travel to the Golden Stair. The journey will be more pleasant with companions." She looked pointedly in my direction. "You, however, need at least another night's rest before we leave. We will not depart until I'm certain you've recovered."

"No doubt Chela loved it when you broke the news to her." Alexander snickered.

"She has no say in the matter," Lydia replied. "The Oracle has spoken, and she cannot argue against it. Besides, Chela is no healer, and she doesn't know how to treat injuries. I do. The spiders are not the only dangers you'll come across on your journey, and your guardian must be well." She studied me with an appraising eye. "It seems your guardian also needs to be more circumspect."

Alexander smirked. "Andrew thinks he's invincible sometimes."

I frowned and shook my head. "No, I don't. I know my limitations—most of the time."

Lydia nodded once in understanding. "We didn't know the Weavers' blood would prove toxic. I don't blame you for acting as you did in this instance, but it isn't the first time you've required a healer's touch since you traveled to the Southlands. Alex told me what you did for him at the Citadel. That was no small matter, and you've only just recovered from it."

I shrugged uncomfortably. "If I had to do it again, I would." I looked directly at Alexander. "My brother is worth it."

Alexander's eyes betrayed a dozen different emotions before he shook his head, adamant in his denial. "You can never go through that again, Andrew. The cost was too high."

"Hmm."

The memory of the pain I'd endured remained fresh in my mind. He was right; I would never willingly repeat the experience, but I wouldn't tell him that. If I were given the opportunity to go back in time and change my decision, I would not. I was content with the outcome.

"Show me the clearing, Alex," I said in an attempt to change the subject. "I'd like to see it for myself."

"If you don't mind, I will join you," Lydia broke in.

I nodded and stood slowly, testing my balance while the table remained within reach. It seemed my legs would carry me without assistance since I'd eaten. Alexander scrutinized my movements, but after a moment, he smiled. I'd be fine on my own.

He led us outside and into the late morning sunlight. He maintained a slow pace that I knew was for my benefit, and though I believed I could have walked faster, I was reluctant to risk it.

We came to the edge of the clearing, where the magical barrier rose in a shimmering field from the ground. Through the undulating curtain of light, I spied dozens of tangled arachnid bodies strewn across the grassy expanse beyond. At the center of the clearing where most of my battle had taken place, the grass had withered and died. There was no visible evidence of the ichor I'd spilled, but I wondered if its toxic properties had caused the plant life to shrivel away.

In all directions of the battle site, bits of gray carapace were scattered amongst the corpses, gleaming dully in the weak sunlight. I recalled tearing blindly at the spiders as wave after wave entered the glade. My claws had shredded their bodies, despite their natural armor. Disembodied legs rose like jagged signposts amongst the wreckage, a testament to the carnage I'd wrought.

It had always been the same. In the midst of battle, I found myself in a rhythm of destruction, my mind attuned to the dual purpose of survival and the defeat of my foes. I was unaware of the damage that I was capable of as I fought, but afterward, I was often stunned by the aftermath.

Today was no different. Even though the Weavers were a seemingly malevolent species, the sight of the devastation gave me pause. Had the spiders truly deserved this massacre? Was I any better than they were? Perhaps the Merael were right to fear my kind.

I sighed and turned away, melancholy and morose by the spectacle.

ELEVEN

My strength rapidly returned, but Lydia chose to err on the side of caution and refused to allow my departure for another two days. Alexander seemed to enjoy the respite; he was in higher spirits than he'd been in weeks. He spent long hours speaking with the various magi who resided within the shield, but Lydia occupied much of his attention. Chela kept her distance, her expression often dour when I spied her from afar.

By our final afternoon in the forest, I was restless and eager to move on. We agreed to leave the next morning, but I needed something to occupy my time. I pulled Emmarie aside and asked if she would like to begin her lessons. She nodded, but appeared hesitant.

"Are you having second thoughts?" I asked gently.

She shook her head vehemently. "No, I want to learn how to fight." She sighed and looked down, clearly uncomfortable. "It's…new for me, and I don't know where to begin."

I nodded, though I suspected she wasn't telling me the whole truth. I recalled Lydia's words, and I believed Emmarie would tell me in time.

"We'll begin with the basics—balance and strength exercises. Sparring will come later." She nodded, the relief so evident in her dark eyes that I laughed aloud. "Did you think we would begin with swords right away?"

She shrugged sheepishly. "Yes."

"We'll work at a pace that's comfortable for you. Based on what the magi have said, we'll be on this journey for a while longer. There will be plenty of time to practice and hone your skills."

I led her to an open space behind the largest building within the shielded area, the shrine. It was quiet and serene. The afternoon sun slanted through the lattice of tree branches overhead, and the day was pleasantly warm. I noted with mild unease that some of the leaves were beginning to yellow at their core, the first mark of autumn's approach.

We spent the next two hours in training. Emmarie had a natural gift for balance, and handled that portion of the lesson well. It would take more time to develop the strength required to wield a sword, so I focused most of our lesson there.

After a while, I looked up to find Alexander and Lydia were observing us as they leaned against the side of the shrine. Alexander had a faint smile on his lips and his eyes were distant, as though he recalled fond memories. Lydia's sharp-eyed gaze was trained on Emmarie, interest evident in her expression.

"I think that's enough for one day," I said. "We can continue tomorrow after we make camp."

She released an explosive sigh filled with frustration. "How long before we can spar?" She demanded, her previous reticence gone.

"Once you're strong enough to hold a sword without wobbling," I replied evenly. "We have time. There's no reason to rush."

She spun around, startled as Alexander approached from behind. "How long were you watching us?"

He laughed. "Long enough. It reminds me of when I was perhaps eight years old and was beginning to train as you are." He looked at me with a smirk. "It always astounds me how patient you become when you're teaching, Andrew. You're usually lacking in that department, but when you teach, it becomes boundless."

I shrugged, which caused him to laugh again.

"I didn't come by to poke fun at you, in any case," he said after a moment. "Lydia has invited us to sup with her again, and I came to extend the invitation."

I glanced behind him, seeking Lydia, but she'd disappeared around the building.

"You've been spending quite a bit of time with her," I replied with a grin. "She seems capable, though I don't look forward to playing mediator between her and Chela."

The women's dislike for one another had become more apparent over the past two days. I hoped they'd remain civil while Lydia accompanied us to the Golden Stair, but I had my reservations. Thankfully, the journey wouldn't take more than a fortnight. Constant bickering was a sure way to exterminate what little patience I possessed.

Alexander sighed. "If you hadn't been unconscious when Chela tried to force us on, you would better understand our position."

I lifted an eyebrow at his use of "our," but didn't comment on it. I was beginning to suspect Alexander had more than a passing interest in the healer. While Chela would certainly disapprove, I felt it would do him good to have someone in his life. Romance was something my brother had never experienced previously.

"Chela was wrong," Emmarie interjected fiercely. "After all her talk before we entered the forest, as soon as we were past the most dangerous portion, she decided to abandon you when you clearly needed time to recover. I won't forget what she tried to do."

"Nor will I," Alexander replied with a firm nod of agreement.

I sighed and rolled my eyes dramatically. "I thought I only had one sibling along for this journey. Now it seems I have two."

Alexander laughed loudly, though Emmarie appeared sheepish.

"We both care for you, brother," Alexander said as he led us toward Lydia's home. "You've looked after us both, you know. And I, for one, wouldn't mind adopting Emmarie as a younger sister. It's a welcome change from so many damned brothers."

Emmarie chewed her lower lip, her dark eyes brimming with questions. "Do you mean it, Alex?"

He flashed a grin. "Of course, I mean it. Andrew agrees with me, don't you, brother?"

While I was not completely certain what Alexander was playing at, I nodded. Lydia had alluded that Emmarie's past had been difficult, and I knew from our brief stay in the Thornhallow she was not close to her uncle. I didn't know if she had any other family but suspected she didn't. I'd become protective of the girl during our travels, and I wanted to see her safe. Perhaps it was this desire that led me to agree with Alexander.

Emmarie's eyes grew shiny, and her bottom lip trembled. She closed her eyes briefly as she struggled with her emotions, then drew a shaky breath. "Thank you. You don't know what this means to me. I've always wanted a real family." She brushed at her eyes, wiping away unshed tears. "Tell Lydia I'll be there soon. I…need a few moments to myself." She turned abruptly and hurried away.

"Well, that wasn't quite what I expected," Alexander said after a moment. "I was only trying to help. I hope you don't mind."

"I don't. It's been clear for a while that she's lonely. She followed us for more reasons than the desire for adventure. I'm certain of that. I hope Lydia was right when she said Emmarie would tell us her story in time. Perhaps your words will give her the courage to finally open up." I managed a weary smile. "We'd best not keep Lydia waiting."

Alexander's face reddened slightly. "Agreed. I'm glad she wants to accompany us, even if it's only for a short while."

I smirked; Alexander was unable to hide his attraction to the healer. "You like her."

"Ah… Um, yes." He cleared his throat and scratched at the back of his neck.

I bellowed a laugh. "Don't be embarrassed. It happens to the best of us. Just be yourself and see where it leads. I won't say a word to the others if that's what you'd prefer."

I opened the door to Lydia's house and motioned for Alexander to enter first. The aroma of cooking vegetables wafted toward us, causing my stomach to rumble.

Alexander chuckled. "At least one thing is certain. I can always count on you to be prepared to eat, brother."

Early the next morning, we said our goodbyes to the magi and the shrine. Chela led us into a subterranean tunnel that would take us from the shrine west, beyond the Venom-weavers' Forest. We wouldn't be forced to endure another harrowing trek through the web-shrouded trees.

I grumbled, frustrated that she'd failed to mention the tunnel previously. The initial trek, as Chela had stated, was solely designed as a part of the magi's challenge. Now that Alexander had completed his trial, the spiders' threat was past.

I should have been grateful, but I was incensed. The Oracle and the magi who assisted her placed their would-be brethren at unnecessary risk. I could see no point to the endeavor, beyond the loss of countless innocents to the ravenous Weavers. It was senseless. *Reckless.*

Lydia had pulled her long locks up into a tight bun, and it was evident Alexander found her new look appealing. She'd traded her long dresses for more practical traveling apparel; a buckskin tunic and trousers that fit her lithe form snugly. Alexander could scarcely keep his eyes from her. His reaction was amusing.

Chela said little, though she no longer appeared angry, merely resigned. She stated we should be through the tunnel before nightfall and that we'd make camp as far away from the borders of the forest as we were able. Given the outcome of our initial journey, no one argued with her. Emmarie walked alongside me as we set out, while Alexander and Lydia followed behind Chela and the cart.

"Andrew," Emmarie said after we'd been walking for a time, "I wanted to thank you—and Alex—again. What you said yesterday... It meant more than you know."

I smiled in response and hoped she'd explain further. She did not, and I was forced to swallow my curiosity. I would not pressure her into speaking of her past if she wasn't ready to share it.

The day passed uneventfully. Emmarie asked me of Novania; what it had been like to grow up in the palace, what the people were like, and what animals lived north of the Barrier. It seemed her questions were endless, but I answered them without complaint. It was a good way to pass the time, and I hoped that by opening up to her, perhaps one day she'd do the same for me.

It was midafternoon when we exited the tunnel. The day had become overcast and faint rumblings of thunder could be heard in the distance. The forest lay behind us, dark and menacing, but the tunnel's exit was perhaps a half mile from the line of trees. I stopped to peer into the murky depths beneath the boughs, but could see no movement within. Perhaps the Weavers had learned their lesson—or perhaps they merely bided their time.

We marched on, into the open plain that sprawled before us. We traveled a few more miles before the first large drops of rain began to fall, then made camp near the road. There were no trees to provide shelter from the weather, and we'd be in for a soggy night if the rain continued.

After we'd set up camp, I drew Emmarie aside for another lesson despite the rain. Later, we supped, and after the others turned in for the night, I remained outside. Alexander had insisted I take the first watch; he believed I'd sleep more soundly when his turn came.

The rain had slackened to a fine mist, and though it was damp, I was not uncomfortable. The night was black since we'd been unable to light a fire in the storm, but I didn't mind. I paced the perimeter of our campsite to keep myself alert, but the night remained peaceful.

Perhaps an hour after the others had turned in, I heard someone stir within the tents. Moments later, Chela emerged. Her eyes swept over the campsite, but it was clear she could see nothing in the darkness. I made my way toward her as she peered into the gloom.

"Chela, are you well?" I kept my voice low to avoid awakening the others.

She nodded. "I wanted to speak with you, Andrew."

I motioned for her to follow, and we began to walk the perimeter of the camp.

"I have no doubt Alexander told you I attempted to move on while you were recovering," she said. Her tone was flat, dull, and lacked her usual spirit.

I frowned in concern. Her gaze was focused on the ground as we walked, her expression drawn.

"Alex said as much, yes," I replied.

"I need you to understand. I didn't want to leave you behind," she continued in a rush. "My primary concern is your brother's welfare, and it always will be. Too many delays may prove dangerous. But he's as stubborn as they come, especially when it involves you."

"I understand. I would have been fine had you gone on without me. I can travel swiftly in the air. I don't hold what you tried to do against you." I chuckled, and she stopped midstride, startled by my response. "You're right about Alex. He's loyal, almost to a fault."

The relief on her face was plain, and she managed a faint smile. "I feared that everyone here disliked me. I know I come across as brash and difficult, but I don't mean any harm. It's just who I am." She released a pained sigh and stared into the darkness. "I won't lose another mage to this journey. Despite his frustration with *me*, I have his best interests at heart."

I recalled Lydia's words from the day we'd met; she didn't like Chela, and it went beyond recent events. While Alexander and Emmarie might have been aghast at leaving me behind, I knew my brother's anger would pass in time and be forgotten. Emmarie had further reason to distrust our guide, but that matter lay between them. I'd do my part to ensure Emmarie's place remained secure within our group. But Lydia's reason for her dislike of our guide was a mystery.

"Alex will calm down, given time," I replied. "I can't speak for the others, but as for myself, I understand your position. Perhaps better than you realize." When she glanced at me, questions in her eyes, I went on. "I commanded the king's armies for years. Leading any group of people—no matter the size—always brings challenges. You can't please everyone, but you also must keep sight of the ultimate goal. Your role in this journey isn't so different."

"Ah, I wish everyone I met was as even-keeled as you seem to be," she replied. "I'm glad you recovered as quickly as you did. And I will always be grateful to you for standing against the Weavers. I haven't properly thanked you for that." She looked down once more. "If you hadn't been there to stall them, I fear what would have happened to the rest of us. They were out for blood that day."

"I've wondered if they would have reacted differently if I'd remained in this form," I mused, thinking of how Emmarie had described the spiders' dialogue. While we'd all been considered "prey," I'd been the largest, an irresistible target for their insatiable appetites.

"Whatever the reason for their attack, I will always be thankful you were there." Chela squared her shoulders and turned to face me. "There are few things in this world I truly fear, and the Venom-weavers are one of them. You saved more than your brother's life that day—you saved mine and Emmarie's."

We'd completed a full circle of the campsite and were near the tent she shared with Emmarie.

"I can rest now, knowing things are well between us. Thank you for speaking with me, Andrew."

I smiled. "Of course."

TWELVE

We reached the settlement of Bradford late the next afternoon. As we neared, we passed numerous farms; it was the beginning of the harvest season, and many people were at work in the fields. We restocked our supplies in Bradford and pressed on, staying only as long as was required. There was no shrine in Bradford for magi to pay homage to, though it lay on the main route of the pilgrimage.

During the journey from the forest, I'd been spending an increasing amount of time marching alone at the head of our group. Alexander was smitten with Lydia and spent most of his time with her. I often heard their laughter as my brother's roguish charm worked its own brand of magic. For his sake, I would be sorry to see her leave.

Chela said little to anyone. I spoke to her only sparingly; she was surly, and conversation with her only soured my mood. Alexander's unabashed attraction to Lydia appeared to be a source of discontent for our guide, and while she kept her thoughts to herself, her irritated glances in their direction were constant. I was marginally grateful for her silence, as I was in no temper to play mediator.

I worked with Emmarie in the evenings, but during the day, she often busied herself with the local wildlife. She had numerous conversations with a variety of birds, several squirrels, and one very persistent raccoon. I suspected she sought the key to speaking with the gray eagles, though she wouldn't share what her discussions entailed.

Left alone with my thoughts, I found myself dwelling on the events at Vinterry. I missed Vera, and my rage with Colin continued to smolder unchecked, just beneath the surface. With the others preoccupied, I brooded and schemed, focused on the day I'd bring my half-brother's corrupt reign to a bloody end. He deserved nothing less.

Eight days passed before we reached Oristan, a sprawling city Lydia referred to as the Blue Port. Long before the city appeared, I detected an unusual tang in the air. It wasn't a scent I was familiar with; it reeked of brine and salt, and when the wind blew from the west, the odor became stronger.

It was only after I glimpsed the city that the source of the smell became apparent. Oristan was perched on a rock-strewn coast, the blue-green waves of the sea lapping at its shores. At the heart of the city, a vast, gleaming structure towered above its whitewashed and stony brethren. It was built to resemble an enormous spiraling staircase, rising toward the endless blue of the sky. In the light of the afternoon sun, it sparkled with a metallic golden sheen.

Our arrival in Oristan was a welcome distraction. Chela led us through the teeming streets toward the shoreline, where she selected an inn that appeared well-kept. It sported an unobstructed view of the sea, and I was entranced by the endless motion of the waves. After we settled in, I was drawn outdoors, mesmerized by the view.

I'd often heard tales of the sea. Novania was bordered on two sides by the ocean, but in all my travels, I'd never beheld its majesty for myself. White birds circled in the air, calling in coarse voices to one another before diving to skim the tops of the waves, only to rise again bearing silvery fish in their beaks. Several long piers stretched away from the shore, where they ended in deeper waters. Dozens of boats bobbed in the currents; most were fishing vessels, but some larger ships floated at a distance.

"It's beautiful, isn't it?"

I turned to find Lydia several paces away. I don't know how long she'd been there, but I didn't mind her presence.

"Yes," I agreed.

"Alex told me you'd never been to the sea."

I managed a smile. "This is my first time. Alex has seen it before. He traveled east from the Capitol a few times, but I was never part of those journeys."

She nodded as she walked forward to stand at my side. "I know. He told me you were often away doing battle with the Corodan." She paused, her gaze fixed on the waves. "I wanted to speak with you while I had the opportunity. Is this a good time?"

I shrugged. Now was as good a time as any, though I was uncertain why she wanted to speak with *me*. It was Alexander who had captured her interest.

"As you can see, I'm not busy. We can speak now."

"When I left the forest, I'd planned to part ways with you here. I have business at the Golden Stair." She paused to chew on her lower lip. "I'd planned to return to the forest once I finished."

I studied her, and she met my gaze unflinchingly. "But you've changed your mind."

"Yes." She shifted her focus to the water once more. "I won't leave Alexander. I… I think I may be in love with him."

I arched an eyebrow, unable to hide my smirk. "Alex has been enamored with you since the day you met. But I'd like to know something first. Alex is twenty-six, and because of our upbringing, he's never been with a woman. He couldn't risk his Mark being discovered. He's unused to courtship… You must be patient with him. Can you do that?"

"I'm a healer, Andrew," she replied with a laugh. "Patience is instilled within my kind during our trials. Alex and I have spoken of his past, and I understand your concerns. Winning his heart will be an undertaking, but he's worth it." She smiled at the waves. "We are of the same age, he and I. I know it's impossible to tell, given that I'm a mage, but it's the truth."

"If you truly care for him, then I give you my blessing," I replied. "Alex has been lonely, though he'll never admit it. I'm happy knowing he's no longer forced to hide who he is."

I sighed inadvertently as my thoughts returned to Vera. The pain of her loss had not diminished over time, and I didn't believe I'd ever remarry. What we'd shared was incomparable.

I'd always hoped Alexander would one day find someone to settle down with, and Lydia seemed a suitable match. He deserved the same level of happiness that I'd once shared with Vera, however fleeting it had been. I wished them the best, and I'd support their union if they planned to wed one day.

Lydia chuckled, drawing me from my thoughts. "I haven't spoken to Alex about my feelings. Perhaps I should do so before you bless anything."

She was teasing me, but I shrugged it off. As was my habit, I was taking matters more seriously than I should have.

"It eases my mind, knowing you approve," she continued. "Alex said you've always been close, even before your exile."

When I merely nodded, she reached over to pat my arm. I was no longer in the mood for conversation; I simply wanted to be alone with my thoughts. She seemed to understand and left a moment later, retracing her steps toward the inn.

I wished Vera were there, that she could see the beauty of the ocean and watch as the sun cast flecks of gold across the surface of the waves. She would have loved the sight.

I imagined we would have walked the length of the beach, hand in hand. She would have removed her shoes to better feel the cool water as it washed over her feet and the coarse sand between her toes. She would have laughed merrily while shoving me into the next wave as it crashed over the sand. We would have spoken of our future, our plans, and perhaps a return to Oristan one day.

Colin had destroyed all that could have been.

Alexander made his way to the Golden Stair with Lydia the next morning.

She planned to conduct her business while Alexander embarked on his next trial, though I suspected the two simply wanted time alone. I wished my half-brother good luck as they departed, then left the inn to walk aimlessly along the beach. Chela departed for the market to replenish our supplies, and I didn't know where Emmarie had gone.

It was just as well. I harbored a deep melancholy sparked by my thoughts the previous evening. I wanted to be alone.

A short time later, several gray eagles appeared overhead. I'd been watching for them, and noted each bird had arrived from a different direction. The sea birds were instinctively wary of their larger kin. Many found roosts amongst the masts of the nearby fishing vessels, leaving the skies to the eagles alone. The eagles paid them no mind as they spiraled through the air above Oristan, drawn to the power Alexander had unwittingly summoned.

I shifted my gaze to the water. I found a measure of peace within the constant motion of the waves, a tranquility I'd long believed unattainable since that night at Vinterry. Once more, I wished Vera were present to see it. Something about the ocean stirred my memories of her. Perhaps it was the color of the water under the partially clouded sky that reminded me of her eyes when the sunlight glinted from them. Or perhaps it was the constant whisper of the water, a sound not unlike that of the wind in the pines north of Vinterry.

But she was gone, and my heart with her. Damn Colin and his petty schemes.

"Andrew!"

Emmarie called from some distance away, but I didn't immediately turn to greet her. I gazed at the waves for several seconds before I peered over my shoulder to acknowledge her presence. I realized with a start that I'd traveled some distance from the inn; it was little more than an outline, obscured by sea mist and haze.

Emmarie raced along the sandy shore, beaming. Flying in her wake was a falcon that appeared familiar, though I didn't immediately understand why. I strode toward her while she slowed her pace and skidded to a halt. When we met, she was winded but smiling.

"Andrew," she said again, breathless, "this falcon was searching for you. She has a message!"

The falcon alighted on Emmarie's outstretched forearm and lifted one of its legs toward me. Attached was a slim roll of paper in a glass tube. As I carefully removed the message, I recalled where I'd last seen this bird—Riversmeet, in Ilia's aviary.

"You found Thomas?" I asked, a smile breaking across my face for the first time in what seemed like weeks.

The bird twittered, and Emmarie laughed. "She said she had no trouble finding him and that you should have more faith in her kind."

I shook my head. "I apologize. I'm not used to this type of message system. But I thank you for finding him and returning to me."

Emmarie laughed again when the bird responded. "She's not angry, but she is a proud creature and would like you to remember that. She wants to return home."

I nodded. "Thank you again."

The bird trilled a response and leapt into the air, eager to be away. It seemed she was unafraid of the eagles.

"Well? What does your message say?" Emmarie asked impatiently.

I managed another smile, then unrolled Thomas' reply.

Andrew,

I'm pleased to hear things seem to be going well for Alex. It's amazing that you continue to find the means to contact me, given the distance that separates us. The falcon is quite a remarkable creature. It seems to know I am writing this message and would like to have it returned to you. I don't know how it can possibly intuit this, but I find it fascinating.

I wish that I were with you now, that I could see the sights and experience all you must have encountered along your journey! Ah, but it is not to be, I suppose.

I'm still hiding in Bridgewaters, but we will be moving on to Calder's Point in a few weeks. Colin has been menacing Bridgewaters—though not seriously—for some time, and it has become unsafe to remain. The duke sent word north. We have allies there. Colin has few friends in the Northern Marches, but he seems to be paying them little mind. He is focused solely on the pursuit of you and has moved much of his army toward the Mage's Gate.

While his attention is focused there, it has given me the opportunity to extricate myself from his reach. I'm afraid I have little else to tell you at this time, but I eagerly await your next missive. Take care, brother, and tell Alex I wish him the best of luck.

Yours, Tom.

I folded the letter carefully and slipped it into a pocket. Emmarie waited impatiently, quivering with anticipation. Alexander and I had spoken of Thomas during our travels, and though she had not yet met our brother, she already considered him a friend.

"Tom's well," I said after a moment. "He didn't have much in the way of news to share, other than Colin is focusing his forces on the Mage's Gate." I scowled. "We still have eight more stops along this path. I hope Colin doesn't find a way through the Barrier before we're finished."

Emmarie shrugged. "The Barrier has held for hundreds of years. It won't fall easily, you know."

I nodded, though I harbored doubts. Emmarie had hoped to comfort me with her words, but she didn't know how relentless Colin could be. He'd continue to press his attacks until he either found a way to break though, or he exhausted his resources in the attempt. Knowing as little as I did about the workings of magic, I didn't put my faith in the Barrier withstanding a prolonged assault. A part of me dared to hope I was wrong.

Alexander's trial lasted a full two days, and night had fallen on the second before he emerged from the spiraling golden structure at the heart of Oristan. He was weary but elated, and his eyes shone with a wild light. Something significant had occurred. He wasn't inclined to speak of it as he rejoined us at the seaside inn, though I believed he'd tell me in time.

For their part, both Chela and Lydia seemed encouraged by the sudden change in Alexander's demeanor. While I didn't understand, I knew enough to realize that they'd taken it as a sign of progress on my brother's part.

Alexander seemed well enough, though it was clear he needed to rest. He supped with us in the inn's common room, but didn't linger afterwards. I followed him upstairs and bade him goodnight at the door to his room. As I turned to leave, he grasped my elbow.

"Wait. There's something I need to tell you."

I nodded and waited for him to continue.

"I didn't want to say this in front of the others," he admitted. "This trial was unlike the others. I feel…different now. Stronger, yet more fragile at the same time. I think I finally understand why the magi worry over me as they do." He frowned and looked down at the floor, troubled.

"Is there anything I can do to help?"

He chuckled and shook his head. "No, brother, you've already done more than enough." He sighed and ran one hand through his hair; he had not yet cut it, and it now fell below his ears. "I'm beginning to understand my power… And it terrifies me." When he lifted his gaze to meet mine, I bore witness to his fear.

"Alex, we'll get through this," I promised. "Remember, we're in this together."

He managed a faint smile. "That we are, brother." He sighed again, and I knew my words had failed to ease his concerns. "I have to be more careful from here on. One wrong move on my part, and I feel as though my mind will snap. The things I've learned… The things I'm capable of… It would drive any normal man to the brink. But *my* choices will determine what I do with my power. It gives me a measure of relief. I'm still in control, but I must fight to remain that way."

I frowned, unable to grasp the importance of his words, but his tone made me uneasy. "Alex, I'll do whatever I can to help you through this."

He nodded. "I know. But there is little more you can do beyond your role as guardian. I may not be on this journey alone, but the trials are something no one can assist me with. For the first time in my life, I can't rely on you to see me safely through. I have to do this myself. Even Lydia can't aid me… My power is too different from hers. She told me on our way to the Stair that it's like trying to read a book in a foreign script without any means of decoding the letters."

"Alex…"

He shook his head and waved one hand dismissively. "I'll be fine, Andrew, at least for now. I am over-tired and I need to sleep. Perhaps in the morning I'll feel more like myself."

I nodded, though I remained unconvinced. He disappeared inside his room, and I made my way back to the common room where we'd left the others. I needed to speak with Lydia and Chela to hear their opinion on what Alexander had revealed. I believed they'd understand his experience far better than I ever would.

By the time I returned to the common room, both women were gone. Emmarie remained, and she waved me over to the table she now occupied alone.

"Chela went outside to check Sienna," Emmarie said as I sat down. "Lydia went outside to gather her thoughts, or so she said." She looked at me pointedly. "They were arguing."

I groaned though the news didn't come as a surprise. "What about?"

"Lydia said she's decided to accompany us for the remainder of Alex's pilgrimage rather than return to the forest."

I knew where her story would lead. "Chela didn't like the news, did she?"

Emmarie stifled her laughter behind a hand. "No. I think they both went outside to cool their tempers. I don't mind Lydia. It's good to have a healer nearby." She scowled as her thoughts turned to Chela. "Chela said it was a mistake to have 'yet another' person to look after during the journey. She thinks my presence is one too many…"

"Don't mind her. She complains more than she ought to, but I believe she tries to do what's best for Alex. In this case, I don't think she could keep Lydia from joining us if she called in a small army to assist her." I was unable to hide my grin. "Alexander wants Lydia with us—and not only because she's a healer."

Emmarie's frown morphed into confusion, and I laughed. I would let her stew over my words. She'd understand my meaning soon enough.

"I'd best go outside and check on them," I said as I rose from my seat. "We can talk in the morning."

I located Chela first. She was in the stable, fretting over the horse and tallying our supplies.

"Chela?" I asked as I approached.

She paused in her work to offer me an apologetic frown. "Emmarie mentioned our disagreement, didn't she? One day, I'll learn to hold my tongue. I seem to make more enemies than friends, and it was not my intention to start an argument. She simply caught me by surprise."

I shrugged. It was best if I left the true reason behind the change unspoken until Alexander and Lydia had shared it with her themselves. "She's proven her skill as a healer. We ought to welcome her."

Chela sighed and adjusted the brim of her hat. "I know, and you're right. If you see Lydia, please give her my apologies. I… I don't believe she'll speak with me if I seek her out."

I arched one eyebrow but didn't press her for details. "I'll talk to her."

Outside, there was little light beyond the torches placed alongside the inn's door. The waves crashed against the shore not far away, but until my eyes adjusted to the gloom, I could see little. Clouds had blanketed the sky, making the darkness nearly absolute.

I stood just beyond the edge of the torchlight for a few moments until my vision grew accustomed to the night. Once it had, I spotted Lydia's slim figure walking slowly along the beach not far away. She'd let her hair down, and it hung in waves below her waist, obscuring her face. I approached and called her name softly once I was near.

She raised her head slowly, and it was obvious she'd been weeping. "Andrew?"

"I heard you'd come outside," I said. "Do you need to talk?"

She shook her head, then turned away to face the dark water. "I want to join you for the remainder of the pilgrimage, but your guide seems certain I'll be nothing more than a burden." Her voice trembled with emotion. "I don't want to leave him, Andrew."

"The decision is not Chela's to make," I replied. "She guides us on the journey because we're unfamiliar with the Southlands, but who accompanies us is our choice." I paused to study her. "I spoke with her a few moments ago. She asked me to give you her apology, for what it's worth."

Lydia sighed in frustration. "That woman! She's caused me more anguish in the short time I've traveled with her than anyone has in many years." She crossed her arms, her eyes hard.

"She's been difficult since we began this journey," I agreed. "But she seemed sincere in her regret when I spoke to her. She knows when she's overstepped her bounds, though often times, it seems the damage is irreparable."

Lydia snorted. "Perhaps it is. I suppose I should accept her apology if it means I may travel with you." She tossed her head, then her expression softened. "I will speak with her tonight."

She turned around, then hesitated. "I didn't realize it had become so dark. How did you find me?"

I chuckled. "I've been told I can see better at night than most."

"Hmm." She took my arm then, and I blinked, startled at the action. "I can scarcely see a thing. I suppose it's fortunate you came looking for me. I need a guide until we reach the light."

I nodded uncertainly and began walking toward the inn. "I wanted to speak with you about Alex."

Now that the spat between the women seemed to be over, perhaps I could learn something about the concerning conversation I'd had with my brother.

"Is something wrong?" she asked.

"I don't know," I admitted. "He said some cryptic things before he turned in for the night. I don't know what to make of them."

"Tell me. If it's about his training, then we must know. He's in a critical period, and we must be vigilant."

"I don't fully understand this business with magic. I suppose I never will." I sighed, then proceeded to tell her of our conversation.

She was silent as she contemplated my words, but didn't appear concerned. As we neared the stables, she released my arm and turned to face me.

"What he feels is normal, Andrew. It will seem overwhelming. What he learns is new and different, unlike anything he's experienced before. It's to be expected. He's excelled in his trials so far, and it gives me hope that he'll finish the pilgrimage successfully. I also find it a relief that he recognizes his fragility. Many would-be magi never see it. They overreach along the way, which leads to failure... That Alexander understands his limitations is a very good sign."

I released a breath, relieved by her words. "Thank you. I would be grateful if you'd continue to travel with us. You understand what Alex is going through, whereas I don't. I'm not sure I ever will."

She smiled patiently. "It's often difficult for those born without the Mark to fully grasp a mage's training. I'll do my best to keep you informed, though Alexander's power is vastly different than my own. Mage-warriors are their own breed... His trials will be largely incomprehensible to me, but I'll do what I can to assist you both."

"Thank you."

She glanced toward the stable as a slight frown creased her features. "I suppose I must speak with Chela. Perhaps we can smooth over our present rift."

THIRTEEN

Alexander slept well into the next morning. When he emerged from his room and found his way to the common room, he appeared rested and in better spirits than he'd been the previous evening. We departed once he'd eaten and gathered his things. It was nearing midday.

Chela was subdued, though it appeared she and Lydia had reconciled. They spoke to one another only when necessary, and while their exchanges weren't friendly, their outright hostility seemed to have abated.

"We'll travel southeast for several days," Chela said from her perch on the cart. "I hope you've had your fill of the sea, for we won't see it again once Oristan is behind us."

Ahead, Alexander said something to Lydia, and she laughed softly in response. I doubted he'd heard anything our guide had just said.

"And then?" I prompted.

"We'll enter old-growth forest and begin the slow ascent to Crystal Crags. That leg of the journey usually takes a week." She shrugged. "Crystal Crags is a mining town. It's nearly the size of Riversmeet, and it's also the site of your brother's next trial."

"I've heard of Crystal Crags," Emmarie chimed in, momentarily distracted from her conversation with a gull. "It's at the base of the Pinnacles."

Chela nodded. "Yes. The Southern Pinnacles may prove treacherous, but we'll worry about the trek through the mountains once we reach Crystal Crags. One step at a time, as they say."

"And the shrine?" I asked.

"The Waterfall Shrine is on the outskirts of the city," she replied. "Crystal Crags is bordered by a lake on one side, and the waterfall fills it. The shrine lies behind the waterfall."

I resisted the urge to frown. I'd hoped for more detail regarding Alexander's next trial, not a bland description of the location. I glanced toward Alexander and decided it was time we spoke; I still hadn't shared the latest message from Thomas with him, but extricating him from Lydia for even a few moments had proved impossible.

"Thank you," I said to Chela before I increased my pace to catch up with Alexander and the object of his attention. "Alex, a moment."

He frowned at my intrusion. "What is it, brother?"

"I'm sorry to interrupt, but I received a message from Tom."

He grinned, his brief irritation forgotten as I passed him the letter.

"We should send Tom another message when we can," he said after he'd finished reading, his mood ebullient. "If this Crags place is as busy as Chela claims, perhaps there will be a mage who can contact him."

I smirked. "So you *were* listening."

He reddened. "A bit."

"Did you meet Bryson Feige while in the Citadel?" Lydia asked from Alexander's other side.

"We did," I replied. "He sent several messages for us."

"He has an older sister with the same talent, you know. Bella. The last time I passed through Crystal Crags, she'd taken up residence there. Perhaps luck will be on our side, and she'll be there still." Lydia's smile was for Alexander alone.

"She was there a year ago," Chela called from behind. "She was set to be married to one of the locals, though I don't recall his name."

"Then there's an excellent chance she'll be there." Lydia smiled once more at Alexander. "I hope one day I can meet this younger brother of yours."

Alexander flushed, but beamed at her attention. "I hope so too."

I took that as my cue to move away. I slowed my pace until I fell in line with Chela and the cart once more.

"They've become rather close." Chela's tone was weary.

I was surprised to see an expression of sorrow on her sun-weathered features. "They have," I replied evenly.

"I've often wondered what love would be like," she said after a pause. "Every time I've begun to harbor feelings for someone, I manage to ruin all that might have been with my critical tongue. Perhaps I'm not meant for it."

I studied her carefully. It was impossible to decipher her age, though I suspected she was older than me. She gazed ahead with an expression of longing directed toward my half-brother and the woman who had occupied his free time of late. Alexander and Lydia made a fine pair, and I hoped they'd remain together.

"Do you care for Alex as she does?" I asked Chela pointedly.

She chuckled bitterly and shook her head. "You need not worry about me, Andrew. I managed to destroy any hope of what might have been early on. Your brother has no interest in me, and I would never drive a wedge between them." She sighed and adjusted her wide-brimmed hat. "I don't know why I mentioned this to you. I usually keep such sentiments to myself."

"When I see them together, it's a reminder of what I've lost," I replied. "When we started this journey, I was determined to see Alexander through to the end. It was a means to returning home, to undo what Colin's done, nothing more. But now…" I shrugged. "Now, it's less about revenge. We must stop Colin so Alexander doesn't suffer as I have. He deserves this chance at happiness."

"You've lost so much at the hands of family." Chela's tone was kind, compassionate. "I must remember the true purpose of this journey. It's not merely for Alexander, but also for you. While his training is important, I must keep in mind that other factors—greater factors—are at work in the world. I'll do my part, and I vow I won't cause any further disagreements amongst our group." Her expression was determined and fierce as she finished speaking.

I believed she'd keep her word.

Our first three days of travel were uneventful, the weather calm, and there were no further disputes to settle between the magi. The morning of the fourth day dawned gray and windy, the chill of autumn no longer a mere hint in the air as the changing of the season made itself known.

We'd entered the forested area nearly two days prior, and our path had become sloped and rocky. The trees were gnarled and twisted, the forest floor carpeted in a riot of thick undergrowth, and a deep sense of *presence* seeped from the shadows. Most of the trees were of broad-leafed varieties, and with each gust of wind rattling their branches, leaves began to fall in a shower of golden-brown. Fallen leaves and detritus gathered along the trunks in mounds as the wind corralled them against knobby roots and twisted brambles.

Our group was subdued as we broke camp, but I attributed the downturn to the weather. Wind was unpleasant at the best of times.

We'd been trudging along, largely silent for nearly an hour, when a pair of sparrows flitted across our path, chirruping insistently in agitation. They darted toward Emmarie, who walked with Lydia at the front of our procession, then both began twittering in concert. I'd become accustomed to the Merael girl's animal visitors and didn't pay them any mind. If something were amiss, she'd tell us.

I resumed my conversation with Alexander as we plodded along behind the cart. We'd been reminiscing about our home and our childhood, on our life prior to Colin's ascension. Life had been so much simpler then.

"The birds certainly seem excited," Alexander commented, unconcerned. "You know, we've made some interesting acquaintances. If someone had told me six months ago that I'd be on this journey, traveling with a Merael and two magi, I'd have told them they were mad."

I chuckled. "And if they would have told you about the skin-changer?"

Alexander laughed. "I knew one day we'd be here, brother. There was never any doubt in my mind that you'd be along for this journey."

I was about to reply but stopped when I noticed Emmarie sprinting toward us. The sparrows were gone, though I'd failed to note their departure. Panic filled Emmarie's dark eyes as the wind whipped her black hair into a frenzy.

"We're being followed," she gasped, breathless, her voice trembling. "I asked the birds around Oristan to warn me if they noticed anything strange. There are three men on the road behind us, about two miles back if I understand the sparrows' distances correctly. The men traveled through the night, and the sparrows overheard them state they were trying to catch up to us. Well, not with *us,* but with *you*, Andrew."

I frowned and glanced at my brother. "More of Colin's men, no doubt." I turned back to Emmarie. "Did they say anything else?"

She shook her head, eyes wild. "They're wearing armor. And they're carrying a strange standard. The birds tried to describe it to me, but all I understood was the coloring. It's red and white."

Alexander and I shared a knowing look. "Red and white is as close to crimson and ivory as a bird's likely to get," he replied. "And armored…"

We couldn't be certain of their origin until we glimpsed their standard, yet its presence alone was telling. In all of our travels through the Southlands, we'd never encountered a group bearing a standard of any sort. It was a formality the southern peoples didn't observe, but one Colin would enforce amongst his cronies. That they wore armor—and were likely armed—came as no surprise.

The more pressing issue was how the three had made it beyond the Mage's Gate and had known what path we'd taken. It was likely my own fault; after our arrival in the Citadel, I'd been less hesitant to reveal my nature. And our arrival there had been no secret—everyone in the city had spoken of the dragon in their midst.

"I'll deal with the followers," I told them. "Go with the others, Alex."

He shook his head adamantly. "No. I'll stand with you."

"No," I stated firmly, recalling Lydia's words—and his own—from our last night in Oristan. "You can't use your power in a fight. Not yet, anyway, and I won't allow you the temptation."

He clenched his jaw in a sudden burst of anger while his eyes flashed dangerously. "I know when to stop, Andrew. I'm in control."

"No, he's right." Lydia said from behind Emmarie. "The Oracle named him your guardian for a reason. Let your brother do his job. You are *not* ready for a confrontation. Your previous skills aside, I won't sit idly by and watch you throw your life away."

Alexander seemed to deflate at her words. I marveled at the effect she had on him and was grateful for it in this case. He squeezed his eyes shut, then released a long sigh.

"Fine. But if they get past you, I won't hesitate to defend the others."

"They won't," I growled. "Now, go! I'll wait for them here and catch up with the rest of you afterward."

Alexander gazed at me stubbornly, but when Lydia placed one hand on his elbow, he turned and allowed himself to be guided away from the pending conflict. If Lydia had not been there, I wasn't certain if I could have persuaded Alexander to follow reason, to allow me to perform the role I'd been assigned alone.

I loosened my sword in its scabbard as I heard the cart begin to trundle away. I hadn't donned my armor that morning, but I didn't want to jeopardize the others with further delays. Perhaps it was for the best; if I needed to shift, I wouldn't have time to remove my armor, and I hated to see such craftsmanship go to waste.

If there were only three men, I might not be forced to shift at all. Even if Colin had sent his best soldiers to intercept me, it was unlikely they'd be a match for my strength, and they certainly couldn't withstand an assault as well as I would. There were few in Novania who'd been able to rival my abilities, and I doubted my arrogant half-brother would have bothered to send his best. He'd made it clear long before our exile that I was beneath them.

He was wrong, and I'd make damned certain he learned not to discount the fury of the dragon-kind.

I stood squarely in the middle of the road while the wind whipped around me, then drew my sword in anticipation of our pursuers. They'd find me ready and waiting once they appeared around the last bend in the road. I glanced over my shoulder to find the others were well out of sight. Leaves rained from the trees, ripped cruelly from the branches that had once given them life. I waited, unmoving, as I listened for our pursuers through the howling of the wind.

I waited another half hour before I heard the trudge of heavy footfalls and the clink of armor above the roar of the gusts. It had intensified since I'd sent the others ahead. The boughs overhead bent and groaned in the onslaught, while the underbrush rippled and danced wildly.

The men shouted to one another in an attempt to be heard. Snatches of their conversation drifted toward me before they rounded the bend and came into view. It seemed they weren't enjoying the weather, and one admitted surprise that they'd failed to catch up with our group so far. The voices were muffled, but even so, one of them was eerily familiar. I adjusted the grip on my sword in anticipation of a fight.

As the men rounded the bend, struggling against the wind in their bulky armor, I understood why their voices had been muted. Each wore a full helm with the visor down. They halted abruptly when they spied me, stunned momentarily by the sight of their quarry.

"It's him!" one shouted. He drew his sword clumsily from its scabbard.

He stood between the others, eyes alight and eager to engage. He was a stout man, but shorter than his companions. The one on the left appeared wary, though his companions were clearly itching for a fight. He was the tallest of the three and carried himself with an air of surety the others lacked. I deemed him the most dangerous.

The man on the right was only scarcely taller than Stout was but had a slender build. He held his blade at an awkward angle; his inexperience with the weapon was apparent in his every motion.

Colin insulted me by sending these men. Only Wary might stand a passing chance, but he would never match my strength. I was at an advantage, and my half-brother's hubris would be repaid with their blood if they chose to strike.

But I would not initiate this battle. I'd wait for them to make the first move.

"You're Andrew, yes?" the slender one asked in a quavering tone.

I didn't answer, but swiveled my gaze in his direction. He stepped backward and swore under his breath.

"He is," Wary replied.

His was the voice that had seemed familiar. Perhaps he'd been a soldier in the king's army or an acquaintance from the castle grounds? I could see nothing of his face, and only a mere glimmer of his eyes beneath his helm.

"Then why are we still standing here?!" Stout demanded, brandishing his blade.

He didn't wait for his companions to reply. He bellowed and charged, a careless move, one borne out of sheer inexperience. Slender hesitated a heartbeat before he followed suit. He waved his sword in the air, leaving his torso undefended and his grip uncertain. Wary called for his companions to stop, but his words were either lost in the wind or ignored.

Stout swung his blade before he was within striking range. As his sword swiped high and wide, I noted the gap his poorly-wrought armor left beneath his arm. I lunged forward and slashed at the opening as he stumbled, carried inelegantly forward by the weight of his weapon. Unlike Stout's, my blade found its mark. He collapsed in a heap as I pivoted to face Slender.

As he watched his friend crumple, Slender roared. His jaw set with angry determination, he grasped the hilt of his blade with both hands and accelerated his charge. I glanced momentarily toward Wary. He strode purposefully in my direction, his eyes emotionless.

Slender's rage pushed him toward recklessness. He charged blindly, swinging his blade in a wide arc. I blocked the strike with a powerful sweep, and our swords collided with a resounding clang. The blade flew from his hand to land at the base of a tree a dozen feet away. He stared after it, stunned, while I pounced on the opportunity the distraction presented.

I smashed my hilt into his temple with a sickening crack. He crumpled and fell at my feet, unmoving. I didn't care if the strike left him unconscious or dead. Colin was a fool to send these men in pursuit, and doubly so if he believed their inexperience would be thwarted by their numbers.

He was a fool thrice over for discounting my heritage.

I turned away from the fallen man in time to note Wary had closed the distance between us. He swung his sword in a deadly arc toward my head. I side-stepped, but not quickly enough. His blade bit sharply into my left bicep as I spun away. Warm blood spilled down my arm, but I ignored the pain. My focus was on Wary alone. I'd deal with the wound later.

"Andrew," he said, voice muffled within his helm, "I never wanted this, but I have no choice. I'm sorry."

He struck again, but this time I was ready. I parried the blow forcefully, but unlike his companions, he knew how to maintain his grip. I glowered, furious that he'd attempt to lay the blame for his actions upon another.

"Everyone has a choice," I growled, circling him.

He shook his head. I wished I could see his eyes, but they were lost within the shadows of his helm. Did he regret this fight, or was he merely disappointed with my response?

When he shifted his blade and swung toward my torso, I recognized the maneuver. I dodged, and while he prepared to strike again, I lunged, my sword angled at his chest. I poured every ounce of strength I possessed into the motion. Even his armor wouldn't protect him from my wrath. I was dragon-kind. He was only human.

My blade pierced his breastplate and cut through flesh, then bone. The sword's fine craftsmanship couldn't withstand the force of my blow. It shattered just below the hilt as its tip struck something deep within the man's body and became lodged in place.

I stumbled backward, momentarily stunned. I'd been prepared to cleave him in two or to wrench my blade free once the damage was inflicted. I'd failed to account for the possibility the steel itself would shatter. Wary fell to his knees, his breathing labored and his fight spent.

I closed my eyes as a maelstrom of emotions rippled through my core. I hated myself for killing the men—even if they'd been acting on Colin's orders. They would have continued to pursue us if I hadn't intervened, but I'd never enjoy taking another's life. I told myself I'd acted out of necessity, that it was the only sure way to keep Alexander safe.

"An…drew…" the man gasped, breaking me from my troubled reverie. I dropped the hilt of my broken blade on the road and knelt at his side. "I'm…sorry…"

I shook my head. Pity warred with frustration as I studied his wound. Even Lydia's skills couldn't hope to save him. "You should not apologize. Rest."

Carefully, I gripped his helm and pulled it from his head to examine the face within. It was Jerrick Vine, the man I'd chosen to replace me as commander before I left for Vinterry. It seemed a lifetime ago.

I released a pained sigh and dropped my gaze. I'd considered Jerrick a friend and believed he'd never bow to Colin's brutality.

"Jerrick?"

"I had…no choice. The king…" He coughed, and a trickle of blood leaked from the corner of his mouth. "I knew…we were not a match…for you. I didn't…didn't want it…to come to this. You were…my friend…"

"Jerrick, you don't have to speak. Please…" Tears stung my eyes. I blinked them away rapidly in order to focus on his final words.

"No…You need to…hear this, while I still…have time."

My heart wrenched at his words. If I'd known who I attacked, I would have held back, reined in my inhuman strength, and settled for a nonlethal blow. Instead, I'd struck without abandon and killed a man who was once my friend. Damn Colin and his twisted orders.

Jerrick coughed again. More blood spilled from his mouth, but he continued. "The king ordered me…to pursue you. He said…you must pay for the insult…you gave him at the…arena. That you must pay…with your life." He gasped and squeezed his eyes closed. An unsettling gurgle issued from within his lungs. "I refused. He killed my wife…"

I swallowed hard, knowing well the pain this man had suffered at the hands of my wicked half-brother. "Jerrick, if I had known…"

He shook his head adamantly. "The king…is insane." He managed a chuckle that resulted in another bout of bloody coughing. "I have…wanted to say those words…for a long time."

"I'm sorry."

"We both know…this wasn't your fault." He drew another rattling breath, then said, "The king doesn't…abide disobedience. He threatened…my sister. And her…family. If I…returned with…your head, they'd be…free…"

"Jerrick…"

After my encounter in Riversmeet, I'd expected Colin to use blackmail and coercion on his subjects, but he'd gone too far. Jerrick was a good man. He didn't deserve this fate, nor did his family.

"He sent others," Jerrick managed between coughs. "Not many… Most…have been avoiding him. He has…few left that remain loyal. I didn't…want to come here…" His breaths hitched and stuttered as his lungs began to fail in earnest. "An…drew… Make him…pay…"

"I will. I'm sorry things turned out this way. It should not have ended like this."

I took one of his gauntleted hands in my own, providing what little comfort I could as his life slipped away. I would bury him before returning to the others; he deserved that remaining scrap of dignity.

The other men weren't as deserving. I'd leave them on the roadside, a warning to others who may yet be on our trail. The man I'd struck in the temple hadn't moved since he'd collapsed, and his chest didn't rise with respiration. He was likely dead. Stout lay in a muddied pool of blood, his flesh gray and eyes glassy in death. They'd be no further trouble.

I remained at Jerrick's side until his final breath faded into the howl of the wind. I regretted what had transpired between us and knew I'd always carry the anguish of his death in the depths of my soul. I'd never believed I'd be responsible for the slaying of a friend.

I buried him beneath the branches of an ancient and sprawling tree, using my bare hands to dig the shallow grave. When my hands became raw, I rested until the pain faded and the skin healed, then resumed. I would not leave his body to the elements or the wildlife.

I planted his sword into the earth at the head of the grave and placed the hilt of my shattered blade at its side. It would serve as a marker, a memorial to the man who had deserved better from life than what he'd received. I apologized and reminisced for a time, the wind the only witness to his impromptu wake. I vowed I'd uphold his final wish. Colin *would* pay.

I dried my eyes roughly as I turned away. The others would have endless questions when I returned, but I wasn't yet prepared to answer them. Just when I'd begun to believe Colin couldn't take any more from me, he'd struck yet again.

As I passed Stout, I collected his sword. His hand had begun to stiffen, and it took some force to pry the weapon loose, but I needed a replacement. I glanced once more at Slender. He would not be rising to pursue us again.

I pushed myself forward. I needed to reach Alexander and the others before night fell. A brief look at the overcast sky told me it was early afternoon. The wind continued to howl, but I largely ignored it in my grief. I mourned not only Jerrick, but Vera, her staff, and so many others who had suffered under Colin's rule.

Colin would pay dearly for the atrocities he'd committed. I'd make certain of it once Alexander's safety was assured.

FOURTEEN

The others had made camp for the evening by the time I reached them. They'd pitched our tents near a small stream where a bend in the road veered toward the water. Dusk was falling as I approached, and the wind had blessedly ceased. Chela and Emmarie were at work preparing our evening meal while Alexander paced the length of the campsite, worry etched across his brow. Lydia was tending the campfire, but abandoned her task when she spotted me. She called my name and broke into a run. Alexander's expression lightened with her outburst, and he followed rapidly in her wake.

I must have looked a mess. Lydia gasped and her eyes widened as she neared. "Andrew, are you hurt?"

I shook my head and frowned at my left arm. My shirt was torn and the sleeve was stiff with dried blood, but my wound had healed hours ago.

She compressed her lips into a thin line. "I want to have a look at you, anyway."

When I rolled my eyes, Alexander chuckled uneasily. I could sense he was eager to hear what had transpired, but I was weary and in no temper to relate my battle with Jerrick Vine.

I allowed Lydia to lead me toward the campfire, then removed my shirt when she demanded more than a cursory examination of my arm. She studied me with a troubled expression, then placed one slender hand on the location where I'd been cut. There was no trace of my injury beyond the smear of dried blood that ran from elbow to wrist. I wished she'd accept that I didn't require the same level of care as the others.

"Satisfied?" I asked gruffly.

I wanted nothing more than to take my cleaner set of garments, a chunk of soap, and dive into the nearby stream. Perhaps after bathing, I'd be less surly and more open to conversation. At present, I simply wanted to be alone.

She nodded, her eyes wide. "You're remarkable. I suppose my skills won't be needed tonight."

I shrugged and rose to my feet, then strode to the cart, leaving her at the fireside. I located the items I sought and made my way toward the stream.

"You can't go in the water!" Chela called, but I ignored her.

Unless she had good reason for me to avoid the stream, I intended to clean myself up.

Rapid footfalls approached from behind, and a hand gripped my elbow a moment later. "Andrew, you can't." It was Chela.

"Why not?" I snarled.

She blinked at my unwarranted hostility and dropped her hand. "You'll freeze. The water is cold as ice."

I turned away from her and pressed on. "I'll be fine. I can handle the cold."

She made a sound of exasperation and reached out to grasp my arm once more. "Andrew, no. Listen to me."

"Leave him be." Alexander's tone was somber. "I've seen him coatless in the dead of winter. If anyone can withstand the cold, it's my brother."

I decided to let Alexander handle the situation and continued on my way. Cold didn't affect me as it did the others. It was part of what I was, yet another unusual attribute I'd inherited from my father. I stripped, piled my clean clothing on the bank, and leapt into the water.

Chela was right; it *was* cold. But as I'd expected, it was a mere sensation against my skin. I didn't succumb to frostbite or hypothermia. I was immune.

After several minutes of vigorous scrubbing, the sweat and blood, mud, and dust had washed away with the current. My back was to the shore, and I was startled to find Lydia perched on the bank when I turned to exit the water. She held a blanket in her hands but set it carefully alongside my clothing.

"Chela thought you'd be blue with cold by now," she said. "I'll leave this for you, regardless."

When I nodded, she turned to depart for the campsite. I remained in the water for a few moments longer, reluctant to return to the others. Finally, I sighed and climbed onto the bank. I used the blanket to dry myself, then dressed and gathered it and my soiled clothing into a bundle. I'd leave it with the rest of my belongings in the back of the cart.

Chela handed me a portion of stew when I joined the others around the campfire. She was perplexed that I'd been unaffected by my time in the stream; for all their knowledge of the dragon-kind, it seemed the magi weren't aware of certain aspects of my physiology. I forced a weary smile and accepted the food before sitting down heavily beside Alexander.

"You look troubled, brother." He spoke in a low tone meant for my ears alone.

I nodded and gulped a mouthful of stew. I savored the flavor of potatoes and rehydrated jerky while I considered my response. I'd planned to wait until morning to tell him what had transpired, but procrastination wouldn't make the discussion any easier. I decided to tell him of Jerrick, our fight, and Colin's recent treachery.

"Jerrick was a good man. You didn't know he lurked beneath that helm, brother. Don't blame yourself." Alexander scratched the nape of his neck and grimaced. "If his words were true, then Colin has set his sights solely on you."

I turned from the campfire to focus on Alexander. His face was grim, his jaw set, and a strange light had entered his eyes. In the growing darkness, they seemed to glow of their own accord. I stiffened as the scent of blood hit my nostrils, nearly overpowering in its proximity. I'd learned enough of magic to understand the scent wasn't from an injury, but from a mage. *From Alexander.*

"Alex?" I asked, unable to hide my concern.

He blinked, and the light in his eyes faded, the metallic stench abruptly gone. "I'm fine," he replied briskly. "I'm furious with Colin, but I'm fine."

I nodded uneasily. Perhaps it had only been a trick of the light, a remnant of memory from the morning's scuffle that brought with it the scent of blood. Without being certain of what I'd witnessed, I didn't want to mention it to Alexander. I'd speak with one of the other magi in the morning.

He studied me for a time, his eyes narrowed in thought. "I ought to ask you the same, brother. Are *you* well?"

I shrugged. "Physically, yes. It's been a trying day, and I'm weary beyond measure." I paused to run one hand through my hair. "Colin is a tyrannical bastard, isn't he?"

Alexander chuckled humorlessly. "That he is. You'll tell me if something's wrong, won't you?"

I hesitated before I gave him a brief nod. "Yes. As I said, I'm tired. And I miss Vera."

Jerrick's story was a poignant reminder of Colin's atrocities, and Alexander's burgeoning attachment to Lydia had catapulted me into the throes of grief more often than I cared to admit.

He clapped a hand on my shoulder. "I know, brother. You haven't been the same since Vinterry." He sighed and looked away. "If only I'd kept my damned mouth shut, we wouldn't be in this situation."

"I don't fault you, Alex. If you had stayed in the Capitol, Colin would have discovered your Mark eventually. It was only a matter of time." I shrugged. "Besides, you would never have met Lydia. You make a fine pair."

He reddened but flashed a grin. "When this journey is finished, I intend to marry her." He stiffened, startled by his own admission. "Please don't tell anyone else...We haven't discussed it yet."

I chuckled. "Your secret is safe with me. It wouldn't be the first I've kept for you." I rose and stretched my arms. "I'm going to turn in. I'll take second watch."

As we departed our campsite the next morning, I drew Lydia aside. Alexander walked ahead with Emmarie, and I waited until I was certain he was out of earshot before I posed my question. We were near enough to the cart that Chela could overhear us, and perhaps she'd provide additional insight. It would be simpler this way, and I wouldn't be forced to voice my concern twice.

"I wanted to ask you—both of you," I said to Chela, "about something that happened last night." I told them of Alexander's reaction during our conversation, the brief glow in his eyes, and the stench of blood.

Both women were silent for some time as they contemplated their answers. Lydia spoke first.

"It was undoubtedly the result of Alexander accessing his power," she said slowly. "He didn't act upon it, which is fortunate, but he may not have been aware of what he'd done. You were right to come to us." She glanced at Chela. "I'll speak with Alex."

She strode purposefully ahead, leaving me alone with Chela. I sighed, unable to conceal my disappointment. I'd hoped to receive a more meaningful reply.

"It happens sometimes," Chela said after a moment. "Most often, it's harmless. What were the two of you speaking of?"

"My encounter yesterday and Colin's involvement." I shook my head sadly. "There has been so much death…"

"Alex was emotional. It's often a trigger. Lydia was right, you know. He may not have realized he'd sought his magic. We'll learn more once she speaks with him."

"When will he be safe?" I asked. "I know he wants to prove himself—and not only to face Colin."

She laughed softly. "Yes, he aims to impress her." Her smile faded as she said, "He will not be safe until he completes his pilgrimage, and he has a long way to go." She titled her head thoughtfully as she studied me. "What happened yesterday? I understand it was more of your half-brother's lackeys, but your reaction is one of grief rather than rage."

I stared at the ground beneath my boots and ran a hand through my hair. I'd hoped to avoid recounting my fight a second time, but it was proving inevitable. I told her everything.

"It's little wonder Alexander reacted as he did," she replied heatedly. "I don't know Colin, but what he's done is abominable. That he is seeking your head for saving Alexander's life is madness!"

I shrugged. "Colin doesn't take well to insult. Real, perceived, or otherwise."

"I can't fault Alexander for his anger, though I hope he'll be more careful from now on." She shifted in the cart's seat and tugged at the brim of her hat. "Do you think there will be more assassins?"

"Yes."

Knowing Colin as I did, he'd continue to send people until one of them returned with news of our whereabouts or evidence of my death. We'd need to remain vigilant no matter how far we strayed from Novania's border.

She fell silent for a time, and when she spoke, her tone was solemn. "Beyond the Frostwake, the path diverges. There are two routes we may take. Most guides choose the route that bends east, then south. It goes through a narrow canyon for miles, but it's the easier path. However, it provides no means of escape and little shelter should we need it. If we are being followed, I don't wish to travel that way."

When I nodded, she continued. "The other route bends west, toward the coast, but doesn't reach the ocean. It leads through a vast marshland that is rife with its own dangers, but I can navigate us safely through. Our pursuers will likely falter if they follow us there. While my ability is not as powerful as Alexander's nor as useful as Lydia's, it is rare. There is only one other who can navigate as I do. He lives far from the roads we've traveled and is far too old to survive a journey away from his home."

I considered her words. "Perhaps it was for this reason the Oracle assigned you as my brother's guide." I crossed my arms as another question entered my mind. "You said the other mage is an old man. I didn't realize magi aged."

She laughed and shook her head with amusement. "That isn't true, Andrew. We age, but it isn't as apparent as it is in non-magical folk. We aren't like the dragon-kind." She offered me a wry smile. "Do you remember the elder we met at the Ashen Shrine?"

I nodded, recalling the woman's snow-white hair.

"She's nearing her end, as is the Oracle. They may not appear aged, but their hair has lost its natural color. It is one of the final signs." She paused to adjust her grip on the horse's reins. "The old man I spoke of is my grandfather. He could have chosen the path of an elder at one of the shrines if he'd wished it, but he's past that point in his life. I doubt he'll be alive when I next return home. He celebrated his ninety-eighth name day in March. As for myself, I'm nearing my sixtieth."

I lifted my eyebrows. I'd assumed Chela was older than I was but was surprised to learn it was by more than two decades.

"The Mark is both a blessing and a curse," she said after a moment's pause. "There have been many times throughout the years when I wished I was more like my siblings and cousins. Life would have been simpler."

The next four and a half days passed uneventfully as we traveled through the forest. The weather was becoming noticeably cooler, the winds sharper, and the skies frequently more threatening.

While I required nothing more than what I had stowed in the cart, Alexander would need warmer clothing soon. I didn't know how well the two magi were prepared for the seasonal change, but Emmarie had run away from the Citadel with very little; she'd require a cloak and thicker garments, as well. I hoped we'd find accommodating merchants in Crystal Crags.

I'd been melancholy for much of the journey. The death of Jerrick Vine weighed heavily on my mind, bringing with it painful memories from Novania. Though speaking with Alexander and Chela helped ease some of my guilt, I was reluctant to forgive myself. I hoped our arrival in Crystal Crags would provide a much-needed distraction from my grief, a respite from my self-loathing.

The forest gradually gave way to rocky slopes, then the steep ridge of mountains known as the Southern Pinnacles came into view, towering over the landscape below. The highest peaks gleamed white with snow where they weren't swathed in a whirl of menacing clouds.

Nestled at the base of the mountains was a sprawling town on the shores of an enormous lake. At the far end of the lake was the tallest waterfall I'd ever seen, streaming down a sheer cliff face to land with a deafening roar in the lake hundreds of feet below. Several wooden piers jutted from the lakeshore into the sapphire-blue water beyond. A handful of small fishing vessels plied the water, though its surface was otherwise still. The city was a tidy array of sturdy buildings, most constructed of pale gray stone with colorful tiled roofs. The streets bustled with activity as citizens and visitors alike conducted business and completed errands.

"Since we've arrived with a few hours left of daylight, I'd like to find Bryson Feige's sister and send a message to Tom," Alexander stated. “I’d also like to find a barber if there happens to be one.” He pushed chin-length strands of hair from his eyes with a scowl.

Lydia laughed softly, then reached up to tug Alexander’s hair gently. “Your hair hasn’t grown that long yet. Besides, I could see you wearing it longer and pulling it back. It would suit you.”

Alexander rolled his eyes. “No, thank you,” he said, though he beamed at her. “I prefer it shorter, and I don’t seem to be as adept at keeping it that way as my brother is.”

Lydia’s gaze swept toward me, and she shook her head, amused. “I don’t believe Andrew trims his hair. He shouldn’t need to.”

Alexander wrinkled his nose. “Of course, I should have realized. I know he doesn’t shave. I can recall a time when we were younger, and he was desperately trying to grow a beard. All the other men his age were doing so, but poor Andrew couldn’t. Even at sixteen, I sported more facial hair than my brother. His frustration was an endless source of amusement for a time.”

I frowned in mock annoyance. “I’m sure we can locate a barber,” I replied evenly.

“Let’s go to the inn first,” Chela interjected from behind. “We can leave our belongings there, then head into the city for our various errands.”

Emmarie scampered alongside me, her dark eyes imploring. “May I go with you when you send the message to your brother? I’d like to write a letter to my uncle to let him know that I’m well.” She bit her lip and looked down, her expression pained. “I’m certain he knows I ran away from the Citadel.”

“Of course.” I offered her a smile which she didn’t return. “We’ll send a message to Tom, and afterwards, I’ll stay with you while you write your uncle. I don’t need to follow Alex to the barber’s, as I’m sure you overheard.”

She giggled and stole a glance toward Alexander and Lydia, who walked a few paces ahead. “I did.” She leaned closer to me and dropped her voice to a conspiratorial whisper. “I think Alex and Lydia are in love.” She stifled another giggle with her hands.

I grinned, amused. Emmarie was perceptive, but I was glad to see she was finally opening up to us. While she still had not divulged her story, I hoped I’d learn the truth of her past one day soon.

We acquired lodgings at an inn near the lakeshore, then stowed our essentials inside. Chela opted to remain behind and stable the horse, while Lydia led us into the city. She navigated through a bustling marketplace toward a quieter sector filled with personal homes. As we walked, Lydia claimed she'd spent several years in Crystal Crags as a child and knew the layout of the city well. She led us unerringly to the small, well-kept home that was our destination, then knocked smartly on the painted wooden door.

A bearded man with a burly physique answered, but when he saw the group gathered on his doorstep, he called inside for Bella. He turned to face us with a weary smile. "I assume you wish to speak with my wife. She has the talent for sending messages, and you have that look about you. She'll be out in a moment. I'm afraid I must be off. I'm due back at the foreman's post soon."

He pushed past us and made his way toward the road beyond as a petite woman with sandy hair appeared in the doorway. The familial resemblance she held with her brother from the Citadel was apparent. She was somewhat disheveled, but offered us a smile and called a farewell to her husband as he departed. A moment later, a small child ran from behind her and grabbed her skirt, tugging insistently. She ignored him and focused on our group.

"I'm Bella Halston," she said by way of introduction, "and that was Jacob, my husband." She gestured to the child. "And this little devil is Devon." She eyed Lydia carefully. "You look familiar, though I'm afraid I don't recall your name."

Lydia introduced herself, then the rest of us, while Bella apologized for her lapse in memory. It seemed the two women had lived only a few houses apart before Lydia had left the city to embark on her pilgrimage as a mage.

"Well, I certainly can send a few messages for you if you don't mind my boy hanging about," she said. "He's only two years old, and I haven't been able to get him down for a nap today. I hope he won't be a bother." She ruffled Devon's blond hair playfully.

She led the others inside, but I remained in the yard. I'd allow Alexander to compose our message to Thomas. If Bella's magic was akin to her brother's, it would irritate my nostrils and send me into a sneezing fit I'd rather do without. It was best if I kept my distance while she worked, and Alexander would fill me in on any news he received from Thomas.

I studied the mountainous peaks that loomed above the city while I waited. Even from a distance, I could see our route could prove perilous. Their craggy sides were steep and rocky, sporting sheer drops in places. The snow I'd spied previously glistened in the afternoon sun; it was beautiful from afar, but treacherous for travel. While Alexander was in the Waterfall Shrine, I'd ensure he was equipped for the journey, no matter how much I detested bartering in the market. His thin shirt and light cloak would never protect him from the elements.

The sound of the door opening and closing drew me from my musings. I turned to find Lydia on the step, her expression one of mild concern.

"Andrew, are you well? Why didn't you come inside?"

I chuckled. I'd failed to mention my reaction to magic, and apparently, so had Alexander. She scowled in frustration before I explained why I'd chosen to remain outside.

"I've heard the dragon-kind are more sensitive to magic than others, but I didn't realize our abilities carried scents!" She laughed with delight. "That's truly something, isn't it?"

"I suppose so."

Her expression became serious once more. "When you witnessed the change in Alexander's eyes that night, you mentioned you smelled blood. I didn't think anything of it, given your fight earlier that day. Was it his?"

"I think so, but I was exhausted at the time. That was a…difficult day." My mood darkened with the reminder of Jerrick's death.

"I trust your judgment. As Alex is constantly reminding me, your natural senses are far keener than ours."

I studied her carefully for a time. Her ageless countenance was drawn with worry, and a shadow lay heavily beneath her eyes. She had not been sleeping well of late.

"What did Alexander tell you when you spoke to him about that night?" I asked.

She rolled her eyes, exasperated. "He was evasive. He assured me he was in complete control, that I had nothing to fear, but he would speak no more of the matter. I fear for his safety, and he acts so cavalier!" She made a sound of disgust. "Sometimes men are more stubborn than cantankerous mules!"

I snorted. "Alex certainly has his moments."

She leveled her gaze at me. "He is not the only one. How long did it take for us to draw out the full story of what happened in the woods? And no one has forgotten your stunt with the Venom-weavers, least of all the mage who healed you. You, I fear, are far more stubborn than your brother. I hope that doesn't prove to be a fatal weakness, Andrew."

"I know my capabilities. I'll be fine."

She shook her head. "Do you hear yourself? This is exactly what I've been speaking of."

At that moment, the door opened and Alexander strode into the sunlight, a sheet of parchment in his hands. He looked between us and frowned. "I feel as though I've interrupted something."

"Oh, we were discussing the stubborn streak that seems to run in your family," Lydia replied tartly with a wave of her hand.

Ignoring her final jibe, I turned my full attention to Alexander. "What does Tom have to say?"

"It seems he's well enough." Alexander grinned and handed me the parchment. "I told him of our latest encounter and of Jerrick Vine. You can read his letter while I find the barber, and we can discuss it later. Emmarie is sending a note to her uncle now. I have to admit, I'm surprised by that."

I nodded in agreement. "I'll wait for her. Go on. I know you've grown tired of looking the part of a ruffian."

He made a face before turning away, while I chuckled in response. I watched as he and Lydia strode down the slope to the cobblestone street and disappeared into the throng of busy people. Alexander seemed more certain of himself when he was with her, as though her mere presence gave him strength. She was kind and seemed to genuinely care about those she met. I hoped Alexander would marry her at the end of his pilgrimage; it was plain to my eye that each needed the other, though perhaps they were unaware of it themselves. I prayed he'd find happiness with her, and that it would be lasting.

The familiar ache in my heart stirred as my memories of Vera resurfaced. Our time together had been fleeting, but I'd cherish it to the end of my days.

With a sigh, I sat down on the step leading into Bella's home and began to study the latest message we'd received from Thomas. His precise handwriting appeared unhurried on the page, a sign he was secure in his location.

Alex,

I'm pleased to receive your message, though its contents trouble me. Give Andrew my condolences regarding Jerrick Vine. I know they were comrades. I've heard rumors Colin was forcing some of his subjects into loyalty by means of bribery or blackmail, but I didn't know he'd resorted to murder as well. I fear I have been away from the Capitol for too long and don't fully know the workings of his plans any longer.

I traveled to Calder's Point with Duke Crossley, and from there, we went farther north. We've made a camp in the caves beyond the borders of Novania and have initiated trade with the Corodan. The new Hive-queen was wary at first — we are trespassers in her lands—but she was open-minded enough to allow us to explain our presence here. She knew I was related to Andrew in some way, and she asked of his whereabouts. I don't know why she holds an interest in him, though her tone has always been deferential when we speak of our brother.

The duke hopes to form an alliance with the Corodan. Without Andrew's presence, she remains reluctant to join forces but is willing to trade. Our camp grows daily. Word has leaked that we are hiding from Colin here. There is talk amongst some folk that I should take up arms against Colin and attempt to oust him from the throne. I am not a warrior as you are, and I was never groomed to lead as Colin was. I don't believe I'm fit for this duty, though the duke claims otherwise.

I don't want to rule. Perhaps when the two of you are finished in the Southlands, we can form a better plan. I look forward to your next message.

– Tom

I sensed Thomas would have continued writing if there had been more space provided on the parchment. The notion of an alliance with the Corodan intrigued me, and the new Hive-queen had seemed reasonable when I'd spoken with her emissary at the end of our war. I didn't have the means to assist Thomas at present, but I would not forget he required my help. I would offer what aid I could once I was in a position to do so. Once Alexander's pilgrimage was at an end.

I was folding Thomas' letter when Emmarie burst outside, sobbing. I rose immediately and went to her, but she turned away. A moment later, Bella exited, her eyes wide and her expression bewildered. Her toddler son writhed in her arms.

"Emmarie, was it something I did? I don't understand—" Bella began, then stopped suddenly as she noted my presence.

Emmarie shook her head and wiped at her eyes. "No, you did nothing wrong, and I should thank you for your help."

Bella nodded uncertainly. "As long as you're sure..."

"I am. Thank you, Bella." She sniffled, wiped her eyes again, and turned to me. "I want to go back to the inn."

"Then that's what we'll do." I turned to thank Bella myself before we departed, then asked if I might stop by once more before we left Crystal Crags. I wanted to reply to Thomas once I had time to think over his message.

"Do you want to talk about what happened?" I asked once we were in the street.

She blinked, startled, then nodded. "My uncle is angry," she said, her voice tremulous. "The Oracle told him I left the Citadel without permission. Even though *she* believes it was the best course of action, *he* doesn't agree." She sighed heavily and hung her head. Her dark hair spilled down to obscure her face as another sob escaped her lips. "I've been named an exile."

While I knew little of the Merael people and what exile might mean, I understood the situation was grave based on her reaction alone. "You are always welcome to stay with us."

She attempted a laugh, but the sound was cut short as another wave of grief overcame her. "You and Alex are too kind. I've broken too many rules, and my uncle will never forgive me. As an elder of the Merael, he said I've brought him great shame."

I pulled her to one side of the street as she broke into sobs once more. Kneeling so I was at eye level with her, I said, "Emma, I know what it's like to be driven from your home. I promise you will always be welcome anywhere I am. I will look after you."

She raised her head long enough to meet my gaze and nod, then threw herself into my arms and sobbed into my shoulder. I don't know how long we remained that way, but she needed someone to comfort her. I would fulfill that role, time and again if needed. As we'd discussed at the forest shrine, she'd become akin to the younger sister I'd never had.

Finally, she pushed away and rubbed her eyes. "I'm sorry," she whispered.

"You don't need to apologize," I replied gently. "Let's get back to the inn. We'll have lunch, and you can tell me the full story if you feel up to it."

FIFTEEN

When we returned to the inn, I led Emmarie to a table in the back corner of the common room. It was secluded, a place where we would not be overheard, and a location that allowed me to observe the other patrons. Emmarie had composed herself during the remainder of our walk, though it was clear she grieved. She didn't speak until after a server had come by to take our order and disappeared into the kitchen.

"I was only a few years old when I came to live with my uncle, Tylmar." Her tone was hollow as she stared at the scarred tabletop between us. "I don't know the truth of what happened to my parents, only what my uncle has told me. I don't know if I should fully believe his account of events."

She sighed and pushed a wayward strand of dark hair behind her ear. "My mother married against the family's wishes. My father was from the forest in the south, the one we call The Green. The Merael from the Green and the Merael from the Thornhallow don't often travel to visit one another, but my father was a merchant. Travel was essential. I don't know what goods he traded. My uncle didn't believe I needed to know. He's never had anything nice to say about my father."

"Believe it or not, I understand," I replied. "My mother had very few kind words to say about my own father."

She gaped, incredulous. "But your father is Zayneldarion Caien! He was one of the greatest dragon-magi the world has ever known. How could she feel that way?"

I chuckled. "He left her—out of necessity, I know, but she never forgave him for it." I shrugged. "My point is, what we hear from our elders is often biased by their perceptions. I've learned it's worth pursuing the truth on my own. When I finally met my father, he wasn't what I'd expected."

She nodded thoughtfully. "Perhaps one day I will seek out my father and learn his side of the story. This is what I know. My parents married, and my mother decided to travel with him. Her family—my uncle in particular—was against it. There was an argument. My mother told my uncle she would never return to Dark Heart, and she left with my father the same day." She sighed. "It was two years later that she sent a letter to my uncle, informing him of my birth. They'd stopped for a time near Oristan. I was born there, near the sea."

Now I understood her fascination with the seabirds. She'd been too young to recall Oristan, but it was a part of her story. I was glad she'd finally chosen to share her past. And, I admitted, it was a relief to focus on something other than my own woes.

"They continued to travel after I was born," she continued after a moment's reflection. "My father did well for himself. He was known to people in most of the cities they stopped to trade in. The letters my mother wrote that my uncle shared with me sounded happy. I'd like to think she enjoyed traveling. She loved my father."

The server returned then, bearing a pair of large bowls filled with fish chowder and a plate of hot, flaky biscuits. Emmarie fell silent and began to eat.

"Did you choose to follow us because of your mother?" I asked as she finished her second biscuit. "You've mentioned you wanted to see more of the world."

She contemplated my question for a moment, then nodded. "I believe so. I've always wanted to see what lay beyond the forest. Perhaps I was thinking of my mother, but I don't know for certain." She managed a small smile. "My uncle forbade me to travel beyond Dark Heart, and I felt trapped. He refused to let me leave unless I went to the Citadel to work for the Oracle or one of her people. I didn't like the prospect of trading one cage for another. When the opportunity arose to flee, I took it. I would have done so sooner, but I've always feared the consequences. I knew he'd be angry, but I never imagined he'd exile me."

She looked down as she struggled to keep her composure. Her lower lip trembled, her face was drawn, and her eyes shone with unshed tears. I understood her exile meant she could not return home, but I had believed she didn't want to return to begin with. I didn't fully understand the situation and all it implied, but I would continue to help her and provide for her as I could. She was so young, so fragile, though she'd never admit it. She needed a mentor and guardian—and that was one role I believed I could fulfill.

"Emma—"

She sniffed and wiped at her face angrily. "No, I'm fine. I should have expected this outcome. Uncle Tylmar doesn't take kindly to disobedience." She crossed her arms and leaned back in her chair, but wouldn't meet my eye. "He often said if I didn't do as told, I'd suffer the same fate as my mother. He was not kind to me. I was relieved when he finally made good on his promise to send me away, even though I didn't want to go to the Citadel. I was fortunate he sent me with you and Alexander. I've finally begun to understand the meaning of friendship." She offered me a wary smile before taking another biscuit from the platter.

"What happened to your mother?" I asked.

"My father's business did well enough, but he wasn't wealthy. He prided himself on his reputation—and with that preceding him, sometimes there was trouble with bandits along the road. My uncle told me their camp was ambushed by a group of men looking to steal his wares. My father and one of his assistants survived the attack, but my mother did not. She died protecting me… I think my uncle blames me. I wasn't even old enough to remember what happened."

"Whatever he may have alluded to, you cannot blame yourself," I replied evenly. "If your uncle blames you, he's wrong. You were only a child. An *infant*."

"I know, and yet…part of me thinks he may be right." She sighed and looked down at her delicate green hands where they were folded in her lap. "Sometimes I think he's just bitter. My father couldn't travel with me once my mother was gone, and he asked my uncle to take me in. I don't believe my uncle wanted the responsibility, and I *know* he viewed me as an inconvenience. He took me in because he was obligated, not because he had any desire to."

"Did your father ever visit you?" I asked her.

She nodded slowly. "He used to when I was small. Once a year, in the summer, he'd make the journey to the Thornhallow, and I would spend time with him for a few weeks. But when I was eight or nine years old, he had an argument with my uncle. I don't know the details, but he left the next day. He apologized and said he didn't know when he'd see me again. I wanted to go with him, but my uncle wouldn't allow it." She clenched her jaw and narrowed her eyes, enraged by the memory. "If it hadn't been for my uncle, perhaps I'd be with my father right now."

"You said the Green is south of here. Will Alexander's journey take us there?" I asked.

"No." She paused to take another biscuit. "Perhaps one day, I can visit my father and learn what truly happened." She laughed bitterly. "I suppose the Green is the only place I can go back to if I want to be amongst my own people again. As an exile of the Thornhallow, I can't return there without risking injury…or worse. The Tree-speakers will have seen to that already."

"What do you mean?" I asked.

She looked up sharply. "Sometimes I forget you aren't from here and don't understand the way of things." She tossed her head with a sigh. "My uncle is a Tree-speaker. It's an ability similar to my own, but he can communicate with the trees and plants of the forest. The forest listens to a Tree-speaker's words and will obey their commands. When someone is exiled, the Tree-speakers inform the forest, and the forest will deny the exile safe passage. If I try to return home, the forest will be hostile. I've seen others lashed by branches and strangled by roots. It's an unpleasant fate."

I struggled to imagine what it would be like to be viciously attacked by *trees*. My perception of the Merael people had been of a peaceful folk attuned to the natural state of the world, though Emmarie's story told me they wouldn't hesitate to defend themselves against perceived threats. Her exile was an overly harsh punishment for the simple act of disobedience, and I told her as much.

"My uncle and I have never truly understood one another," she replied bitterly. "This is his way of ensuring he doesn't have to see me again unless it's on his terms."

I nodded, though I sensed there was something more she'd chosen to omit. With Emmarie, I'd have to be patient, no matter how difficult that might prove. She'd tell me the rest of her story only when she was ready and not a moment sooner.

Emmarie frowned, her gaze drawn to something across the room. I turned to find Alexander and Lydia had returned and were making their way toward us. It seemed my half-brother had found the barber he'd sought; his hair was once again cut almost as short as my own. He flashed a grin as he caught my eye.

"It looks like we'll have to finish our conversation another day," I told Emmarie, who merely nodded. I sensed she was not as comfortable talking with Alexander as she was with me.

"You look presentable again," I teased as Alexander took the open chair beside me.

He laughed. "Much to the lady's disappointment, I must admit." He gestured toward Lydia, who arched an eyebrow and shook her head. "Ah, but I feel like myself again."

"You look too much like Andrew with your hair so short," Lydia replied, then with a startled glance in my direction, added, "I meant no offense, of course."

I chuckled. "Of course."

We remained in the common room for some time, speaking of what was to come next. Alexander planned to enter the waterfall shrine in the morning. Lydia and I both wanted to see him off and wish him well, and he readily agreed. After Alexander began his trial, we'd visit the marketplace to acquire warmer garments for those who required them.

Chela joined us after a time and seemed content with our plans. "I anticipate we'll be leaving the Crags within three days' time," she said. "The trials of the waterfall usually pass swiftly."

Noting a trace of anxiety on Alexander's features, Lydia reached across the table and took his hand in her own. "You're doing well so far. You'll pass this trial, just as you've passed the others. You'll see."

Alexander nodded, though uncertainty was clear in his green eyes. I was grateful to Lydia for her words; her encouragement meant far more to my brother than anything I could have hoped to say. They understood one another in a way I didn't comprehend, drawn as they were by their magical abilities.

"She's right," Chela agreed. "You'll pass this trial, and the next after it. The elder at the Ashen Shrine saw that much of your path clearly, and she is seldom wrong."

Alexander frowned and looked away. "And after that? The path was no longer certain…"

"Alex, the path is rarely as clear as yours has been thus far," Lydia replied gently. "I believe you'll succeed—not simply in tomorrow's trials, but in the pilgrimage as a whole. Even though you must enter the trials alone, know that we are *all* with you on this journey. You are never truly alone."

He drew a slow breath and nodded. "You're right, as usual. Sometimes I'm a damned fool."

Lydia's gaze flicked toward me briefly before she returned her attention to Alexander. "You strive too hard to be like your brother. It's not a bad trait to aspire to be like him. Andrew is a good man. But you are not your brother—you're a mage, and therefore your path is different. You must remember this."

Alexander looked at me with a sheepish grin. I didn't know what to say; I'd always been there to protect him, but I'd never realized he'd been emulating me.

"Alex—" I began, but he shook his head.

"You don't have to say anything. What she says is true, though I never realized it until recently." He managed a laugh. "I wish my life had been simpler, that I'd never been born cursed with the Mark. I'd still be back home, and we'd have put a stop to Colin's tyranny by now."

"You are not cursed," I said evenly. "I'll admit, your ability is strange to me, but we will deal with Colin one day. You have my word."

"If you continue to impress the elders as you've done so far, you'll be unmatched in battle—except perhaps by the dragon-kind," Chela added. "That mad brother of yours won't stand a chance, even with an army at his back. As much as I fear the coming war, your presence gives me hope."

"It brings hope to us all." Lydia smiled and squeezed Alexander's hand. "We're all here for *you*, Alex. That will never change."

After I'd turned in for the evening, there was an unexpected knock on the door. My room was small but clean, with just enough space for a single bed, a three-legged wooden stool, and a brazier. I'd left the brazier unlit and cold as I didn't require its warmth. The room was illuminated by a single candle that I'd left on the stool.

I pulled the shirt I'd just removed over my head once more and went to the door. I had not been expecting visitors.

I was surprised to find Alexander alone in the hall.

He offered me a weary smile. "May I come in, brother?"

I moved aside to allow him passage into the room, but frowned when I noted his uncharacteristically troubled expression. He sat on the end of the bed while I remained standing. His eyes stared at the planks of the floor, unseeing as his mind grappled with unspoken concerns.

"Alex?" I asked after several long moments.

"I hope nothing is wrong, but I needed to speak with you." He scratched his neck and sighed. "I've been thinking over our conversation. When we first returned to the inn." His frown deepened.

"We spoke of many things, brother."

The topics had ranged from his upcoming trial to Colin to preparing for the next leg of the journey. We'd spoken of Thomas and memories from our childhood, as well. Nothing stood out to me that should have brought him to my door with a heavy conscience.

"When Lydia mentioned I've modeled my life after yours, I thought she'd gone too far." He leaned forward to rest his elbows on his knees while he rubbed his temples. "We've discussed it, but I'd hoped to keep those conversations private. I'm doing my best to be *me*, but you're my brother." He groaned. "I'm not making any sense, am I?"

I laughed, relieved he was worried about something so trivial. He looked up, startled, then managed a smile. The tension had been broken.

"Alex," I said, still laughing, "I never realized you looked up to me as you do. If you're concerned I was offended by her words, you don't need to worry." I studied him carefully for a moment in the flickering candlelight. "You speak to her about many things, don't you?"

He nodded. "I meant what I said in Oristan. I want to marry her… But not until this journey is over, in case things don't go as planned. I don't want to leave her a widow. She deserves better than that." He looked up at me then. "What was it like for you with Vera? Did you speak with her often?"

"Yes."

We'd spent many long evenings together in her library during the winter, had taken countless walks through the vineyards and the woods surrounding Vinterry. We'd always been open with one another, and there had been no secrets between us.

"Vera and I talked often. Every day," I added.

"I feel as though I can tell her anything, but I don't know if she's capable of keeping my secrets half as well as Vera kept yours." He scratched at the nape of his neck again. "That's what troubles me most. I wasn't prepared for her to speak as she did today."

"Have you talked with her?" I asked.

He nodded and released a weary sigh. "Yes. She was unapologetic and claimed she did nothing wrong. But I feel slighted."

"I don't think she meant any harm," I replied. "She genuinely cares for you. Perhaps it's best to let this go."

"I suppose compromise is something I ought to get used to if I want to make a life with her." Alexander groaned and looked away.

I chuckled. "You'll have to get used to it no matter who you choose to make a life with. Some are more willing to compromise than others." My thoughts flashed to Claire; she'd been proud and stubborn, often unwilling to yield.

"You would know better than I." With a sigh, he rose to his feet. "I should turn in. Tomorrow will be a tiring day. Good night, brother."

"Good night."

I watched him leave, thinking over all we'd been through during the past two years. So much had happened, and yet, there was still so much left undone. So many things demanded our attention.

He was resilient, but more fragile than he'd admit—and he could not afford distractions if he hoped to succeed in becoming a mage. I needed to pay closer attention to Alexander and push my own grief to the wayside. I had wallowed in it far too long.

The morning dawned gray and cold, bringing with it a chill wind that hinted of winter, and lowering clouds that threatened snow. I walked with Alexander and Lydia to the waterfall on the far side of the lake. We stood near enough that I could feel its icy spray on my skin as we said our goodbyes to Alexander. A small crack in the stone cliff face was visible along one side of the roaring water, which Lydia indicated was the entrance to the trial chamber.

Alexander shuddered and drew his cloak firmly around his shoulders as he strode away. He walked with purpose, though uncertainty dogged his steps. I placed my faith in Chela's predictions and planned to count the hours until he returned to the inn. I was certain he would.

As we turned away from the waterfall and Alexander, Lydia began to weep silently. She'd maintained her composure for my brother's sake, but now that he was gone, her emotions spilled forth unchecked.

"Alex will be fine," I assured her. "He'll get through this."

She sniffled and released a sigh. "I know. I didn't know how difficult it would be to say goodbye. I've never allowed myself to care so deeply for anyone…"

"If he hasn't managed to tell you yet, my brother feels the same." I smiled, recalling our conversation from the previous evening.

We fell silent as we retraced our steps to the inn. We met Chela and Emmarie outside. They'd been awaiting us, and we departed for the marketplace where I took it upon myself to find warm garments for Alexander. When I declined to purchase anything for myself, I received disapproving scowls from all three women. After a while, I caved and allowed Lydia to select a woolen cloak large enough to accommodate my frame.

The air grew steadily colder as the day wore on, and I believed we'd be facing snow before long. One glance at the nearby mountains confirmed my suspicions; the highest peaks were wreathed in gray clouds, their rocky faces obscured by wind and weather.

"The weather bodes ill for our journey," Chela said as we returned to the inn. Her tone was low, for my ears alone. "The passes are rarely closed between here and the Frostwake, but snow will prove an unwelcome burden as we make the trek. The magi of the Frostwake are diligent in keeping the passes clear, but it takes time to do so, even with magic to aid them."

"We have all the supplies we need," I replied. "Alexander and I are no strangers to winter travel. It's the three of you I'm most concerned for."

Chela arched one eyebrow. "Save your concern for those who require it, Andrew. I've made this journey several times and in far worse conditions. Your Merael friend, I fear, will struggle with this part of the journey far more than the rest of us."

"I'll look after her."

"I know you will," she replied evenly, "but don't allow her presence to become a distraction from your role as Alexander's guardian. Seeing him safely to the Frostwake is your first priority."

I glowered. I didn't need yet another reminder that my brother was to come first above all else. I'd given my word I would see him through to the end of his journey, and I'd make good on it. I knew Chela meant well, and though her remark irked me, I didn't argue my point. Words wouldn't appease her—she required proof through action.

I helped Chela stow our newly purchased supplies in the cart while the others scurried inside. I paused to study the lake once I'd finished and noted that despite the wind and the pending storm, a number of gray eagles had appeared to circle purposefully above the rough water. Their presence was drawing a crowd of onlookers near the lakeshore.

"They've returned," I remarked.

Chela moved to my side and smiled. "As I told you before, they're attracted to power."

I frowned, unsatisfied with the answer. "Shouldn't there be something more to this? Why fly so far simply to circle about, then disappear again once it's over? It doesn't make sense."

She studied me carefully for a time before making her reply. "I suppose *you* would understand the strength and stamina required to fly long distances. The eagles have a purpose, but my knowledge on this matter is limited. It has been many years since we've witnessed them flock to the shrines in such numbers. I know only what I've been told by others. I have no first-hand experience beyond what we've seen on this journey so far."

"And what *have* others told you?" I pressed, unwilling to let the matter lie.

"It doesn't matter," she replied evasively. "I don't wish to speculate."

I scowled and crossed my arms; I'd get nothing more from her.

I watched as the eagles swooped and soared above the storm-darkened waters, occasionally diving to snag fish from the waves. Whatever the meaning behind their presence, one thing was certain: My half-brother possessed a power unrivaled by any other living mage, and the birds could sense it.

SIXTEEN

Snow was beginning to fall the next morning when Alexander returned from the Waterfall Shrine. I met him inside the common room, and moments later, Lydia and Chela appeared at our side.

"You've finished rather quickly," Lydia said with a smile.

He shrugged. "Everything went well, but I'm tired."

He retired to his room and didn't venture out again until midafternoon. By that time, a soft blanket of snow had covered the streets of Crystal Crags and continued to drop from the leaden skies in a deluge of wide, feathery flakes.

"We must remain here until the storm passes," Chela said as Alexander joined us.

We were seated at an oval table near the hearth in the common room. Only a handful of locals had braved the weather, leaving the room largely empty. It was cozy near the fireplace, yet quiet. Chela rose to pace as she gazed out the nearest window and frowned at the falling snow.

"The weather will only grow worse the longer we delay," Lydia countered. "We should leave tomorrow as we originally planned."

"Perhaps we should evaluate the weather in the morning, then determine if it's best to leave or stay," I suggested.

I hoped to avoid another spat between the pair. While Chela had kept her word so far, I didn't know if it would truly last for the remainder of our journey. It was best to keep the two on even footing and intervene before the discussion became heated.

"That's a sound plan," Chela agreed, and to my relief, Lydia nodded. "In the meantime, I suggest you remain indoors. I don't want anyone succumbing to the cold."

Murmured agreements followed her statement, and not long afterward, our group dispersed. I trudged to my room, planning to rifle through my belongings a final time before our departure. I believed we'd be leaving the next morning, regardless of the weather. If it was Lydia's wish to depart, Alexander would take her side even if the suggestion flew in the face of reason. He was smitten.

Once I'd ensured my pack was in order, my stolen sword was sharpened and oiled, and the cloak the women had insisted I purchased was folded, I deemed myself ready. I kicked off my boots, then lay down to sleep fully clothed. It was the first night I recalled sleeping soundly since our encounter in the woods.

When I awakened the next morning, the storm had abated, and the early morning sun shone brilliantly, sparkling across layers of snow. I collected my personal effects before I made my way downstairs; we'd be leaving as I'd anticipated. By midmorning, the others had gathered in the common room with their things, bundled against the cold. We ate a brief meal, then departed the inn, and soon after, Crystal Crags was behind us.

As we approached the base of the pass ascending into the mountains, the snow that had crunched underfoot while we traveled through the city disappeared from the road. The bare earth was dry, while only paces away, drifts were piled on either side.

"We are fortunate," Chela said as she took note of my confusion. "The pass was cleared by one of the magi from the Frostwake. They must have been in the city when the storm came. Otherwise, this lower stretch would be covered in snow."

"Do you believe we'll meet this person as we travel?" I asked.

She shrugged. "It's possible. The mages responsible for clearing the pass are quick and usually don't tarry. If they're not encumbered by a cart of supplies as we are, they'll no doubt make better time." She paused a moment, contemplative, then said, "The pair I refer to are twin brothers. I'm certain they'll be quite interested in you and Alexander. They've always been keen to learn of familial ties between magi, and given what *you* are…" She trailed off with a smirk.

"If they wish to speak with me, I'll oblige them. It will give me something to pass the time with." It was my turn to shrug. "I'd like to learn more about my own family, and you've mentioned you believe our mother must have been Marked, though how she hid that from my step-father, I'll never know."

"If the twins learn you're open to indulging their curiosity, they may never allow you to leave," she replied, amused. "That you're Alexander's guardian won't matter. They're passionate about history, family heritage, *and* the dragon-kind."

The ascent to the Frostwake was uneventful. Though the temperatures continued to drop as we gained elevation, the weather held until the last few hours of our journey, and only then did snow begin to fall once more. The pass through the Southern Pinnacles had been rocky and arduous, and I was grateful to the unmet twins whose job it was to clear the pass. If our way had been blocked by snow and ice, the journey would have been miserable.

During the second day of our trek, I managed to pry Alexander away from Lydia for a few hours. I asked him about his trials and his thoughts on the journey so far. He was uncharacteristically evasive, and I grew frustrated. I was merely trying to understand the process and his experiences, but he didn't seem to comprehend why I posed the questions I did. My patience eroded, and his temper flared. It wasn't long before I gave up and he returned to Lydia's side. I didn't broach the subject again.

As we neared the Frostwake, the pass widened and spread onto an immense plateau. We'd risen above the tree line the afternoon before; the plain was dotted by small, evergreen shrubs where the landscape wasn't encrusted with snow. Near the center of the plateau, a massive structure loomed, and a cursory glance told me it was constructed of solid blocks of ice. A low stone wall surrounded the structure, only just visible above the snowdrifts.

I walked with Emmarie alongside the cart as we made our way across the plateau. Chela gestured toward the ice-building in the distance with one hand while she adjusted the horse's reins in the other.

"That's the Frostwake," she said, her tone somber. "This land holds great meaning for the magi. Many of our forebears have come here to end their days and are buried on this plateau. It's a site of remembrance, and of sorrow for some."

I scanned the landscape again and noted a number of stone pinnacles jutting above the snow. Each pinnacle was the same color and shape, the same height and breadth. The longer I looked, the more markers I located. Grave markers. There must have been thousands of magi buried across the plateau.

"Why was this location chosen?" I asked, mystified.

The environment was harsh, and the snow would have been an obstacle for the burials, even for magi. I couldn't imagine the strength it would require to dig a proper grave in the frozen earth.

Chela shrugged, but it was Lydia, walking ahead with Alexander, who answered. "Long ago, a battle was waged here. It was during the final days of the Mage War when hostilities between factions were at their peak. Many died and were laid to rest here."

"The battle was fought between rival factions of magi," Chela continued. "If the stories are true, the destruction caused was indescribable. Mage fought mage. They rent the land in their wake, and countless innocents were killed. It was your father's people, Andrew—the dragons—who put an end to the fight and forced an uneasy peace between them, but the damage had already been wrought. We lost more than magi during the war. We lost our sense of compassion, our tolerance for differences, and our civility. It's been a thousand years, perhaps more, and our land still hasn't fully recovered."

"The pilgrimage passes through the Frostwake so the would-be mage can learn this history," Lydia said after a moment's reflection. "Sometimes, we return to remember what we've lost so we won't repeat our ancestors' mistakes. Since the end of the Mage War, many have come here to join their predecessors in death. It is not merely a site for the pilgrimage, which is why the passes are kept clear. Many seek this place for their own reasons."

We continued in silence for a time, each lost in their own thoughts. I studied Alexander as he walked ahead with Lydia; he'd been uncharacteristically silent since our last conversation. It troubled me, yet I didn't know what to do. He'd begun to confide in Lydia more often, and I couldn't claim to know his thoughts as well as I once had. Though I was happy they'd met, I felt more like an outsider with each day.

Snow began to fall as we crossed the distance to the Frostwake. Emmarie huddled in her cloak, misery etched across her green features. I pulled mine from the cart bed and draped it around her shoulders. She had more need of it than I ever would.

As we neared the low stone wall at the Frostwake's perimeter, Alexander stopped abruptly and turned to stare intently across the snow-covered expanse of the plateau. Chela cursed as she was forced to rein in Sienna unexpectedly.

"Alex?" I asked.

When he failed to respond, I broke into a jog to cover the distance between us. I could not see anything that would have drawn his attention, but his gaze was fixed. He didn't react to my approach, didn't blink, didn't flinch.

"Alex!" I reached toward his shoulder, but Lydia swatted my hand away, her eyes wide.

"Do not break him from this trance!" she cried, while at the same time, Chela said, "Andrew, no!"

I dropped my hand and released a frustrated sigh before glancing between the two women. I was weary of being left in the dark when it came to their damned magic and Alexander's burgeoning power.

"Damn it, explain this to me! He's my brother and *my* responsibility. How am I supposed to help him if I don't know what this is?" I clenched my jaw and seethed as I looked between them.

Lydia bit her lip and Chela shrugged. Neither would meet my furious gaze.

"We don't know for certain what he's experiencing," Lydia said haltingly after a moment. She wrung her hands and continued to chew on her lip. "Sometimes these things happen, particularly when we are near a site that resonates with our brands of magic. This was the site of a horrific battle. He is becoming a mage-warrior, and warfare is in his blood…Whether we like it or not."

"Is it dangerous?" I demanded.

We'd been told time and again that magi could lose themselves within their power before their training was complete, and such experiences could strip away their sanity. I feared for Alexander, and I loathed that I was powerless to protect him from it.

Lydia's blue eyes were wide with fear. "It could be, but we won't know until he awakens."

I tore my eyes from hers and turned to face Alexander. He continued to stare across the plain, but his expression was no longer bland. Horror was written in his features and tears leaked from his eyes. I didn't doubt he was in danger, but this was a battle I couldn't fight for him.

Damn it, what use was I to this confounding mission? I was a protector who could do little but observe. It was maddening.

"To startle a mage from a vision, particularly when they haven't completed their training, is dangerous," Chela stated evenly. "It's best for Alex if he wakes on his own, undisturbed."

I bottled my anger and bit back the heated words I longed to say. Lashing out at those who were attempting to help us would do me no good, and I'd vowed to do better when it came to my temper. I had no choice but to trust them and hope Alexander wasn't harmed in the process.

Alexander's eyes darted rapidly, as if he witnessed a spectacle unfolding throughout the plateau. His expression flickered between awe and terror, sorrow and shock. Though I could not see as he did, I was certain the experience would leave a profound impression. The falling snow was beginning to accumulate in his blond hair, but he was unmoved by it.

I shifted my gaze to meet Lydia's. "Will he awaken soon?"

She shrugged helplessly in response.

Then, as rapidly as his encounter had begun, it was over. He blinked slowly, a dazed expression on his face. When his eyes refocused, he shook his head slowly and peered at me.

"Andrew? I…" he shook his head again. "I saw…"

As I watched, his expression crumpled into anguish. He blinked rapidly as he tried to clear unwanted tears from his eyes. He looked around, noted Lydia at his side and Chela perched in the cart just beyond. Emmarie stood silently alongside our loyal horse, her young features etched with concern.

Alexander shuddered and scratched at the nape of his neck. "I don't know if I can continue on this path." His voice was strained. "I've come so far, but…if what I saw was a glimpse of my future, I want no part in it!"

He was on the brink of hysteria, and one look at the two magi told me they didn't know how to calm him. I stepped forward and placed one hand on each of Alexander's shoulders, turning his body to face me.

"I don't know what you saw, but until you tell me, I can't help you." I kept my voice even despite the crushing terror that gripped my soul. I *would not* lose him. "Whatever it was, we both know walking away—giving up—isn't an option."

He ground his teeth together as he waged an internal struggle. He wanted to tell me what he'd witnessed, yet something gave him pause. He was afraid to tell me, the only person who had been with him since his Mark had been revealed. I swallowed the bitter realization and forced myself to remain calm—for his sake.

"Alex, I'm here to help you in any way that I can," I said in a voice laden with raw emotion.

"I know, brother." His voice was subdued, a mere whisper in the frigid air. He looked up slowly, fear in his clear, green eyes. "I saw the battle that was waged here… There were magi—many magi—like myself. They were merciless and terrible, capable of such horrors…" His voice cracked as he lapsed into silence and hung his head.

At least now, I understood.

"What you saw happened centuries ago. And those magi were not *you*." I sighed, uncertain if what I was about to say would make sense, but I hoped he'd understand. "*You* are in control of your actions, brother. Whatever you might be capable of, I know you'd never use your ability to harm anyone who didn't deserve it. That you fear such an outcome tells me you won't become like those of the past."

He drew a breath. Nodded. I watched as his fear transformed into iron-clad determination. "You're right, brother. I'm not like them, and I will never be. I won't allow it."

I released his shoulders and stepped away. "Then you know what you must do."

Again, he nodded, then turned to face the ice-structure looming not far ahead. "Yes. Let's go."

The building of ice was far larger than I'd anticipated. From a distance, it appeared the same size as a common inn, but as we approached, I realized it was at least three stories high and stretched farther through the snowfield than it had seemed from afar. There was a stable attached, also constructed of ice, but the interior was insulated from the weather and was pleasantly warmed by a series of braziers. There were more than two dozen horses housed within the stable and a handful of carts much like our own. Two men worked within, and once we collected our belongings, they took over Sienna's care and the storage of our cart.

Immediately inside the main structure was a vast room. The interior was comprised of conventional materials; the exterior was simply fortified by ice. The floor was stone, and intricately woven rugs were placed artfully throughout. At precise intervals along the perimeter of the main room were several large stone hearths, each stoked with a blazing fire. At each of the hearths, people gathered to speak in hushed tones. Some glanced in our direction as we entered, though most paid us no heed. The room was warm, and the others shed their bulky winter cloaks as we walked toward the room's far end.

A pair of magi were stationed there, and behind them was an enormous oaken door. One was a tall, thin man with friendly and open features; the other was a dour woman who appeared displeased by our arrival. She crossed her arms and frowned at our approach.

"More visitors, and this a large group," she complained. "We are already nearing capacity! Bah, I will fetch the quartermaster." She turned and stalked away without introduction or greeting.

"My sincerest apologies for Rathwyn's behavior. She's been in a foul temper lately," the man said. He had pale blue eyes and light, freckled skin. His hair was a startling shade of red-orange, which he wore pulled back into a shoulder-length ponytail. He cleared his throat. "Regardless, welcome to the Frostwake. My name is Niall Roche. Why have you come at the onset of winter?"

"I've come for a trial," Alexander said as he stepped forward. Hard determination marked his stance. He gestured to me and said, "This is my half-brother, Andrew. He was named my guardian, and Chela is our guide." He introduced Lydia and Emmarie as well, though he didn't share their reason for joining us.

Niall smiled. "I hope some of you don't mind sharing a room for the nights to come. As you've heard, we are nearing capacity. Rathwyn will be in better spirits when she learns you're here on a pilgrimage. She hosts the trials at the Frostwake, you see. All of our other guests are here for…different matters."

It was several minutes before Rathwyn returned with the man she referred to only as "the quartermaster." He'd located rooms for us, though Lydia and Emmarie were forced to share, as were Alexander and I. I took my brother's belongings to the room for him when he made it clear he wanted to speak with Rathwyn regarding his next trial. I was relieved he seemed to have regained his sense of purpose, and the incident outside had not shaken his resolve beyond repair.

I was stowing our belongings when a light tap came on the door. I called for the person to enter but didn't look away from my chore as I was nearly finished. I knelt before a chest of drawers, stuffing my few articles of clothing inside as the door opened.

"I must thank you." Lydia sat down carefully on the end of what would be Alexander's bed. She'd taken her long hair down since our arrival, but began to braid it as she spoke.

"I've done nothing more than what was required." Satisfied that our things were stored sufficiently, I stood and turned to face her.

"I suppose that's true. You did exactly what was needed." She sighed. "Alex is fortunate you were named as his guardian. Chela and myself…We didn't know how best to handle the situation outside. He would have given in to his despair, and I would have lost him." She stared at the floor, her expression pensive. "Losing him would have destroyed everything I've dreamed of for the future."

I knelt so we were closer to eye level. "I know Alex as I do simply because we're brothers. I've always looked out for him, protected him, and I've watched him go down that very path before. It's only because I have such experience that I knew what to say."

Her hands continued to work at her hair as she blinked away tears. "Will I have the opportunity to know him as well as you? I want it to be so, but…there are too many unknowns. Too many things may happen long before we reach the end of his journey."

"The only advice I can give is that you must take this one day at a time. Make the most of what you have with my brother. You'll never know how long you may have together, and if you care for him as much as I believe you do, you should seize every opportunity you have. Don't wait. As I know far too well, happiness can be torn from you savagely and without warning." I sighed as my thoughts turned to Vera. I looked away in an attempt to hide my grief.

Lydia reached out to take one of my hands in hers. Her skin was cool and soft. "I hope one day you will find happiness again. It pains me to see your sorrow." She squeezed my hand in a gesture of comfort, then slowly let go. "I hope the man I marry—whether he is Alexander or someone else—harbors as much love for me as you do for the woman you lost. Any woman would be so fortunate. Of that, I am certain." She rose and moved toward the door.

"Lydia… Thank you," I managed, my voice roughened by emotion.

She offered me a sad smile before she exited and closed the door softly behind her.

When Alexander entered some time later, I was still kneeling on the floor, just as I had been when Lydia left. I didn't know how long I'd been there, though my knees had begun to ache. My thoughts were focused on Vera, Vinterry, her staff, the life I'd been forced to flee… and the interminable grief I'd been unable to cast aside.

Lydia's words had been meant in kindness, but my wounds remained raw.

Alexander studied me briefly, but he knew what had been running through my mind. His welcoming smile vanished as he sat heavily on the bed.

"I miss her too, brother," he said. "Together, we'll make certain she's avenged."

SEVENTEEN

I walked to the main hall the next morning alone. Alexander had awakened early, eager for his trial, and had left without waking me.

A large group was gathered for a memorial service in the main hall, and they clustered along the hearths nearest the door. They were collectively somber in their shared grief while they listened to a pair of magi give a prepared oration.

I walked to one of the hearths farthest from the activity as I didn't want to disturb the mourners. The man whom we'd met the previous evening, Niall, sat near the fire, a thick book in his hands. He offered me a knowing smile as I approached, then carefully closed the tome, marking his place amongst the yellowed pages with a length of faded blue ribbon.

"I spoke to several of your party this morning as your brother was preparing to begin his trial," he said. "Chela mentioned you were interested in your family's ancestry, though she would not elaborate, much to my chagrin." He chuckled. "Niall will be here shortly. We may speak more on the subject then."

I blinked as I realized rather belatedly the man I'd approached wasn't Niall, as I'd believed, but his twin. "I thought you were—"

"Niall?" he asked, amused. "Yes, I know. We haven't been introduced properly, have we? I'm Nevin Roche, the elder twin."

As I introduced myself, the entry door burst open and banged loudly against the interior wall as an errant gust of wind caught it. A flurry of snow swirled inside as a woman dressed in leather pants and a jerkin strode inside. She was pretty, with curly blond hair that spiraled on either side of her face, and the most intensely blue eyes I'd ever seen. She was clearly a mage and wasn't dressed warmly enough for the wintery conditions outside. She appeared frustrated as she struggled with the heavy door. I rose and crossed the room to assist, as my strength far surpassed hers.

Once the door was closed securely, I turned to face her. She backed several paces away, but smiled warily. "Thank you," she said before she turned on her heel and strode away.

I frowned, puzzled at the brief exchange, then returned to the hearth where Nevin waited.

"That was Rynn." He flashed a brief grin. "She's the mage responsible for the ice shield protecting the exterior of the Frostwake. The blocks serve as an additional layer of insulation. It may not seem like much, but it helps tremendously with keeping the interior warm."

My eyes grazed the room, seeking another glimpse of the strange woman, but she was gone. "I didn't have the time to ask her name."

Nevin chuckled. "Such is her way. Her Mark is very powerful, and when she completed her trials, she was physically changed. It happens from time to time." He narrowed his eyes in thought. "It may well happen to your brother. His Mark is the most powerful I've encountered yet. Rynn's is but a shadow in comparison."

"What do you mean she was physically changed?"

Nevin smiled, though his eyes were sad. "Her power lies with ice and snow. She can freeze or thaw items at will. In a place like this, her magic is immensely useful, but the strength of her talent came with a steep price. When she became fully attuned to her abilities, she became as cold as the ice she manipulates. I don't mean in an unfriendly sense—Rynn is a vibrant and wonderful person once you come to know her. What I mean is she's physically cold to the touch. So much so that until she understood what happened during her last trial, she gave several people serious cases of frostbite merely by shaking hands or offering hugs." His gaze traveled toward the group of mourners at the far end of the hall. "She left as she did because she feared you'd come too close. She doesn't wish to harm anyone."

"She would not have harmed me," I replied automatically. "She simply doesn't know it."

He opened his mouth to respond, but stopped and flashed a grin at someone behind me. Turning, I noted Niall was walking toward us.

It was remarkable how similar the two were, even down to how they wore their hair. The two greeted one another, and Niall sat down at a point equidistant between Nevin and myself.

"Your last statement has given me pause for consideration," Nevin said after a moment. "You aren't what you seem to be, are you?"

"He is not," Niall agreed with a nod before I could muster a response. "Not Marked, though not an ordinary man, either."

The two peered at me expectantly, and I knew this would be where our conversation must start. "I'm not Marked," I confirmed. "I'm a skin-changer. Dragon-kind."

Both of the men's eyes widened in identical expressions of genuine surprise.

"I can't believe this!" Niall exclaimed with a grin. "Some of the dragon-kind still remain!" He glanced at his brother, who nodded, his eyes alight with wonder.

I shrugged uncomfortably, though I'd been expecting their reaction. I'd never grow used to the attention.

"Now I understand why Chela said you were interested in learning of your ancestry," Nevin said after a moment. "Alexander is your brother… Nay, he must be your half-brother, for he has no dragon's blood in his veins."

"I *knew* the two of you must be brothers," Niall stated. "You share many of the same physical traits, but there was something I sensed that was markedly different about you. I believed I merely sensed the magnitude of Alexander's burgeoning power, and that was where the difference lay." He shook his head, amused. "I'm pleased to be wrong! The dragon-kind yet live!"

"If we can help you learn of your family's history, you must tell us what you know already," Nevin continued. "Start with your parents, then tell us of Alexander's. I assume you must share a mother."

"We do," I conceded. "How did you guess we shared a mother rather than a father?"

Both of the men laughed, but it was Niall who answered. "A skin-changer can only be born of a dragon-mage father and a non-dragon mother. They aren't conceived any other way. It simply doesn't happen."

"He forgot to mention the dragon-mage father must be powerful," Nevin added. "Only a handful throughout history were graced with the ability to change their form to appear human. They were known as the emissaries."

"Since you're a skin-changer," Niall continued, "it can only be deduced that Alexander is your half-brother through your mother."

Once I recovered from my initial shock, I found myself telling the two what I knew of my family without further prompting. My father was Zayneldarion Caein, who I learned had an impeccable reputation amongst the magi. My mother was Carra Winston, a human woman from the northern reaches of Novania. When I mentioned Alexander's father was the late king of Novania, Carlton Marsden, both of the men gaped, stunned and appalled by the news.

"How is it he didn't know of Alexander's Mark?" Nevin asked. "We've heard tales since we were children regarding the laws of Novania. If his Mark had been discovered, your brother would have been killed."

"Our mother protected us both," I replied. "Under Carlton's rule, the laws weren't enforced except in rare cases. Now that he's gone, I fear it's no longer true."

"The implications are chilling," Niall stated as he tapped one finger against his lower lip. "I've studied the laws of succession in Novania. The king will name his eldest legitimate son as successor and heir. That means you must have a brother who now occupies the throne."

I nodded grimly. I didn't want to speak of Colin and the growing list of atrocities he'd committed.

"Alexander wasn't his first-born," Niall continued. "That means there are more years between the two of you than what appears." He tilted his head to one side thoughtfully. "I've heard stories of skin-changers appearing youthful even after several hundred years. You appear no older than your brother, though it can't be true."

I gaped at him. Had he truly said *several hundred years?* Was I doomed to live so long, filled with sorrow and continual loss, condemned to outlive everyone I cared for, everyone I loved? I'd known I was no longer aging for the better part of a decade, but I'd never considered the implications. I looked away, suddenly desperate for an escape. I needed to be alone with my thoughts.

"I'm sorry," Niall said gently. "You didn't know, did you?"

I turned toward him and shook my head. How could I have known? The scant conversations I'd managed to have with my father never touched on the topic, and I'd never asked him for specifics. I didn't know what the typical lifespan of a dragon was, let alone someone like myself.

"Niall, we should get to work," Nevin said quietly after a moment. "I sense Andrew would like space to clear his head, and we have snow to clear from the passes."

"Yes, you're right," Niall agreed as he stood. "If you feel up to continuing our conversation at a later time, all you need do is ask."

I merely nodded as the twins took their leave. I stared into the nearby fire as my thoughts circled endlessly. I'd always assumed I would have an average lifespan—*for a human.* In mere seconds, my lifelong assumption was shattered; I would outlive everyone I knew, Alexander included, if I didn't succumb to a violent death in battle. Given the other natural abilities I possessed, the chances of even that fate were slim. I'd already experienced so much loss in my life, and I didn't relish the thought of never having an end to my anguish. But such was my lot, it seemed.

I wished more than ever that my father was nearby. I desperately wanted to speak with him, but it would take days to reach him, even if I were to assume my dragon form and fly the entire distance. The more I stewed over the revelation, the angrier I became. I'd never wished for this existence, and I didn't want it now. I needed an outlet for my anger.

After a few more moments spent glaring into the fire, I rose and stalked outside. It wouldn't be wise to release my pent-up rage within the confines of the building.

The frigid air struck me as I opened the door, but it did little to diminish the fire burning in my gut. Some distance away, I spied the twins clearing the path through the plateau, a blaze of fire arcing along the road ahead of them.

I stomped away from the main building and off the path. The snow was more than knee-deep, and the most recent layer was heavy with moisture. I picked up a handful of snow and hurled it into the distance with as much force as I could muster. The action served no purpose other than to release my rage, but I had no other outlet. I picked up another handful of snow and tossed it after the first while my thoughts continued to swirl around the twins' revelation.

What had I expected? I was dragon-kind, the son of my father. Why had I foolishly clung to the notion I'd have a human's lifespan? Holy hell, there was so much I still didn't understand about my nature, and it was infuriating. I couldn't blame my father, not truly. He'd spent the previous thirty-eight years trapped in stone, and our conversations, while meaningful, had been limited by Lileen's magical ability and stamina. The topic had never come up, yet I remained angry. A part of me insisted I should have known.

"Andrew, what are you doing out here?"

The voice startled me back into reality. I'd been lobbing snowballs into the distance for some time, oblivious to what anyone observing might think of the behavior. I dropped the latest handful of snow and paused to survey the area. I must have been more furious than I'd realized; I'd cleared a circle in the snow nearly the width of my outspread arms.

I turned to find Lydia at the edge of the nearby path. Her blue eyes were filled with concern, and she was bundled in several layers against the cold. I sighed and ran a hand through my hair. I could only speculate what must have been running through her mind.

I grimaced and related my conversation with the twins.

"It's fortunate you turned your anger toward the snow and not something else," she replied cautiously, "but I'm concerned about you. I…We were all under the impression you *knew*. You've spoken with your father."

I suppressed a growl. "I didn't know *this*. I suppose it should not have come as a surprise, given my other attributes." I picked up another handful of snow, turned, and threw it hard.

"You should come inside," she pressed. "You've been out here for over an hour with no protection. Surely even *you* grow cold at times."

"I'm fine," I snarled.

The momentary terror and concern on her features forced me to relent. She was not at fault, and my anger was misplaced.

"I'm sorry," I said. "It looks as though you need to sit near the fire, but the cold doesn't affect me. At least I was aware of *that* aspect of what I am."

She shivered and pulled her cloak more tightly around her shoulders. "I would not have come out if you hadn't been foolish enough to start tossing snow about. You've alarmed some of the others."

Her tone was sharp, unyielding. She was right; I'd been acting the fool, and my temper had once again bested me.

When I made no response, she sighed in exasperation. "Sometimes you men are just like children. Luckily for you, we women are capable of keeping our senses long enough to drag you back to reality."

I frowned and stomped ahead. I wrenched the door open more forcefully than necessary and felt one of the hinges threaten to give way. I growled low in my throat and swallowed my rage once more. It wouldn't help matters if I damaged the building and forced everyone else present to experience unnecessary discomfort. With exaggerated caution, I closed the door behind us.

Lydia made her way directly to the nearest hearth, but I chose not to follow her. Her barbed comments had done nothing to diminish my ire, and I was in no mood for conversation. I found a place on one side of the door and leaned against the wall, where I scanned the room with my arms crossed. Chela was at the far end, sitting at another hearth with Rathwyn and Emmarie. They chatted amiably, and each held a steaming mug between their hands. Other hearths were occupied by people whom I didn't know or recognize. Some spoke softly amongst themselves, though a few cast wary glances in my direction. I'd caused more of a stir than I'd intended.

"You were outside for quite some time," a woman said from beside me. I hadn't heard her approach, but I looked to my left and was surprised to see Rynn, the woman I'd encountered earlier in the day. "Most people would have been blue with cold an hour ago. You seem to be unaffected—albeit angry."

I frowned and looked away, hoping that she'd understand I didn't want to talk. I kept my gaze fixed on the other side of the room, but she stubbornly remained nearby. I felt her eyes on me, and eventually I succumbed to my own curiosity and peered at her once more.

"What do you want?" I demanded, my tone more severe than I'd intended.

She arched one eyebrow, but her expression was unreadable. "Are you always this hostile to those you've just met?"

I rolled my eyes and sighed. "No," I conceded, feeling some of the anger drain away. I offered her my hand. "My name is Andrew Caein."

She nodded, staring at my outstretched hand for several long moments. After speaking with the twins, I understood her hesitation.

"I know who you are," she replied slowly. "I'm Rynn Gwyllias."

"You can't harm me," I assured her. "I'm not like the others here."

Her eyes met mine, vibrant and blue and filled with a dozen questions. Finally, she reached out and took my hand. The contact was brief, but I understood immediately why she'd feared to make it—her hand was far colder than the snow outside. If I'd been anyone else, I would have sustained frostbite, but since I was invulnerable, no harm was done.

Tears filled her eyes as she withdrew her hand. "It has been eleven years," she whispered, drawing one hand up to touch her lips in a gesture of wonder. When the tears spilled onto her cheeks, they froze upon contact with her skin.

"Have I done something wrong?" I asked, perplexed by her reaction.

She shook her head as a tremulous smile stretched across her features. "No, Andrew, quite the opposite." She brushed the ice from her face with a strained laugh. "I must go, but we'll speak later. I will seek you."

The twins sought me out after they'd finished clearing the road near the Frostwake. It was nearing evening, and my temper had cooled sufficiently that I was once more amenable to conversation. I could not blame them for my lack of knowledge.

As we settled near a hearth, I began with an apology. I was certain they'd heard what had transpired after they'd departed, and I needed to make certain they knew I wasn't angry with them. I'd never handled surprises well.

Nevin chuckled, and Niall shook his head, amused. "There is no need for apologies, my friend," Niall replied. "You were caught off guard. As I understand it, that will always put a warrior into a foul temper."

"Nevertheless—" I began but was cut off by Nevin.

He held up one hand. "We won't hear any more of this. It's in the past. You sought our knowledge of ancestry, and we'll tell you what we know."

"Yes," Niall agreed. "We know many tales of your father, and of his father as well. The Caein line was filled with magi, most of them powerful."

"Truthfully," Nevin added, "if you wish to learn more about your father's family, your best resource is in the Dragonlands. Your brother's final trial—the last shrine—is there, in the ancestral home of all dragon-kind. You should seek the library when you arrive. You will have no trouble gaining entrance."

"What do you mean?" I asked.

The twins laughed. "My mistake," Nevin replied. "It will take us some time to remember you aren't from this land and don't know her history."

"What my inadequate brother is attempting to say," Niall interjected, "is there are many areas within the Dragonlands that can't be accessed by anyone, save dragon-kind. There is much magic there, and your forebears guarded their secrets carefully. The library will not open for humans—we've both tried. But as a skin-changer, you should be allowed entry."

I considered the last conversation I had with my father. He'd asked me to seek the Caein family vault when we reached the Dragonlands; a set of armor made from his own scales was stowed within. It had been his desire that I take it for myself and use it when the time came to face the armies of Novania. He'd indicated I would be granted access, given that I was dragon-kind—and a Caein.

He had not mentioned the library, but time had been short, and I hadn't known what to ask. I surmised the library was similarly enchanted.

"Inside the library, there is rumored to be a room dedicated solely to the lineage of the dragon-kind," Nevin said after a moment. "The history of each clan is supposedly contained within. Few have ever been allowed within the library, and since your people left this world, none have found their way inside."

"It's a shame, truly," Niall added. "So much knowledge, so much history… All lost to us because of our unfortunate mistakes as men."

I narrowed my eyes, puzzled. "What do you mean?"

"It's our fault the dragons chose to leave," Niall replied. "The rules of men harbored little love for the dragon-kind beyond the Southlands. Dragons weren't meant to be penned as they were. They were meant to roam the skies."

"You're familiar with the rules of Novania," Nevin added. "Should you return, the laws allow that you may be hunted and killed like a beast. It's cruel and demeaning. The dragon-kind are more intelligent than humans could ever aspire to be."

"There are other lands, far to the east and across the sea," Niall continued. "The dragons once had homes there as well, but the men of those lands became unfriendly, just as the Novanians did. Their last refuge was here, within the protection of the Barrier."

"It took many years before the dragons acquired the means to carry out their plan to leave this world behind," Nevin stated. "The magic required to open the gateway was powerful beyond measure. You've seen what it did to the three dragon-magi who summoned it—and to the forest surrounding them." He shook his head thoughtfully. "No human has ever been born with a Mark to rival any of the three dragons who remain in the glade. Even your brother, powerful as he is, would have been no match for any one of them."

"My father referred to what happened as a curse." I stared into the flames of the nearby hearth as I absorbed the twins' words.

"Yes," Niall agreed. "To be aware of oneself, but trapped within stone, unable to move, to speak… It is the worst of fates. The dragons felt there was no hope of regaining true freedom here. The sacrifice of the three was the only way to break the cycle, and opening the gateway to another world was an act of last resort. They tried countless times to make peace, but beyond the Southlands, their attempts at diplomacy were met with scorn."

"We've spoken to Caelmarion on occasion," Nevin said after a moment's silence. "He and the others—Miranetha and your father—knew the price of the magic they summoned. They believed their sacrifice was worth the cost if it meant their people were granted freedom once more."

"Yes," Niall said with a sigh. "Caelmarion said, 'An eternity trapped in stone was but a small price to pay,' if it meant his children and grandchildren weren't forced to hide from the larger world. He dreamed of a place where they could live in peace, freely, as they'd long desired."

"Do you think the dragons found such a world?" I mused.

"I would like to believe so," Nevin replied. "The alternative is they are no better off than they were before."

"The alternative means the sacrifice made in the Stone Grove was in vain," Niall said. "I fervently hope it was not. The dragon-kind deserved better than what this world ultimately gave them."

We fell silent, each lost in his own thoughts. I hoped the twins were right and the dragons had found peace at long last, but our conversation caused me to wonder about the three who remained behind, sacrificed for the greater good of their people. *Our* people.

I'd never asked my father or Caelmarion if the petrification could be reversed. Perhaps after Alexander's trials were over and Colin had been dealt with, I could return to the Stone Grove and seek answers to some of the questions that now rattled through my brain. I'd been focused solely on the immediate future when last I'd spoken with them and had failed to seek information regarding their past.

"You lot look far too serious." I turned from the fire to find Rynn had appeared, her eyes locked onto my own. "I'd like to speak with you, if I'm not interrupting."

The twins shared a knowing glance and stood in unison. "I think we're finished for this evening," Niall replied. "There is much to think upon."

"Indeed," Nevin agreed. "We'll speak again before you leave the Frostwake."

Once the pair were gone, Rynn sat down in the space Nevin had vacated. She studied me for some time but said nothing. Her expression was one of mild curiosity.

I became restless and uncomfortable under her silent scrutiny. "I thought you wished to speak with me. So far, you've done nothing but stare."

A flicker of a smile crossed her lips, and she tossed her head, causing her curls to bounce and sway. "I'm trying to decide where to begin."

I lifted an eyebrow. "Perhaps from the beginning?"

She smirked. "You have a sense of humor, I see." She shifted slightly in her chair and turned to face me directly. "I suppose you're right. Starting from the beginning is best."

I nodded my encouragement, my curiosity piqued. "I have nothing else to do but wait for Alex to complete his trial. We have plenty of time."

Her eyes narrowed slightly. Even in the flickering light of the fire, they were a startling shade of blue. "Alex must be the mage who has attracted so much attention today," she replied. "I've never witnessed so many eagles gathered. Surely you saw them while you were out tossing snow."

I felt my face flush and offered her a sheepish grin. "I was…preoccupied."

"So it would seem." She laughed softly. "Tell me, how is it you are unaffected by the cold? I sense it has something to do with the twins' interest in you."

The intensity of her gaze was a force unto itself, and I blinked. "I sought them out, truthfully," I replied. "I was told they knew much about history, and I hoped they might help me learn more about my own family."

"An odd request from a guardian," she replied, her gaze never wavering from mine. "Most guardians are warrior-types, as you so obviously are, though you're different. Certainly, you're taller than most, and you carry yourself with more authority. But there is more. A normal man wouldn't have lasted ten minutes in the cold, and you were outside for more than an hour. Without a cloak."

I frowned. "I thought you'd come to tell me *your* story, but now you're interested in my past?"

I broke away from her gaze to stare into the fire once more but was compelled to tell her. She was an enigma, and I needed to solve the puzzle she presented. Perhaps if I answered her question, she would reciprocate.

When I turned to look at her once more, she still gazed at me with an intensity I was unaccustomed to. "I'm a skin-changer."

A smile spread across her features, and her eyes sparkled with excitement. "I suspected as much!" She looked down, and her smile stretched into a grin. "This confirms everything."

"What?"

She laughed. "I'm sorry, but I've been waiting for this day for many years. You are the one I've been waiting for, and I must leave the Frostwake with you."

I chewed my lower lip. Chela wouldn't be pleased with another addition to our party. Even though Rynn had considerable power as a mage, I didn't believe our guide would be amenable.

"This isn't my decision alone. It affects the others as well—"

"It is *not* their decision, and it isn't yours either," she stated. "The Oracle had a vision when I last spoke with her, and it was clear." She reached into the pocket of her jerkin to remove a folded slip of paper, then handed it to me. "Read that. It is the Oracle's vision. She penned it for when this day arrived. Read it, and you'll understand."

I sighed and took the sheet of paper begrudgingly. Once again, I'd been pulled in an unanticipated direction by something the Oracle had said. I'd grown weary of her while in the Citadel, but it seemed her visions continued to plague me, despite the distance separating us.

I frowned as I unfolded the paper to read its contents, convinced I wouldn't like the message within. The ink was faded, but the handwriting was clear and legible. I glanced above the edge of the paper before I began to find Rynn staring intensely.

Rynn Gwyllias, daughter of Bryt and Sera –

To you, I inscribe the vision I have seen upon this page.

You shall go to the Frostwake, where your ability will be needed for a time. You shall remain there, awaiting one whom you cannot harm, one of the dragon-kind. When he arrives, you must depart with him, for he shall need your aid, though he will not understand at first.

My vision also revealed a powerful mage, though I could not discern his face and I could not determine his tie to the other. I have no doubt they will arrive together, the dragon-kind and the mage. Their paths are as one. In this regard, your aid shall be required by them both.

Do not allow either to persuade you to remain behind. You must go with them.

At the bottom of the page, the Oracle's crescent-and-stars symbol was drawn in green ink, while the rest had been penned in black. As was true of all correspondence with the Oracle, the missive was terribly vague. The only certainty was her reference to the dragon-kind—it could only be me. And the mage must be Alexander since neither Chela nor Lydia considered themselves powerful. The Oracle seemed to believe we would need Rynn's help.

I sighed, frustrated, and handed the sheet back to Rynn.

"Now you understand," she said. "You will need my abilities. Or perhaps it is Alexander who will need them. Either way, your paths are one as the Oracle claimed, and I must accompany you."

"Chela is our guide," I replied. "You'll need to speak with her. I advise you to show her that message when you do. She's unlikely to accept your word alone."

Rynn smirked. "Chela has come here before, and we have an understanding. But I will do as you ask and show her this." She tilted her head to one side as a shadow seemed to pass over her features. "When we spoke earlier, I know I left rather abruptly. I was nearly overcome. I want to apologize."

"You don't need to," I replied, but she held up one hand for silence.

"Please, I need to say this." She looked down briefly to collect her thoughts. "It has been over eleven years since I completed my trials. I hurt several people without meaning to, simply with my touch, before I realized what I'd become. I've always believed the Oracle sent me to the Frostwake, not because I'm uniquely adapted to the weather, but because it's far away from most people, and I could not pose a danger to them. And I *am* a danger to anyone who comes too close."

"Rynn…" I wanted to say something to comfort her, but I was at a loss for words. Clearly, she'd suffered due to the effects of her magic.

She locked her eyes on mine. "You're immune to the cold, and because of that, I was able to shake your hand. It has been eleven years since I last made physical contact with anyone. *Eleven years…*" She paused to stare into the fire, then shook her head. "I believed I'd never experience human contact again. I believed the Oracle's vision was mistaken. The dragons fled before my mother met my father, and twice she wrote of the dragon-kind. It was an impossibility. And yet, here you are."

I forced a tired smile. "Perhaps I can tell you the rest of my story while we travel, but I don't feel up to repeating it a second time tonight. Once with the twins was enough."

She snickered. "They can be a bit overwhelming when their curiosity is engaged." She looked down at the folded sheet of paper in her hands. "For the first time in many years, I'm hopeful for the future. Your presence here and the confirmation of the Oracle's vision… It means a great deal to me." She met my gaze once more. "I'm certain we'll have much to speak of while we travel. It's growing late, and I have many things to do tomorrow." She stood slowly and smiled. "Good night, Andrew Caein."

During the next few days, I spoke with the twins, though their interest in my ancestry finally began to wane. They started to ask questions about Alexander, then moved on to the topic of laws in Novania. Their appetite for knowledge was nearly insatiable. Thomas would have loved speaking with the pair.

I didn't see any more of Rynn during that time, though I was approached by Chela the day after our conversation. She was resigned, but didn't argue. The Oracle's word carried more weight than anything I could have said.

When Lydia learned another mage planned to join us, she was genuinely happy with the prospect. She believed it would be good to have Rynn along to assist if Alexander had any more episodes like the one he'd endured on the plateau. She was clearly impressed with Rynn's power.

During our final afternoon at the Frostwake, Lydia sought Rynn of her own accord. I watched from across the main hall as the two chatted and laughed. I sensed it was the beginning of a lasting friendship.

I didn't know what it was about Rynn, but she intrigued me. I wanted to learn all I could of her and was pleased she was joining us, though I wouldn't voice my opinion to the others. That was a secret I wouldn't divulge to anyone until I understood why she'd captured my attention.

I hoped I'd be granted the opportunity to know her better, given time.

EIGHTEEN

The twins met us at the stable as we prepared to depart the Frostwake. "The road south is clear," Niall said with a grin. "I know it's been snowing, but we've found time to work around our many conversations with Andrew."

I chuckled. "And I'm grateful you've taken the time."

Nevin turned to Rynn while his twin spoke briefly to Alexander. "We'll miss you," Nevin said. "You've done good work here, and I'm not certain how well we'll cope without your special brand of magic."

"We'll cope," Niall cut in, "but we won't like it."

Rynn laughed, though tears gleamed in her eyes. "I'll visit when I can," she promised. "This has been home—and you've been as close to family as I've had here."

Chela took up her position on the cart and glanced pointedly in our direction. Emmarie was huddled in the back of the cart beneath her cloak and mine, clearly ready to depart. We said our final goodbyes to the twins, then joined the others to begin the long descent from the Frostwake.

Lydia emerged from within the main structure last, bundled in multiple layers against the frigid air. Alexander offered his arm, which she accepted, and the pair began to walk at the head of our procession.

I studied them for a time as I brought up the rear with Rynn. During his trial, Alexander had experienced something that renewed his resolve to continue, strengthening it beyond the words I'd imparted after his vision. He was determined in a way I'd seldom witnessed from my brother, confident in his path, and fierce in his desire to see his journey through.

For her part, Rynn appeared contemplative. When I asked what weighed on her mind, she assured me she looked forward to the journey but said little more. I was once again left alone with my thoughts.

Our first day of travel passed uneventfully, but on the morning of the second day, it began to snow. We'd broken camp only an hour prior.

"I'd hoped we wouldn't be delayed by the weather," Chela grumbled from the cart.

Rynn laughed. "I'm a frost mage. This storm won't stop us."

She grinned and assumed the lead confidently. As she drew on her power, a spicy scent akin to wintergreen permeated the air. Even though I allowed the others to walk ahead, the smell was strong enough to irritate my nostrils, and I began to sneeze. Alexander glanced over his shoulder with a knowing smirk. I glowered in return.

Rynn moved the snow from our path efficiently, and we made significant progress down the mountainside despite the storm. After a time, my repeated bouts of sneezing mercifully ceased. I was uncertain if I'd grown used to the scent, or if the wind had changed direction and pushed it away from me. Regardless, it was a welcome relief.

The snow tapered off during the afternoon, and an hour later, the pale disc of the sun emerged from behind the clouds. We stopped to make camp not long after. Once the tents had been pitched, Rynn worked more of her magic, using it to build walls of snow to shelter our camp from the biting gusts of wind.

I set about building a fire while Alexander took his turn sparring with Emmarie. I watched the pair, noting with satisfaction our Merael friend was rapidly improving. She'd grown stronger and had learned to detect the telling movements that indicated whether she should parry or dodge her opponent's next swing. Alexander grinned all the while, pleased with the activity and clearly enjoying his role as mentor.

Once the fire was blazing, Alexander halted the lesson and joined Lydia to help prepare our evening meal. I sat a short distance away from the fire to keep out of their way while they worked. After a time, Rynn joined me. She offered a smile, her eyes dancing with amusement.

"We didn't have time to speak as I'd hoped the last two days," she said, her tone matter-of-fact. "Clearing the way of snow took much of my energy and focus, but I believe we have time now. Don't you agree?"

Reluctantly, I nodded. She expected me to tell her my life's story—or as much of it as I could manage in the few hours we had. I could convince Alexander to take the second watch if my tale ran too late into the evening, and I knew he'd appreciate the extra rest.

"Good," she replied. "You owe me a story. I've been waiting years for your appearance at the Frostwake. I'd like to know why you're still here while the rest of the dragon-kind have fled."

I watched Alexander and Emmarie for a few moments before I formed a response. She watched me intently but said nothing as I gathered my thoughts. I appreciated her patience.

I began with what I'd managed to piece together from the brief conversations with my father. Although I'd been reticent at first, I found something about Rynn's demeanor put me at ease. I told her why I'd failed to flee with the rest of the dragon-kind, but didn't explain why Alexander and I had been forced to flee Novania, only that we'd gone. There was time enough for that tale later.

When I finished, she drew her knees up to her chest and stared into the fire. "Your father didn't know your mother had conceived, so you remained here. What astonishes me is that you survived as long as you did in Novania."

"We plan to return when this journey is over," I replied. "We have unfinished business with our brother… The king."

She studied me carefully for some time. It had grown dark while I'd been speaking, and her face was now illuminated by the flickering campfire.

"We received some disturbing reports at the Frostwake only a few weeks ago," she said. "Tales of assassins that managed to fool the guardians at the Mage's Gate. At first, I didn't believe the rumors, but then a pair of strange men passed through. They were poorly equipped for the weather in the pass, and they sought information on fellow travelers. They didn't stay long. The people they sought weren't at the Frostwake. They were searching for a man from Novania, though they didn't specify a name."

I clenched my jaw in frustration. I'd been a fool to hope we'd outpaced all of the damned villains Colin had sent after us.

"They were seeking you, weren't they?" Rynn asked pointedly. "Your reaction tells me it's not the first time assassins have been in pursuit of you."

I met her gaze steadily for a few moments, then nodded. I'd hoped to avoid spilling our whole story yet again, but if the Oracle's message to Rynn meant anything, she deserved to know what she'd become entangled in.

"This will take some time," I warned her.

She arched an eyebrow, though I couldn't read her expression. "I have nothing else to do," she replied dismissively. "Let's get supper. Afterward, you can share your story in its entirety."

Rynn proved an ardent listener. She asked few questions and allowed me to tell the tale with minimal interruptions. Alexander agreed to take the second watch and turned in early. The others followed suit not long afterward, leaving us alone at the edge of the dying campfire. I talked long into the night and stopped only when I came to our arrival at the Frostwake.

To my surprise, it had been a relief to share our story and relate some of my internalized frustrations with someone. I'd long relied on Alexander for that purpose, but his infatuation with Lydia had altered our dynamic significantly.

"I was correct to believe the Oracle's message," she said thoughtfully after a time.

The fire had faded to mere embers, though the sky had cleared, and a three-quarter moon provided pale illumination as its light reflected on the snow. Even in the darkness, I was struck by how vibrant her eyes were.

She gazed at a point some distance away as she continued. "You and your brother need my help."

"You seem very certain," I replied.

"Yes. We don't muster armies in the Southlands—not since the Mage Wars. What we lack in soldiers, we make up for with magical power. If you plan to confront Colin, you'll need as many magi as you can summon. My ability will be an asset to you. I can do much more than move snow and build walls, you know."

I smiled faintly. "I have no doubt of your abilities."

She shifted to face me directly. "Good, because I intend to help you whether you agree to it or not." She laughed, but the sound was cut short by an expansive yawn. "I think I ought to turn in for the night."

When I nodded, she rose and walked to the small tent she'd brought along for herself. I looked up at the sky and judged by the position of the moon that it was nearly time to wake Alexander for his portion of the watch. I rebuilt the fire before rousing him, then turned in myself.

I was awakened by Alexander. Daylight had broken some time ago, and I could see through the canvas of the tent that the sun was shining. Puffs of steam issued from Alexander's mouth as he grinned.

"I see why you always take the second watch," he grumbled good-naturedly. "You'd sleep the whole day if you were allowed."

I sat up and stretched, mildly annoyed by the intrusion. I'd been dreaming of Vinterry, of Vera; it had been an uncommonly pleasant dream.

"I suppose you came to tell me everyone is waiting," I replied.

Alexander laughed. "No, I haven't let you sleep that late. Lydia made breakfast and insisted I wake you so you can eat before we depart."

As he finished speaking, excited voices arose outside. I scrambled to my feet and began pulling on my clothing. Alexander ducked outside to learn the source of the commotion, and I followed moments later.

I didn't immediately understand what had occurred to cause the excitement. The campsite was in the process of being packed, and Lydia stood near the campfire, stirring a pot of porridge. There were no strangers present, and nothing appeared out of place.

Emmarie stood near the wall of snow ringing the camp, her gaze fixed on the sky. Following her line of sight, I spotted a solitary gray eagle above. It flew low and released a piercing shriek as it glided above the treetops and prepared to land.

As the bird made its descent, its true size became apparent. Its wingspan neared six feet in length, and its body was almost three feet high. It was slate-gray, though some of its tailfeathers sported a reddish hue. It landed gracefully on the lip of the snow wall and gazed at us with brilliant yellow eyes. It released a single cry that pierced the chill morning air.

Emmarie approached it, her eyes wide with wonder. I smiled as I watched her; this was the moment she'd been seeking for weeks. She spoke to the eagle as she approached. The eagle's gaze landed on Alexander, and though it didn't focus on Emmarie, it responded to her inquiry.

Emmarie spun around, her dark eyes wider than they'd been moments before. "Alex, he's here for you." She was breathless.

I glanced at my brother. He eyed the eagle warily, then turned to Emmarie. "Why?"

The eagle responded with a series of shrill cries. Its gaze never wavered from Alexander.

Emmarie nodded in understanding. "His name is Galewing, and he has been chosen by the council of eagles to be your…ambassador? I'm uncertain if that's the correct term." She frowned for a moment, then continued. "He says it has been over four hundred years since the council deemed a mage worthy of an ambassador. He is honored to have been selected as yours."

Alexander shook his head. "I don't understand."

Rynn strode toward him but remained just beyond arm's length. "Every mage-warrior was said to have a gray eagle as an ally. What we know of those days is captured in the histories, in tales passed down from previous generations. None of us fully understands what this means, but it *is* significant. Go to him."

He looked at the others, uncertain and bewildered, then finally turned to me. "Andrew, I don't know what to do."

I smiled and motioned to Galewing. "There is only one way to find out what this means, and that's to go to him as Rynn suggested. You'll be a mage-warrior, and if this is part of your role, what can it hurt?" I kept my tone light, though I shared his anxiety.

He chewed on his lower lip, then drew a breath. It was clear he was uncomfortable with the situation, but he began to move hesitantly toward the eagle. As he drew near, Galewing ruffled his wings in anticipation. The eagle released another cry just as Alexander stopped in front of him.

"He says you will form a bond," Emmarie translated. "You won't need me to speak for him once you do. You will have…an understanding."

Alexander turned to her, helplessness written across his features. "What must I do?"

The eagle's cry pierced the air once more, and he took to the air briefly, only to land on Alexander's shoulder. Alexander stumbled, surprised at the action and unprepared for the bird's weight. As he recovered his balance, Galewing arched his neck and touched his forehead to Alexander's temple. A moment later, Galewing leapt into the air to resume his perch on the wall of snow. Alexander stood unmoving for some time, staring at the bird, his expression unreadable and his eyes wide.

I moved forward, concerned for my brother's well-being, but stopped when Rynn grasped my forearm in her icy grip. "I think we should leave Alexander alone for a time. He needs to process what happened."

I frowned. "And what *did* happen?" I asked, unable to keep frustration from seeping into my tone.

"It's as Emmarie said," Chela replied from a few feet away. "He has formed a bond with the eagle. They are coming to know one another."

I shook my head, mystified and confused, then turned away to begin packing my belongings and breaking down the tent. I hoped Alexander would explain his experience. Surrounded by so many magi, I was an outsider, and it left me impatient and irritable. I would never comprehend their experiences, and as I was continually forced to remind them, I had not grown up in an area where magic was allowed and embraced.

I did my best to avoid becoming bitter, but with each new magical anomaly that came our way, my frustration mounted. None of the women had taken the time to explain half of my questions, and this business with Galewing was yet another instance where I was left grasping for answers while they remained shrouded in mystery.

Seething, I focused my attention on my tent, then moved on to the one Lydia shared with Emmarie. Their belongings were already stowed in the cart, which left only the task of dismantling it for travel. I glanced at my brother once I'd finished. Alexander remained unmoving.

I swallowed a litany of curses and continued my work.

As I stowed Chela's tent in the cart, Alexander turned away from the eagle and fell to his knees. Ignoring the cries of the others, I ran to him and knelt at his side. His face was pale and drawn, but he offered me a smile all the same.

"It's the strangest thing, brother," he said with a shake of his head. "I know what Galewing wants, what he *feels*. He senses the same from me. I never imagined anything like *this* was possible."

"Believe me when I say I feel the same," I replied dryly. "This entire journey seems a thing of folklore. And yet, here we are."

Alexander chuckled. "You should know better than I what it means to be an object of folklore, Lord Dragon."

I rolled my eyes, exasperated. "Never call me that, Alex."

He shrugged, undeterred, and flashed a grin. "Perhaps my jest was in poor taste, but my point remains the same. You are just as much a strange part of this journey as Galewing or the magi around us." His grin widened. "I wouldn't change it for the world."

I nodded as I rose to my feet. It was a rare occurrence when Alexander was compelled to reassure me, but I was thankful he'd done so. My previous ire evaporated, and I forced a tight smile.

Perhaps he was right, and I had a place within the group, after all.

NINETEEN

The weather steadily improved as we descended from the mountains, as did my mood. I found myself spending more time speaking with Rynn than I'd anticipated. It was comforting to have someone I could talk with while Alexander spent his time with Lydia and Emmarie spent hers with Galewing or the local wildlife. I'd begun to consider her a tentative friend.

By the fifth day out from the Frostwake, the snow was a mere memory. Our surroundings appeared to be in the final fading stages of late summer; the trees were leafy, the grass was green, the weather calm. The terrain began to level out, the air was warmer, and everyone in our party was in better spirits. In the far distance, I could make out the glimmer of a large body of water as the sun's rays danced across its surface; a lake, I believed. It was late afternoon, and we'd be stopping to make camp soon, but I mentioned the lake to Chela anyway.

She adjusted the brim of her hat, then shielded her eyes with one hand from the sun. "Your vision must be far better than mine. I can't see it yet, but it's Lake Dwymm. A city of the same name lies on the far side. It's our next destination."

"Dwymm is my hometown," Rynn said after a moment. "Like your brother, I was on the pilgrimage when last I was there." She tilted her head to one side thoughtfully, but her eyes twinkled with unspoken amusement. "I didn't tell my brothers I'd be visiting from the mountains. I wonder what they'll do when I appear on their doorstep unannounced?"

"You plan to visit your family while we're there?" Chela asked, clearly surprised.

Rynn shrugged. "Why shouldn't I? I've kept to the Frostwake for long enough. And they know of my…condition. They'll keep their distance. But it will be nice to see them again. It has been too long."

"You'll have time," Chela replied. "Alexander will be in the trials for a day or two at least."

At the mention of Alexander, I looked ahead to where he walked hand-in-hand with Lydia. Galewing was gone, presumably to hunt, and the two were taking the time for themselves. The eagle's presence was still something of a mystery to me, though Alexander had attempted to explain the connection between himself and the raptor. The gray eagles had made a pledge to the magi of ancient times; an eagle would be chosen to accompany each mage-warrior, and upon first meeting, a life-long bond would be forged between the two.

Alexander described the bond as something sensed within his mind. It was an almost tangible thing, something he was not only aware of, but could physically see and feel. I didn't understand and doubted I ever would, though I tried.

The eagle's presence was a source of continued wonder for the magi and Emmarie. Each had heard legends of the gray eagles, but this was the first time one of the proud birds had deigned to descend from the heights to interact with one of their own. Emmarie had spoken at length with Galewing as well, delighted to be the first Merael in generations to have done so. Galewing appeared endlessly patient, but it was impossible to determine emotion from his keen yellow-eyed gaze. Alexander assured us Galewing was pleased to accompany us, and the eagle was as curious about us as we were of him.

We made camp that night some distance away from Dwymm. The lake was only just visible to the others when Chela indicated we should stop. The night passed peacefully, and we departed the next morning before the sun had risen more than a handspan above the horizon. Alexander was restless until we were on the road, eager to begin his next trial.

"Dwymm is home to the Red Pyramid," Rynn said.

She'd chosen to walk alongside me at the head of the column that morning. Alexander and Lydia were not far behind, speaking quietly. Chela and the cart brought up the rear, and Emmarie walked alongside her, deep in conversation with Galewing, who perched on its railing.

"Is there something significant about the shrine?" I asked.

She shrugged. "It's no different than any of the others you've visited. Perhaps it seems more important to me since it resides in my hometown." Her gaze traveled to the distant sparkle of sunlight reflecting off the surface of the lake, her expression melancholy.

I studied her for a time, considering the source of her troubled demeanor. After a time, she looked up, startled I'd been watching her. I averted my gaze and felt my face flush.

"I know you've been away from your home for many years," I said slowly, eyes fixed on the horizon. "But I feel there's something more to your story." When she sighed, I knew my assumption was correct. "You can trust me."

"I suppose I owe you that much. After all, you've shared your story." She frowned and stared down at her boots.

"I'll help if I'm able," I offered.

She laughed. "You should not offer your services so readily. You may regret the kindness in the end. You don't understand what you've just promised." She shook her head, amused.

I shrugged. "Nevertheless, the offer has been made."

She frowned slightly. "We hardly know one another, and yet you offer to help me with a problem you know nothing of. Why?"

I didn't have a reason; I simply wanted to help. I would have done the same for any of the others.

"I'd help anyone in our group if asked."

"Hmm." Her gaze traveled to the distant lake once more. "Your unexpected kindness is touching, but it may prove your downfall should someone wish to exploit it. Given everything you and Alex have been through, I'm surprised you remain so trusting. I wouldn't be."

"If you weren't a mage and hadn't been instructed by the Oracle to follow us, I would never have offered," I replied. "Colin would never employ a mage to pursue me. He'd sooner execute someone bearing the Mark than speak with them. It's those who lack magic we must be wary of. I don't believe I have anything to fear from you."

She turned to face me once more, a faint smile playing upon her lips. "Those are words few have uttered in my presence since I completed my trials eleven years ago. None have yet been able to stand by such a claim… But you aren't like them." Her eyes narrowed as she raked them across my form. "You aren't boasting. You truly believe I can't harm you."

"I'm not affected by the cold, Rynn. Besides, if I can't withstand an assault in this form, I'll shift. As a dragon, I'm stronger in every way."

"I know, and perhaps that's what I'm afraid of." She grimaced and looked away. "While I'd like to visit my brothers in Dwymm, there is still the matter of my father… We haven't spoken since I left for the Citadel. He knew I bore the Mark, but he hoped I wouldn't pursue this path. He arranged a marriage for me—one I didn't want, I might add—in an attempt to keep me in Dwymm. When I learned what he'd done, I was livid. I left that night, determined to make it to the Citadel on my own. I couldn't remain here, knowing that I could do something more with my life."

"Why did he try to prevent you from becoming a mage?" I asked.

Since coming through the Mage's Gate, Alexander and I had been regaled with stories of the magi. The people we'd met were in awe of magic if they weren't Marked themselves. Rynn's story contradicted every tale we'd been told, and if I was going to help her as I'd promised, I needed to understand why.

"My father had two siblings, both of whom were Marked," she replied. "His elder brother died during his pilgrimage. His sister survived half of the trials, but was lost to the madness. I don't know what became of her." She paused to gather her thoughts. "I believe he wanted to keep me safe, but his methods were flawed. I needed to choose my own path, to see for myself what I was capable of. He didn't understand."

"You hope to see him again, but you're uncertain how to approach him."

She nodded. "The last message I received from my brothers bore troubling news. Father's health is fading, and I want to visit him one last time. Even if it means reliving my past anger." Her shoulders slumped, and she seemed to deflate. "I wanted to see my brothers first. Perhaps they can prepare me for what might ensue when I visit my father." She peered at me, and I could see a plan forming in her mind. "Perhaps there is something you *can* do, Andrew."

"Tell me."

"My brothers have indicated that our father lamented what I've become. He referred to my attunement, of course. Perhaps if they are made to see there *is* someone I can interact with normally, he'll be less…disappointed." She bit her lower lip, eyes pleading. "Would you…accompany me?"

I hesitated. She was right; we didn't know one another well, and to be introduced to her family… The very notion was awkward.

"You won't have to do anything," she implored. "I only need you to be there, so they can see I'm not isolated any longer. I'll speak to them and make them understand that I don't have to remain—" She stopped abruptly and flushed crimson before drawing a breath with a shake of her head. "What I mean to say is, I'm not relegated to the Frostwake any longer."

I wanted to know what she'd been going to say before she stopped herself, but I didn't press her. If she needed my presence when she met with her father, it was something I could provide—and I'd given my word that I'd help. She'd already offered to fight alongside us when we left to face Colin, and assisting her with this matter was paltry in comparison. I'd survived worse social interactions while married to Claire.

"I'll accompany you," I replied evenly.

A sudden smile illuminated her face and she clapped her hands together in delight. "Oh, thank you, Andrew! You don't know how much this means to me."

Dwymm was ringed by a wooden palisade, and armed guards were stationed at the entrances when we arrived that afternoon. We learned it was a precaution against a violent band of brigands that had taken up residence in the hills nearby.

"It became necessary to build the palisade a year ago," Rynn said. "When I was a child, we had no such concerns. I don't know what has drawn the brigands' attention here."

"There have always been brigands in the Great Marsh," Chela replied. "Perhaps they've moved north where the climate is more pleasant."

Rynn nodded, though she appeared distracted. I knew she was concerned about meeting her family, but since she hadn't mentioned it to the others, I held my tongue.

"You're likely correct," she said and allowed the subject to drop.

Chela led us to an inn near the heart of the city. As we drew near, the top of the Red Pyramid became visible, rising above the other buildings that comprised Dwymm. It was exactly as its name described; a large, four-sided pyramid constructed of crimson stone. The remainder of the city was built of wood or gray brick, which made the pyramid all the more prominent.

Alexander announced he would present himself at the pyramid immediately. Galewing shrieked his approval and took to the sky while Alexander and Lydia departed, leaving the rest of us to settle into our rooms. I helped Chela stable the horse before carrying Alexander's personal effects up to the room we were to share on the third floor.

When I arrived, Rynn awaited me. She leaned against the doorframe as though she'd been there for some time. She straightened as I approached, but said nothing while I stowed my brother's belongings.

"I think it's best if I visit my brothers today," she said. "They'll be furious if they learn I didn't come immediately."

I nodded and followed her outside. She led me through Dwymm toward the lakeshore.

"They're fishermen," she explained as we began to thread our way through a congested marketplace. "Petyr is older than I am and has a family of his own. He should have returned from the lake by now and should be at home. Syllas is the youngest. When he last wrote to me, he'd taken to selling the days' catch here in the market." She glanced at the various vendors and their wares, but we had not yet come upon any men offering fresh fish.

"Do you think he'll be here?" I asked.

"I don't know. Syllas has never been predictable. He may be here, or he may be at home. Who can say until we find him?" She laughed, seemingly carefree. "Syllas writes to me most often. He was the only one who supported my decision to become a mage. Syllas will be glad to see me, though Petyr will likely keep his distance. He thinks I betrayed our father by leaving as I did, but I hope time has tempered his anger. He has written to me more often over the past few years, and I want to believe it's a sign of his acceptance."

I hoped for her sake it was; she'd seemed genuinely distressed by the rift within her family, and it was clear she blamed herself for its formation.

I admired her determination to follow her own path. It was not something I'd been afforded while in Novania—even Alexander hadn't been allowed to choose his future. Our paths had been determined almost since birth, and if Carlton had still been in power, our lives would have continued as they once had—I as the former soldier and Alexander as the prince, both duty-bound to our roles and the terms of tradition.

Rynn proved adept at avoiding contact with others, even in the crowded confines of the marketplace. She'd donned a pair of leather gloves, though if the tales she'd told were true, I was doubtful of their effectiveness. I followed her through the crowd, having little trouble keeping sight of her since I was at least a head taller than everyone we passed.

As the lakeshore came into view at the far end of the market, we came upon several merchants trading in fresh fish. Rynn slowed her pace to examine each stall before moving on to the next. Syllas was not present.

Rynn continued, undeterred. She led me along the lakeshore toward a collection of quaint homes clustered at the end of the long wooden pier. A pair of small fishing boats were tied on one side, and two young boys perched along the opposite edge, fishing poles in hand. A man sat on the steps outside the nearest home mending a fishing net, while another worked in the yard, splitting a stack of firewood.

Rynn glanced at me briefly, grinned, and quickened her pace. "Fortune is with us today. Both of my brothers are home. Petyr is mending the net, and Syllas is cutting wood. The boys on the pier must be Petyr's sons."

As we approached the fishermen's homes, Petyr set aside the net and stood, shading his eyes against the sun's glare. His eyes widened as he called to the other man. Both sported the same light blond hair and vibrantly blue eyes as Rynn. They kept their hair cropped short, but it was still distinctly curly, and the younger of the pair sported a bushy beard.

"Damn me, brother, but I think our long-lost sister has finally come home to pay us a visit!" Petyr laughed and strode toward Rynn. He stopped a few paces away, uncertain how to approach her. But he smiled and appeared pleased she was there.

Syllas set aside his axe and jogged to our location. "Rynn!" He strode past his older brother, but stopped before he touched her. "Damn, but I wish I could give you a hug," he said after a moment. "I know I can't based on what you've told us."

"I'm glad to be here, however briefly," Rynn replied. "I've missed you both." She looked down, an array of emotions playing across her features.

"It's apparent you're a mage, but you haven't changed a bit otherwise," Petyr stated, peering at her over Syllas' shoulder. His keen gaze flicked up to meet mine. "Who is your companion?"

Rynn straightened and gestured to me. "This is Andrew Caein. He's accompanying his brother along the pilgrimage as the mage's guardian."

Syllas narrowed his eyes briefly as he considered her words while Petyr nodded a greeting.

"I can see you're thinking, Sy," Rynn teased, arching an eyebrow.

"You've said many times you were unable to leave the Frostwake until the Oracle's vision came to pass," Syllas replied. "Does your appearance here mean—?"

Rynn laughed and cut him off. "Yes, the vision has been fulfilled. I no longer have to remain at the Frostwake, though my time here will be short. Once Andrew's brother has finished his trial, we'll be leaving again."

"Rynn, may we speak privately for a moment?" Petyr asked, and when she nodded, he motioned her to follow him into the nearest house.

Syllas remained outside for a few moments, studying me closely with a piercing gaze. "She's been waiting for the day she could leave the Frostwake for many years, you know," he said before he disappeared into the house with his siblings.

Left alone, I walked toward the lakeshore and the accompanying pier to gaze across the water. The surface sparkled in the afternoon sunlight; it was calm, serene, and smooth as glass.

"Who are you, mister?" I turned at the sound of the child's voice, and found I'd captured the attention of the two boys fishing on the pier. Both had the same light blond hair and blue eyes as Rynn's family.

I smiled at them. "My name is Andrew," I replied, amused. "How's the catch today?"

The younger boy shrugged. "We caught one fish earlier. Uncle Sy said it would be slow going from the shore today."

The other made a face at his brother. "And father said we ought to try anyway. You never know when a fish might bite."

His tone became superior while he spoke to his younger sibling, and I chuckled. Alexander and Thomas had been similar when they'd been the same age.

"Who was the lady?" the younger boy asked. "The one who went inside with father and Uncle Sy?"

"Her name is Rynn," I replied. "She's your aunt, if I'm not mistaken."

The two looked at one another with wide eyes, clearly excited, and immediately abandoned their fishing equipment. They raced the length of the pier toward the house. It was apparent they'd heard of their aunt and were eager to meet her, though I knew Rynn and her brothers most likely didn't need their interruption.

"Wait!" I called, jogging to catch up. They stopped halfway up the stairs leading to the door of the house. "We should give them a few minutes alone. I imagine they have much to discuss."

The boys looked at one another and seemed to come to an unspoken agreement. The oldest nodded once, then sat down heavily on the wooden steps, his younger brother following suit a moment later. I smiled; the two seemed to have a relationship not unlike the one I shared with Alexander.

"Did you travel here with our aunt?" the younger one asked, quivering with excitement. "My pa says she's a mage. I've never met her."

I nodded. "I met her at the Frostwake, and we traveled here with my brother and a few others."

They shared a knowing glance, and the elder of the two spoke up. "Is your brother a mage?" he asked eagerly. "My name's Darynn, by the way."

I laughed, reveling in their enthusiasm. "Yes, my brother is becoming a mage. He's here for his trial."

The younger boy bounced up from his seat, unable to remain still any longer. "My name's Altynn. If you're with your brother, does that mean you're a guardian? We saw you walking to the house earlier, and I said to Darynn that you were bigger than our pa. And our pa is one of the tallest men in Dwymm! You look like you should be a guardian."

Laughing again, I nodded. "Yes, I'm Alexander's guardian."

Darynn rose from his seat, and the two began to pepper me with questions so rapidly I could only manage brief answers before the next was delivered. Did I have a sword? Had I fought any brigands? What was the Frostwake like? Were the trials difficult? Where had we come from? Could I teach them how to swing a sword? Had we met the Oracle? On and on it went, with the two boys racing across the small yard, bounding in circles in their excitement.

I had little experience with children, but I was enjoying the brief time I had with them. They were curious and excitable, thrilled with the prospect of news from outside, and eager for tales of adventure.

We were interrupted when the door to the house slammed open, banging hard against the wooden siding. My back was to the house, but I spun to find Rynn striding down the steps, her head down, anguish on her fair features. Tears spilled from her eyes, freezing moments later on her cheeks. She walked directly toward me and collapsed into my arms, where she began to sob uncontrollably.

I was stunned. I didn't know what had occurred to upset her so badly, and I was uncertain how to comfort her. Awkwardly, I put my hand across her shoulders as she buried her face against my shoulder. I looked over her head toward the door. Syllas and Petyr stood on the steps watching us carefully. Both men appeared aggrieved as well.

"Rynn," I said gently, looking down at her head full of curls, "what happened?"

She sniffed loudly and looked up at me, her eyes rimmed in red. Where her face had touched my vest, the tears had melted, but they rapidly refroze as she pulled away. "I've come too late, Andrew. I've come here too late!" Her voice broke, and she began to sob once more.

Helplessly, I looked up at her brothers. Petyr had drawn nearer, though he remained beyond arm's length of his sister. Syllas gathered the two boys and ushered them inside where they would not become a nuisance.

"Our father passed away ten days ago," Petyr explained, his voice roughened with emotion. "We asked Rynn to travel from the Frostwake as soon as she was able, though we knew she may not reach us in time." He reached one hand toward her, then drew it back. Even in her grief, he could not risk touching her. He sighed heavily and dropped the hand to his side.

It was several minutes before Rynn regained her composure. She pulled away from me and apologized for placing me in an awkward situation. I understood why she'd come to me, though; in her grief, she wanted—*needed*—to feel human contact, and there was no one else who could provide it.

"I understand what it's like to lose a parent," I said gently. "The grief can be overwhelming. You need not apologize."

Blinking away a fresh wave of tears, she nodded. "I knew you would understand, but all the same, I should have said something before throwing myself into your embrace. But my brothers can't…" Her voice cracked, and she looked down at the ground between her boots, refusing to make eye contact.

"Let's go inside," Petyr said after a moment of tense silence. "Myra will be home from the market any time, and perhaps you can share a meal with us. It seems my boys have already taken a liking to you, Andrew. They can be incessant with their questions if you allow it." He smiled wearily. "There are many days I wish I had half the energy they possess."

I agreed and guided Rynn inside. She was distraught, continually fighting off more tears, her heart broken at the news she'd come too late to reconcile with her father. The two boys, sensing her grief, remained quiet at first, then ventured toward her after a while. When their curiosity could no longer be contained, Altynn initiated the next round of questions. Their youthful enthusiasm drew Rynn from her despair as she began to speak with them.

We learned Altynn also bore the Mark, though his was small. He proudly rolled up his left sleeve to reveal the crescent on his bicep. The coloration was different than Alexander's; Altynn's was purplish, almost the color of a bruise.

"I'm going to be a mage one day, too," he declared with a grin. "Can I see your Mark, auntie?"

Rynn laughed. "I'm afraid not," she replied. "It covers the whole of my back, and you don't want to see that, do you?"

Altynn's face fell, but he snapped his head up a split second later, his eyes meeting mine. I was seated beside Rynn on a cushioned bench, a mere observer.

"What about your brother's?" he asked eagerly. "He has a Mark. Do you think he would let me see it?"

I laughed. "Perhaps, but you'll have to ask him," I replied. "He's in the pyramid even as we speak, so it may be a few days before you'll have the chance."

Altynn nodded vigorously. "I will! Does he look like you? I'll wait at the pyramid for him and then—"

"You will do no such thing," Petyr interjected from across the room, though he smiled. "Perhaps Andrew will be kind enough to introduce you to his brother. You don't need to go stalking the poor man." He shook his head, amused. "Myra informs me that supper is ready, so please, join us in the kitchen."

"Food!" Darynn cried happily and raced from the room, nearly crashing headlong into his father's legs. Altynn followed his older brother moments later, though he avoided any near-collisions.

Rynn laughed wearily as she stood up. "Thank you, Pete," she said. "I've been dreading this meeting, fearing what the outcome would be. I know you never approved of my decision, just as father never did. But you've shown me great kindness, and your sons are beautiful."

Petyr smiled as he ushered us toward the kitchen and the delicious aromas emanating from within.

"Sy always believed you should have had a say in father's plans," he said after a moment. "I understand why you left, though I also understand why father hoped you'd remain here. He feared for you. But seeing you today has been a wonderful thing. Don't berate yourself for being unable to come home sooner. We understand you are obligated to follow the Oracle's direction. We harbor no anger toward you."

She nodded, and I noted the spark that usually danced in her eyes was beginning to return. The interaction with her family had been welcome, even though they mourned their loss.

"You don't know how much your words mean to me, Pete. If I were able, I would hug you right now."

He smiled. "We also understand why you can't, but it gladdens my heart to know there is someone in the world you can turn to." He flicked a glance in my direction, his expression meaningful.

I shrugged and feigned ignorance to his supposition. I'd acted as needed, and I would have done the same for any of the others we traveled with. Rynn was a friend, but I doubted she'd become anything more.

TWENTY

Alexander remained in his trials for another two days. Rynn spent most of that time with her brothers and nephews, reacquainting herself with the family she'd long been separated from. When she returned to the fishermen's pier on the first day alone, her nephews were sorely disappointed. She asked me to return with her on the second day and to bring along the practice swords I used when sparring with Emmarie. It seemed the two boys were desperate to learn a bit of swordplay before our departure. When Emmarie learned of our plans, she insisted on coming as well; she would not relinquish an opportunity to hone her skills.

When we arrived at the pier, we were met by Syllas and his two nephews. Petyr was out on the lake, and Myra was perched on the steps of their home, mending a fishing net as she watched her sons chase one another around their small yard. I introduced Emmarie, who was an immediate object of fascination—they'd never met a Merael. She was rapidly inundated with queries by the curious youngsters.

Rynn sat near Myra and began working on the net, keeping her distance from the other woman while she and Syllas chatted. She was in better spirits, though at times, the deep ache of sorrow was reflected in her sapphire eyes. I knew she'd be grieving for some time, and I vowed I'd be there to see her through it. I understood grief better than most.

I stepped toward Darynn and Altynn, brandishing the pair of practice swords I'd brought along. The boys released whoops of anticipation, eager to begin. I knew they weren't serious about learning the art of the sword, but I hoped it would prove a welcome diversion if I indulged them. Rynn needed time to speak with her brother without interruption.

We began with a demonstration. I sparred with Emmarie for a time while the boys observed. Darynn's attention was rapt, though Altynn's flagged. Darynn took a turn next, and while Altynn fidgeted impatiently for his opportunity, he rapidly surrendered his blade to his brother. Swordplay clearly wasn't to his liking.

The day passed pleasantly. I felt almost at home amongst the fishermen, something I had not experienced since my last days at Vinterry. They were good folk; hard-working, stalwart, and always ready with a smile and a laugh.

Chela arrived unexpectedly during the afternoon. She was introduced to Rynn's family, but insisted she could not stay.

"I've only come to tell you that Alex has returned," she said. "He's resting, but mentioned he'll be ready to depart in the morning."

With an inexplicable sense of melancholy, I said my goodbyes to Petyr and Syllas and thanked them for allowing me to spend the day with them. Darynn and Altynn were unhappy to see us leave and begged their father for practice swords of their own.

Rynn was silent and contemplative while we navigated the marketplace and made our way back to the inn, but Emmarie chattered animatedly. She'd enjoyed her time with the boys immensely and, I suspected, had been thrilled at the opportunity to demonstrate her new-found skills. I nodded distractedly as she spoke, but didn't truly hear her words. Rynn's sudden shift in demeanor concerned me.

Rynn grasped my elbow and drew me aside as we reached the inn. "I must speak with you a moment. Let's go to the green space beyond the inn where it isn't as noisome."

She held my arm until we reached the grassy lawn that spanned the distance between the inn and the Red Pyramid. Trees grew along the perimeter of the green space, providing a sense of privacy within the busy city's center. It was empty of people when we arrived, and it was peaceful, quiet, almost serene.

Rynn released my arm only when she was certain we were alone, but seemed reluctant to do so. When she turned to face me, I was struck by the intensity of her gaze.

"I must travel with you wherever your path may lead, but the last few days have been wonderful, and I'd like to return here again one day. I've been away from my family far too long. I've sorely missed them."

I frowned, puzzled. Why was she compelled to reiterate what I already knew? I welcomed her assistance along Alexander's journey—and beyond if she was willing—but I would never stand in her way if she wanted to visit her family. I understood the yearning, the need to be surrounded by loved ones. She was free to see them as often as she wished.

After a moment, she released an explosive sigh. "It's difficult to leave so soon after our reunion," she explained. "If I were able, I'd stay here forever. But I can't. It's my duty to accompany you, even after your brother's trials are complete. The Oracle's vision may not have stated it in such bold terms, but I can *feel* it, Andrew. My place is with you."

"What are you trying to say?"

I took a step back, placing distance between us as the moment became awkward. I wanted to escape, to return to the inn and speak with Alexander. It was an excuse, one she'd see through in an instant, but I wasn't prepared for this. My wounds were too raw, and it was too soon.

She laughed merrily, breaking the tension. "What I meant to say is I know I must continue to travel with you. You've both expressed the desire to return to Novania and confront your brother. I will be there to help as I may. It's the Oracle's will. I assure you, I meant nothing more."

She wouldn't meet my gaze. I knew she wasn't completely truthful, but it wasn't an outright lie, either. I pushed my misgivings aside and focused on what I believed was true—she would keep her promise and prove a staunch ally when we marched north to face Colin.

"I'd like to return to the inn," I said after a moment. "I'd like to speak with my brother."

She nodded. "Of course. I've kept you away too long as it is."

Alexander was asleep when we returned and didn't awaken until after noon the following day. Lydia scarcely let him out of her sight, and I began to fear something had occurred during his latest trial that was a cause for concern. When I pressed her for answers, she claimed Alexander was well, and there was no reason to worry. Yet her behavior led me to believe otherwise.

We didn't depart that day as planned, but prepared to do so the next day. Syllas, Petyr, and his two sons met us outside the inn as dawn broke and we loaded our belongings into the cart. They'd come to say a final goodbye to Rynn, who was overcome with emotion.

When Alexander emerged from the inn, Altynn rushed toward him without introduction. "Can I see your Mark? Andrew said you're a mage!"

Alexander, bewildered by his enthusiasm, lifted his eyebrows and turned to me. "Brother…?"

"Altynn," I said evenly as I knelt in front of him, "Alex doesn't know of our conversation. I haven't had the opportunity to talk with him."

Altynn pouted, and for a moment, I feared he'd burst into tears. He clenched his jaw, then nodded and stared at me expectantly. I explained the situation, while Altynn pushed up his sleeve to reveal his own Mark.

Alexander laughed once he understood. "I suppose I can show you since you've been so kind as to show off your own." He grinned at Altynn, who bounced on his toes with unabashed excitement.

"Thank you! Auntie Rynn wouldn't show me her Mark, and I have never seen someone else's, only my own." Altynn turned to stick his tongue out at Rynn, who shook her head and laughed.

I stepped back to observe the interaction between Altynn and Alexander. Alexander unbuttoned his shirt and pulled the fabric aside so the boy could see the Mark emblazoned across his torso. Altynn tilted his head to one side thoughtfully while he studied it.

"It's not the same color as mine," he said, confused. "And it's so *big!*"

We shared a laugh as Alexander buttoned his shirt once more. "I've been told the coloration has something to do with the nature of your power," he told the boy. "Mine is shades of gray and white, and I'm on the path to becoming a mage-warrior. Yours is another color, meaning your ability is different than my own."

Altynn nodded, his small face remarkably solemn. "Thank you." He turned to face Rynn, who stood alongside his father. "Do you see, auntie? Alexander showed me his Mark like I wanted! I like him better than you." He stuck out his tongue again, then broke into a peal of laughter.

Interacting with Altynn and Darynn had been far more enjoyable than I'd imagined. They would no doubt grow up to be fine young men one day, and it was heartening to see they still had some of their childhood left ahead of them. I thought of Vera and her lasting desire to have children—even if that meant we'd adopted them from an orphanage. To my sorrow, we never had the opportunity before she perished, and without her, I doubted I'd ever entertain the notion again.

Perhaps one day, Alexander and Lydia would have a family of their own. I could imagine spending time with nieces or nephews, of sharing tales of my adventures with them. But I would never have children of my own.

Rynn made a final round of goodbyes to her brothers and promised to return when she was able.

Before they left for the lakeshore, Syllas drew me aside. "Please take care of Rynn for us," he said. "She's more fragile than she lets on, and she has come to rely on you. I hope I can as well."

I blinked in surprise, then managed a stiff nod. "I'll see that she remains safe," I promised.

What had Rynn told her brothers of me? What did they believe I was to her?

We reached a crossroads that afternoon. A small and tidy inn was located nearby. We'd stay for the night, rather than press forward. It would give us time to decide which path to take before we reached the fork in the road ahead. As we settled into the common room for supper, the discussion grew heated.

"If the southeastern road is safer, why would anyone bother taking the other route?" Lydia asked. "I myself took the canyon path, and even in early summer, the heat was not unbearable. And we're well past the hottest days of the year."

Alexander scowled and crossed his arms. "The marshlands would prove treacherous for someone trying to pursue us. While I don't relish the idea of trekking through the muck, it may be in our best interest to do so." He scratched at the back of his neck and tossed his head. "Holy hell, we've been over this."

She narrowed her eyes as they flashed in momentary anger. "We can make better time reaching the next shrine if we take the canyon road. The faster we travel, the less likely it will be that Colin's men reach us."

"Men passed through the Frostwake ahead of us," I cut in. "They may already be lying in wait, ready to spring their trap. I have no doubt they were more of Colin's cronies, and I will not see Alexander walk into an ambush."

Alexander snorted. "Good. Walking into ambushes is *your* specialty, Andrew."

I suppressed a growl, irritated by his harsh tone.

Lydia's eyes blazed. "How long have you known this? This is the first I've heard of it, and we should have known before leaving the Frostwake!"

While I had relayed my conversation with Rynn to Alexander, I'd assumed he'd tell Lydia. The two had grown so close that I was surprised she *didn't* know. I glanced at Alexander, who looked down at his half-empty plate and reddened. Lydia took note of his reaction and fixed him with an icy stare.

"You knew and didn't bother to inform me?" she demanded, incensed. "After all we've been through together, the two of you still harbor secrets!" She rose from the table, her hands visibly shaking with rage. "We will discuss this later. *At length.* I've had enough of this for one day." She spun on her heel and strode across the room toward the stairs leading to the guest quarters.

An awkward silence descended over the table. I sensed there was more to the argument than what had just occurred. Lydia's outburst was decidedly out of character, and though I wanted to pry, I held my tongue.

Chela stood up not long afterwards, pushing her plate away. "I'll tend Sienna," she murmured. Emmarie offered to assist her, and the two departed, leaving Alexander, myself, and Rynn at the table.

"Would you like me to speak with her?" Rynn asked. "I believe I understand why she's upset."

He shook his head miserably. "No, that won't be necessary. I'll speak with her."

I flicked my glaze between the two. "Alex, what's going on?"

He sighed heavily. "I never told Lydia the full story of what happened between myself and the Oracle. I've been feeling guilty, so I finally shared the truth. I truly believed she'd understand… I didn't mean for it to cause a rift between us, but she's furious. She's scarcely said a word since this morning."

I nodded my understanding. Though most of the magi we'd met believed his liaison with the Oracle was an honor, Alexander had left the encounter feeling utterly used. I didn't blame him, but clearly, Lydia did.

I frowned. "I suppose I don't fully understand her reasoning. You didn't know what the Oracle wanted when you agreed to spend time with her, and I was witness to your bitterness afterward."

Alexander barked a laugh. "I still resent her for it, but that wasn't enough. I must find some way to placate Lydia. I love her. I don't want this to drive us apart."

"She's angry you'll have a child with the Oracle before you'll have one with her," Rynn interjected. "She cares for you as much—if not more—than you care for her. Your confession wounded her deeply. The news you both knew of the men at the Frostwake pushed her beyond the limit of tolerance. My advice to you, my friend, is to give her time to think things over. Leave her be for now, and when she's ready to speak to you, she will. No doubt she'll be in a calmer state of mind by then."

"I didn't tell her about the Frostwake because I didn't want her to worry needlessly," Alexander explained. "Holy hell, I can't win in this situation! Andrew, you've been married twice. What do you suggest?"

I arched an eyebrow. "Lydia is a different woman than either Claire or Vera were," I replied slowly. "I think Rynn's advice is sound, though if you're prepared with an apology, it will do much to appease her."

"But I've already apologized—more than once!" Alexander pounded his fist on the tabletop in frustration. "Simply telling her I'm sincerely sorry *again* is not going to have an effect."

"Let me explain, brother," I said evenly. "An apology can consist of more than simple words. Do something for her that she's been waiting for, or perhaps give her a gift. Be thoughtful and considerate. She'll be pleased with your efforts."

Alexander sighed and ran one hand through his hair. "I'll think on it, but I don't know what I can do *here*. Perhaps something will come to mind if I give it some time." He glanced around the room, then stood. "I'd like to take a walk and clear my head."

Rynn rose swiftly from her seat. "I'll join you. We know there are at least two men seeking us. We shouldn't go off alone." She fixed me in her piercing gaze. "If we haven't returned in an hour, we've gone north along the road we traveled earlier in the day. I trust you will come looking should we be late."

When I nodded, she motioned for Alexander to follow. He appeared bewildered, but made his way outside with Rynn. I suspected she had come up with an idea; she'd been speaking to Lydia for a good portion of the day. It was unsurprising, now that I understood the spat between Lydia and Alexander. Lydia held a wary dislike of Chela, and Emmarie was still too young to fully understand such relationships, so she'd turned to Rynn.

I remained in the common room where I could observe the other patrons while I awaited their return. There were only a handful of other guests at the inn, and all seemed familiar with the servers and barmaids. They were locals, farmers perhaps. The men who pursued us would have been strangers. If they were near, they weren't at the inn.

When Alexander and Rynn returned a half-hour later, Alexander went directly to the stairs and bounded up two at a time. Rynn rejoined me at the table. I gave her a questioning look, hoping she'd tell me what had transpired outside.

"Your brother has little experience with women, it seems," she said with a chuckle. "The poor man didn't fully understand why Lydia reacted as she did. I've set him on a path to make it right." She flashed a grin, her eyes glittering in the semi-darkness.

"Before we fled Novania, Alex kept as much distance as he could muster between himself and most women," I replied. "He feared what would happen should someone see his Mark."

"Oh, I understand the situation," she replied. "I hope my advice helps him mend the hurt he's inadvertently caused. Did you know he has not yet told her he loves her?" She shook her head, amused. "It's no wonder she's furious."

I arched an eyebrow, surprised by the news. "I hope you told him he'd best tell her."

Rynn laughed. "Of course I did." Her expression became serious, and she studied me intently for a moment. "I also advised him to tell her of his intentions. He says he will wed her after he completes his trials, but I doubt she's aware of it. She deserves to know."

I nodded. "That she does. I hope they're able to reconcile tonight. While I haven't seen anyone who looks out of place, I still believe the men you saw at the Frostwake have something planned for us. Or, rather, for me. We don't need infighting to distract us from the true dangers ahead."

"I agree," she replied. "I hope all will be settled by morning." She stood up and briefly touched the back of my hand. Her fingers were still icy, despite our proximity to the hearth. "Good night, Andrew."

I watched her leave, reeling at the unexpected contact. She was a friend and I respected her, but my senses told me she craved more.

I was unable to muster the same sentiments. I hoped she'd understand.

TWENTY-ONE

Banging issued from the door to my room, loud and persistent. I sat up blearily as I blinked away the last vestiges of sleep. One glance out the tiny window my room afforded told me the sun had not yet risen. I scowled and swung my legs over the edge of the bed, irked by the interruption. The knocking resumed, somehow more insistent, more urgent.

I glowered at the door. "Give me a damned minute!" I bellowed. Whoever lurked in the hall had better have important business, else my temper would flare further.

I felt I'd only closed my eyes moments before. My sleep had not been restful, and I'd tossed and turned for most of the night. To be awakened so soon after drifting into fitful slumber placed my nerves on a razor's edge. I was irritable, and in my present temper, I didn't care.

My dreams had featured the day I'd rescued Alexander from the headsman's axe, but on this occasion, Colin had worn the executioner's black. I'd been frozen with fear in the nightmare, unable to cross the distance between us. I'd watched helplessly as Alexander's blood spurted from wound after wound while Colin cackled in delight. Such dreams had plagued me on occasion, but rarely were they so vivid.

And this one left me surly and unsettled.

I ran a hand through my hair and stood up, thankful the knocking had ceased as I purged the nightmare from my mind. I pulled on my trousers and made my way to the door, then yanked it open more forcefully than I'd intended. The knob crumpled and fell from the wood to roll across the floor.

I glowered at it. The day was not going well so far.

Alexander paced in the hall, a finely fletched arrow clutched in his fist. He stopped midstride as my door opened and turned to face me, his features drawn.

"Alex, what in hell—?" I began, but he shook his head.

"Andrew, listen to me. This is important."

"It had better be," I growled. I crossed my arms as I waited for him to continue, making my displeasure with the early awakening known.

"Galewing was scouting. He found the location of Colin's men," he said, undeterred by my foul mood. "They've set up an ambush along the road to the canyon. While they slept, he stole this."

He held the arrow up for my inspection. The shaft was straight and evenly balanced, while the fletching was expertly done with tawny goose feathers. With his free hand, he pointed at its tip. It was a broadhead forged of steel, though it glistened strangely in the dim candlelight of the hallway. When I leaned forward to inspect it more closely, an acrid scent assaulted my nose. I stepped back, stunned. It was poisoned.

"It's—"

"It's poisoned, I know," he replied in a flat tone, then resumed pacing. "Whoever these men are, they're not seeking a friendly round of negotiations. I don't think we should travel by way of the canyon."

I nodded in agreement. "Yes, I think this settles the debate. We go through the marshlands."

I looked up as rapid footfalls approached. Lydia raced toward us, her eyes wide with concern.

"I spoke to Chela about the arrow, and she'd like to look at it." She glanced briefly in my direction, unable to suppress a smirk. "We'll continue this discussion downstairs once you've made yourself presentable."

Lydia led Alexander away. With a sigh, I retreated into my room to finish dressing. I plucked the broken doorknob from the floor and placed it on the small bedside table, then gathered my belongings. I wouldn't return to the room once I'd gone downstairs to meet with the others. Alexander's revelation had driven all hope for further sleep from my thoughts.

When I arrived in the common room, Alexander and the three magi were gathered around a table. The arrow had been placed in the center, and they took turns examining it. Emmarie sat off to one side, her head against the wall and her eyes closed.

"I'm unfamiliar with this substance," Lydia said as I approached. "As a healer, I've come to recognize many natural poisons, but this one is strange."

"The feathers are also unfamiliar," Chela stated. "They're similar to some of the goose feathers I have seen, but if you look carefully here—" she indicated a series of dark spots that ran in a straight line along the outer edge of the fletching, "—they are unlike those of common geese." She looked up to meet my gaze, then glanced at Alexander. "But you have seen such feathers before, if I'm not mistaken."

I nodded. I'd recognized the feathers immediately; they were commonly used by the fletchers who supplied the king's garrison in the Capitol.

"They come from a tawny goose," I replied. "They're common in the Northern Marches of Novania."

Lydia chewed her lip, Chela muttered under her breath, but it was Rynn who spoke next. "There is no longer any doubt these men seek you. That they've tipped their arrows with poison tells me they mean only harm. We must avoid the canyon."

"They'll realize we've gone into the Great Marsh within a day's time," Chela replied wearily. "I don't doubt they'll pursue us. There is little room for error when navigating the marshes, even with my ability to guide us, but the cart will leave its mark as we pass. We must move swiftly and hope they're unable to catch up."

"I can assist you in the marsh," Rynn offered. "I can freeze the ground temporarily so we may hasten our travel—"

"No," Chela interrupted firmly. "We can't take that approach. It's safest to travel on solid ground, and I can find that. I know you mean to help, but such tactics could leave us stranded and you exhausted. I'm unwilling to take the risk."

Rynn narrowed her eyes and frowned in displeasure. "We'll do it your way, then. But if speed becomes imperative, I'll do what I feel necessary to expedite our travel."

"If it comes down to it, I'll head them off." My words were met with silence. "After all, if they've come from Colin as we suspect, they are here for *me*."

"Andrew..." Alexander groaned. "Don't. *Please*."

"We both know I can handle two men," I stated.

Though I'd kept my tone even and confident, I harbored doubts. I didn't know how my body would tolerate poison. The after-effects of my battle with the Venom-weavers had shown that even I would succumb if a toxin was potent enough, but I kept the uncertainty to myself. After all, it was my duty to protect Alexander, and I'd vowed to protect the others as well.

Alexander heaved a sigh. "Very well. We should leave as soon as we're able. I'd like to put as much distance between us and those men as we can while we have the chance." He glanced toward the doors leading outside, then nodded to himself. "I've asked Galewing to keep watch behind us. I'll know if he sees them—or anyone else who might follow our tracks."

Less than an hour later, I was armed and armored as I walked alongside Alexander. We brought up the rear of our group, with Chela and the cart at the head. Upon my insistence, both Emmarie and Lydia rode inside the cart, crammed between our belongings. If we ran into trouble, they could use it to rapidly flee for safety. Rynn refused to join them, but I understood. She walked alongside Chela at the front of the cart while Galewing soared overhead, circling back toward the inn at intervals as he scoured the ground for signs of pursuit. No one spoke.

By midday, the road veered into a densely wooded area. The trees were unlike any I'd encountered before, tall and gnarled, with wide, arching branches and sharp-edged leaves. Among the tangled roots protruding from the soft loam were patches of bright green moss. The air became stifling and oppressive beneath the canopy, and the drone of insects accompanied the sound of our passage.

Not long after we entered the woods, the first traces of marshland became apparent. Stands of reeds poked between the trees, and the ground became increasingly soft and muddy. The road began to disappear amidst the muck, and Chela's grip on Sienna's reins intensified. A single misstep could land one knee-deep in mud or worse.

The faint scent of cinnamon wafted to me periodically as Chela channeled her magic, seeking solid ground. I slowed my pace to allow the spicy odor more time to dissipate before it reached my nostrils. I'd never forgive myself if we were discovered due to a sneeze.

By the time evening began to fall, firm ground had become increasingly scarce. As we set up camp for the night, Chela placed stones around the perimeter to indicate where the ground became unstable. Our tents were pitched in a tight circle, and as the sun disappeared behind the veil of trees, biting insects swarmed. The gnats and mosquitos were indiscriminate, and we all suffered, save for Rynn.

"A fire would keep these pests away," Chela grumbled.

I shook my head. "We'll have to live with the bugs. I won't risk them locating us in the dark and catching us unaware. A fire will serve as a beacon to Colin's men."

She groaned but didn't press the issue further.

A short time later, Galewing returned to perch on the railing of the cart. Alexander went to him, and they stared intently at one another for several moments. I imagined they spoke through their strange bond, and once finished, Galewing took flight once more. As Alexander turned toward the fire, I shot him a questioning glance.

"He plans to spend the night over there," Alexander replied, indicating a tall tree some distance away. "The insects are a bother to him as well." He chuckled. "I wish I could fly to get away from these damned biters too. There's nothing to be done about it, I suppose."

"What news does he have, Alex?" I asked as I swatted a pair of mosquitos on my forearm.

"None, yet," he replied. "He saw no sign of pursuit today, but like you, he believes those men will follow us. He'll resume scouting with the dawn."

I allowed myself to relax after hearing the news. While it was a relief to learn Colin's men had not yet made their way into the marshes, I didn't believe they'd delay long. I expected we'd receive word of our pursuers by the next afternoon, if not sooner. The cart had left deep ruts in the mud, and our trail would not be difficult to follow. Without the burden of a cartload of supplies, the men would make far better time than we did. Even with advanced warning from Galewing, I didn't know how long we'd have to prepare. The forest canopy was thick and would obscure the eagle's vision.

"Hmm," Chela murmured to herself. "I think I'll turn in early tonight. With the darkness, I can scarcely see a thing, and perhaps the tent will provide a respite from the insects."

"I'll take first watch, brother," Alexander said after a moment. "While I might not be able to see much, I can listen to the night sounds. And if Galewing notices anything, I'll know." He shrugged. "I'm not certain if this was the right path. Perhaps it would have been better to risk a confrontation than slog through this mire and be eaten alive by the biters."

"This was the right choice," Lydia countered. "Their arrows concern me. I don't know if I am capable of healing an injury fouled by that poison. The marsh is unpleasant, but it's safer."

I nodded in agreement. "This is the best path forward. It may not seem so at present, but if we stay ahead of the assassins, it's for the better."

Alexander frowned. "I'd rather not spend the rest of my journey looking over my shoulder while waiting for an arrow in the back."

I wouldn't contradict him; I felt the same. If it had only been the pair of us making the journey, I would have been less reluctant. But there were others to consider—Lydia and Chela had few skills that would help them in a fight, and Emmarie was young and inexperienced. I believed Rynn was capable of holding her own, but the others concerned me. I'd do everything in my power to ensure they reached the Ebon Spire unharmed.

"If we're forced to face them, then we'll do so. But we must consider the others." I sat back and crossed my arms. "I'd like to be rid of Colin's lackeys as much as you, but I won't put their welfare at risk."

He slumped, but managed a nod. "You're right, brother."

We sat in silence while the others turned in one by one. A short time after she'd entered her tent, Emmarie exited and came toward us. While I could see her movements in the dark, Alexander could not. When she spoke, he was startled.

"I'd like to join you on your watch," she said.

"Emmarie! Holy hell, I didn't hear you." Alexander laughed, a nervous, unsettled sound.

"I'm sorry." She paused to giggle. "I knew Andrew could see me. Sometimes I forget he isn't like the rest of you." She glanced in my direction briefly, then returned her gaze to Alexander. "I can see better in the dark than you, and I can speak with some of the creatures nearby. The toads can see better at night than Galewing."

"I think it's a wise idea," I replied before Alexander could object. "Perhaps it's time we post two for each watch, rather than one."

"And who will take the second watch alongside you?" Alexander asked pointedly. "I don't plan to stay awake the whole night."

"Rynn asked me to wake her for second watch," Emmarie replied. "I hope that isn't a problem?"

I smiled wryly. I was unsurprised Rynn would volunteer herself without informing anyone of her plans. And she'd asked to take second watch, knowing I'd be with her. What was she playing at?

I pushed my misgivings aside once more and focused on Emmarie. "That will be fine. Now that watch duty is settled, I'm going to turn in as well."

My slumber was dreamless, or rather, if I dreamt, I recalled nothing. It was a relief when I realized this upon being awakened by my brother in the dark hours of the night. Weeks had passed since I'd managed a single night without visions of Colin's atrocities haunting me. I felt more rested than I had in some time.

When I emerged from my tent, Rynn was outside, her back toward me as she stood unmoving in the darkness. She peered into the night, though I wondered how much she could truly see. The moon was not visible and only the faint starlight illuminated our camp, dampened by the thick canopy overhead. She turned slowly as she heard my approach.

"Andrew?" Her voice was a bare whisper.

"Yes." I stood beside her, perhaps two paces away.

She chuckled softly. "I knew it must have been you, but I can't see a thing."

"I can see some," I replied. "On a night like this, I rely on my other senses more heavily. Even my night vision has limits."

"Alex said you see better in the darkness than we can. I suppose it's part of what you are."

"Hmm."

I listened to the sounds of the night creatures for a time, contemplating her intentions. I was uncertain why she'd chosen to assist with the watch at all when we had not discussed doubling up. Around us, the marshlands were filled with the drone of insects and the hooting calls of nocturnal birds, the croaking chorus of toads, and the rustle of reeds as stealthier creatures crawled past. I could see only a short distance from the campsite, but my other senses assured me the night remained calm.

"I wanted to speak with you alone," Rynn whispered after a time.

I shifted my gaze to study her features in the darkness. Her jaw was set in determination, her eyes were fierce, her stance rigid. She feared the outcome of our pending conversation. But why?

"Now is a perfect time to talk," I replied. "The others are soundly asleep."

A faint smile crossed her lips. "You continue to surprise me. You have a sense of humor at times when I least expect it." She paused, and her momentary smile fled. "Traveling as we are, it has been difficult to have a private conversation with anyone. There is always someone nearby, someone to overhear. Perhaps I have merely grown used to the isolation of the Frostwake, and it will simply take time to adjust. I haven't traveled with a group since my pilgrimage ended."

"Eleven years is a long time," I replied. "I don't fault you for your struggle now."

"Ah, but that is the least of my hardships," she replied. "Since meeting you, I find myself drawing too near the others. I've become careless in my interactions. I nearly touched Chela's hand this morning as we loaded the cart, and I was shocked by my lapse. I pride myself on my vigilance, yet I've become almost cavalier." A frown creased her pretty features. "Now that I've found one person I need not fear, it has become something of a distraction."

I arched an eyebrow and swallowed, taken aback. "I…distract you?"

She laughed merrily. "I suppose that's one way to put it, yes." She laughed again. "What I mean is this: I don't have to fear *everyone*, and I have become lax. For the first time in many years, I'm almost comfortable with other people, and the feeling is utterly foreign. I wasn't expecting to feel this way about traveling with them. With you."

We fell silent as I contemplated her admission. I was troubled by her words, by the implication inherent in her final statement. I didn't believe I could be what she hoped for—my heart had been shattered by Claire, decimated by Colin. Time had not yet healed my wounds, and I'd carry the scars for eternity. Perhaps in time… No, I pushed the notion firmly away.

After a few minutes, she took several steps forward. Her back was to me as she stared skyward, studying the faint stars twinkling in the hazy sky above.

She sighed after a time and lowered her gaze. "I never properly apologized for the scene I dragged you into with my brothers. I was heartbroken when I learned my father had passed and I'd never have the opportunity to make amends. I needed human contact, and there was no one else I could turn to. I didn't mean to seem forward. I'm sorry if it was awkward."

I understood why she'd hoped to speak without the others present. To my knowledge, no one else knew what had transpired, and part of me wished to keep it that way. Grief was a difficult thing to bear alone, and it wasn't my place to share her sorrows with the others.

"I don't fault you for it, Rynn," I replied softly.

"Thank you. You're a better man than I expected."

I frowned, uncertain what she meant, but decided against pressing her for details.

"I consider you a friend," I said evenly. "I understand the various forms grief may take all too well. I've experienced a great deal of it recently."

She moved closer and stretched one hand toward me. She wanted me to take her hand, but I pretended I'd failed to see her movement. After a moment, she dropped it to her side.

"I'm glad I have finally spoken with you. I'm relieved knowing you aren't bothered by the events in Dwymm. I consider you a friend as well."

TWENTY-TWO

"It's too damned early," Alexander grumbled as I roused him the next morning.

"Would you rather I let you sleep until Colin's people arrive?" I countered, nonplussed.

He groaned and pushed himself to sitting. "No. You're right. I'll be out in a moment." He reached for his discarded shirt, then paused. "Galewing didn't see anything worth noting last night. I think we've remained ahead of them for now, but he's left to scout again."

I nodded once and ducked outside, relieved by his news but unsettled by the nonchalant admission he'd been speaking with the eagle during our conversation. I still didn't understand the nature of the bond between them. Magic would continue to baffle and confound me unless one of the others finally explained their experiences in a way I could comprehend. Combat was straightforward and more to my preference.

Chela was outside when I emerged from our tent, as were Lydia and Emmarie. Rynn dismantled her tent while Chela hitched Sienna to the cart and the others stowed their belongings. Once finished with the horse, Chela rummaged in the cart and withdrew a sack, then approached me.

She thrust an apple and a chunk of day-old bread into my hands. "Eat, then don your armor. It's too quiet this morning, and I have a feeling you'll need it."

I nodded. The insects had begun their incessant drone, but the birds and other creatures remained unheard. I hoped Galewing would provide us ample warning if Chela's premonition proved true.

Within the hour, the camp was packed, we'd eaten, and Alexander and I had both strapped on our armor. Lydia and Emmarie clambered into the cart and we set off.

As we traveled deeper into the marshes, our pace rapidly decreased to a crawl. The route we followed was solid enough to bear our weight, but the ground was saturated. Mud and grime sucked at our boots with each footstep, and the cart became lodged in the muck several times. A well-placed shove on my part dislodged it from the mire each time, and we pressed on.

By midday, the top of a black spire became visible above the canopy. I hoped it was an indication we'd neared our next destination.

"I think I see the Ebon Spire." I flashed a grin at Chela as I swatted away a cloud of gnats.

She adjusted the brim of her hat and gazed in the direction I'd indicated. "Ah, yes, I see it now. We don't have much farther."

"Holy hell, it's about time," Alexander muttered under his breath. "These damned biters are almost worse than the mud."

A quarter-hour later, Galewing's piercing cry alerted us to his presence. Alexander craned his neck skyward, and the eagle landed gracefully on the edge of the cart seconds later. A heartbeat later, Alexander spoke, his tone grave.

"They're almost upon us," he stated, eyes wide. "Galewing apologizes for the lack of warning, but there are so many damned trees. We don't have much time."

I unsheathed my sword and nodded to Alexander. "Emma, you and Lydia stay in the cart. I want you to drive as fast as you can—"

My words were cut short by the whistle of an arrow as it whizzed past my left ear. I spun around with a grimace and spotted the archer not far behind, half hidden behind the bole of a tree.

"Go, now!" I shouted as another arrow shot past me, again only just missing its mark.

I dove behind the trunk of the nearest tree. I'd draw the archer out of hiding and force him into a proper fight. Alexander ducked behind a nearby bush and drew his sword.

Chela screamed, an agonized sound that made my blood run cold. I couldn't risk returning to the cart and hoped the women were unhurt, but there was no time to be certain. My focus was on our adversaries as they approached.

I heard Rynn's voice, urgent, yet decisive as it rapidly dwindled behind us. I hoped she and Chela could get the others to safety. I wished Alexander had remained with them where he wouldn't be tempted to use his unstable power, but it couldn't be helped now.

Galewing's cry pierced the air. Alexander chewed his lip, then whispered, "They're coming this direction, brother. What's your plan?"

He pulled on his helm, and I could just make out his eyes behind the dark dragon scale. I cursed myself silently; I'd left my helm in the cart.

"We stay where we are. We'll bring the ambush to them this time." I adjusted the grip on my sword and tensed in preparation.

Alexander nodded once, grim determination in the set of his jaw. I spied no foreign glow in his eyes and suppressed a sigh of relief. He was in control.

Within moments, the men's rapid footfalls came toward us, mud sucking loudly at the soles of their boots as they followed the cart tracks. I nodded to Alexander as the first man ran into view. He lunged toward me, but I parried his strike and held my ground. Though his weapon was forged steel and finely crafted, he'd forgone armor. His leather jerkin would do little against our weapons.

While the man focused on me, his back was to my brother. Alexander buried his blade deep in the man's left side. His eyes widened in shock as he fell, and I shoved him away to face his companion.

The second man carried the bow. He nocked an arrow and drew as I turned toward him. I dove behind the tree as he loosed, and the arrow missed its mark.

Alexander swore. I peered at my brother to find the arrow had landed in the muck near his feet. I ducked behind the trunk again, uncertain if he'd been hit as another arrow whizzed past my head. Alexander began to laugh wickedly, then sprinted toward the archer.

I swallowed the bile in my throat. Was this the madness the magi feared?

"Alex, no!" I roared.

My words came too late. The archer fired again. From his distance and aim, the shot should have been lethal.

I watched, horrified, as it struck Alexander squarely in the abdomen. The arrow fell away as he continued to charge forward, undeterred by the attack. I stared helplessly as my brother bore down on the man in a battle-induced rage. Alexander continued to laugh, a cold, mirthless sound that chilled me to the core.

In all our years together, I'd never witnessed this side of my brother. And I didn't like it.

I shook my head, recovering my wits, and raced toward the two, my sword raised. Alexander released a wordless roar and struck the man with a savage blow as I was a mere four steps away. His sword cleaved through flesh and bone, severing the man's head cleanly from his torso. Alexander stepped backwards and dropped his sword. He bent forward, hands on his knees, as he gasped for breath.

"Alex! Are you hurt?"

It no longer mattered who the men were. My only concern was Alexander's welfare. His actions may have spared me an injury, but they'd been reckless. If he was wounded, it was my fault. I should have done more to protect him.

Alexander removed his helm and grinned. "I'm fine. This dragon scale is a wonder! The first arrow hit me square in the shoulder and bounced right off. Then I knew what I must do." He snickered. "Your scales make me nearly invincible."

I stared at him, dumbfounded. It took several moments before I understood his meaning. I joined in his laughter as relief washed over me. I should have known he'd be better protected than I was; my scales had protected me from arrows and Corodan blades alike. I'd discounted the advantage he'd have wearing the dragon scale.

"I think you saved my damned skin, brother," I said as my laughter abated. "As idiotic as your charge was, I'm glad you made it."

"I'd do it again." His smile faltered, and he looked away with a grimace. "Why is Colin so determined to have your head and not mine? It's almost as though he's forgotten me, but I doubt it. Colin may be a drunken sod half the time and a right bastard the rest, but he's not one to ignore a threat. What else does he have in store, I wonder?"

I shrugged. “There will be time enough for speculation later. For now, we need to find the others.”

“I’m not certain we can,” he replied, his expression troubled. Galewing landed in the soft mud beside him and eyed him sharply. “Galewing says Chela was hit. Rynn led them through the marsh, but she froze the ground along the way. I don’t think we can follow their tracks.”

I surveyed our surroundings. We’d managed to remain close to the cart’s tracks during the fight, but I didn’t know how solid the ground was beyond our present location. I was uncertain if I should risk shifting to get us safely to the spire. Would the ground support my weight in dragon form? I chewed my lower lip, contemplating what must be done, yet unable to decide on the right course of action.

I groaned and sheathed my sword. “We can wait for Rynn’s return. I have no doubt she’ll come back… Or I can shift, and we’ll fly to the spire. The trouble is, I don’t know how well the ground will hold under my weight.”

“The spire isn’t far. Galewing offers to speak with Emmarie for us. He believes they should be nearly out of the marshes by now.” Alexander’s frown deepened. “I’d rather not risk you sinking and becoming stuck. I don’t know if we’d manage to free you. You’re so damned *big* as a dragon.”

“Then we’ll wait here for Rynn’s return.”

Galewing shrieked and soared into the air, flying swiftly in the direction of the spire. Alexander and I walked to the point where the cart tracks abruptly ended. He sighed and sat down heavily in the mud.

“It’s as I thought,” he stated. “When Rynn began to freeze the ground, the cart left no tracks. I suppose it was foolish to hope it would be otherwise.”

“If the spire is as close as Galewing says, we won’t have to wait long.” I narrowed my eyes as I considered his previous words. “You said Chela was hit?”

He nodded. “Galewing didn’t elaborate, but it’s why Rynn took over as guide for the horse. As much as I dislike the woman, she’s done well by us so far. I hope she’ll recover.”

“As do I, brother. With Lydia present, she’ll be in good hands.”

Alexander smiled fondly. "Yes. She saved you from the spiders' venom, though she continues to insist you healed on your own. I'm not certain I believe her. She's overly modest when it comes to her magic."

I arched an eyebrow as I sat down alongside him. "I believe I was unconscious for two days. I'm fairly certain she must have had a hand in the healing process, otherwise I would have awakened later, yes?"

He chuckled. "That's exactly what I've told her, but she seems to think it was simply your body's response to the healing it managed on its own." He shrugged. "I wouldn't know. My abilities lay in the opposite direction of hers."

"What do you mean?" I asked.

He gazed up toward a small patch of sky, frowning thoughtfully. "I'm a warrior, and my abilities will enhance my effectiveness in battle. I don't fully understand how it works yet, or what exactly will happen, though I can tell you that during my trials, I have experienced…*things*…" He looked at me out of the corners of his eyes. "My reflexes were faster. So much so that I wonder what I'll be capable of. I became stronger and more resilient each time." He paused to scratch at the nape of his neck. "I sorely wanted to test some of my abilities today, but I didn't. It would have been…unsafe."

I nodded, relieved he'd resisted the temptation. Lydia would undoubtedly ask me what had transpired, and I was pleased I could reassure her Alexander had not put himself in unnecessary danger. His diabolical laughter had merely been a side-effect of his surprise with the dragon scale's protection.

"I understand why the gray eagles ally with mage-warriors," he said after a few moments of silence. "When we were fighting, I could see as I normally do, but I could also see as Galewing does. It gave me an overhead perspective of the battlefield."

"Alex, that's incredible."

He laughed, giddy. "Our bond allows us to communicate, but until that fight, I didn't know he would share his sight with me. It will be an advantage when we face Colin's forces."

I studied him for a moment, thinking over his words. "You sound as though you plan to raise an army against him, brother."

He nodded. "That's exactly what I plan to do. An army of magi from the Southlands. Or the Corodan and Tom's allies from the north. Or a bit of both. We'll see. Colin is unfit to rule, but we both know he won't willingly give up the throne."

"Should you need an experienced commander, I'm at your service."

He grinned. "I wouldn't have it any other way. But let's not get ahead of ourselves. We still have this journey to finish first."

"That we do."

I lapsed into silence as I thought over everything we'd need to put in place. Forces must be gathered, supplies acquired, armor and weapons procured, and a staging area determined. We'd need to contact Thomas, find a way for his forces to join ours, or coordinate our movements from a distance. That aspect might prove difficult, with the whole of Colin's kingdom separating us. And then there was the matter of who would rule should we succeed in ending Colin's reign. Who would take the throne in the tyrant's place? Who would the people accept?

Alexander's laughter drew me from my thoughts, and I glanced toward him questioningly.

"I don't even have to ask what you were thinking of, brother," he said with a smirk. "It was clear in your expression. I realize there is much to prepare for, but we're not ready yet."

I snorted. "I was thinking… If we remove Colin from the throne, what then? Will you become king?"

He gaped at me. "I…haven't considered it. I never wanted to rule, and honestly, I think I'd be rubbish." He shook his head. "No, I bear the Mark. I don't think it would be wise. If anyone should take the throne, it's Tom."

His explanation was sound. The Mark would be a source of fear amongst the people and a detriment to our cause. Whoever took the mantle of kingship in Colin's stead must be respected, revered, a benevolent force to undo his wickedness. The Mark would sow mistrust. Alexander was right; it must be Thomas.

"I often wonder what would have happened if my father had kept your secret…well, a secret." Alexander sighed. "So many of the kingdom's noblemen respected you, and you've always striven to do what is right and just."

"It was never my place to rule. I've known that all my life." I leaned back and stretched. "Even if he had named me his heir, it would have become apparent within a few years that I'm not… That I'm different."

He clapped my shoulder with a nod of understanding. "Father didn't know *that* secret. Truly, no one did until you finally bothered to tell me. And that was *after* you slaughtered the Hive-queen and her cronies. Even if it had been but a few years, you could have done Novania some good…"

I chuckled. "Perhaps. In the end, the throne would have passed to Colin anyway. I'll never have children, Alex. I…can't. And it doesn't do any good to speculate—we can't change the past."

He sighed. "I know. But sometimes, I like to think about what might have been. I miss our home."

"As do I, brother. But I don't know if I can live there again. There are too many unpleasant memories that continue to haunt me." I stood up and grimaced. My armor was caked with mud, and the chore of cleaning it would likely take hours.

Alexander rose and managed a tired laugh. "We must look a mess. I hope Rynn won't be much longer."

The afternoon was waning toward dusk by the time Rynn returned, following Galewing's lead. She was relieved to find us unharmed, though her blue eyes were troubled and guarded. The news regarding Chela could not be good. She stopped a few paces away. The toll the day had taken was marked on her features; her face was drawn and pale.

"If we are to reach the spire before dark, we must hurry." She glanced beyond us, a worried frown on her lips. "I suppose those men won't be troubling us any further. Were either of you hurt?"

Alexander shook his head as I said, "No, we're fine."

"Good."

She turned away and motioned for us to follow. She held her hands out on either side, palms toward the ground. The marsh solidified in a wide radius around her, and a thin rime of frost appeared on its surface.

Rynn set a quick pace, but I could see her energy was rapidly fading. She made no complaints and continued to press on through the mire.

We didn't speak again until we'd cleared the line of trees and the spire loomed ahead, no longer unobstructed by the foliage.

Alexander whistled. "Would you look at that!"

The Ebon Spire was a tall, slender tower formed of three segments. Each segment was comprised of a shiny, black material reminiscent of polished obsidian that twisted around the others in an impossible tangle as it rose toward the evening sky. How the magi managed to create such architecture was beyond my understanding, but the sight was a wonder to behold.

As I pulled my gaze from the tower, Rynn stumbled and fell to her knees. I was at her side in an instant, as was Alexander.

"I'm sorry," she mumbled through a grimace. She squeezed her eyes shut and appeared to be in pain.

I knelt at her side. "Are you hurt?"

She shook her head stubbornly. "No, I'm…exhausted. I've expended the last of my energy." She peered at me through narrowed eyelids. "I didn't want you to worry."

"She needs to rest, Andrew." I was startled by the sudden authority I heard in my brother's tone, but I nodded.

"I can help you reach the spire." I offered my arm. "Can you walk?"

She sighed and grasped my hand feebly. Slowly, she regained her feet, but swayed unsteadily as soon as she'd risen. She collapsed into my side, unconscious. I lifted her into my arms and glanced at Alexander. Even through my steel plate, I could sense the frigidity of her body.

As we crossed the distance to the spire, Galewing flew ahead to alert the others of our imminent arrival. By the time we reached the small courtyard at the tower's base, Emmarie and one of the resident magi awaited us. Emmarie led me inside and directed me to a room that had been designated for Rynn, while the mage stopped Alexander to speak with him privately before he followed us inside.

Rynn's room was large enough to accommodate a single mattress and little else. I noted her personal belongings were stowed in one corner as I lay her down as gently as I could. Despite the relative warmth of the day, she'd left a thin film of frost on my breastplate.

"I'll stay with her," Emmarie volunteered.

I nodded my thanks. I sorely wanted out of my armor, mud-caked as it was, and perhaps I'd take a bath if the spire had such amenities.

As I exited the room and entered the hallway, Alexander appeared at the far end with the mage we'd met outside. I strode toward them, intuiting they had news. My personal discomforts could wait.

"Andrew, this is Korvus," Alexander said by way of introduction. "He has been assisting Lydia where he can, but…the spire doesn't have a healer." He looked away. "Chela has asked for us."

I nodded once. "It's not good, is it?"

Korvus gestured toward another door along the hall. "She's within. I'm afraid there's little more to be done."

I glanced at Alexander, and when he nodded, I led the way to Chela's room. It was larger than the one Rynn had been given, with a proper bed and a chest of drawers. Chela lay on the mattress, her skin waxy and pale, her eyes glassy, a thin sheen of sweat visible on her forehead. Lydia knelt at her side. Her hands hovered over Chela's body, her eyes closed as the green scent of herbs permeated the air.

Chela's eyes rolled in our direction as we entered. "Who's there?"

Her voice was weak, a dry whisper. She tried to sit up but immediately fell back against the sheets.

"Chela, be still," I said quietly. "You need to rest."

"Andrew…you've made it here." A faint smile crept across her face as she closed her eyes. "Is Alex safe?"

"I'm here, Chela," he replied from beside me. "I'm well."

She nodded, the movement almost imperceptible. "Then I have not…failed…" She breathed a sigh and lay still.

Lydia rocked back on her heels and dropped her hands to her side. "I've done all I can for her," she said, eyes shining with unshed tears. "She needs to rest. Let me speak with her for a moment. I'll meet you in the courtyard presently."

Dismissed, we trudged outside. I located the cart and noted someone had unharnessed Sienna and provided her with a bag of oats. I located our packs and handed Alexander his. A few moments later, Lydia joined us.

"She won't last the night." Tears leaked from her eyes. "I can't determine what fuels the poison. If I knew its source, I could counteract it, but it's foreign to me. I've never been so helpless before." A sob escaped her throat, and she covered her face with her hands.

Alexander darted toward her and drew her into his arms. "What matters is you've done your best," he said.

"I fear she was clinging to life only until she knew you were safe," Lydia replied, pushing away from him gently. "She took her position as your guide seriously. Your safety has always been her priority." She wiped at her eyes. "I feel terrible for the dislike I held for her. She meant well."

"You can't blame yourself," Alexander insisted. "You aren't the one who fired the arrow, nor were you responsible for his orders."

She wiped away a fresh wave of tears. "I must return. She shouldn't be alone in her final moments. I'll stay with her. Perhaps she'll forgive me for our past disagreements."

Three hours later, Chela drew her final breath. I was in my appointed room alone when Korvus arrived with the news. Another friend lost, thanks to Colin. Another life needlessly extinguished. I followed him to the foyer where we'd entered.

The others were already there, save Rynn. Two magi whom I didn't recognize stood on either side of Chela's shrouded body.

"We'll inter her in the mausoleum beneath the shrine," one woman said. "It's an honor for any mage to be laid to rest at a pilgrimage site, but as a guide to so many, Chela is deserving."

"Thank you," I murmured while Lydia whispered the same.

"She took her duty seriously," Alexander said, his voice strained.

"She'll be missed," I added. "We wouldn't have reached this point without her."

Lydia was distraught and dissolved into sobs. "I did all I could," she stammered. "This is my fault. I should have… Should have…done more."

Alexander attempted to console her, but she shook her head and pushed him away as the shrine's resident magi carried Chela's body through a doorway at the rear of the foyer. She retreated to her room moments later. I heard her weeping long into the night.

After I turned in, my dreams were filled with people from my past, friends and foes, each caught in the web of deceit and madness Colin had spun. Colin's hands were irrevocably stained, bloody and swollen as he cut down each familiar face.

When I awakened some time before dawn, I was convinced Alexander had been correct: We must take the fight to Colin—and soon. He must face justice, and our lost friends and family must be avenged.

There was no way to remove him from power except by force, and it would be up to us—and perhaps Thomas—to do so.

TWENTY-THREE

When I went to Rynn's room the next morning, she was still unconscious, but her expression was peaceful, and she no longer appeared drawn and haggard.

The others had busied themselves elsewhere. Emmarie had taken over the care of Sienna, Alexander had predictably entered his next trial, and Lydia was shut away in her room. She claimed she needed time to study the arrow to learn the nature of the poison on its tip, but I suspected she simply wanted to mourn in solitude. The arrow was merely a convenient excuse.

While I needed to give my armor a thorough cleaning and I'd promised Alexander I would do the same for his, someone should be present when Rynn awakened. Since the others were busy, the task fell to me. She needed to learn of Chela's death, and it was best the news came from a friend rather than one of the spire's unfamiliar magi.

I sat carefully beside the mattress she lay on, moving slowly so I wouldn't disturb her. One of the spire's magi entered not long after and was pleased to find me there.

"You are Andrew, yes?" she asked hopefully. When I nodded, she said, "My name is Elianna. Elder Carridan asked me to look in on her, but how can I, given her unusual condition? Korvus tried to check her vitals last evening and came away with a nasty case of frostbite." She hesitated and bit her lip, her eyes fixed on my own. "You carried her inside. She doesn't affect you as she does everyone else."

I groaned. The spire's magi were unaware of what I was. Perhaps I could keep it that way, though I was certain they'd begin to question why Rynn's condition didn't harm me. It was only a matter of time.

"That's right," I replied. "Do you need me to assist?"

"Typically, we'd check the mage's temperature to look for fever, but I don't think she suffers those." Elianna sighed and looked around the room helplessly. "I don't know what to do. It's a classic case of over-extension, but we can't treat her as we do other mages."

I smiled, amused, and decided to humor the poor woman. Gently, I placed the back of my hand across Rynn's forehead. She was just as frigid as I remembered. I sat back with a shrug.

"I don't believe she has a fever."

"Well, thank you," Elianna replied, flustered. "There is one more thing you might do for me before I go. Can you check her heartbeat? If it's calm, there is no danger, but if it races, we may have a problem."

"I'm afraid I don't know what to do."

Elianna laughed softly and took my right hand in hers. She extended my first two fingers. "Take these and place them on her wrist, just so," she said, pressing my fingers against her wrist. "Hold your fingers there for a few moments, and you should feel her pulse, just as you do mine. Can you do this?"

I nodded. The task was simple enough. When I took Rynn's hand in my own, she gasped and sat up with a start, reflexively jerking away from me. Only then did she notice who knelt at her side.

"Andrew? I'm sorry, I was afraid—" she glanced toward Elianna. "Oh, I see now. She asked for your help. How long was I asleep?" Her blue eyes narrowed with concern.

"Long enough the elders were becoming concerned," Elianna replied. "It's morning now, on the day after your arrival." Her gaze shifted between me and Rynn. "I'll leave you alone since it seems you have awakened without incident. I'm certain there is much you'd like to discuss."

Once Elianna was gone, Rynn turned to face me, her expression unreadable. "The last thing I recall was kneeling on the ground between you and Alex. I tried to stand, and then…nothing."

"You fainted," I replied. "Luckily for you, I was there to break your fall."

She smiled sheepishly. "I pushed myself too far yesterday. Perhaps if we'd been a bit closer to the spire when those men came, I would not have depleted all of my energy. Speaking of which, is there anything for breakfast? I could eat an entire banquet on my own."

I chuckled. "There should be some bread and jam left over from earlier. Can you walk?"

She narrowed her eyes and frowned. "Today, I can say with confidence that yes, I can. I should have told you how exhausted I truly was. I'm sorry." She reached toward the foot of the mattress and pulled her boots toward her. "Who took these from me? Was it you?"

I shook my head. "I don't know who did, but Elianna mentioned Korvus ended up with frostbite."

She shook her head and sighed in frustration. "When we first arrived, I told them of my condition and that under no circumstances should anyone attempt to touch me. Some people never listen." She stood up of her own volition and smiled victoriously. "It seems I'll be fine."

When I failed to return her smile, her face fell and she became somber. "What is it? What's wrong?"

I drew a breath. "Chela passed during the night."

She looked down, her shoulders slumped. "I'm sorry. I didn't know her long, but I can only imagine Lydia's reaction. They didn't usually agree, but Lydia vowed she'd do her best to heal the wound. She began as we fled the marshes and only stopped her ministrations when the elders asked her to, so Chela could be moved inside. She must be in anguish."

"She's taken it very hard. I wish there was something I could do."

Rynn chuckled as a gleam of mischief returned to her eyes. "No, leave this to me! But first, show me to the kitchen. I'll talk to her after breakfast. I think I can ease some of her suffering."

Once Rynn had eaten and I was certain she wouldn't collapse a second time, I left her for the outdoors while she paid a visit to Lydia. Emmarie sat on the ground near Sienna, and Galewing perched on the side of the cart, watching her intently. They seemed to be engaged in a private conversation, and rather than disturb them with my presence, I walked a short distance away from the spire and paused to study the landscape.

It was quiet. We were less than a mile away from the edge of the dense trees that marked the border of the marshland. The land immediately surrounding the spire was carpeted in short grass, interspersed with the occasional clump of late-summer wildflowers in shades of red and gold. Beyond the marsh, the Southern Pinnacles jutted into the sky, capped white with snow. Above, a dozen other gray eagles circled the Ebon Spire. Idly, I wondered why Galewing did not join his brethren.

I didn't know how long I'd stood there, simply observing the landscape while my thoughts roamed.

"Andrew?"

I turned to find Emmarie. I nodded and shifted my gaze back toward the horizon.

"I hoped we could spar today while we wait for Alex."

I smiled faintly, pleased she was eager to continue learning how to wield a blade. "Of course. It will give us something productive to do."

Alexander emerged from his eighth trial late the next afternoon. During the time he'd been occupied, Rynn managed to coax Lydia from her room, and the two had taken several long walks around the perimeter of the spire. I insisted on following them from a distance, in case more assassins pursued us, but I'd spotted no one. I hoped there would be no further attempts on my life for the remainder of our journey, but it was foolish to let my guard down. Not after we'd come so far.

When not acting the part of sentinel for them, I sparred with Emmarie, cleaned my armor and Alexander's, and sharpened our swords. Galewing returned to the sky while I worked, soaring above the spire with his brethren. He didn't return until Alexander emerged, then remained only long enough to relay a message. My brother smiled fondly, then announced he needed to rest. He remained inside his room until late the next morning.

While Alexander slept, the rest of us ensured we were ready for the next leg of our journey. Without Chela's guidance, I was uncertain what provisions we may need beyond food, and I didn't know where we'd next be able to resupply. Alexander and I would have been lost in this land without the aid of the others, and I felt a deep pang of regret that I'd been denied the opportunity to thank Chela properly. She would be sorely missed, despite her sometimes abrasive demeanor.

Lydia acquired a map from one of the shrine's elders, and with his help, we determined the route we must take. We'd go southeast, where we'd come upon the settlement of Stillwell in two days' time. Elder Carridan encouraged us to resupply there and purchase as many provisions as we could load into the cart. There were no more settlements for leagues beyond Stillwell.

After that, we'd travel east across a vast plain. At its heart was the next site along Alexander's journey, an area marked on the map with the sketch of a tree. When I asked about the marking, Lydia beamed with delight.

"It's known as the Oracle's Tree," she replied. "Legends claim it was planted by the first Oracle after the end of the Mage Wars as a symbol of peace. It's said to be protected by magic that has not been seen since that time, and the first Oracle's spirit lives on within the tree. I don't know if it's true, but I recall from my own pilgrimage the tree was by far my favorite site. It's beautiful. You'll see."

Rynn smirked. "We could attempt to describe it to you, but I don't feel words are adequate. You must see it for yourself. Even non-magi find the site stunning. It's unlike anywhere in the world."

She flashed a bright smile, and I was unable to do anything but smile in return.

"My people also have stories of the Oracle's Tree," Emmarie added. "My uncle once told me his greatest wish was to visit the place himself, but I don't believe he will ever make the journey. He's a Tree-speaker," she added when she noted Rynn's puzzled expression.

Rynn nodded, understanding. "Of course. I met another Tree-speaker once at the Frostwake. He was likewise thrilled with the prospect of seeing the Oracle's Tree, though I don't know if he ever reached it. He was traveling alone. It's a long distance to go without the support of friends."

Emmarie nodded, her dark eyes filled with immeasurable sadness. "I'm going to check Sienna one more time."

She stood to leave, and I rose with her. "I'll accompany you, Emma."

I followed her outside into the evening air while ignoring the strange looks I received from the other women. I knew speaking of her uncle was painful, and Emmarie had not yet told anyone else of her exile. We walked in silence toward the packhorse, where she was tethered near our cart.

"You didn't have to come," Emmarie sniffed, her voice thick with emotion.

"But I did. Someone has to make certain you're alright."

I glanced toward the door of the spire as its hinges creaked. I could make out Rynn silhouetted by the yellow light spilling from within, though I doubted she could see us from her position. The night was dark; the moon had not yet risen, but it would be little more than a sliver once it did.

"I suppose I ought to thank you, then. For always looking out for me, I mean." Emmarie sighed. "When this journey is over, I don't know what I'll do. I can't return home."

"You can always seek your father," I reminded her. "You've said you'd like to see him again."

She shrugged, her gaze fixed on the ground. "I could, but what good will it do after so many years? When my mother died, he disappeared. Perhaps he believed he was doing the right thing by leaving me in my uncle's care, but sometimes I think I would have been better off fending for myself."

"You're welcome to stay with us," I offered. "Alex and I have plans. We'll need all the help we can muster, and your skills with a sword have improved greatly."

I didn't want to divulge anything further. Alexander and I still had many things to discuss, though a plan was beginning to form. She'd be in danger if she traveled with us, but she'd be no better off living in exile, alone. I believed she was old enough to make the decision herself, and with us, she'd have someone to ensure her welfare.

She looked up, hope gleaming in her eyes. "If you'd have me along, then yes, I will travel with you." She pursed her lips thoughtfully, then asked, "This is about your brother, isn't it? The king."

"Yes."

"After everything you've done for me, it's the least I can do in return," she replied. "I will fight alongside you when it becomes necessary. You and Alex have become a better family to me than anyone related by blood."

My heart ached for her plight. The only blood relative she knew was responsible for her exile. Belatedly, I realized her situation was not unlike my own. Perhaps it fueled my desire to help and protect her.

Emmarie cast a wary glance toward the door of the spire, where Rynn remained in the doorway. "Andrew, can I ask you something?"

"Of course."

"Why does Rynn always seek you out?"

I cleared my throat, suddenly uncomfortable. I believed I knew the reason, but I feigned ignorance. "She does?"

Emmarie laughed. "You haven't noticed? Everyone else has."

I shrugged and glanced toward Rynn. She continued to peer through the darkness, her eyes seeking our location.

"What do you suppose she wants?" Emmarie's tone was contemplative.

I watched Rynn for a few moments while I thought over the girl's question. As I began to speak, Rynn turned to disappear inside.

"I believe she's seeking a friend. I'd like to believe I can be that for her." I shifted my weight and sighed.

I hoped for Rynn's sake friendship was the extent of her interest, but I kept my thoughts to myself.

It took the better part of two days to reach Stillwell. It was a small community made up of sprawling farms surrounding a central marketplace. Most of the people we encountered were locals seeking trade with neighbors. We received a wary, yet interested, welcome from most of the folk we encountered, and the farmers were eager to trade. Several years had passed since a mage had traveled through the settlement while on their pilgrimage, according to those we spoke to.

After we replenished our stores, we made camp just beyond the town's perimeter, as the settlement was too small to host a proper inn. It was just as well. The coin we'd been given by the Oracle at the start of our journey was starting to run low. We didn't linger past the night.

The farther we traveled from Stillwell, the fewer trees we encountered. Soon, we traveled a path that cut through waist-high grass. From horizon to horizon, there was nothing but the vast expanse of flat grassland and the nearly cloudless sky above. The weather was moderate, though I suspected in high summer it would have been sweltering. Autumn was an excellent season to traverse the open plains.

Occasionally, I glimpsed herds of large animals moving in the far distance. The beasts remained beyond the visible range of the others; only Galewing and I possessed keen enough eyesight to spot them as they trundled across the landscape. Neither Lydia nor Rynn knew what the creatures might be, for they had never encountered the beasts during their previous travels. Emmarie, who had taken to driving the cart in Chela's stead, hoped one would draw near enough that she might speak with it. To her disappointment, no such encounter occurred.

Though we spoke during the journey, our conversations were often subdued. Chela's death remained at the forefront of our minds, and Lydia could not shake her misplaced sense of failure, despite our collective efforts to console her. Had circumstances been different, the journey might have been enjoyable, but we found little happiness along the way.

During our fourth day of travel, I spied what could have only been the Oracle's Tree in the far distance. Something truly massive rose from the surrounding plain, and as we drew nearer, there was no doubt it was a single tree towering above the landscape to an impossible height. It was another day before we drew near enough to make out the details of its nature.

It was similar in appearance to an oak, though the trunk had a circumference larger than most cities we'd encountered in the Southlands. The branches rose into the sky, seemingly thousands of feet above our heads, to spread in a vast, tangled canopy. Dappled shadows covered the plain for miles in every direction. Enormous roots, larger than our supply cart and immeasurably long, broke through the soil to form massive, twisted arches large enough to span the roadway. Birdsong drifted from overhead as countless sparrows, finches, and other species I didn't recognize communed with one another in the vast network of branches.

While I'd encountered some spectacular sights along our journey, the Oracle's Tree left me speechless. I'd never imagined such a thing could exist in nature.

"There's a shrine carved into the trunk of the tree itself," Lydia said as we drew near the base, her tone reverent. "It's where we must go next."

"I understand why my uncle spoke of coming here," Emmarie breathed. "It's so beautiful. To speak with such a tree…What stories must it have to share?"

"Perhaps some of the birds who reside here will share their tales with you," Alexander suggested. He craned his neck to gaze at the web of intertwined branches above. "This place… It's utterly amazing."

I smiled as the phrase reminded me of something Thomas had once said to me regarding a tale he'd read in the castle's library. "What do you suppose Tom would say if he were here?" I mused. "He'd be enthralled by this tree. More than you or I."

Alexander laughed with delight. "That he would. Ah, Tom. I hope he fares well. I wish we could contact him again." He grinned at me then, his eyes alight. "The stories we'll have when next we meet!"

"There may be another Feige along our route," Rynn said slowly. "The father of Bryson and Bella used to live in Dragon's Feet. If he still lives, you can send a message to your brother there. He possesses the same talent as his children."

"Dragon's Feet?" Alexander snorted. "That's an odd name."

I chuckled. "You haven't bothered to look very closely at our map, have you?"

He shrugged and cast a furtive glance at Lydia. "I've been otherwise occupied."

I smiled as a flutter of anticipation stirred in my core. "Dragon's Feet is the last city we'll stop in. It lies at the base of the pass that leads into the Dragonlands."

I'd been awaiting this portion of the pilgrimage since before we'd embarked on it. The Dragonlands—my father's homeland—held as much meaning for me as it did for Alexander. I'd visit the library, as the Roche twins had suggested, and hoped I'd glean answers to some of my questions. Then there was the matter of the Caein family vault and the dragon scale armor my father had spoken of. There would be much to do once we finally reached the Dragonlands, and I was eager to arrive.

Our final destination had always seemed so far away, but now, only a handful of stops remained. A thrill of excitement ran through me as I considered what I might learn of the dragons—and of myself.

Emmarie's voice broke through my silent reverie. "If only the birds weren't so high. I don't believe they can hear me from the ground."

"Perhaps I can remedy that," I replied with a grin. "It's been some time since I last stretched my wings."

Her eyes widened with delight. "Truly, Andrew? You would allow me to fly with you so that I might speak with the birds?"

I laughed, carefree in a way that I'd not felt in months. "Of course. What else will I do while Alex is in his trial? I'd rather spend time doing something worthwhile than sit idly about."

"You mean…you'll change forms?" Rynn asked, her blue eyes ablaze with a fierce fascination.

I nodded. "Flying has become one of my favorite pastimes. If my dragon form wasn't so awkward, I'd take to the air more often."

Alexander chuckled. "At least one of us will have fun while we're here. Enjoy yourself, brother."

His words were spoken lightly, but his expression was troubled. With each trial, his anxiety grew, though I doubted he'd speak of it in front of the others. His worry put a damper on my own buoyant mood, and we traveled the remainder of the distance to the shrine's entrance in relative silence. I would wait until he began his trial before taking to the sky with Emmarie.

The shrine at the Oracle's Tree was a marvel within a wonder. The entrance was little more than an oversized crack in the tree's gray-brown bark. Upon crossing the threshold, we were greeted with an exquisite interior carved from the living wood itself. Intricate designs decorated the walls and ceiling, depicting figures of animals, people, and various places. I recognized the image of the Ebon Spire and the Golden Stair as we passed. The floor was smooth and polished to a sheen, and a row of lanterns hung along the curved outer wall to illuminate the space in a warm light. The shrine within the tree was nothing short of an artistic masterpiece.

We encountered a mage after we'd walked some distance. He stood before a heavy door carved with the crescent-and-stars symbol belonging to the Oracle and crossed his arms with a stern frown as he spied us. His loose hair was white, the only indication of his advanced age.

"I'm afraid the three guest rooms are presently occupied," he said by way of greeting. "Your group is welcome to pitch tents outside."

"Is there another mage within the trials?" Lydia asked.

The elder shook his head. "There have been no other mages here for quite some time. It has been over a year, in fact. A pity."

He paused to study each of us in turn. There was something in his gaze I found unsettling, and I was immediately mistrustful. He emitted an aura of superiority, yet I sensed darkness lurking beneath his genial façade.

"It won't do any harm to tell you of the others who came before you," he continued after a moment. "Two are scholars from the Citadel, here on the pretense of studying the tree. They are outside, making drawings and charts, taking notes, and the like. The third is one of your people," he said to Emmarie. "Not a Tree-speaker, however. He is merely…curious."

Emmarie met his gaze for the briefest of moments before looking down at her hands. "I'm no Tree-speaker either."

He nodded as the faint scent of something faintly sweet, reminiscent of dried apples, wafted toward me. I knew he used his magical ability, whatever it might be. My tension rose; why did he deem it necessary to channel his magic during a mere introduction? What did he hope to gain?

"An unusual group you have," he said to Alexander. "I see your guardian—your brother— and a pair of magi… Strange, that. Both so young too. Surely the Oracle didn't choose one of you to be the guide?" He asked, his gaze flitting between Lydia and Rynn. After a moment, he focused on Lydia, with an appraising expression. "I seem to recall your last visit, perhaps four years ago?"

Lydia nodded but made no reply.

"If you want to hear our story, it will take some time," Alexander cut in. "But to answer your first question, our guide is no longer with us. She was…killed, and is buried at the Ebon Spire."

The elder nodded once more, but his expression soured. "Tragedy follows you wherever you tread. And it is not of your doing, no… Hmm." He shook his head, suddenly agitated, his dark eyes flashing dangerously. "Such is the way of your kind. No! Don't look at me with such surprise—I know what you are. The eagle who accompanies you is but the most obvious sign. A mage-warrior. We haven't seen one live to complete the trials in several centuries. No doubt others along your path have shown you a measure of fear. As they should."

Alexander tensed and clenched his fists. I was uncertain what he planned to do, but I was familiar with the warning signs; his temper was primed to flare. I watched the elder warily, suspicious of his motive. The faint, fruity scent lingered in the air. While his magic wasn't obvious to the others, I knew he channeled it—but to what end?

"What are you playing at, old man?" I growled. I placed one hand on the hilt of my sword, prepared to defend my brother if need be.

He laughed heartily and tipped his head back while the scent quickly faded. "I see. There is no fooling *you*, is there?"

He studied me closely for a moment, and when I didn't relax my guard, he sighed. "I should not have used my power to peer into the minds of your companions. It has been many years since any of *your* kind have graced us with their presence."

I dropped my hand and nodded curtly. "Your ability gives you some insight into what others are thinking."

"And you are more finely attuned to the essence of magic than those around you realize," he countered. "Perhaps I've acted unfairly to those who travel here, peeking into their minds as I so often do. But you must understand, this site is remote and receives few visitors. I find using my ability on my guests stems the tide of boredom I face each day."

"That's a sorry excuse," Rynn replied, her tone like acid. "No one should be subjected to one such as *you*, peering into their minds unannounced and unwanted."

The elder's gaze swept to meet Rynn's, a tight smile on his lips. "Strong words for someone who has been so cursed by her own power. Shall I tell the others what I saw in your thoughts?"

Rynn snarled as her face flushed crimson. She turned on her heel and stormed toward the entry.

He chuckled. "I thought not." Turning to Alexander, he said, "Don't mind me. I'm but an old man, prone to senseless amusements.

I'll leave your friends be from now on. After all, I must focus on seeing you through your trial."

He chuckled again, and the tension in the room eased, but when he next spoke, his tone was grave. "Your power is vast, young man, and you're in a very precarious situation. But you know this. There is but one path forward: To complete that which you have started. Are you ready to begin?"

TWENTY-FOUR

While Alexander made his final preparations to enter the trial chamber, I went outside to start setting up our campsite before night fell. Rynn was pacing between the shrine's entrance and our cart, seething at the elder's words. Though I didn't know what he'd glimpsed when spying on her mind, I didn't fault her for her explosive reaction. It had been an unwarranted intrusion and a breach of trust.

As I walked toward the cart, she turned sharply to match my stride. I glanced at her curiously. Her jaw was set in anger, and her blue eyes flashed as she began to speak.

"That man should never have been allowed to become an elder, let alone at a sacred site like this." Her voice wavered with unconcealed rage. "He wasn't here when I came through on my own trials, though it seems he remembers Lydia. He is vile…arrogant. Ugh!"

"If it's any consolation, he didn't say anything further after you left." I hoped my words would calm her.

She laughed, a bitter, mirthless sound. "The damage has been done. He knows what my thoughts were, and now the rest of you are left to wonder what he saw and why I'm now livid." She paused as the others began to emerge from the tree, then shook her head in frustration. "Now is not the time. Perhaps one day, I'll summon the courage to tell you. But not today."

I nodded and removed the tents from the cart. Wordlessly, Rynn took the stakes and began to assist with the task. I didn't know what to say. I wouldn't press the issue; she'd tell me in time, and it wasn't my business to pry.

Later that evening, as the others were turning in for the night, Lydia sat beside me as I stoked the campfire. She was pensive as she gazed into the dancing flames. I suspected she wanted to speak of Alexander, but was surprised to learn her thoughts were on other matters.

"I've been meaning to ask you this for quite some time." She turned to face me, the firelight casting odd shadows across her face.

"Now is as good a time as any," I replied. "The others are asleep, or will be soon. Is this about Alex?"

She smiled warmly. "Alex will be fine. I'm not concerned about him tonight, though I wish I understood his intentions better." She sighed. "No, I didn't want to talk about Alex. We'll work out our differences, given time."

I nodded. "I'm glad to hear that. My brother cares for you a great deal."

"What I've been meaning to ask *is* related to Alex in a small way." She faced the flames once more and drew a breath before she continued. "I've come to know him well. He speaks very highly of you. But I have not taken the time to truly get to know *you*, and… I suppose what I wanted to ask you is…" She sighed and peered toward the night-darkened plains beyond our camp. "I'm sorry, Andrew. I didn't realize this would be so difficult."

I watched her warily, uncertain of where she was headed with the conversation. "Obviously, something is troubling you, but I can't answer your question unless it's asked."

She laughed softly and shook her head. "I know, but I'm afraid of the answer." She looked at me then. "It's silly, isn't it?"

"You have nothing to fear from me. If this is about Alex, as you say—"

"No, it's about me. Or, rather, *us*. Alexander and myself." She steeled herself, and her next words spilled forth in a rush. "I told you once before I thought I was in love with him. That was weeks ago, but sometimes it seems as if it's been a lifetime. I'm certain now that I *do* love him. I wanted to ask…Do you approve? Of us being together?"

I grinned, then broke into a laugh. "Of course, I approve. Alex has never been so happy, and I can assure you that's your doing. Did Alex spin some wild tale about me? I don't understand why you'd be afraid to ask."

She managed a laugh, then shook her head. "No, I suppose I was merely concerned when I didn't need to be. Alex thinks the world of you. He would follow you to the ends of the earth if you asked him. That alone made this conversation rather intimidating."

I chuckled. "As I said, you have nothing to fear from me. If you recall our conversation in Oristan, I already gave you my blessing. He's happy. Besides, you understand him in a way I no longer can...You're a mage, and frankly, I don't comprehend the nuances of your abilities. I can't talk with him regarding what he's going through—it's foreign to me. But you can."

I paused and ran a hand through my hair. It was a relief to finally share my mounting frustration with her.

She beamed and placed one hand lightly on my arm. "You can count on me. I'll watch over him to the best of my ability. Once his trials are complete, he will be different...We are all changed in the end. It's evident in our faces, our eyes." She paused to draw a breath and squared her shoulders. "He'll be fully in control of his power by then and will no longer be a danger to himself. I'll admit I was sick with worry when he stayed behind with you in the marshes. But it all happened so quickly. There was no time to consider what to do..."

"He told me something after the battle was over," I replied thoughtfully. "He said he didn't use his power that day, that he knew it wasn't safe to do so. I was...relieved." I looked down for a moment, then said, "He saved my life."

"He told me what happened. He was a reckless fool, charging headlong toward the archer as he did." She snorted indignantly. "The armor he wears is a remarkable thing, but I fear he puts too much faith in its ability to protect him. It is only armor, after all. Given the right circumstance, it can be rent asunder, dragon scale or not."

I nodded. "I was afraid if I shifted, I'd sink into the mire. If I had, perhaps he would not have been compelled to act as he did." I shrugged. "Alex has always been a bit reckless. He's skilled with a blade, but there have been too many times when I've been forced to rush to his rescue. He has a habit of charging into situations without regard to his own safety."

I paused to offer her a grin. "Since he met you, he's changed. He's calmer. More willing to listen to reason. Perhaps your influence will prevent him from repeating that stunt."

"Hmm, perhaps." She smiled, then stifled a yawn with the back of her hand. "I'm sorry, but I must go to sleep. Thank you for speaking with me. It has put my mind at ease."

I made good on my promise to Emmarie after we'd breakfasted the next morning. I walked around the expanse of the Oracle's Tree until the curve of the trunk hid the campsite from view, then undressed and shifted, stretching my wings expansively. It had been weeks since I'd last taken my dragon form, and I came to the pleasant conclusion that I'd missed it. It was not the rush of power that I'd been longing for, but the sense of freedom—freedom upon land and air, but above all, the freedom to be *myself.*

With a grin, I leapt into the air and flew the short distance to our camp. I relished flying; there was nothing in the world akin to soaring through the air with the wind against my scales.

Emmarie awaited my return, eager to introduce herself to the birds in the canopy high above. I didn't see Lydia, but Rynn stood between the tents. She studied me in silence, her blue eyes alight with an inner fire. I wondered what her thoughts must be to provoke such intensity in her gaze.

As Emmarie clambered up my side and perched between my spines, Rynn strode forward. She stopped several paces away, her expression a mixture of wonder and trepidation.

"Andrew… It's really you, isn't it?"

I smiled, then nodded.

"Would you like to fly with us?" Emmarie called down to her. "It's great fun!"

Rynn shook her head adamantly, her blond curls bobbing with the motion. "No, I don't believe that would be wise. I'll keep my feet firmly on the ground, thank you." She arched an eyebrow at me quizzically. "I don't suppose you'll be back for the midday meal?"

"We'll return before then," Emmarie assured her.

She nodded and backed away as I prepared to leap into the sky. Emmarie's hand tapped my back twice. With her signal, I rose toward the interwoven branches overhead, pumping my wings powerfully. The wind rushed past, cool and refreshing. I smiled, elated by the simple act of taking to the air.

We soared beneath the canopy and toward the rim of sky beyond. As we burst forth into bright sunlight, I banked upward and slowed my speed. Birds darted from the leaves beneath us, startled by our passage. I laughed, caught up in the moment, my concerns set aside for a time.

It was the first flight I'd taken simply for the sheer pleasure of it. On previous occasions, it had been of necessity, our troubles overshadowing the delight I might have experienced otherwise. I reveled in the moment. *This* is what the dragon-kind had been born for.

The birds continued to flee from my proximity as my vast shadow fell across their leafy perches. Emmarie called to them persistently. After a while, a solitary sparrow overcame its innate dread, beating its tiny wings at a furious rate to keep pace with me. Emmarie continued to speak, and finally, the bird alighted on her hand. She beamed, delighted.

I continued to soar above the tree's enormous branches, spiraling toward its top, then winding down toward the lower canopy while Emmarie conversed with the bird. It had been many months since I'd last felt so carefree, and I was loath to see it end. But as the sun neared its zenith, I knew we must return to camp. I'd promised Rynn we'd be back, after all.

Emmarie said her farewells to the sparrow, then tapped my back twice. I released a contented sigh and grinned. There were few other ways I could envision spending the morning that would have left me feeling such peace afterwards.

I landed a short distance from our tents. Emmarie slid down my side to land nimbly on her feet.

She beamed at me. "Thank you! When you return, I'll tell you all I learned from the sparrow. This is a wondrous place!"

I smiled and watched as she scampered toward the others where they stood near the campfire. Rynn looked up at her approach, then her gaze flicked beyond the Merael girl to meet mine. She arched an eyebrow, an amused smile playing on her lips, and shook her head. She pointed at a cookpot set over the fire, and I understood she expected me to return as soon as I'd shifted and dressed once more. I flew to the area I'd left my clothing and boots, then retraced my steps to the camp, human again.

"I wasn't certain you'd return in time to eat with us," Lydia stated as I approached. "You were gone for hours. It seems Emmarie found what she sought. She's done nothing but gush about a certain sparrow and the incredible view from the treetops above."

"You would have been welcome to come along," I replied.

I continued to smile, relaxed and at ease. Perhaps I should consider flying more often; it had relieved my tension in a way nothing else could have done.

"I would rather be here in case Alexander returns." Lydia offered me a smile. "Someone must look after him while his guardian is away."

I winced as a pang of guilt shot twisted my gut. I'd taken far too much pleasure in the morning while my brother toiled away. "I should have remained here, as well."

Lydia laughed. "Oh, Andrew, everyone knows you'd do everything in your power to see Alex succeed. You've already done so much for him—for all of us, truly. If what you've alluded to is true, these moments of joy will become fewer as time marches on. If anyone deserves a few hours of relaxation, it's you. Now stop fretting and eat."

I sparred with Emmarie after lunch. She was still energized from our flight and surprised me with several creative moves as our wooden practice swords clashed. She grinned mischievously each time, and I laughed in response.

We'd just finished the day's lesson and returned the practice swords to their place in the cart when Lydia cried out and fled from the campsite. Startled, I turned to follow her path to find Alexander had emerged from the Oracle's Tree and was making his way toward us, smiling but clearly exhausted.

I greeted him as he approached, then stopped to study his face more closely, struck by a subtle change. While he didn't have the ageless countenance of the others yet, his face no longer appeared as young as it had on the previous afternoon. He truly was becoming a mage.

He frowned, his eyes narrowed in concern. "What is it, brother?"

I shook my head, bemused. "You're…changing."

Alexander tipped his head back and roared with laughter. "The irony of your statement isn't lost on me. *You're* the expert on changing." He smirked. "It was going to happen sometime, you know."

Lydia beamed at him. "It's a sign that all should go well with your final trials. It gladdens my heart."

He smiled at her fondly. "I've been telling you not to worry." He hooked one finger beneath her chin as he gazed at her, while she stared at him in adoration. "I'll get through this and more. You'll see."

Alexander spent the remainder of the afternoon lounging about camp. Lydia prepared an early meal, and as soon as he'd eaten his fill, Alexander turned in. He would no doubt sleep the night through and continue well into the next morning. Rynn offered to take the first watch in Alexander's stead and would awaken me when it was time for the second.

When I turned in a few hours later, Alexander was sleeping soundly. I noted with some amusement he'd fallen asleep fully clothed with his boots on. Knowing that I'd be called to watch at midnight, I removed my boots but remained fully dressed as well. I fell asleep to the sound of Alexander's rhythmic breathing and was mercifully spared from dreams.

I awoke to the sound of raised voices. I lay still, listening to the argument as it began to unfold. Rynn's voice was unmistakable, but the other voice, while familiar, I could not immediately place. It was a male voice, but not Alexander's. He remained asleep a few feet away. I frowned, my sleep-addled brain unable to recall where I'd encountered the speaker previously.

"…suggest you turn around this instant," Rynn stated forcefully. "I'll not let you come any closer."

The other voice dripped with condescension. "Your men are asleep. I'd like to see you try to stop me. I'll have what I want, girl, and you won't stand in my way."

Rynn was in trouble. Instantly alert, I fumbled for my boots and pulled them on, then scrambled toward the exit.

"I *said* you will not come any closer! You will not harm them so long as I draw breath, you lecherous bastard!" Rynn seethed.

When I burst from the tent, Rynn stood at the entrance to the tent Lydia shared with Emmarie. Her body was rigid, her blue eyes alight with an eerie inner glow. The sharp tang of wintergreen hit my nostrils as she channeled her magic. The elder mage from the Oracle's Tree was before her, his back toward me. Why was he here, and what had he done to spark Rynn's unmitigated rage?

"I'll go where I want, girl, and take whom I want."

A flare of hot anger shot through my core as I understood. Lecherous bastard, indeed.

He stepped forward as I charged toward him. I'd kill the bastard if he so much as touched any of the women. Before I reached his location, his body suddenly stiffened and became immobile.

I skidded to a halt a few steps away. Rynn stretched her hands toward him, pure loathing twisting her features. The elder's skin became pale and took on a bluish cast in the firelight as frost coated his body. His eyes clouded white as they were frozen from the inside out.

Stunned, I gaped as he fell to one side with a solid thud, then stared at Rynn, shocked by her power. It had been different when she froze the marshes for our passage or moved drifts of snow, but I'd never considered what her magic would do to a human being.

Rynn collapsed to her knees and drew her hands over her face as she began to sob, the wintergreen scent rapidly dissipating. I could make out the glitter of frozen tears on her skin as I moved toward her and knelt at her side.

"Rynn? What happened?"

She dropped her hands, revealing eyes rimmed in red and filled with unspoken torment.

"He… He wanted… He wanted Lydia." Her voice cracked as she choked back another sob. "I don't think he knew anyone was awake… He planned to defile her…" Her breath hitched and fresh tears spilled from her eyes, only to freeze moments later. "I couldn't let him. No woman deserves such treatment… And Alex. What would he say? I… I had to stop him."

I drew her into a rough embrace. "You did what was necessary," I replied. "He won't hurt anyone again."

She gasped and wrenched free of my arms to stare at the elder, paces away. Her eyes were haunted, horrified. "I…killed him?"

I rocked back on my heels to look at the man, his limbs stiffened from the unnatural cold. He looked as though he'd been lost in a blizzard, buried beneath snow for countless weeks, one of cruel winter's casualties. No man could have survived such extremes.

"Yes."

"I only meant to stop him," she whispered, her voice tight with anguish. "I never meant to…to kill him."

Her face paled, then she leapt to her feet and bolted into the darkness. Moments later, I heard the sound of her retching.

I knew what she was going through. I'd endured a similar experience years ago during one of my first campaigns. The first kill, even if it was a matter of life or death, was the hardest to bear. Over the years, I'd grown calloused, and while I regretted the taking of each life, I no longer became physically ill afterward.

While Rynn was away, Lydia emerged, shaken. Even in the firelight, her complexion was ashen.

"I heard everything," she said, unable to take her eyes from the fallen elder. "If Rynn had not been here, he would have…accomplished what he'd come to do." She swallowed hard as her tears began to fall. "Why would he attempt such a horrific thing?"

I shook my head helplessly. I couldn't explain why some men chose to force themselves on women when they were neither wanted nor invited. "I don't know, but I'm glad you're unharmed. Is Emma…?"

Lydia forced a smile. "She sleeps. It's fortunate she didn't overhear him or bear witness to this tragedy. She's lucky to have you as her protector."

I frowned. "Had Rynn not been on watch, things would have ended far differently, I'm afraid."

"She will always have my thanks," Lydia replied, her tone meaningful.

At that moment, Rynn stumbled toward us. Her face remained pale, but she seemed to have regained her composure.

Lydia rushed toward her to stop abruptly a handspan away. "I owe you a great debt."

Rynn studied her before making her reply. "No woman should be forced to suffer such indignities. I would not stand for it." She drew a breath and sneered in the direction of the corpse, her eyes hard and unyielding. "I would do it again too. He deserved his fate."

I admired her resolve and her courage. In that moment, I knew I could count on her to fight when circumstances demanded, to do what was necessary in the face of adversity.

"How many others has he defiled during the years he spent here?" Rynn continued, her voice tight with rage. She paced near the dwindling fire, speaking to us and to no one. "I'm certain this wasn't his first foray into someone's camp. He wasn't expecting anyone to be awake, nor was he expecting me to stand up to him. He made his intentions clear, the vile shit. He couldn't touch me, so he focused his attention on those less equipped to defend themselves." She made a sound of disgust.

"Rynn," Lydia said solemnly, "thank you."

While the two women spoke, I gathered the elder's remains and carried his body from the campsite. I located a snarl of roots near the base of the tree some distance away from the shrine's entrance. A hollow space filled with leaves and debris lay beneath the roots, large enough to accommodate the body. I placed it inside and covered the corpse with the tree's detritus.

He didn't deserve a proper burial, and I doubted anyone would come looking for him.

I glanced toward the sky, catching a glimpse of the moon through the interwoven branches. It was well past midnight. I fully expected to return to camp to find Rynn and Lydia had turned in, but as I approached, Rynn's solitary figure stood at the edge of the firelight. Perhaps sleep eluded her after the ordeal.

She didn't speak until I settled down to sit beside the fire. Her eyes never left my face. "Lydia has gone back to sleep. Thank you for cleaning up my mess. I'm still in shock. I didn't mean for him to die, even though the bastard deserved it."

"As I said, he can't harm anyone again. That's what matters."

She nodded, unconvinced, then sat down beside me. "I don't believe I'll be able to sleep tonight. I'm too shaken."

"That's understandable," I replied. "If you'd like to talk, I'm here."

"Thank you. I—" She stopped suddenly, bit her lip, then looked away. "Let's talk of other things. I don't want to dwell on what happened. Tell me of your homeland, of your brothers, anything… Just not this."

"Of course."

I spoke of Vinterry; the vineyards, the processes I'd learned from Hiram, and tasting the year's first batch of wine. I spoke of Giles and his grandson, Gregor, who dreamed of becoming a soldier when he was older. I spoke of Vera, our times spent walking through her estate, the nights we'd spent in the library, and her insistence that I learn more of my heritage. Those were happier times, and it did my heart some good to speak of them.

Rynn said little but listened attentively. Before I knew where the time had fled, the first light of dawn was breaking over the eastern horizon.

"I must thank you," I said as we watched the sunrise together.

She shook her head, her eyes on the lightening sky. "I've done nothing to deserve your thanks, Andrew."

"You listened to me talk for hours." I offered her a smile. "I haven't spoken with anyone like this since I lost Vera. It's…comforting, I suppose. I'm glad to find there's someone I can still talk to."

When she turned to face me, her eyes shone with unshed tears. "I didn't know you felt so alone. If you ever wish to speak, I'm here."

"And that's why I thanked you," I replied. "You've helped me remember I'm not alone. It's a relief."

She smiled enigmatically, her blue eyes sparkling in the first rays of the rising sun. "After all you've done for us—and for me—I'm pleased I can return the favor."

TWENTY-FIVE

Though Alexander slept until nearly midday, we didn't linger at the Oracle's Tree. What had begun as a wondrous experience had ended in tragedy, and none of us wished to remain any longer than necessary. From the tree, we'd travel northeast across the grassy plains.

The others the elder had mentioned on our first meeting—the scholars and the Merael—remained elusive. I'd begun to suspect he'd fabricated the story to keep us out of the shrine. There was no one left to mourn the man, and I believed his fate was justified. Rynn struggled with the memory of the confrontation, though I assured her she'd done nothing wrong. The elder had been a damned monster.

As we passed beneath the last of the great tree's canopy, Lydia drew Alexander aside. I knew she planned to tell him what had transpired, and I believed he deserved to know. He'd be furious, but his rage would be mitigated by the outcome. He'd likely turn the anger upon himself since he'd been exhausted and slept through the ordeal.

I hoped Lydia could convince him that he was not to blame.

We reached an unspoken agreement regarding the events with the elder at the Oracle's Tree. After our first day of travel, the subject wasn't broached again. We spoke of many things, but the elder wasn't one of them.

It took five days to make the journey across the plains. The land began to rise and became hummocked, while small shrubs began to dot the landscape, most bare of leaves. The weather had grown colder, and a biting wind blew toward us from the mountains in the north.

Though Rynn and I were unaffected by the turn in the weather, the others sought cloaks and blankets for warmth.

Two more days passed before we reached our next destination. A vast plateau rose above the surrounding hills, its flat top and sheer, rocky sides an anomaly against the rest of the landscape.

Lydia led us to a narrow dirt track that zig-zagged up the plateau's western side. It took most of an afternoon to hike to the summit. Once there, we were greeted by a maze of ancient stone walls. The dark stone was worn smooth where it remained exposed to the elements, spotted with green-brown lichen in places, and reduced to fine rubble in others.

"We should make camp here," Rynn said. "The maze can be difficult to navigate, and without Chela, it may take hours to find the path to its center."

"The shrine is there, I take it?" Alexander asked as he pulled a tent and stakes from the cart. I took another tent and its set of stakes, prepared to set to work as well.

Rynn nodded. "We call this the Ancient Maze for obvious reasons. At its heart is a small structure the magi erected here many generations after the maze itself was discovered. We don't know who the original builders were."

Lydia lugged a cookpot from the cart and said, "Before the Oracles, there were fewer sites on the pilgrimage. Some were destroyed during the Mage Wars, while others remained. Most of the sites we've visited were built after the first Oracle appeared, but this one is ancient. This, and the two after it." Lydia shot a meaningful glance in my direction. "The final two sites were created by the dragon-magi."

"How old is this place?" Alexander asked.

Lydia shrugged. "We don't know. When I was here, there were two elders in residence at the shrine and there was one at the cave near Dragon's Feet. No one remains to watch over the last site in the heart of the Dragonlands."

"You're forgetting the road to the last site is grueling," Rynn added. "Since there are no dragons left to greet us at the gate—" she stopped mid-sentence and spun around to study me carefully. "Perhaps I'm getting ahead of myself."

Lydia had stopped what she was doing to study me as well. "Rynn, I don't know if it will work. But we should try…"

Rynn nodded, her blue-eyed gaze intense. "Yes, we should. It will save us a week of travel if it works."

With a frown, I abandoned the tent I'd been setting up. "Will one of you please explain?"

I crossed my arms, irked that I should be scrutinized like an insect under a glass. I suspected they referred to the gate at the entrance to the Dragonlands. Chela had mentioned it on occasion, but I needed to hear it from one of them. A pang of sadness shot through me at the memory of our lost guide.

"There's a gate leading into the Dragonlands a few miles up the road from Dragon's Feet," Rynn replied. "The gate is sealed with powerful magic. It will respond to no one but the dragon-kind. Since your people departed, there has been no way to open the gate. Each mage seeking the final site of the pilgrimage must journey days out of the way and navigate a rather unpleasant system of caves before they reach the summit."

It was as I'd suspected. "And you believe I can open this gate? Chela mentioned it as well."

Both women nodded, but it was Lydia who spoke. "You are dragon-kind, Andrew. It should open for you if the stories are true."

"I'll try," I promised. "There is still the matter of this maze and reaching Dragon's Feet before we concern ourselves with the gate."

Alexander chuckled. "Perhaps it wasn't that you're my brother, but that you're a skin-changer that caused the Oracle to name you as my guardian."

I frowned, uncomfortable with the sudden scrutiny. "We may never know. That woman was too damned vague. And I doubt she'll be any more forthcoming when next we meet with her." Frustrated, I turned away to finish setting up the tent.

"The Oracle only speaks of her visions when times require it," Lydia replied defensively. "She sees many things, but much of that will never come to pass. The Oracle sees *possible* futures and will only reveal those she believes are a certainty."

"And you believe she *wasn't* certain I'd be capable of opening the gate?" I asked, exasperated. "That she *wasn't* certain we'd make it this far? I find that difficult to believe, based on what she *did* tell us."

"Andrew…" Alexander's voice weary.

As I looked up, I was met with his frown. He knew my stance regarding the Oracle and her visions; I was not only skeptical, but the mysticism she surrounded herself with was a source of endless aggravation. I was surprised he'd chosen to defend her, given she'd used him to produce an heir he would never see. I glared at him. Finally, he averted his gaze and released a heavy sigh.

"I know you don't fully understand the business between magi and the Oracle," Alexander said after a moment. "But your anger is unwarranted, brother. She told us enough to guide us through this journey. It was all she was obligated to say. That she told us more was…unusual."

"It was a breach of the Oracle's code," Lydia replied with emphasis. "When Alex told me of her other visions and what she'd revealed to you… It was a shock. The Oracles live by a code, and to reveal possible futures to a mage who has yet to prove himself goes against it. And to further relate what she saw of *you*—a person who is not a mage at all—is unheard of. It should not have been done."

"Then why did she do it?" I demanded. "She spoke of battles to come, of the destruction and death that would lie in our wake. There was no doubt she saw *me* in her visions. She claimed she saw a black dragon. I am the *only* dragon left, in case you've forgotten. If all of this was against her 'code,' why was she compelled to tell us at all?"

Over the past months, I'd put the Oracle's words out of my mind. I didn't want to be the source of such destruction if it meant the lives of innocents would be lost. While we'd decided Colin must be dealt with, what that would entail was yet to be seen.

I found myself at the epicenter of a series of events that would yield consequences for many years to come, and much of what the Oracle had told us was hazy, warped by a future she couldn't fully visualize. Alexander's pilgrimage had been my priority; now that it was nearly finished, perhaps that possible future wasn't so distant after all.

"I can't answer for her," Lydia said after a moment. "What is done can't be undone, and you've learned more than you should have regarding your future."

"We know what we must do, brother," Alexander added. "About Colin, I mean. And to do that, we'll be forced to fight. He won't give up his throne easily, but he must be ousted. That much is clear."

"Then we should begin making official plans." I sighed and stood up, finished with the tent.

"After the last of my trials, I must return to the Citadel," Alexander continued. "I know you don't want to hear this, but I must speak with the Oracle again. It's expected that I do so."

I bit back a groan. I'd anticipated the outcome, but I didn't have to be pleased about it. As with many long journeys, the final destination was the same point we'd started from.

"I've suspected it," I growled. "Perhaps she'll have advice for you regarding Colin. When we spoke with her last, she was unwavering in her belief that our arrival meant the onset of war. Perhaps that's why she's chosen to break her own damned rules."

"She truly saw war in your future?" Rynn asked, eyes wide. When I nodded, she frowned. "We've always believed the northerners would leave us in peace. Most magi don't share my view, but given the history of our lands, war should be inevitable. It's simply a matter of when."

Lydia's expression soured. "Sometimes you are so depressing, Rynn!"

Rynn laughed. "I state the facts as I see them. Complacency can only last so long before something happens to bring it crashing down." She shrugged, indifferent. "If it were not during our time, it would occur during the next generation's or the next after that."

Lydia sighed in exasperation and turned her back on us. She began to arrange kindling to make a campfire, clearly finished with the conversation. Alexander shook his head, a puzzled expression on his face, and went to help her. I had enough experience with women to know it wouldn't be long before she sent him away, but she'd also appreciate the sentiment behind his actions. She wasn't angry with him, but with the situation.

I walked away from the camp toward the outer wall of the maze. The walls, though crumbling, stood almost ten feet high and were several feet thick. They were constructed of stone and mortar, and had been built to exacting dimensions, each block fitted perfectly amongst those surrounding it. Even after so many years, the craftsmanship was evident.

"I've heard stories of people becoming hopelessly lost in the maze."

I turned to find Rynn had followed me from the campsite. She stood a few paces away, gazing up at the weathered stones. "Lydia and I have been here. There are markings to guide the way, if you know what to look for. Luckily for your brother, I do." She offered me a knowing grin.

I lifted an eyebrow. "Why tell me others have become lost if there is no risk for us?"

She shrugged. "It gave me something to say other than, 'I followed you from camp,' although my words were true. When I was here previously, we found a skeleton. It had been there for some time, poor soul."

I crossed my arms and tilted my head as I studied her. "And why *have* you followed me, Rynn?"

"I…don't rightly know," she said before she looked away.

A blush rose in her cheeks, and I knew she wasn't being truthful. I decided to let the matter rest. There was little harm in seeking conversation.

The next day dawned gray and cold, made miserable by a biting wind from the north. It would not be long before snow began to fall in this region, and on the plateau, there was little shelter outside the maze's ancient walls. We broke camp hurriedly and made our way to the entrance, an arched opening within the stone.

Alexander communicated with Galewing briefly after we'd gone inside, and he nodded thoughtfully as the eagle took flight. "I believe I—*we*—can navigate this," he said, chewing his lower lip in thought. "Galewing believes if he can share his sight as he did during our fight in the marshes, I should see the path we must take to reach the shrine at the center. It should save us time."

Rynn narrowed her eyes in thought. "It will if it works. While Lydia and I know what markings to look for, they're not always readily apparent. We'll try your way first." She flashed a grin at Alexander. "You may end up being more useful than the rest of us. Besides your brother, of course."

I frowned. "What does that mean?"

She laughed good-naturedly. "What I meant is, like Galewing, you have the advantage of flight. An aerial view of the maze is superior."

"Yes, well, I suppose that's true," I muttered.

I didn't understand why, but she flustered me at times. I looked helplessly at Alexander, but he merely smirked, mischief in his eyes.

To my immense relief, Lydia intervened. "Let's just be on our way. With Galewing's help, we should be to the center before nightfall."

With Alexander in the lead, I took the rear, following Emmarie as she guided Sienna and the cart. She'd proven adept at handling the animal, though since the encounter at the Oracle's Tree, she'd become subdued. I decided to speak with her once we had reached the shrine and Alexander had entered his trial. I wanted to ensure she was well.

Rynn kept pace with Alexander as we traversed the twists and turns of the stone maze. Lydia followed them for a time, but after a while, slowed her pace and allowed Emmarie to overtake her. She fell into step alongside me. I raised my eyebrows in question at her approach.

We walked in silence for several minutes before she spoke, though she appeared thoughtful. "I don't know what Rynn and Alex were goading you about earlier, but I've seldom seen you appear so…flummoxed. Are you well?"

I blinked, surprised by her concern. I thought over the brief conversation but couldn't pinpoint the source of my discomfort. I felt well enough.

"I believe I am," I replied slowly. "I believe… Ah, never mind."

I'd been about to explain I disliked being the center of attention when it came to my innate abilities. I still had much to learn, and I didn't like that others seemed certain I could solve problems for them when I didn't know if I could do so myself. And Rynn… She'd become a puzzle of late.

She nodded, unconvinced, but didn't press further. "Very well. But you will tell me if you are unwell? I'd like to help if I can."

I chuckled. "I'm fine. Don't trouble yourself."

"Hmm." She was silent for a few moments, then said, "Alex and Rynn have been discussing you this morning."

I glowered in their direction. "Why?"

Lydia laughed. "I may be a mage, but I don't have the ability to know their thoughts. Rynn began by asking questions about Novania but quickly steered the conversation toward you. I don't know what she hopes to achieve, but Alex was amused by the situation. He enjoys telling tales of your exploits, though I think he has a tendency to embellish the truth at times."

I rolled my eyes. It was typical of Alexander, though the last time I recalled him acting this way was just after I'd begun courting Vera. Perhaps her loss had affected him more than I'd realized.

"I'd have to know which tale he's spinning to know how much truth he tells."

"It was your battle with the Corodan and their Hive-queen when I parted from them."

I nodded. It was one of Alexander's favorite stories. He particularly enjoyed the part where he'd arrived at the rim of the pit and found every last Corodan slain, with me standing in the midst of the carnage, stark naked. I sighed and ran a hand through my hair.

"He likes that tale. He seems to enjoy seeing my face redden while he tells a certain part of it." I shook my head but couldn't stop myself from smiling in his direction.

"I must have walked away before he reached that portion," Lydia replied. "But now you've piqued my curiosity…"

"Oh, hell, no wonder my brother likes you so much." I laughed. "The short version is that I went to face the Corodan alone. It was before Alex knew what I was. I was sorely outnumbered, and the only way to survive the situation was to shift into my dragon form. When I shift while wearing armor—or any clothing, for that matter—the garments are instantly destroyed, rent beyond repair. By the time Alex arrived, I'd shifted again, but my armor was a lost cause. Only my cloak survived the transformation."

Lydia bit her lower lip for a moment, but was unable to contain her laughter for long. "You are not the storyteller Alex is, but I can see why he likes that tale. I'm surprised he hasn't told it sooner." She laughed again. "I can envision the expression he wore when he found you."

"Believe me, he was at a loss to explain what he saw. It was one of the soldiers who came up with an explanation." I chuckled. "That day seems a lifetime ago. So much has happened since then."

She nodded, understanding. "You've been through more in the past year than most people endure in a lifetime. While there are times when your anger takes the forefront, you both manage to retain a positive outlook. It's not only revenge that drives you, but some deeper purpose. Am I correct?"

I thought over her words carefully. "Colin must face his crimes, but that isn't the whole reason why I've chosen to oppose him. Alex and I have been forced to hide what we are for most of our lives. I want the people of Novania to see we aren't monsters, that we should be allowed to live just as they do. To be forced into exile simply for *existing*… It isn't right."

"When you speak that way, I understand why the army respected you and followed you as they did." She smiled faintly. "It wasn't that they were ordered to, or that they believed you were of royal birth. It's because you have a way of making people *believe* as you do. It's a gift."

I frowned, making my skepticism known. "I only speak my mind."

"Ah, but that is where you're mistaken," she countered. "It isn't simply that you speak your mind, it is *how* you speak it that makes a difference."

We lapsed into silence as I pondered her words. I didn't feel I was particularly eloquent, and I detested making public speeches. There had been times when I'd spoken out of necessity, but I'd always ensured the soldiers under my command knew they could approach me, no matter their rank or experience. I'd been more at home in the barracks than I'd ever been in the castle. Life had been so much simpler when I was merely a soldier in service to the king.

I wondered what the garrison would think of me now. I was certain news of the tourney field would have spread like wildfire through Novania. They must have known the man they'd so willingly followed was not a *man* at all. Would they choose to follow the king's laws, the same laws that would have seen me put to death even as I'd drawn my first breath of life?

I'd encountered men and women throughout my life who believed the superstitions that people Marked were inherently evil. And the stories told of dragons were no better—the dragon-kind were a species to be feared—and hunted. I'd distanced myself from those conversations, afraid I might say something that would give them reason to suspect my loyalties.

Would the soldiers who had willingly followed me into battle against the Corodan still hold the same respect for me now that my true nature had been revealed? It was a question I needed an answer to before we faced Colin.

With Galewing's help, Alexander navigated the stone paths unerringly, and we reached the shrine at its heart well before noon. Rynn paused to appraise him as we came to a stop outside its entrance, clearly impressed with his newfound skill. Galewing descended from the sky long enough to share another silent conversation with Alexander, then took to the air once more. I watched the bird longingly, though I knew my place was on the ground for at least a while longer.

A trio of magi emerged from the shrine and extended their welcome to our group. A bald man with bushy white eyebrows who introduced himself as Wynmar Solais spoke first. "Good day, friends. My assistants will see to your horse and belongings. Please, come inside."

He ushered us through the door with a genuine smile and without any trace of magic use. I relaxed; we would not experience a repeat of the events from the Oracle's Tree.

"It has been months since a mage last arrived for a pilgrimage," he said as he led us to a cozy sitting room adorned with cushioned benches arranged around a stone fireplace. "It seems you were expected to reach this point. A message came four days past from the Citadel, addressed to one, Andrew Caein."

I frowned in confusion. Why should I receive a letter, and from the Citadel, of all places?

"I'm Andrew."

He withdrew a carefully folded sheet of parchment from within a pocket. It was sealed on one end with red wax, which had been impressed with a signet, but I was unfamiliar with the design.

"I don't believe the message is urgent. You may read it later if you wish," Wynmar said, though he appeared perplexed. "I believed the message was for your mage. I find it surprising it's for his guardian."

I nodded. "As do I."

While Wynmar spoke to Alexander, I stared at the letter. Rather than paying heed to the conversation, my mind wandered as I attempted to puzzle out who the sender might have been. There were a number of people we'd met while in the Citadel, but I doubted any of them would send a message—most had been far more interested in Alexander. This left me to conclude it had likely come from the Oracle. With that conclusion, I became less interested in reading its contents and merely resigned myself to doing so.

A few minutes later, one of the younger magi entered the room to announce that our quarters had been made ready for our stay. Wynmar excused himself after imploring Alexander to seek him once he'd eaten breakfast the next morning. We had the remainder of the afternoon and the evening to ourselves.

I remained where I was as the others prepared to leave, turning the letter over in my hands. Alexander spoke briefly to Lydia, then sat down at my side.

"Why don't you open it and see what it has to say?" he asked.

I frowned. "If it's from the Oracle, I'm not sure I want to read it."

He chuckled. "And if it's not from her?"

"Then I suppose I ought to open it." I sighed. "I don't know who else might have sent it, and sent it *here*, of all places."

Alexander snickered. "It will bother you until you know for certain what it says. I know you, brother. You can't abide *not* knowing."

I grunted. "Very well."

I turned the letter over once more and broke the wax seal, then unfolded the message. It was written in a flowery script that reminded me of Claire's hand, though on closer inspection, it was not her handwriting but another woman's.

Andrew –

I'm writing this message on behalf of your father, who cannot do so on his own. I visited the Stone Grove on business for the Oracle, and once that was complete, Zayneldarion asked if I might share his words. I obliged him, of course. It would be foolish to deny one of the great dragons of our time, even given his current circumstance.

Zayneldarion sends his regards, and he sincerely hopes this letter finds you well. He wished that I remind you of your last conversation with him and hopes you will find time to visit the Caein vault in the Dragonlands. Based on our calculation, you should arrive there soon.

I will ask the Oracle for an appropriate destination in which to send this once I return to the tower. If you return to the Citadel, please visit your father. He speaks

highly of you, and I can sense through his words he is very proud. He would enjoy another visit. May your travels be safe and swift.
– Lileen.

Five distinct symbols had been painstakingly drawn at the bottom of the message. I didn't recognize them, nor did I understand their meaning.

"Well?" Alexander asked after a moment.

"It was from my father, in a way." I smiled through my sudden melancholy.

I handed him the message and sat back while he read.

"You're fortunate, brother." He handed the message back to me.

"How so?"

"Your father didn't know you existed until a few months ago," he replied. "Yet he's taken to you as though he's known you since birth. I know he can't deny he's your father—seeing you in dragon form alongside him made that abundantly clear. What I'm trying to say is many other men would have treated you with indifference or outright hostility. Your father *accepted* you. He seems to genuinely care for you. It's a lucky thing."

My smiled widened. "You're right. And since you must return to the Citadel once this is over, I'll return to the Stone Grove. I need to speak with him again. I think… Rather, I *know* I'll enjoy my time with him."

TWENTY-SIX

I'd been restless throughout the morning, unable to remain still. After a time, I left the others where they lingered near the shrine's hearth and moved outside. The weather was brisk and hinted of snow, but the chill hadn't deterred the gray eagles. A dozen soared through the overcast sky above, and I wished I could join them.

I shook my head and made my way to the stable where Sienna was hitched. She appeared comfortable; the interior of the stable was warm and dry, and a bag of oats was within her reach. I was certain Emmarie had seen to her care, but the elder's assistants had done their part as well. There was nothing to occupy my time there.

I returned outside and was surprised to find Galewing had landed on the roof of the shrine. He eyed me sharply, then released a shrill cry. I frowned, perplexed by his presence, until Rynn appeared in the shrine's door.

"Alex has finished his trial."

I stared at her for several seconds, uncomprehending, then understood the eagle's return. I glanced skyward to find his brethren were gone. "That was fast."

Rynn nodded. "He's gone to his room to recover, but Wynmar seems to think he'll have no further obstacles in the rest of his trials. We can leave tomorrow, weather permitting."

I grinned, relieved by the news and excited by the prospect of traveling ever closer to the Dragonlands. "Dragon's Feet is next."

A faint smile appeared on her lips. "Yes. He's nearly finished, and you're… You're nearly home."

I paused to glance at the sky once more. "I've never considered the Dragonlands my home."

"It's the birthplace of your ancestors," she replied. "It was your father's home."

Home. I experienced an unanticipated rush of emotion as I contemplated her words.

It was another four days before we reached the city of Dragon's Feet. During the journey, I often found myself speaking with Rynn. I learned much about her; she spoke of her family, of her time at the Frostwake, of her various likes and dislikes. She was ready with laughter and smiles, and I grew comfortable with her presence. She didn't allude to seeking anything more than friendship, and I was content.

We had no encounters with Colin's assassins, and the weather remained amenable to travel, though it steadily grew colder.

Once in Dragon's Feet, we sought an inn Lydia recommended. It was a three-story affair, freshly painted inside and out, with a clean stable attached to the rear. As we made arrangements for our stay, the first flakes of snow began to fall outside.

"Your way to the trial cave will be clear enough," the innkeeper said as he made notes in his ledger. "The people of Dragon's Feet are diligent when it comes to keeping our streets clear. Your route to the Dragonlands may prove difficult, however. It's treacherous, even in summer. I hope you're prepared for a nasty trek."

"We're ready," Alexander replied with a pointed glance in my direction.

He held onto the hope I could open the gate, but I harbored doubts. I was only *half* dragon, after all. The women had only heard tales, none of which could be corroborated, but I'd given them my word I'd attempt to open it. It was best to be prepared for the worst should I fail, and I hoped Alexander understood.

"We'll need to resupply," I said to the innkeeper.

"A wise decision. The market is always open, no matter the weather."

Our first night at the inn was comfortable, and Alexander departed the next morning for the trial cave. Lydia insisted she accompany him to the cave's entrance, though he assured the rest of us we need not follow.

An inch of snow had fallen overnight, and though the day was cold, the storm had passed and the sky was clear. I watched from the window of the common room as Alexander and Lydia departed, their boots leaving distinct prints in the freshly fallen snow.

"He'll be alright, you know."

I turned to find Rynn a few steps away, leaning against the wall with her arms crossed. I didn't know how long she'd been there, silently observing as I watched my brother leave.

"I know."

"And yet here you are, brooding." Her expression was unreadable.

"I made a promise to watch over him," I replied. "It's hard to step back and allow him to go off on his own. He's no longer my kid-brother—he's grown up. A man. I must let him do this, and yet I feel irresponsible. I should be with him." I managed a weary smile. "That must sound ridiculous."

Rynn's expression softened. "I understand some of what is running through your mind. Syllas is seven years younger than I am. There are times I still think of him as a child, though he's old enough to have a family if he wished it." She sighed. "Sometimes when I see you with Alex, it makes me pine for the company of my own brothers."

At that moment, Emmarie bounded into the room, a wellspring of youthful energy. "Andrew, there you are!" She flashed a grin. "I'd like to train today. I know it's cold, but I think I can manage for a while."

I chuckled. "If you'd like to work on your sword-arm, we can plan for it. But let's wait until this afternoon, when it's warmer."

"Thank you!" She spun around, prepared to rush back the way she'd come, and nearly ran headlong into Rynn. "Oh, I didn't realize you were there. My apologies."

Rynn waved her away with a laugh before turning back to me. "That's the most animated I've seen the poor girl since we left the Oracle's Tree."

I nodded. "I spoke to her a few days ago. She was upset by what happened, as can be expected, but not in the way I'd anticipated. She was angrier about having slept through the encounter than at what might have happened had you not been there." I shook my head, baffled. "While I believe she'll be adept with a blade one day, she's not ready for a confrontation yet."

"Perhaps she was angry because she was unaware of the situation," Rynn replied. "I don't know if she would have fought that man, but if I'd been in her place, I would have been rattled. To sleep through something like that…" She shuddered.

"Perhaps you should speak with her as well," I replied. "A woman's perspective might be what she needs to hear."

Rynn shrugged. "Lydia and I have spoken to her, but it didn't have any affect. She's been in better spirits since we left the maze, and I believe it was *your* words that gave her comfort. That girl idolizes you and Alexander both."

Lydia returned a short time later to find us chatting near the windows.

"It will likely be a few days before he returns," she said with a pained expression.

Rynn nodded knowingly.

"That will give me time enough to seek out the elder Feige," I said after a moment. "I'd like to write Tom again."

"I know where his residence used to be," Rynn replied with a smile. "I doubt he's moved since then. I'll take you there."

Lydia appeared amused by our exchange. I was puzzled by her expression, but didn't have time to inquire. Rynn was on her feet and moving toward the door, beckoning me to follow. Once we were outside, she led me purposefully through the snow-dusted streets. Some of the townspeople gave us startled looks as we passed; we weren't dressed for the weather.

She said nothing for several minutes, then stopped abruptly and whirled to face me. We were on a quiet street that ran between a row of small, well-kept cottages. There were no townspeople nearby, and the only other creature I could see was a cat, who darted away at our approach.

"I've been meaning to speak to you about something, and now is as good a time as any." Her usual confidence was gone, replaced by uncertainty—and perhaps fear.

"What's wrong?" I asked, confused by her sudden change in her demeanor.

She bit her lip and looked around helplessly, though there was no one nearby to assist her. "Andrew, I… I know you've been through hardship and hell the past few months. And I know you aren't prepared for what I'm about to tell you." She grimaced in momentary frustration. "This is proving a more difficult conversation than I'd anticipated."

I stared at her, at a loss for explanation. "Whatever it is, you can tell me."

She laughed bitterly and shook her head. "One would think that, but something holds me back. I…fear your reaction."

"Why?" The question was out of my mouth before I'd fully registered the thought.

She frowned and looked at the trampled snow between her boots, studying it as though it was more interesting than the remainder of the world around us. "You've said you consider me a friend. I suppose…I want more than mere friendship. I want what Lydia has with Alexander—but with you."

I averted my gaze. I'd suspected this for some time, but I'd hoped it wouldn't come to this. I couldn't be what she wanted, not while I continued to mourn Vera.

She laughed nervously. "I've been trying to catch your attention since we met. There have been times I was certain you felt *something* more than mere friendship, but your reaction tells me that I've been mistaken." She paused and stared at her feet. "Where do we go from here, now that you know what I feel?"

I couldn't meet her eye. I didn't want to hurt her, though a part of me felt the damage had already been done. I wasn't ready to move on, and I didn't know if I'd ever be. Honesty would slice her heart like a knife, but it was best she learned now. I wouldn't lie to her.

"I can't give you what you seek. Not yet. Perhaps not ever."

"Alex warned me you'd say that." Her voice came out in a choked whisper, strangled by grief and disappointment. "He said it was too soon, that you'd need more time. I thought I was prepared for this outcome, but I'm not." She drew a shaky breath and seemed to steel herself. "If I must wait another decade or longer, I will. To me, you are worth waiting for."

I didn't know how to respond to her declaration, so rather than fumble for a response, I held my tongue. After a few moments, she sighed heavily and turned away.

"Come. I'll take you to the elder Feige." Her voice was subdued, her expression defeated.

"Rynn… I'm sorry."

It pained me to see her downcast, and knowing it was my fault only made the situation worse. I liked her and held her in high regard, but I wouldn't let her believe there was anything more between us. It wasn't fair to her, no matter how difficult my words had been.

She shrugged but didn't reply. She led me past a half dozen cottages before stopping in front of one with a small wooden sign above the door. The sign was hand-carved to show a scroll and quill.

Rynn gestured toward the door. "This is the house. I… Can you make it back to the inn on your own?" When I nodded, she appeared relieved, perhaps even grateful. "Then I'll see you again once you return. I'd like some time alone. To think."

"Of course."

I watched her stride purposefully back the way we'd come, my heart heavy. She deserved better than what I could offer, better than the broken shell I'd become in the wake of Vera's murder.

I stood outside Feige's home for a few moments while I attempted to sort out my thoughts. When I finally turned toward the residence, my energy was depleted, gone with Rynn's departure.

When I returned to the inn, I carried two different messages from Thomas. The first wished Alexander luck in the last of his trials, then went into a detailed account of Thomas' activities in the secret encampment he'd established in the Gloaming Highlands. He'd gathered more allies since we'd last written, though the Corodan still remained staunchly opposed to an alliance without my presence to facilitate it. Thomas ended the first message with a plea for my assistance. He needed the Corodan if we hoped to raise an army capable of opposing Colin's forces.

I'd replied with a promise I'd return north once Alexander was safely through his pilgrimage. I'd travel to his location with as much speed as I could muster once my role as guardian was at its end. I'd fly if necessary. I understood his desperation, and I could outpace Colin's men. I'd done so before.

Thomas' second letter stated he feared Colin knew of his current location; the duke's soldiers had captured a pair of scouts wearing the garb of the royal guard only a few miles from their camp. While they were unable to return to their superiors, their presence had struck a chord of anxiety in those assembled to support Thomas. The scouts had been taken captive, and Duke Crossley had interrogated them, though it seemed he'd learned very little. Thomas concluded the message with a renewed plea for urgency in my travels and a brief description of his location.

I would share the messages with Alexander once he returned. He'd understand my position, though I wasn't certain he'd agree to travel with me. He wouldn't leave Lydia behind, and I suspected he had plans involving the Southlands that he hadn't yet shared with me. We needed to discuss a true strategy once his training was complete.

I didn't see Rynn when I entered the inn's common room, though Lydia fixed me with a disapproving stare each time I crossed her path. I didn't doubt the two had spoken, and Rynn had been devastated by my refusal.

I believed I'd done the right thing when I'd spoken honestly, but given Lydia's dark looks, I began to question my decision.

I sparred with Emmarie for several hours that afternoon in an attempt to focus my thoughts elsewhere, but I was distracted. After a time, Emmarie began to take notice. I apologized and cut her lesson short.

I didn't see Rynn until that evening. I'd begun to suspect she was avoiding me, but I didn't fault her. I was in the common room with Lydia and Emmarie awaiting supper, when Rynn entered and moved toward us purposefully. Our eyes met, and she held my gaze as she took the open seat across from me.

I knew I should say something, but words eluded me. After several seconds of increasingly awkward silence, I managed, "Are you alright?"

She nodded. "Yes, thank you." She glanced down at the table for a moment, then reached across to take each of my hands in her own.

I raised my eyebrows. "Rynn?"

She held my gaze, her blue eyes fierce. "Andrew Caein," she began slowly, "I have come to a decision. Wherever your travels may take you, I will accompany you. I can't allow you to walk out of my life now that I know you—even if it means we remain only friends."

I looked down at the polished tabletop, uncomfortable with the situation, made more awkward by the presence of Lydia and Emmarie—but a small part of me was decidedly pleased.

When I looked up, her eyes were fixed on mine. I had no choice but to tell her of Thomas' messages and what they meant for my future.

"I won't be staying in the Southlands much longer," I said evenly. "Once Alex is safely through his trials, I must go north. Tom asked for my help, and I've agreed to assist him."

She nodded. "Then he'll have my help as well." She released my hands and sat back in her chair. "Where you go, I will follow."

Lydia was aghast. "You can't be serious! You're a mage. To go north means a death sentence—"

Rynn's laughter cut her off. "Who better to venture north with than someone who knows the lands and its ways?"

"I won't be staying in Novania," I added, hoping to ease Lydia's fears. The sudden urge to defend Rynn's decision was undeniable; despite my innate misgivings, I rather liked the idea of traveling with a companion. "We'll only be passing through. Tom is hiding in the Corodan lands. I gave Alex my word that I'd travel with him as far as the Citadel, and I still intend to do so. I'll inform Tom once we're there when he should expect us… And I'll tell him I won't be arriving alone."

"I'd like to come along as well," Emmarie said.

I smiled at her, but shook my head. "I think Alex will need your skills more than I do. You should remain with him."

What I didn't tell her was she'd be taking an even greater risk than Rynn if she followed me into Novania. Rynn was human, and as long as she didn't use her abilities, I doubted anyone would question her. Emmarie wouldn't blend in, no matter how hard she tried.

Her face fell, but she nodded. "I thought you'd say that. But you'll write to us, won't you?"

I laughed. "Yes. As often as I'm able."

Rynn appeared content with the outcome of the conversation. When she caught my gaze, she smiled. My tension began to erode, and I leaned back in my seat, relaxed. I'd feared I would lose her friendship, but she was more resilient than I'd anticipated. I was grateful she understood.

And I was pleased I wouldn't be making the long journey to Thomas' camp alone.

I sprawled in front of the hearth in my room the next afternoon, studying the map we'd acquired from the elders at the Ebon Spire. The Dragonlands was only a short distance away from our present location, the gate less than a day's journey from the inn. I traced my finger across the depiction of the gate and silently prayed I'd manage to open it.

A rapid knock drew my attention, and I set the map aside. "Andrew?" Lydia called from the hall, her voice strained.

I rose and strode to the door. "What's wrong?" I asked as I pulled it open.

She wrung her hands and wouldn't meet my gaze. "There's a messenger in the common room from the…the shrine. He's asked for you."

Dread's icy fingers stabbed through my core. I nodded and followed her downstairs, refusing to voice my concerns. We both knew a messenger from the shrine meant something unusual had occurred in Alexander's trial, and it was unlikely he bore good news.

The messenger stood stiffly just within the entrance door. He nodded a greeting as I approached. "I'm Lewis. I've been sent to escort you to the shrine."

"What happened?" I asked as I followed him into the frosty afternoon.

He shook his head, then held one hand up in Lydia's direction. "This involves the mage and his guardian. You shouldn't come."

Lydia bristled. "There is no one and nothing that will keep me apart from Alex," she hissed. "I won't interfere in the shrine's business, but I intend to be near the man I love."

"It's—" he began.

"Let her come," I cut him off.

He appeared uncomfortable by the demand, but nodded. "Fine. But you must remain outside once we arrive."

Lewis set a brisk pace, and at times I believed he'd break into an outright run. The urgency of the situation was clear, and I hoped with every fiber of my being that my brother was well. As we approached the mouth of the cave, he stopped and spun to face us.

"The elders are inside," he replied. "There are a pair of guards at the entrance. They'll allow you to pass, guardian, but the cave is closed to others until this…situation is resolved."

"Why can't you tell us what happened?" Lydia demanded shrilly.

He sighed. "I don't know the details, but I can't allow you to follow him inside. The elders were explicit. You must wait here."

"I'll return with Alex," I promised. Lydia nodded tearfully.

The guards at the mouth of the cave parted as I approached and studied me solemnly. A flickering torch held in an iron bracket on the wall behind them lit the chamber beyond.

"The elders await you outside the trial chamber," one of the guards stated as I passed. "The path leads directly to it. You won't become lost."

"Thank you."

I strode past them and entered the cavern. The walls were rough and slick with moisture, but more torches lit the way at intervals. The path wound through several narrow passages to end in a domed chamber adorned with dozens of natural columns. At the center of the chamber, a pair of white-haired elders knelt beside an unmoving form. They stood at my approach.

Even from a distance, I recognized Alexander. Something metallic glinted in his hands, but it wasn't until I neared his location that I understood what he held. A curved single-edged sword forged of a strange, silvery metal was clasped in his hands. It glinted red along the blade edge and sported a hilt constructed of dark wood. I'd never encountered a weapon of its nature.

"You must be Alexander's guardian." The man who addressed me was tall but frail. His watery blue eyes met mine with a measure of compassion, yet uncertainty and unease flickered through his expression.

I nodded. "What happened? And what is that sword?"

He sighed and glanced at his colleague. "Kella, please tend him for a time. We must speak."

Kella nodded and knelt beside Alexander. Her hands began to massage the air a hair's breadth above him.

"I'm Ramos," he said as we walked a short distance away. "I've seen many things in my time, but never anything like this. Alexander completed his trial, but upon returning from the chamber, he fell into a deep sleep. As you can see, he hasn't awakened. That isn't what concerns me, as it happens on occasion." He glanced toward Alexander once more, a troubled look crossing his features.

"What *does* concern you?" I pressed.

He shook his head. "That sword… He held it when he left the trial chamber. I don't know what spirit he encountered, but it must have given him the weapon. I don't know what to make of it."

The Oracle's words came back to me then, spoken months before. She'd been speaking to Alexander when she'd said, *"And I saw you, as well. Standing in the midst of the destruction, bodies piled around you, while you brandished an ancient sword. A cursed blade, if I'm not mistaken."*

I stared at Ramos, certain I knew what Alexander held in his hands. "She said it was cursed…" When he gave me a strange look, I repeated the Oracle's words.

Understanding came over his features then, and his eyes lit with a burst of excitement. "A cursed blade! They were forged in ancient times for use by mage-warriors. They aren't cursed in the manner you suspect—it's simply the name they were given. They can be safely handled by mage-warriors, but no one else. If another mage were to touch the blade, it would consume their mind. The mage-warriors' powers are markedly different than most, and we've never fully understood the workings of them. But that blade…Yes, the description I'm familiar with matches this weapon."

"It won't pose a danger to him?" I asked, reeling with the news.

"Not to him, no." He shook his head, and his tone became grave. "To his foes, however, that will be a very different story."

"You mentioned it was a gift from a spirit," I said. "I don't understand."

"When a spirit gifts an object to a mage during the trials, there is always cause for concern," Ramos replied patiently. "It is my duty to keep a mage's guardian apprised of any unusual developments. I'm relieved you were aware of this blade, as was the Oracle."

I snorted. "I knew only the fragments the Oracle saw fit to tell me. I still don't understand the nature of this weapon."

"I've told you all I can, I'm afraid." Ramos sighed. "It has been centuries since a mage-warrior reached this point in their trials, and much of our knowledge has been lost. Knowing he bears a cursed blade as his predecessors did is something of a relief. The blade won't cause him harm."

"Will Alex know more when he awakens?" I asked.

"I hope so," he replied. "I'd like to know more about this weapon, myself."

TWENTY-SEVEN

I returned to Lydia a short time later, even though Alexander had not yet awakened. She was huddled near the side of the cave's mouth, her fur-lined cloak drawn tightly around her shoulders while she continued to shiver. When she saw me exit the cave, she rose swiftly and rushed to intercept me.

"Alex, is he—?" Her voice trembled.

I smiled gently. "He'll be fine. He's resting."

The relief in her expression was undeniable. "Oh, thank you." She paused to shoot a heated glare toward the messenger. "If he's fine, why was I made to stand out here in the cold? Why was I unable to see him?"

"Let's head back to the inn. I'll tell you on the way," I replied. "They sent for me because something happened that was…unusual."

As we walked through the darkening streets, I explained what I'd witnessed within the trial chambers, what Ramos had said, and what the Oracle had told us before we'd embarked on our journey.

"A cursed blade? I've never heard of such a thing." She was thoughtful for a time, then shrugged. "I'm no scholar. There is much about magic I don't know."

She sighed and looked skyward. The first pinpricks of starlight had begun to twinkle while the last of the sun's rays faded away. Above the city were a number of gray eagles, though it was impossible to tell which of the dark silhouettes belonged to Galewing.

"If Alex had been in any real danger, Galewing would have known." Lydia dropped her gaze and offered me a weary smile. "I still don't understand the connection he has with that bird. He's tried time and again to explain it to me, but it's a foreign concept. I can't seem to grasp his meaning. But Galewing would have warned us if Alexander was in danger. Since he didn't, perhaps I panicked without good cause."

"Don't be so hard on yourself. I know you love my brother, and your reaction was natural." I raked a hand through my hair. "I was worried as well."

She narrowed her eyes and scowled. "I've been meaning to talk to you about that, you know. Love. You and Rynn. She wouldn't tell me what you said two days ago, but she was *very* upset. All she'd say was Alexander was right. I don't know what she meant, but she's my good friend, and I don't like seeing her hurt." She crossed her arms and tossed her head indignantly. "I know her pain was *your* fault. While she seemed better yesterday and you seem to be on even footing once more, I will not see her hurt again. *Do you understand me, Andrew Caein?*"

I nodded automatically, stunned by her outburst. I'd never witnessed Lydia—kind, caring, gentle Lydia—lose her temper so thoroughly. Even her spat with Alexander at the crossroads was paltry compared to the wrath she currently spewed in my direction.

"She's determined to follow through on her ridiculous notion of traveling with you into the north, you know." Her voice dropped in volume, and while much of the ferocity was gone from her tone, a core of steel remained. "I spent most of the morning trying—and failing—to talk her out of it. She's insistent. She claims you've come to an understanding, that all will be well, but… Should I find out otherwise, you *will* deal with me. And I *will not* be as forgiving a second time."

"Lydia, I swear I didn't upset her intentionally." I swallowed and looked away, helpless in the face of her anger. "Things are…complicated."

Lydia's glare could have boiled water. We were nearly to the entrance of the inn, and she stopped in front of me, blocking my path to the door. "Then tell me what happened since she would not."

I grimaced and averted my gaze. If Rynn had chosen to keep silent, it wouldn't help matters if I spilled the details to Lydia. I didn't know why Rynn would keep our conversation to herself, but I respected her; it wasn't my place to explain.

When I didn't respond, Lydia's scowl deepened. "You'd best not hurt her again, Andrew, or so help me, you will live to regret it." She turned on her heel and stormed inside, leaving me alone to grapple with my tangled web of emotions.

I turned away from the inn and stared at the darkening sky. I didn't want to join the others, not with Lydia in a foul mood and Rynn… I wasn't certain what she felt. Lydia would tell the others Alexander was well if they asked. My presence wasn't required.

A handful of townsfolk passed. Some moved toward the residential areas, a few stepped around me to enter the inn, and others scurried toward the business district on last-minute errands. I paid them no heed, despite their curious stares.

I don't know how long I stood there, but after a time, I became aware someone had approached and stopped at my side. I was surprised to find Rynn, gazing toward the sky in the same manner I had been, her hands clasped behind her back. She glanced in my direction and offered a strained smile.

"I heard you've suffered Lydia's wrath."

I shrugged. "I wouldn't tell her what we discussed. As close as the two of you have become, it wasn't right for me to do so. I didn't want to make matters any worse than I already have."

"I spoke to her." Rynn's eyes focused on the night sky once more. "She was rather mortified at her own behavior once she was apprised of the details." She laughed softly. "She said I was a fool for ignoring your brother's advice."

"You are no fool, Rynn."

I studied her in the faint light spilling from the inn's windows as she watched the stars appear above. Her expression was serene, at peace with the outcome, despite the heartbreak I'd wrought. She was stronger than any woman I'd met, and I was glad we'd remained friends.

After a moment, I said, "If our roles had been reversed, I would have acted just as you did. Though you handled my reaction with far more grace than I could have managed." I chuckled. "Alexander likes to remind me I lack patience and my temper often gets the better of me."

She peered at me, her expression unreadable. "When you say things like that, it only serves to reinforce these maddening feelings I have. I know you're not ready to move on. Alex told me you still dream of her most nights. She was a lucky woman to be so loved by someone like you."

I averted my gaze. I didn't want her to witness the warring emotions I was unable to keep from my expression. What she'd said was true; I still dreamed of Vera often, though my dreams weren't as pleasant as she seemed to believe. I often woke in anguish, forced to relive my search of Vinterry and the discovery of Vera's body, bloody and broken, face-down amongst the grapevines. I'd failed to protect her, the woman I'd loved and cherished above all others.

But Rynn's words were a balm to my troubled soul. I had not yet forgiven myself for my failure, and perhaps I never would. To complicate matters, a part of me was convinced that if I moved on, Vera's memory would become tarnished and faded. I couldn't allow that to happen. She deserved to be remembered, to be loved, even long after she'd departed this life.

I wanted to believe Rynn understood some of what I was feeling, though I didn't think I'd ever be able to express to her—or anyone else—the depth to which Vera's loss had truly affected me. I'd lost a part of myself that night in the vineyard, a part I'd never recover.

I was startled when I felt the icy touch of Rynn's hand on my arm, her brilliant blue eyes filled with concern.

"It tears at my heart to see such sadness in you. I wish there were some way I could help you through this, if only you would allow it." She shook her head. "I will *always* be your friend. I'll be here for you should you need to talk."

She squeezed my arm before turning away. I watched her go, and after a time, I followed her lead. Rather than join the others in the common room, I took the stairs to my room, alone.

Alexander returned just after dawn the next morning. I'd been awake for some time, plagued once more by dreams of Vinterry's ruin. I'd gone to the inn's common room and took a seat at the table nearest the windows to watch for my brother. When I saw him striding along the nearly deserted street with the strange sword sheathed at his hip, I rose from my seat and moved to the door to greet him.

His eyes were bright. He flashed a knowing grin as I pushed open the door and held it for him.

"Ramos said you'd paid me a visit," he said, forgoing a greeting. "This sword… They didn't know what to make of it, brother. I'm glad you explained the Oracle's vision." He chuckled. "No, in truth, I'm glad you remembered at all. Until Ramos mentioned it, her words had completely slipped my mind."

I led him toward the table I'd just vacated, and we sat down as the first rays of sunlight began to illuminate the city outside.

"I ought to warn you about something else that happened while I still have the opportunity," I said. When he arched an eyebrow, I said, "Lydia is rather furious with me… I'm certain she'll tell you everything once you're alone."

Alexander shook his head, an amused smile playing at the corner of his mouth. "What have you done this time, brother?"

I told him the full story and finished with, "I had no idea your beloved could be so damned terrifying when she's angry."

Alexander roared with laughter. "I almost wish I could have seen that. You, the mighty skin-changer, brought down by the kindly healer and her vicious temper."

I rolled my eyes in mock exasperation.

"Perhaps it's best all of this came to light before more time passed. I've known for some time Rynn's harbored feelings for you—and in typical Andrew fashion, you were downright oblivious. I told her to give you more time. While I'm not pleased she ignored my advice, at least I don't have to dance around the subject while I'm talking with you." Alexander frowned. "Why is it women always want us to keep their damned secrets? I'll never understand."

I shrugged. Even after two marriages, I continued to be confounded by the women in my life. "We may never know, Alex."

He laughed, then stood up. "Speaking of women, I'd best tell Lydia I've returned, else we'll both be targets of her ire."

"Once you're finished and rested, find me again. I have messages from Tom." I didn't tell him what my plans were. There would be time enough for that later.

He nodded. "I will, brother. We can depart today if everyone is ready. I had plenty of sleep at the cave overnight. I would have come back last evening had Ramos not insisted I stay. They wanted to monitor me a bit longer." He glanced toward the staircase, yearning in his green eyes.

"Go. I'm sure she'll be thrilled to see you."

We departed midmorning, following a route leading toward the sheer rocky cliff-face looming behind Dragon's Feet. The cliff marked the western edge of a vast plateau, and as we drew nearer to the formation, we were eclipsed by its shadow.

I passed the messages from Thomas to my brother, and afterward, he explained how he'd come into possession of the cursed blade.

"I encountered the spirit of an ancient mage in the trial chamber," he said, his voice filled with wonder. "You could say she was one of my predecessors. The blade once belonged to her."

"Why?" Rynn asked, clearly puzzled. "The entities of the trial chambers don't typically gift us anything—let alone ancient weapons."

Alexander shrugged. "She was a mage-warrior during the time of the Mage Wars. She didn't have an heir to pass it on to and… She'd been waiting for another mage-warrior to arrive for centuries. She was exhausted and desperately wanted a final release." He bit his lip and wouldn't meet our eyes.

I narrowed my eyes as dread coursed through my veins. "Do you mean this spirit couldn't find peace until she parted with that weapon?"

He nodded, his expression troubled. "When Ramos said the blade wasn't truly cursed, he was mistaken. It's unsafe for anyone but a mage-warrior to handle, and it will be a boon to me, but… It doesn't come without cost. If another mage-warrior doesn't come along, I'll share the same fate as she did. The blade will hold my spirit long after I've passed unless I can gift it to another."

Lydia shook her head as tears began to leak from her eyes. "Alex, no… You should cast it aside. Be rid of it, I say! You can't agree to this fate."

He managed a smile, but his eyes were filled with sorrow. "It's too late, I'm afraid. The blade is mine, whether I want it or not." He drew a breath and said, "I owe it to the spirit—Liari—to wield this blade, no matter the uncertainty it brings to my future."

He sighed, then suddenly brightened and hastened to the cart. He rummaged inside for a moment, then withdrew the sword we'd purchased in the Citadel. He trotted forward to where Emmarie sat perched in the driver's seat.

"Emma, I want you to have this," he said, offering the sword to her hilt-first.

Her eyes widened as a delighted smile spread across her face. "Truly?"

He chuckled and nodded. "Yes. I won't need it any longer, and I think your skills have proven themselves. You should have your own blade. I know you feel Andrew has the final say when it comes to your training, but just between us, his opinion doesn't count." He winked at her conspiratorially, and she giggled.

I shook my head, amused, but said nothing in my defense. I'd planned to find her a suitable weapon once we returned to the Citadel regardless, and Alexander's gesture was touching.

"Thank you," she said. She halted Sienna briefly to stow the sword alongside her personal belongings.

Once we began moving again, Rynn found her way to my side. Alexander and Lydia walked ahead of the cart while I had fallen to the rear.

"I wanted to speak with you about the Dragonlands before we reach the gate." She glanced at the towering cliff-face that loomed ever nearer.

"Is this about opening said gate?"

She nodded. "At least in part, yes."

I shrugged. "I've already promised I'll try to open it, though I don't know how it works… Or if it will respond to me. I'm only *half* dragon."

"And that's *half* more than anyone else can claim," she countered, a gleam of mischief in her eyes. "I've seen the mechanism once before. It doesn't require any skill to use, nor does it take magic. I believe it will open at your touch. There's an impression on the mechanism, but you may have to assume your dragon form to make it work. The impression isn't a handprint and doesn't work for humans. It's in the shape of your…talons? I'm not sure if that's the correct term."

I looked at my hands, turning the right over to examine the palm. I'd never considered calling it anything other than a hand, even in my dragon form, but she wasn't wrong. The shape of the same appendage was markedly different when I shifted. Talon was as good a word as any to describe them, though I suspected my father would have termed them differently.

"I'll try to make this 'mechanism' work while human, and if it doesn't, I'll shift." I shrugged again. "My father never mentioned the gate. I can't be certain it will even respond."

"There is magic in the gate," Rynn replied. "It was attuned to work for the dragon-kind. You may not be a *dragon*, Andrew, but you are *dragon-kind*."

I looked away. Until we reached the gate, we wouldn't know if the magic would respond to my touch. And if my father's people were as secretive as the Roche twins believed, I couldn't discount the possibility they'd deny skin-changers access to their lands.

"You'll see when we arrive," Rynn continued animatedly. "It will open for you. I'm certain of it."

I smiled in spite of myself; her enthusiasm was contagious. "I hope you're right."

When we reached the gate late that afternoon, I was immediately enthralled.

It was built into a large crevice that split the cliff face and was carved of the same reddish stone that comprised the hillside. Two enormous panels spanned the gate, designed to swing inward on opening. Each panel was the same height as the sheer rockface surrounding the gate, towering high above the road and held firmly in place by interlocking facets embedded in the stone. An array of strange symbols decorated each panel, but they were unfamiliar, foreign even to Lydia and Rynn. A pedestal sat near the righthand side of the gate. It stood waist-high, its flat top marked with the impression of a dragon's forefoot.

There was no way to bypass the gate unless one could fly. The cliffs on either side had no visible handholds or cracks, while the gate, despite the intricate symbols decorating its surface, appeared too smooth to allow for climbing. I understood why the magi had been forced to use the treacherous cave system and journey days out of the way simply to reach their final destination. The gate was inaccessible.

I stared at the monumental stonework for countless minutes, transfixed. This was the gate that would lead me to my father's homeland, the home of the dragon-kind. While I'd known our journey would bring us to the Dragonlands eventually, the awe it evoked was indescribable. The gate was the work of dragon-magi, the work of my ancestors. It was unlike anything we'd come across on our journey so far.

But there was another sensation, a thrumming of power that emanated from the stone itself. It vibrated through the air, through *me*, tangible, yet unseen. Magic. Ancient magic, certainly, but its power remained, embedded in the earth itself.

I don't know how long I stared at the gate before Alexander spoke. His voice was subdued, reverent.

"I know this place has much more meaning for you than it does for the rest of us. It's truly an amazing piece of craftsmanship."

I blinked as though I'd just awakened from a powerful dream. "Alex, I… I don't know what to say. Being here is unlike anything I've ever experienced." I looked around to take in our surroundings once more. "I can feel the power within this place. My father's people—my ancestors—built it with magic. I can *sense* it…"

"I can as well," Alexander replied. "Not as keenly as you seem to, but we all—the magi, I mean—can feel the power that remains here."

My gaze landed on the pedestal, and my previous doubts vanished. I could sense it deep within my core, a strange resonance I couldn't explain. If I placed my hand on the pedestal, the gate would swing inward to allow us passage. It truly was a place for all dragon-kind, no matter what form they might take.

"I'll open the gate," I told my brother. I was confident it would respond to my touch now that I better understood its essence.

I placed my right hand atop the impression in the stone. It was dwarfed by the outline of the dragon's talons. Was I truly so much larger when I shifted?

As my palm touched the stone, a warm, tingle swept across my skin, more of my ancestors' magic. A moment later, the gate swung open to the sound of stone grinding upon stone.

TWENTY-EIGHT

The gates to the Dragonlands had remained open for several minutes after I'd placed my hand on the pedestal, but closed once more of their own accord after we'd passed through. It was a clear indication the dragons had not meant for the gate to stand open in welcome; given what I knew of their history, they'd likely designed it as a measure of protection, a final safeguard surrounding their homeland.

The road leading from the gate to the summit was paved with perfectly square blocks of stone, each larger than the cart. The stones were adorned with more of the strange symbols that had been carved on the gate. The road ascended gently, following the course of the crevice as it cut its jagged course through the rock. Its depth became shallower as it rose in elevation and would eventually level out at the top of the plateau.

We chose to make camp rather than travel any further. It would be dark soon enough, and the daylight would vanish from the depths of the crevice well before the sun set in the western sky.

"By my estimation, it will take most of the day tomorrow to reach the summit," Rynn said as she helped me set up the tents. "I think you've saved us at least a week's worth of travel, Andrew." She paused to flash a grin.

"I'm relieved the gate opened for you," Lydia agreed. She and Alexander were preparing supper, working side by side. "The caves are difficult to traverse. They're also dark, smell of mildew, and when last I was here, they were filled with bats." She shuddered. "I don't like bats."

Alexander stopped what he was doing with a laugh, then slipped one arm around her waist. "I would have protected you from the bats, my dear."

Lydia rolled her eyes and feigned annoyance, but after a moment, she smiled, basking in his attention.

"What are your plans?" Rynn asked me quietly.

I wanted to explore as much as I could, to learn as much of my father's people as possible while in their homeland. I recalled the twins had encouraged me to seek the library, and I needed to find the Caein family vault. But if time permitted, I'd do more. I related my desire to Rynn.

She nodded. "I know the structure the twins refer to as the library. It's adjacent to the trial tower. Perhaps we can find information there that will lead us to the vault." She studied me carefully for a moment. "What's so important that you must find this vault?"

"There's a suit of armor within the vault that my father hoped I'd take for my own." When she looked at me curiously, I added, "It's dragon scale armor. *His* dragon scale."

"It's his legacy to you. His way of protecting you when he can't do so himself." She smiled then, her gaze flicking toward Alexander. "You've done the same for Alex, you know. Perhaps you're more like your father than you realize."

"I can't say. I hardly know him, though I'm grateful he's accepted me." I sighed, suddenly melancholy. "I wish I could spend more time in the Stone Grove. I'd like to learn more from him, learn of our people. Perhaps one day I can, but I fear it's some time off."

She nodded, her vibrant blue eyes fixed on mine. "We'll help Tom once this is finished."

"Thank you," I replied solemnly. "I'm glad I won't have to make the journey alone."

I hadn't shared my concerns with the others about the next leg of my journey. I didn't know if Colin had soldiers near the Mage's Gate, though there had been rumors. If he did, their orders were likely to subdue and kill me on sight. Reaching the highlands where Thomas was camped would take at least a week if I flew the entire distance, and if I were pursued for the duration of my journey, I wouldn't stop for rest or risk hunting. I wasn't certain how long I would last without food to sustain my dragon form.

The news I'd gleaned from Thomas told me little of Colin's recent movements, but I believed Colin would not leave the Mage's Gate unwatched. Perhaps it wouldn't be an army that awaited me, but there would be someone. My human face was known throughout Novania, I couldn't easily hide in my dragon form, and sport-hunting of dragons was permitted in my homeland.

There were too many unknown variables to state with certainty that I'd survive the trip.

"You look troubled." Rynn's voice cut through my reverie.

I shrugged. There would be time enough to explain my thoughts later, when I was certain Alexander was no longer in danger.

"It's nothing," I replied dismissively.

Her expression was skeptical. "I don't believe that, but I won't press you."

The rest of the evening passed uneventfully. With the gate closed behind us, I believed we were safer than we'd been in some time. Colin's assassins—if any remained—couldn't hope to open it. Alexander and I agreed to take the night watches, though I believed all would remain quiet. For the first time since leaving Riversmeet, we were truly secure.

When I next awoke, the faint light of dawn blushed the sky. I glowered, angry that I'd overslept and irked that Alexander hadn't bothered to wake me. I glanced across the tent to note he wasn't inside and his blanket roll remained untouched. I frowned, the first pangs of worry clawing at my chest. I hadn't forgotten Chela's story of the mage she'd lost at the same point in the pilgrimage.

I dressed hurriedly and burst from the tent to find Rynn tending the campfire. She looked up, startled at the sudden noise, then smiled. Her eyes glinted with mischief.

"Good morning. I took over your watch last night. Alex and I both thought you could use the extra sleep."

My frown intensified. "Where *is* Alex? He wasn't—"

"In your tent? No," she replied with a smirk. "He has been otherwise…detained." Her eyes flicked to the tent that belonged to Lydia.

I burst into laughter, relieved Alexander was safe and amused by the lengths he'd gone to conceal his planned tryst. I shook my head as I sat down near the fire.

"I told Emmarie to sleep in my tent last night," Rynn continued. "I knew they'd need their privacy." Her tone was light, but there was a deep longing in her eyes. "Lydia confided in me weeks ago she'd hoped for this. She's *quite* enamored with your brother."

I chuckled. "And he is with her. I don't know if he finally mustered the courage to formally ask her, and truly, I shouldn't tell you this at all, but… He hopes to marry her."

Rynn beamed. "She won't deny him, should he ask. She's been waiting for him…Why has he taken so long, I wonder? It's obvious what they feel for one another."

I shrugged. "Alex has little experience with women, and he wanted to be certain he'd survive this journey first. I'm happy for him and thankful she hasn't lost her patience and moved on. It would have devastated him."

Rynn's eyes were locked on the campfire, her expression thoughtful. "I'm pleased for them. Do you know why Lydia was living at the forest shrine where you met her?"

I shook my head. I'd never asked about her past, and she hadn't been forthcoming.

"When she left on her pilgrimage, she was betrothed to a man from the Citadel. She received word at Crystal Crags that he'd fallen gravely ill. His sister implored her to return home. A healer can do much to remediate illness, even if not fully trained." Rynn sighed with a shake of her head. "Her guardian wouldn't allow her to return. She'd put herself in danger by doing so. He wasn't wrong—it's the way of magic. She followed his advice, but by the time she returned to the Citadel, her betrothed had passed. She never forgave herself. As a form of self-punishment, she requested the post in the Venom-weavers' forest."

"She tended me there, you know," I replied.

Rynn smiled. "Lydia told me that story. She claims there was little she did to help you recover, but she monitored your progress. I suspect it wasn't out of a desire to see you healed, but rather to satisfy her curiosity." She looked up, her eyes twinkling. "When you arrived at the Frostwake, the twins told me of you almost as soon as they'd finished speaking to you. I didn't believe them—nor you—until the moment you shook my hand. I'd always assumed a skin-changer would prefer to remain in dragon form. Why bother passing oneself off as a human, when a dragon is so powerful, so exotic? Yet, I have seen you change forms but once in all the time we've traveled together."

I shifted uncomfortably in my seat. "You know my story. You know where I grew up… Even here, I still can't shake my ingrained fear. In my mind, it's safer to blend in rather than make a spectacle of myself, but I suppose it's too late for that, given what happened at the tourney field." I sighed and raked a hand through my hair. "Colin gave me no choice in the matter. I couldn't allow his farce to play out. I couldn't watch Alexander die. And I don't know what will happen when I return now that my secret is common knowledge."

Rynn reached over to take my hand. "You will not be alone. And you need not worry about me—I can take care of myself, as you know." She released my hand and sat back. "Have you spoken with Alex?"

I shook my head. "I meant to speak with him yesterday. I gave him the messages from Tom, but once we left the inn, there were other things on his mind. Obviously, one was Lydia, though I know the cursed blade also preoccupied his thoughts." I looked at her sharply. "Is that blade truly as dangerous as Lydia's reaction made it out to be?"

"The power it contains is unlike anything I can describe. It feels *wrong*, somehow," Rynn said. "Alex can handle it safely because it's attuned to his magic—but *his* power feels wrong to me too. I don't have the correct words to describe what I sense about him or the blade. I *know* he's a good person, and that won't change simply because he's a mage-warrior. I don't mean to say your brother is wrong or that there is anything wrong about him," she added, noting my concern. "His magic is just so…*different* from my own, different from anyone else I've encountered. It's…foreign. And he is incredibly powerful. I don't think he fully comprehends it." She sighed, frustrated. "I'm sorry. I must seem incoherent."

"Not at all. I only ask because I'm trying to understand. It must be difficult for you to explain it to someone like me. When the three of you begin discussing magic, I'm at a loss. The whole concept confounds me."

She smiled gently. "We appreciate that you've been trying. Your brother, in particular. Without your support, he would not have made it this far."

After Emmarie emerged that morning, I began to take down the unoccupied tents while Rynn rummaged through our supplies and located some dried fruit and hard cheese for breakfast. Emmarie assisted me, and by the time Lydia and Alexander finally exited their tent, we were nearly ready to depart. Alexander's face promptly flushed crimson when he realized he'd overslept and his secret was exposed. Lydia smiled and went about her morning without any sign of embarrassment.

Once the last tent was stowed in the cart and we started off, Alexander drew me aside, his face flushed. "I don't know what to say… I'm—"

I cut him off with a laugh. "Alex, don't worry about it. I'm happy for you. For both of you."

He grinned sheepishly, then ran one hand through his hair, which had grown longish once more. I wondered if he planned to allow it to grow since it seemed to be Lydia's preference.

"Thank you, brother. I've never been happier." His eyes sought Lydia as she walked alongside the cart. His gaze lingered on her slender form. "I need your advice."

I arched an eyebrow. "What about?"

He looked down, decidedly uncomfortable. "I want to marry her. I need to ask her properly, but I don't know *how*. I hoped you'd have a suggestion or two."

I chuckled. "To be honest, I have no experience with asking a woman for her hand in marriage. The marriage with Claire was arranged by her father and yours. I had no hand in it. And Vera… Well, *she* asked *me*."

Alexander's eyes widened. "Vera asked you? I thought—"

I smiled at the memory. "I think everyone thought as you did. I'd lost my title, my damned name, and Colin did all he could to humiliate me. I was hesitant to ask. She was a noblewoman, and I had nothing to offer. I was the late queen's bastard. She saw past all of it and didn't care if there was court scandal."

"I understand why you loved her. She was never interested in the petty dealings of the other court ladies. She truly loved you." He shook his head sadly. "I know you miss her, but I hope one day you'll find the means to move on."

I shrugged. "Perhaps. I don't know. But back to your original question, I'm afraid I don't have any advice."

"It's just as well, I suppose. If I just ask her, do you believe it'll be enough?"

I nodded. "She loves you. I'm certain if you ask, she'll accept. In fact, she's been waiting for you to do so for quite some time."

He spun to face me, startled. "Do you truly believe that?" When I nodded, he grinned. "Then I'll ask her tonight. Thank you, brother."

We traveled through the crevice as it gently sloped toward the center of the plateau, and it was midafternoon by the time we reached the summit. The paved road opened into a wide plaza surrounded by stone buildings that were clearly built for a race much larger than mere humans. If I were to shift, I would have no trouble passing through the monumental, arched doorways into the massive rooms beyond, but in my present form, I felt small and insignificant.

The doors to each building were closed, and on closer inspection, I noticed they had similar mechanisms to the gate below. A small stone pedestal was placed outside each, topped with the impression of a dragon's forefoot. Amongst our group, I alone could access what lay inside. What would I find? Excitement shot through my core at the prospect.

Lydia and Alexander walked ahead of the cart, and Lydia pointed to various structures as we passed. Rynn had been speaking quietly to Emmarie for a time, but as we arrived at the plaza, she paused to allow me to catch up with her.

"The stories say these were the homes of the various dragon clans," she said, gesturing around us. "I don't know if it's true, but it seems a likely explanation." She pointed to an area above one of the doors as we passed, indicating a row of symbols etched into the stone. "If one of us could read the dragons' script, I believe they spell the various surnames. One of these must belong to the Caeins."

I frowned thoughtfully. "Can no one read it?"

She shook her head. “It’s the language of the dragons. I’m afraid they didn’t share their language with humans, nor did they with the Merael, the Sevanni, or the Corodan.” She studied me carefully, her eyes compassionate. “They would have taught you their language if they’d remained here.”

I gaped at her for a moment as I realized I had a partial key. I dug into one of my pockets, seeking the letter I’d received from my father at the Ancient Maze. There had been several symbols drawn at the end, symbols much like these. I took out the letter and unfolded it carefully, pointing to the series of symbols Lileen had drawn.

“Rynn, my father sent this. At the time, I didn’t understand, but—”

“Five symbols. Caein is five letters, is it not?” She looked at me, eyes alight with the prospect of adventure.

I nodded. “He asked me to find the vault. Do you think these spell our family’s name?”

“What else could it mean?” She spun around to study each building around the plaza in turn. As she came nearly full circle, she pointed suddenly to the structure immediately to my left. “There! It matches your letter!”

I laughed aloud. “Then we’ll visit it tomorrow. For now, we should catch up with the others and help set up camp. There will be time enough to explore while we wait for Alex.”

She grinned, eyes sparkling in the afternoon sun. “If I return to the Frostwake one day, what a story I’ll have for the twins! Not only did you open the gate, but we’ll learn what lies within some of these structures. What do you suppose we’ll find?”

I smiled, pleased I had someone to share the moment with. “I wonder that myself. Whatever we find, I look forward to it.”

The road led away from the plaza and through what appeared to have once been a garden that was now in a state of wild overgrowth. The plants were green and many were in bloom, despite the late season and the chill wind that brought with it the promise of snow. Like the gate, the garden emanated power. I assumed the plant life thrived due to the residual magic within the earth and would continue to do so indefinitely. The garden stretched to a low stone wall that overlooked the sheer cliffs on one side.

The road widened again as we exited the garden, flanked on either side by a series of buildings that were even larger than those we'd passed earlier. They were lined with massive stone columns, each carved in the likeness of a dragon.

Rynn gestured to the structure on the right. "This is the building we call the library. I don't know if it's truly a library. No one has been inside since the dragons passed through the gateway." Pointing to the building on the left, she said, "We believe that's an armory."

The road ended not far ahead at the foot of another enormous structure. It was a tower, rising high into the sky to overlook the lands surrounding the plateau. The tower was square with a flat roof, but was rather plain when compared to the other buildings we'd passed. It lacked the detailed carvings and symbols I'd come to recognize as dragon script, while its entrance was open to the elements, the only structure we'd encountered that was not sealed.

"And this is the Tower of the Final Trial." Rynn paused to gaze at its apex. "Magi must ascend it, and only there can the final trial begin. It's said when the dragons were here, they would often fly around the tower when a mage was within their trial." She smiled faintly and shook her head. "There were a half dozen gray eagles during my trial. I can only imagine what it must have been like to see dragons as well."

I studied her for a moment and on an impulse, said, "I can arrange for one dragon. And perhaps he would even allow for a passenger or two to join him."

She laughed, then shook her head, suddenly nervous. "No… Perhaps Lydia will join you, but I'd rather my feet remain on the ground."

It wasn't the first time she'd mentioned this, I realized. "Do you fear of heights?"

She chewed her lip uncertainly, then nodded.

"You do realize that I plan to fly most of the distance north when I leave to meet up with Tom?" I asked gently.

She nodded once more. "I know. And the very idea terrifies me." She sighed and looked away, embarrassed. "I must learn to conquer this fear. It won't be long before I'm forced to face it."

"Know that my offer stands," I replied, "but it will be your choice. I suspect Lydia will want to check on Alex from time to time, and Emmarie loves flying. You won't be alone if you choose to go."

"I'll think on it." She managed a tight smile before turning away.

We made camp near the tower, and once that task was complete, Alexander made good on his plans. He drew Lydia aside, and they walked a short distance away from the tents, where we'd be unable to overhear their words. I set to work peeling potatoes, positioning myself so I could watch the pair. They spoke for a few moments, then Lydia threw herself into Alexander's arms. They kissed rather passionately.

I grinned, elated Alexander had found Lydia and that she'd agreed to his proposal. They made a fine pair.

Rynn also watched them, and though she smiled, her eyes shone with unshed tears. There was sorrow in her expression and a longing I'd seldom seen from her. I wondered what she was thinking and realized belatedly her reaction was likely the result of our conversation in the streets of Dragon's Feet.

I suppressed a sigh and focused on Alexander and Lydia. They walked toward camp, hand in hand, beaming.

"Did she say yes?" Emmarie blurted excitedly as soon as they were within earshot.

We shared a laugh, and Alexander said, "She did. We plan to marry once we return to the Citadel."

TWENTY-NINE

Alexander entered the tower with the dawn. His mood was buoyant and optimistic, yet determined. As he disappeared inside, I turned to Lydia.

"If you'd like to fly later, I'm willing," I offered.

She smiled, her eyes trained on the tower's dark entrance. "Perhaps this afternoon. It will take time for him to reach the top."

I nodded and glanced at Rynn. "I'd like to visit the library this morning."

Rynn studied me in silence, then followed wordlessly as I began to walk away from our camp.

The entrance to the library was painted in shades of rose and gold as the sun's first rays reached its columns. As we walked between the towering stones, I noted each carved dragon was unique to those surrounding it. Perhaps they'd been important figures in the dragonkind's history? I added the question to the growing list of items I hoped to ask my father. There was so much I still didn't know.

We passed between the towering columns and beneath the roof's overhang, cast in deep shadow where the sun's light failed to reach. A door large enough to accommodate three or four dragons walking abreast lay in a recess beyond. Near the right side of the door was another stone pedestal, the impression of a dragon's foot visible despite the poor light.

"I feel insignificant," Rynn whispered. "Between the enormity of the buildings and the raw power I sense… I'm nothing more than an insect crawling in the dirt."

"You are no insect, Rynn," I replied with a chuckle.

When I placed my hand on the pedestal, the same warm tingle coursed through my hand that I'd experienced at the gate. The door swung inward, silent on its magical hinges.

Rynn's eyes widened with delight and wonder as the interior was revealed. "Oh! This is… This is incredible."

Soft golden light spilled from within. I gaped as we entered; the ceiling had been manipulated to produce the light of its own accord. In the center of the room was an oval table, clearly designed for use by people far larger than mere humans. Several enormous leather-bound books were spread across its surface, their size on a scale I was unaccustomed to. Each book was nearly as tall as I was in my present form and nearly as thick. One book had been left open, but I couldn't read the contents of the page—it was written in the dragons' symbolic language.

Rynn growled in frustration. I glanced toward her and stifled a laugh. She wasn't tall enough to peer over the rim of the table.

"I can't read it," I said.

"I suspected as much," she replied, a hint of disappointment in her tone. "Without a codex or a key, I don't know if we'll ever learn what the books here contain." She turned away from the pedestal, then pointed excitedly toward the walls surrounding us. "Andrew, look!"

The walls were constructed of numerous stone panels. Across each surface were a series of what appeared to be genealogical charts. At the top of each panel was a series of symbols, and below were etchings; most depicted dragons, but there were a few with a strange, curving line bisecting them. Below each etching was another series of symbols. Vertical lines connected some etched dragons with others, which gave me the impression they were family charts.

"Andrew," Rynn breathed. "That one there, do you see? The symbols at the top match those from your letter."

I turned to study the panel she indicated, then moved across the vast room, drawn inexplicably toward it. I wished I understood what the symbols meant; I desperately wanted to know more of my ancestry.

If the panels were a depiction of each family's lineage as I suspected, the Caein line was one of the oldest of the dragon clans. The panel boasted more etchings than most of the others, some rows packed so tightly the symbols beneath each dragon were nearly too small to read. Given the longevity of dragons, I didn't know where my father's placement would have been within the many generations. He could have been listed anywhere.

I stopped within arm's reach of the panel to study each etched dragon and the rows of symbols, seeking understanding. None bore the curved line I'd spied on the other panels. What did the line indicate, and why was it missing from *this* panel?

A single dragon was positioned level with my eye. On an impulse, I ran my fingers over it. A warm sensation spread through my hand and up my arm as the stone reacted to my touch.

Startled, I tried to pull away, but was enveloped by darkness. A single light shone upon me from overhead, its glare casting everything beyond the beam into shadow. I turned around and swallowed my panic. I wasn't in the library any longer.

"Rynn?" I called. My voice quavered. Where was I? Where was she?

"Relax, child, you're safe here."

The voice was a deep baritone. It emanated from the shadows, but I couldn't determine the direction of the speaker. I spun around, searching blindly for the source.

"Who's there?" I demanded.

"I'm Davereth, the keeper of histories," the voice replied. "It's my duty to record each birth, to chronicle each descendant borne to the dragon clans. My body is long dead, but my spirit remains here, awaiting the next generation."

"What is this place?" I asked, calmed by Davereth's voice. My momentary panic dissolved, replaced by curiosity.

"It's a magical construct. It's not a physical 'place.' Your body remains in the chamber of history. Only your mind was brought here."

"Why?"

A low chuckle issued from the shadows. "Did no one tell you of this ritual? Was it mere chance you placed your hand on the stone?"

"Ritual?" I asked, confounded. "I know of no ritual…"

"Ah, it's as I suspected then. Allow me to explain." There was a pause, and I imagined the spirit gathered his thoughts. "It was tradition that brought your forebears here. Each child would come to the chamber of history, where they would touch the stone panels. It has been my duty for thousands of years to assess each child and record their place in the stone outside. None have come here in years. Was the gateway finally opened?"

Stunned, my mind struggled to comprehend his words. My voice eluded me. I managed a nod.

A sad sigh emanated from the darkness. "Then the elders have gone, as have the rest. Tell me, young one: Why do you remain behind?"

"My father didn't know I'd been conceived. He's one of the three who opened the gateway."

"The elders were so set upon fleeing that they didn't consider the price of summoning such magic. I counseled against opening the gateway. I witnessed the consequences first-hand ages ago. Did you know your ancestors were not originally from this world, child? A gateway was opened once previously, and we came through it to find ourselves here. It suited us for a time, but the elders grew restless and disillusioned." Another sigh, like a faint gust of wind, passed through the shadows. "Have you spoken with what remains of your father?"

"Yes. He and the others were petrified by the magic."

"It's as I feared. It's a shame. A waste of talent." Davereth fell silent for a few moments, then said, "I will record your place in the stone, as is deserving of the dragon-kind. I thank you for indulging my questions. Let me have a look at your other side."

I frowned in confusion, then understood. Davereth was asking me to shift. I obliged, then wondered belatedly if I had done the same in the physical world. I hoped Rynn was at a safe distance and hadn't been hurt by the sudden transformation if it had occurred.

"Ah, a Caein," Davereth said, his tone pleased. "The first skin-changer to grace the clan in our long history." There was a pause, then, "Zayneldarion's son. I should have guessed. He was ever considered a pariah. He didn't share their beliefs regarding our people's interactions with humans, nor did he abide by many of your clan's rules. It comes as no surprise he was a part of opening the gateway. If your existence had come to light, he would have been disowned by your clan's elders."

"What do you mean?" I asked. "There were others like me in the past—"

"Yes, child, there have been," Davereth replied patiently. "Most dragon clans were tolerant of the other species, but not the proud Caein line. To indulge in a dalliance with a human would have been considered disgraceful, a stain on their proud heritage. Perhaps it's fortunate your father didn't know of your existence while the other Caeins still roamed this world. He may have been exiled, and you with him—if they didn't kill both of you first."

I looked down, at a loss for words. For most of my life, I'd entertained the notion of learning about my father's people, but the truth wasn't what I'd imagined. I would have been no better off amongst the dragon-kind than I'd been in Novania. The stories I'd heard as a child made dragons seem noble and benevolent when they weren't erroneously depicted as monsters or the object of misguided laws. But it seemed they possessed a dark side too.

"The truth can prove a burden," Davereth said after a time, "but I don't believe in spinning falsehoods. I exist to record our history and do so accurately. I will not apologize for sharing the truth with you."

I drew a breath and continued to stare at the floor. "I'm grateful you've told me."

It was yet another item I needed to speak with my father about. His clan, our *family*, would have shunned me. Perhaps it was fortunate the rest of the Caein line was gone.

"I will record your name in the stone as Zayneldarion's son. You will be marked as what you are, a skin-changer. What is your name, child?"

"Andrew."

"A human name. I shouldn't be surprised. When next you speak with your father, be certain to tell him you've spoken with me."

"I will." I wanted to say more, but was forcefully ejected from the construct.

I staggered backward from the stone panel, surprised to find myself in my human form once more. I landed hard on my backside and gaped as the stone panel began to change in order to accommodate another etching near the base of the Caein family line. It bore the same curving mark I'd seen elsewhere—the mark of a skin-changer.

Rynn knelt at my side, her eyes wide. "Are you well? When you touched the stone, I could sense the magic, then you became unresponsive. And now…"

I was fixated on the stone. Symbols appeared beneath my mark—my name, carved in dragon-script. A vertical line formed between my etching and what must have been my father's. Rynn followed my gaze and stared at the panel in wonder.

"It's a family chart," I explained. "There's a spirit here whose sole purpose is to record each new addition."

"Does that mean the new mark is yours?" she asked, her voice excited. "That means this one—" she stood up and indicated the etching above mine, "—must be your father's." She studied the panel for a moment, then nodded. "The symbols below each mark must be the dragon's name. What does this line mean?" she asked, pointing at the curving shape that bisected my mark.

"It means I'm a skin-changer."

I frowned, troubled by Davereth's revelations regarding my father's clan. If the dragons had still been part of our world, I would have been an outcast even more so than I was now. I rose to my feet slowly and looked around the room. I needed time to think, and the chamber of histories had abruptly become stifling.

"Let's go back to the others. I've learned enough of my family for one day."

She gave me a puzzled look, and I shook my head.

My father had been accepting of me, and I'd assumed the other dragons would have been as well. To learn I would have been shunned had come as an unwelcome surprise. I'd truly believed the dragons were different than humans, that they were beyond petty matters of race or upbringing. I'd believed they were *better*. I'd been wrong, and the knowledge stung.

As we exited the building, the doors closed of their own accord. Rynn glanced back, an expression of longing on her face. "If we could have stayed just a bit longer, I may have come up with a sort of codex for these symbols. Knowing your name and your father's is a start."

"Perhaps one day I'll return."

"Andrew, what happened? What did the spirit tell you?" She stepped in front of me and peered into my face, concern lining her features.

I couldn't withhold the story. She'd been there, worried and frantic as my mind was drawn into the magical space with Davereth. She deserved to know why I'd become so morose despite what should have been a momentous event. While we walked toward the camp, I related my experience.

"I'm so sorry," she said as I finished. "At least your father accepted you. That's what truly matters, isn't it? The others are gone."

I forced a strained smile. Her positivity buoyed my spirits, something I sorely needed in that moment. "You're right. Thank you for listening to me. You're a good friend."

She smiled. "I will always be your friend, no matter what may happen between us. I…" She shook her head, then forced an even brighter smile. "It looks as though Lydia has been waiting for our return."

Lydia sat near the campfire, watching our approach with interest. Emmarie chattered excitedly, and when she noticed our return, she waved and flashed a grin. Lydia laughed as Emmarie bounded away from her side and charged toward us.

"Lydia said you promised to take us flying!"

I laughed despite my melancholy. Her unabashed enthusiasm was endearing. "I did. Does this mean she's ready?"

"I am." Lydia had walked toward us during the exchange. She smiled as she gestured toward the sky. "The eagles began circling not long ago, and Galewing departed to join them. It means Alex has reached the tower's roof and has begun his trial. He may be there a few days. Still, I'd like to see him, and I must admit, I've been looking forward to flying with you. Emmarie says it's a thrill."

I glanced at Rynn, who stared at her boots, an anguished expression on her face. I knew she'd tell me when she was ready to face her fears, so I didn't press her. I groaned, disappointed, when Emmarie voiced the question instead.

"Will you join us, Rynn?"

"Emma…" She didn't understand the source of Rynn's hesitation.

"It's alright." Rynn managed a smile. "She meant no harm, and I suppose there's no use waiting any longer, is there? I must face this some time." She drew a breath and appeared to steel herself. "Yes, I will join you."

Emmarie tilted her head as she gave Rynn a quizzical look. "You're always so brave. How can you be afraid of flying? Andrew will keep us safe!"

Rynn shrugged uncomfortably. "I've always feared high places, but if I am to travel north, I must overcome it."

The women entered one of the tents to allow me privacy while I undressed and shifted, though Rynn lingered a moment after the others disappeared within. I didn't notice she was outside until I'd pulled my shirt off, and when my eyes met hers, her face flushed crimson. She hurriedly ducked inside. I shook my head with a smile, amused and a bit flattered.

I left my clothing piled outside my tent and walked a short distance away from the camp. I shifted with a grin, exhilarated by the prospect of taking to the air. It was precisely what I needed to clear my head after speaking with Davereth.

I stretched my wings in anticipation, watching as my shadow fell over the campsite. Moments later, Emmarie burst from the tent and sprinted toward me, dark hair streaming behind her. Lydia and Rynn approached more cautiously and stopped a few paces away. Rynn's face was pale, though she did her utmost to keep her composure.

"Rynn should sit in the space between your wings," Emmarie stated with a surprising measure of authority. "It's the safest spot, and I don't notice your movement as much there. Lydia can sit in front of her, and I'll sit behind." She flashed a grin. "This is exciting!"

I lowered myself so they could climb up my side. Lydia and Emmarie went first and took their places between the dark spines on my back, but Rynn hesitated. She stared at the ground, clearly struggling with herself and the situation.

"If you are not ready, we can do thisss another time."

She looked up, startled. "Andrew, your voice… It's you, but it's so much deeper. I suppose that shouldn't be surprising, given your current size." She laughed nervously. "No, I need to do this. Waiting will only make it more difficult."

Carefully, she climbed up to the space Emmarie had indicated. I could feel her trembling even as she gripped the spine in front of her with both arms. I craned my neck to look back at my passengers, ensuring each was secure. Lydia offered me a smile, and Emmarie's grin split her face. Rynn appeared miserable; her eyes were squeezed shut and she grimaced, even though we remained firmly on the ground.

"Rynn, are you—?" I began.

She nodded without looking up or opening her eyes. "Yes. I must."

I sighed heavily. I didn't know how to alleviate her fear other than take flight and prove she was safe. I wouldn't allow any of them to be harmed, but I didn't believe my words would calm her.

Emmarie patted my side twice, indicating she believed they were ready. I waited a heartbeat, then sprang into the air. I gained altitude while flying around the tower in a wide arc. As I increased in elevation, I tightened the circle. When we were even with the tower's rooftop, we were within a stone's throw of the tower itself. As I drew near, most of the gray eagles gave me a wide berth, though Galewing showed no fear. He flew alongside me for a time, calling shrilly.

Behind me, Emmarie laughed with delight. "Galewing welcomes you to the skies, Andrew!"

Alexander knelt on the tower's roof, his head bowed and his eyes closed. The cursed blade was sheathed at his side, and his hands were folded calmly in his lap. A breeze ruffled his blond hair, but he paid no attention to the wind, nor did he look into the sky. He appeared serene, at peace.

I glanced over my shoulder. Rynn had loosened her grip and had finally opened her eyes. Her face was ashen, but her trembling had subsided. Perhaps she was winning the battle against her fear.

Lydia's gaze was fixed on Alexander, and a fond smile played across her fair features. She'd left her hair down, and it whipped around her in wild eddies. I was certain she'd spend a lengthy amount of time combing her tresses once we returned to camp.

I circled the tower a few more times before deciding it was time to land. I was concerned for Rynn and didn't want to prolong her discomfort on her first foray into the sky.

As soon as I touched down, she slid along my side to land gracefully on her feet, then immediately planted her hands on her knees. She panted as though she'd just run a mile and was desperate to replenish her breath.

"Rynn?" I asked as the others dismounted.

She rolled her eyes toward me, then began to laugh. "That was terrifying! And yet… It was worth every second." She offered me a weary smile. "Once I forced my eyes open, I could see…*everything*. What an incredible view! But it will take me some time. I may never grow used to traveling like that."

I grinned. "I'm glad to have made a good firssst impresssion."

She shook her head. "I'm merely thankful to have my feet back on the ground!"

THIRTY

I flew with Lydia again that evening. Rynn declined a second flight, and Emmarie elected to remain with her—out of guilt, I suspected. Lydia had pulled her long hair up into a tight bun for our second flight, having spent over an hour combing the tangles from her locks after our first. As we came abreast of the tower's flat roof, I noticed Alexander seemed to be in the same position as before.

Puzzled, I turned my head slightly so Lydia might hear me over the rush of the wind. "Isss it normal for a mage to remain unmoving for ssso long?"

She laughed cheerfully. "Oh, yes." She spoke loudly, but I had to strain to make out her words; her voice didn't carry well over the wind. "There are spirits at every pilgrimage site, and to commune with the spirits, we must enter a trance. That is what you see now."

"Hmm." I circled the tower again, studying my half-brother carefully in the fading light. "What happened with the blade wasss not wholly unexsspected, then?"

Lydia didn't speak for several moments. "No, it was not. If one of the spirits is especially attuned to the new mage's talent, sometimes it will impart a gift… Or a curse, as it may prove to be for Alex." Her tone was filled with despair. "Most of the spirits have chosen to stay, to act as mentors for the next generations of magi. I believe the one he encountered at Dragon's Feet was there only to pass on her blade. Alex believes she departed as soon as his trial was complete."

I considered her words for a time. "You told him the blade and the connection with it isss unnatural."

"It is. That blade is bound to Alexander's spirit, his very essence. He wasn't given a choice in the matter. And as you know, mage-warriors are scarce." She paused to gather her thoughts. "Alex is a good man. It pains me to know he may suffer centuries beyond his natural death simply because he acquired a sword."

We fell silent, and after another two passes around the tower, I turned back toward our campsite. By the time we returned, Emmarie and Rynn had built a fire and were preparing a meal from vegetables Emmarie had discovered in the overgrown garden. I shifted into my human form and dressed with my back to the others.

When I approached the fireside, Emmarie was stirring the cooking pot; the aroma was delicious, and I realized I was ravenous. A short time later, we shared a meal. While we ate, I discussed my plans to visit the vault the next day.

"I'd like to retrieve my father's armor in the morning," I said around a mouthful of perfectly cooked squash.

"I'll accompany you," Rynn offered.

I nodded in silent thanks. I'd expected she'd join me whether I asked her to or not.

"Will you return to the chamber of histories?" she asked after a time.

I shrugged. "If time permits, I'd like to. It will depend on Alex's return."

"I truly believe I can create a codex based on what we've learned of the dragons' symbols so far." She grinned. "What the twins wouldn't do for something like that!"

The night passed uneventfully. The next morning, we made our way to the plaza, retracing our steps past the chamber of histories and through the wild tangle that was the garden. While I didn't know if the vault was within the building that bore my family's name, it seemed a logical place to begin our search.

When I placed my hand atop the stone pedestal near the double doors, the warm, tingling sensation I'd come to expect was accompanied by the sound of a deep baritone voice that seemed to issue from within the stone itself. "Enter."

Startled, I backed away and collided with Rynn. The doors swung inward to allow us entry as I recovered from my momentary shock.

When we were only a few steps inside, the doors closed noiselessly behind us. I spun around, fearing we'd been inexplicably trapped, but a second pedestal stood on the interior side of the door.

The room was illuminated only by the sun as it streamed through a series of skylights high above. Each was large enough that I could have flown through them in my dragon form, though I suspected there was glass—or perhaps magic—sealing the building from the elements.

The room was empty. There wasn't a trace of the dragons who had occupied it only a few decades ago. Our footfalls echoed against the stone floor, and our voices carried strangely through the stale air. A coat of dust lay across every surface, while spiderwebs clung stubbornly to the corners.

"It looks like they took everything with them," Rynn whispered as she surveyed the empty space. "They didn't plan to return."

"I was certain the vault would be here," I replied, swallowing my frustration. "My father didn't tell me how to find it, only that I should. If it isn't here, I don't know where to begin the search."

"Just because the first room is empty doesn't mean the entire building is," she pointed out. "Come. Let's explore a bit before we give up."

We walked through several more rooms, each as empty as the first. The only residents were the tiny brown spiders who made their homes in the corners. As we arrived in the final room, I was thoroughly disheartened. There was nothing left of my father's family but dust and legends.

"I don't think it's here." I released a sigh and glowered at the walls. "We've been through every room—"

"Wait a moment," she said, holding one hand up in a gesture of silence. She bent to study one of the walls more closely, her face only a hairsbreadth from the stone. "Look at this… There's a fine crack in the stone, nearly invisible."

She traced her finger along its length. It rose in an unbroken line from the floor to well above her head. Her eyes followed the crack upwards, then she took several steps to her left, and her hand traced another fine crack down to the floor. The lines were too straight, too precise to be a result of the building's age.

"There's another crack here, joined to the first by the one above." She turned to me and smiled, her eyes ablaze with the thrill of her discovery. "I think it's a door. But how does one open it?"

"An excellent question."

There wasn't a pedestal as there had been at the entrance. The wall was unblemished between the cracks, and I could see nothing that might help us solve the mystery. But I was certain something of importance lay beyond.

Suddenly, Rynn grasped my wrist and pressed my palm against the wall. She held it there for several seconds, but when nothing happened, she released her icy grip.

"I had to try something," she said with a shrug. "Your method of glaring and sighing hasn't done anything useful."

I dropped my hand to my side with a chuckle. "You're right. What else can we do? I can't see any means of forcing it open."

Her eyes widened with excitement. "Forcing it open? Alex said when you can't solve a problem, you often resort to brute force."

I snorted. "Of course, he'd say that. What do you think I should do? Break the stone?"

She shrugged. "Why not? After all, you're far stronger than you appear. Perhaps something will happen."

I laughed nervously. I felt foolish for entertaining the idea. "I don't know…"

She rolled her eyes. "You can be incredibly stubborn. Humor me, if you will. Something may come of it."

I sighed, convinced it was an act of futility, but I'd do as she asked. When nothing happened, she'd at least focus on a more reasonable approach to solving the puzzle.

I made a fist, raised it above my head, and pounded on the stone with as much force as I could muster. My bones screamed at the impact, and the meaty side of my fist was instantly bruised. I turned to face her once more.

"You see? There was nothing."

I tilted my head as an idea came to me. The Caein clan's history might be the key to unlocking the vault. Perhaps the wall wouldn't open at a human's touch, but only that of a dragon's.

"You've thought of something." Rynn grinned. "Tell me."

"I'm going to shift."

"I think I understand," she said. "Would you like me to go—"

I chuckled. "It isn't necessary, though you'll need to give me more space."

I began to undress as she stepped across the room. I sensed her eyes on me, but I didn't turn to face her. I tossed my clothing against the nearest wall, then shifted. Suddenly, the room didn't feel as vast.

I peered over my shoulder at her. "I don't know if it will work, but I'm going to try."

When she nodded, I pressed my left forefoot against the wall. Several seconds passed without movement. As I was about to give up, a low rumble issued from behind the wall. I grinned as the wall slid open to reveal another room beyond.

Rynn laughed as she walked across the room to rejoin me. "You were right."

"I can't believe it worked."

"I wasn't certain it would," she admitted. "But it makes sense, given what we learned of your ancestors."

I nodded and peered into the room beyond. It was pitch dark within, void of the skylights the other chambers sported. I edged forward, allowing my eyes to adjust as I passed from sunlight to shadow. After a few moments, shapes became clear in the darkness, but even my superior eyesight could not fully pierce the gloom.

"We should get a torch from camp," I said.

"I may have a faster solution," Rynn replied thoughtfully. "Allow me to try something. It will only take a moment."

I backed out of the darkened room, ducking out of habit though the top of the door was well above my head.

Rynn moved past me to stop at the threshold. She closed her eyes in concentration and moved her hands slowly along the wall. I wrinkled my nose as the scent of wintergreen hit my nostrils and elicited a sneeze. While I'd sometimes considered my sneezes explosive in human form, they were minor compared to what I released now.

Rynn laughed in amusement as she worked her magic, undeterred by my thunderous racket. She built a smooth sheet of ice at a slight angle to the opening, and as it grew in size, the light from above was reflected into the darkened room beyond.

"I didn't think to try that," I said as I admired her work.

She beamed at me and dropped her hands. "I wasn't certain it would help, but it seems to have done the trick." She looked at me curiously for a moment, then shook her head. "What is it about magic that makes you react so? Your eyes are watering."

I shrugged. The effects would dissipate now that she'd finished. "I'll be fine. I've been told it happensss to people like me."

She arched an eyebrow. "You mean it happens to skin-changers."

I nodded and moved past her makeshift mirror. Enough light pierced the gloom that I could now make out various items. There were a pair of tables laden with books the size of those we'd discovered in the chamber of histories, a collection of urns that stood taller than I did in my present form, and several immense wooden chests. An array of swords adorned a rack on one wall, and opposite them were several dozen shields, each emblazoned with a different emblem. In the far corner, partially obscured from view by one of the urns, was an armor stand. A finely crafted set of plate mail rested upon it. Even in the dim light, I knew it was dragon scale. *Black* dragon scale.

I'd located the armor my father had spoken of.

Ignoring the other items in the vault, I went to the armor stand and dragged the contraption from the corner toward the opening in the wall. The armor was light-weight and looked large enough to fit my human form. I brushed a few strands of cobweb from the armor and placed it carefully on the floor of the outer room.

I stepped out of the vault and shifted. While I dressed, Rynn inspected the helm and gauntlets. She ran her hands over their surface, her expression unreadable.

I picked up the remaining pieces and smiled, grateful she'd accompanied me. "I would not have found this without you. I'm in your debt."

She blushed prettily and shook her head with a smile. "I'm happy to help. That's what friends do." She studied me for a moment before turning to walk back the way we'd come. "Let's go back to the camp. I have a feeling Lydia would like to check on Alexander again."

By the time we returned to camp, the eagles were no longer circling in the sky and Galewing had returned to perch on the side of the cart.

Emmarie was speaking with him, though even to my untrained ear, his responses were clipped. He merely humored her, but Emmarie didn't seem to mind. Lydia stood at the tower's entrance, peering inside.

We stowed my armor and moved to join her. The chamber of histories must wait for another day.

Lydia turned at our approach but didn't smile. Concern etched her features, and I dreaded something had gone awry.

"Lydia, is he—?" I began, but she shook her head.

"The trial is complete. We'll know how he fares soon enough," she replied. "There are only two outcomes. He will walk through this door, hale and whole, or not at all."

I glanced over my shoulder toward the camp, and my eyes fell on Galewing. His presence assured me Alexander had survived. If he had not, the eagle would have departed to rejoin his brethren in the skies.

"He'll appear soon," I said. "Alex was prepared for this."

"I wish I shared your confidence." She wrung her hands and averted her gaze. "There are many unknowns at work, and until I see him, I won't rest. I can't."

I turned to Rynn for reassurance, but she merely shook her head. "There is nothing we can do but wait. Galewing's presence is a welcome sign, but Lydia's right. It may mean nothing."

Lydia turned then, shading her eyes with one hand. "Galewing has returned. I hadn't noticed…"

It was another half hour before the sound of footfalls echoed within the tower. I broke into a grin, certain Alexander would be walking through the door any second, his pilgrimage complete. It was another minute before the others heard the footsteps as well. Moments later, Alexander's silhouette filled the doorway.

With a sudden burst of speed, Lydia rushed forward to gather him in her arms. He embraced her gently and smiled as he bent his head to kiss her. When he looked up once more and his eyes met mine, I was startled at the change in his features. No longer was he merely my younger brother; he was without a doubt a mage in full possession of their ageless countenance. While I'd expected the outcome, it still came as a shock.

Alexander disengaged from Lydia's embrace and strode toward me with a mischievous grin. He extended his hand, and we clasped forearms. He applied more pressure, and I gaped at him. He was far stronger than he'd been, and I sensed no magic in the air.

"Alex, what happened?" I asked.

He glanced at Rynn, then said, "My Mark is more powerful than hers, and you've seen what magic did to her. I've also been physically changed, though perhaps in a less dramatic fashion." He chuckled. "Care to arm-wrestle, brother?"

I arched an eyebrow, uncertain if he was serious or merely jesting. "You know I won't compete with—" I began, but he cut me off with a laugh.

"I'm not so certain that you'll win." He flashed a grin. "Come on. We'll go back to camp and see how our strength matches up now."

"Does this happen often?" I asked Rynn as we followed Alexander toward camp. He had one arm looped around Lydia's waist and seemed to be in high spirits. I was bewildered.

"Are you asking about his euphoria or the physical change?"

I laughed uneasily. "Both, I suppose."

"I believe all magi are triumphant at the end," she replied. "As Lydia mentioned, there are many unknowns, and to overcome all of them and be fully in control of one's powers is…extraordinary. Exhilarating. I lack the proper words to describe it." She shrugged, then added, "Beyond the look of a trained mage, the physical changes that occurred with us are exceptionally rare. Do you truly think his strength is a match for yours?"

I shook my head. "No. But he's far stronger than any other man I've encountered. I sensed that much in his grip. I'll humor him, but it may end up bruising his newfound ego."

She laughed. "I must say, this could prove an interesting match. The mage-warrior versus the skin-changer. Who shall win? My wager is on the skin-changer."

Ahead, Alexander shook his head, amused. "Don't be so certain he'll win, lady of frost!" he called over his shoulder.

She rolled her eyes. "I suppose I deserved that, teasing you both as I did. Lady of frost, ha!" She muttered under her breath.

We set up for his arm-wrestling match, using an empty crate as our table. His terms were best of three, though I doubted we'd go beyond two. His newfound strength was considerable, but he was not dragon-kind.

"Don't hold back, brother." He smirked. "You'll lose."

I arched an eyebrow. "Be careful what you wish for, Alex. And I'll know if you use your power for assistance."

He laughed then. "Hmm, what's the worse fate? To lose a few matches to my big brother, or endure him sneezing in my face? I'll take my chances with losing, never fear."

We sat across from one another, and as we grasped hands, I glanced at Lydia. "Will you count down from three?" I asked, certain Alexander could not win. This was merely an exercise in formality.

"Certainly," she replied with a smile for Alexander alone. "Three…Two…One…Go!"

Alexander's strength proved greater than I'd anticipated. I failed to brace myself in preparation for the match, and he had nearly won before I managed to recover. I exerted my own strength then, though not fully—I didn't want to hurt him during this ridiculous endeavor. A moment later, his arm was pinned.

He laughed. "Damn. Again, brother!"

I sighed as we reset our positions, and I nodded to Lydia once more. The second time I was prepared, and it was over in a heartbeat.

Alexander grinned. "I'll admit defeat."

"If you were to compete with anyone else, you'd win without breaking a sweat," I replied. "But I have an unfair advantage."

He snorted. "I'll say. I suppose I never realized the true depth of your strength. You've always held yourself back—with everyone."

"I don't like the notion of harming people."

He rose to his feet. "Walk with me, brother. We have things we should discuss before we depart for the Citadel."

I nodded and stood up as well. With a glance at the three women, I said, "We'll return before nightfall."

I didn't know how long our discussion would take, but there was much that needed to be said. Between Alexander's focus on his trials and his courtship with Lydia, we'd scarcely had any time to speak alone.

We walked along the road toward the overgrown garden. "I have something of a plan," he said after a time.

"As do I, brother. But you speak first."

"It's tradition that I return to the Citadel after the completion of my pilgrimage. We discussed this previously, and I know you plan to accompany me at least that far." He kicked at a loose stone, sending the fragment skittering ahead of us. "What I didn't tell you is it's also tradition for the Oracle to grant a favor to each mage who completes their trials. The mage may request nearly anything of her. I plan to ask that she send a summons to all willing magi. She owes me that much after what she coerced from us both. I'm going to build an army, Andrew."

I nodded thoughtfully. "If she agrees, it will speed up the process of gathering your forces."

He looked at me sharply. "You speak as though this will be my undertaking alone. I hoped you would stay true to your word and take up the role of commander—"

"Alex, Tom needs my help. While you go through the process of recruiting others to your cause—which will take time, even with the Oracle's help—I must go north. I'll be your commander if that's your wish, but I must help Tom first."

He deflated. "You did mention you'd contacted him." He scratched the nape of his neck and groaned. "I've been so preoccupied, I'd forgotten. I didn't read his messages yet, though I still have them."

I chuckled. I wasn't surprised he'd forgotten. "Tom is taking refuge in the Gloaming Highlands. He's been attempting to forge an alliance with the Corodan, but they won't speak to him. The Hive-queen refuses to negotiate with anyone but me."

Alexander appeared thoughtful. "If you think about it, this whole cascade of events began that day when you confronted the old Hive-queen alone. If you hadn't fallen into their trap, I would never have known you were a skin-changer, and we'd still be at war with the Corodan. If that day had ended differently, Colin might not be sitting on the throne, and father would still be alive." He frowned, then said, "It's strange how far we've come, and yet, you're returning to the place it all began. A part of me wishes I could accompany you, but I can't. I have work to do here."

"It will take both of us and all the forces we can muster to oust Colin," I replied. "He has the entire kingdom at his disposal, and we have little more than hope on our side. But if you can muster a sizeable force in the Southlands and I can convince the Corodan to accept Tom's alliance, we might just pull this off."

We walked into the heart of the garden, where a small pond was located. The water was green with algae, but the surface was dotted with delicate yellow flowers. Alexander stopped abruptly as he spied our reflection in the water, then turned to peer at himself more closely.

"I hardly recognize myself," he murmured. "Holy hell, next to me, you look younger. I..." He turned from the pond, his expression one of disbelief. "You truly don't age, do you, brother?"

I managed an uneasy smile and shook my head. "I began to notice it a few years ago. I knew I'd be forced to leave Novania eventually. Someone was bound to start asking questions sooner rather than later." I paused to study our reflections again. "And you may have been able to hide then, but now...You have the look of a mage. There's no denying what you are."

We walked in silence for a time, each lost in his own thoughts. There was much yet to be done.

Our paths would lead us to the Citadel, but there they would diverge. I'd stay long enough to speak with my father and bear witness to Alexander's wedding. I didn't believe I could tarry any longer; Thomas was at risk of discovery, and I'd never forgive myself if he was captured.

"I've asked Emmarie to stay with you," I said after a time. "She expressed her desire to travel with me, but I fear it's too dangerous. The people of Novania don't know the Merael."

"She has proven adept with a sword, if only in practice. I'll continue her lessons, never fear." He grinned. "It's fortunate she followed us from the Citadel. She'll be a great asset to our communications if I can't convince the Feige family to join me." He paused to study me carefully. "Lydia told me Rynn plans to travel with you—and you've agreed."

I nodded slowly. "She was rather insistent."

"What do you plan to do about her, brother?" he asked pointedly.

"I don't know."

"She'll be risking much simply by going with you. If anything were to happen to upset the fragile balance you seem to have, she'll have nowhere to run." He crossed his arms. "And I fear if you continue to string her along, she'll become miserable and may even resent you. You need to make a decision. Commit yourself, or let her go."

I arched an eyebrow, surprised to receive advice of this sort from Alexander. I wondered how much of his speech had been dictated by Lydia. While a part of me was insulted by the insinuation, another part grudgingly acknowledged he may have been right. I couldn't continue to lead her along, hoping one day I'd sort out the complicated tangle of emotions that ensnared my heart. I genuinely liked Rynn, but after Vera and Claire, I feared risking another attachment. My wounds were still too raw.

I shook my head. It was too soon after Vera's death, and I didn't know what I planned to do.

After a moment, Alexander shrugged. "Think on it, brother. That's all I ask."

We walked to the edge of the garden, to the overlook that offered a spectacular view of the lands below the plateau. Far below was the city of Dragon's Feet, and in the distance, I could make out the smaller plateau that sported the stone maze at its top. I marveled at how far we'd traveled and the wonders we'd encountered in these unfamiliar southern lands.

Alexander stood at my side, his arms crossed as he gazed down at the vast expanse of landscape. His eyes were fierce, his jaw set in determination.

"We have much to do," he said. "I hope we're both up to the task."

The Caein Legacy will continue in Harbinger

THANK YOU FOR READING GUARDIAN!

If you enjoyed reading this book, please consider leaving a review.

Information about new books and their release dates will be posted on my website (www.ajcalvin.net), as well as shared via my newsletter. If interested, you can subscribe by visiting my website and clicking on the "Subscribe" tab.

ACKNOWLEDGMENTS

First, I'd like to thank my biggest supporter in my writing endeavors, my husband. His endless patience (particularly when I'm grumbling about formatting or revisions) means the world to me. There are certainly times when I'm not fun to be around when I'm working on book projects, but he has always been understanding.

And then there's the team of various people who also helped make this book come to life:

Jamie Noble, whose artwork is on the cover,

Dewi Hargreaves, who drew up the map from my scrawling attempts at it,

Sheena Sampsel, my editor and comma-wrangler,

My brother, Patrick, a major inspiration behind Alexander's personality and his interactions with Andrew throughout the series,

And lastly, but most importantly, my readers. Without you, none of this would be worthwhile. I truly hope you enjoyed reading Guardian and will continue with the series from here.

NOW AVAILABLE:

HARBINGER: BOOK THREE OF THE CAEIN LEGACY

The Novanian king has gathered an army in the north with the intent to make war upon the magi. He has exiled all three of his brothers. Andrew and Alexander fled to the Southlands, while Thomas escaped into the hostile northern highlands, the land of Novania's ancient foe, the insectile Corodan. While Alexander prepares to face Colin's army in the south, Andrew makes the perilous journey through Novania to seek Thomas' whereabouts and offer what aid he can.

Traveling at his side is Rynn, a powerful mage with the ability to manipulate and form ice. When they fail to locate Thomas after days of searching, Andrew is forced to seek the aid of the Corodan. He has a long and bloody history with their people, and was responsible for the death of their previous Hive-queen. Uncertain if the Corodan will cooperate, but faced with no other hope of locating his brother, he ventures into the heart of the Corodan lands.

Without Thomas, the brothers have no hope of overthrowing Colin and his tyranny. Without Thomas, Novania will continue to execute innocent citizens simply for bearing the Mark of the Magi. Without Thomas, the kingdom will be lost.

ABOUT THE AUTHOR

A.J. Calvin is a science fiction/fantasy novelist from Loveland, Colorado known best for The Caein Legacy series and The Relics of War series. A former microbiologist, A.J. lives with her husband, along with a turtle, a bearded dragon, and a salt water aquarium.

When she is not working or writing, she enjoys scuba diving, hiking, and playing video games.

For more information on the author and news about her writing, please visit her website at www.ajcalvin.net.

www.ingramcontent.com/pod-product-compliance
Lightning Source LLC
Chambersburg PA
CBHW020257030826
48979CB00026B/1375/J

* 9 7 9 8 9 8 8 3 1 9 3 5 1 *